BLACK WINGS OF CTHULHU

ALSO EDITED BY S. T. JOSHI:

Black Wings Of Cthulhu 2
Black Wings Of Cthulhu 3
Black Wings Of Cthulhu 4
Black Wings of Cthulhu 5
Black Wings of Cthulhu 6

The Madness Of Cthulhu
The Madness Of Cthulhu 2

Acolyte of Cthulhu

Black Wings of Cthulhu

TWENTY-ONE NEW TALES OF LOVECRAFTIAN HORROR

EDITED BY S. T. JOSHI

TITAN BOOKS

Black Wings of Cthulhu: Volume 1
Print edition ISBN: 9780857687821
E-book edition ISBN: 9780857687838

Published by Titan Books
A division of Titan Publishing Group Ltd
144 Southwark St, London SE1 0UP

First edition: March 2012
5 7 9 10 8 6

With thanks to PS Publishing.

A CIP catalogue record for this title is available from the British Library.

Printed and bound by CPI Group (UK) Ltd, Croydon CR0 4YY.

CONTENTS

Introduction

S. T. JOSHI

HE FACT THAT H. P. LOVECRAFT'S WORK HAS INSPIRED writers ranging from Jorge Luis Borges to Hugh B. Cave, from Thomas Pynchon to Brian Lumley, suggests at a minimum a widely diverse appeal ranging from the highest of highbrow writers to the lowest of the low. In his own day, Lovecraft attracted a cadre of colleagues and disciples—Clark Ashton Smith, Robert E. Howard, August Derleth, Donald Wandrei, Robert Bloch, Fritz Leiber, and many others—who readily borrowed his manner, his style, and some of the components of his evolving pseudomythology; in several cases, Lovecraft returned the favor by lifting elements from their own tales. After his death in 1937, his work—first issued in hardcover by Arkham House and, over the course of the next seventy years, distributed in the millions of copies in paperback and translated in as many as thirty languages—continued to nurture the imaginations of successive generations of writers, chiefly but by no means exclusively in the realms of horror and science fiction.

What is it about Lovecraft's work that writers find so compelling? A generation or two ago the answer would have been relatively simple: his somewhat flamboyant style mingled with his bizarre theogony of Cthulhu, Yog-Sothoth, Nyarlathotep, and so forth. Today the answer is not so straightforward. We have, mercifully, gone beyond the stage where Lovecraft's prose style is an object of emulation—not because it is a "poor" style, but precisely because it is so intimately fused with his conceptions and worldview that imitation becomes both impossible and absurd. It is as if one were to imitate a painter's distinctive pigments without any attempt to duplicate his models or landscapes. Similarly, the pseudomythology that Lovecraft developed in story after story is so quintessential an expression of his cosmic vision that the mere citation of a deity or place-name, without the strong philosophical foundation that Lovecraft was always careful to establish, can quickly cause a story to become a caricature of Lovecraft rather than an homage to him. It is to be noted how many stories in this anthology do not mention a single such name from the Lovecraft corpus; and yet they remain intimately Lovecraftian on a far deeper level. Indeed, the very notion of writing a "pastiche" that does little but rework Lovecraft's own themes and ideas has now become *passé* in serious weird writing. Contemporary writers feel the need to express their own conceptions in their own language. The concerns of our own day demand to be treated in the language of our time, but Lovecraft's core tenets—cosmicism; the horrors of human and cosmic history; the overtaking of the human psyche by alien incursion—remain eternally viable and can even gain a surprising relevance in the wake of such cosmic phenomena as global warming or the continuing probing of deep space.

The epigraph from "Supernatural Horror in Literature" from which I have derived the title of this book was meant by Lovecraft to be a general formula governing the best weird fiction from the dawn of time to his own day; but it is clear, from such phrases as "contact with unknown spheres and powers" and "the scratching of outside shapes and entities on the known universe's utmost rim," that the formula applies most particularly to his own work. The core of that work, as Lovecraft well recognized, was cosmicism—a conception expressed in his now celebrated letter to Farnsworth Wright of July 5, 1927, accompanying the resubmission of his seminal tale "The Call of Cthulhu" to *Weird Tales:* "All my tales are based on the fundamental premise that common human laws and interests and emotions have no validity or significance in the vast cosmos-at-large." It was this single statement that led me, in soliciting stories for this book, to suggest that straightforward "Cthulhu Mythos" stories were not the only ones that would be considered for inclusion. It can readily be seen that some writers have chosen to play ingenious variations off of other Lovecraft tales whose relation to his mythos is tangential at best. The fact that three separate writers in this volume (Caitlín R. Kiernan, W. H. Pugmire, and Brian Stableford) have chosen to compose ingenious and widely differing riffs on such a story as "Pickman's Model"—a tale that has only the most remote connection to the "Cthulhu Mythos" as conventionally conceived—suggests that they do not require the presence of Cthulhu or Arkham to justify their tributes. It is for this reason that I have carefully chosen my subtitle, "New Tales of *Lovecraftian* Horror."

It is of interest that some of these tales effect a distinctive union between Lovecraftian horror and what seem at the outset to be very different modes of writing—the hard-boiled crime story (Norman Partridge's "Lesser Demons"), the tale of psychological terror (Michael Cisco's "Violence, Child of Trust"), the contemporary tale of urban blight and crime (Michael Shea's "Copping Squid"; Joseph S. Pulver, Sr.'s "Engravings"). What this suggests is that the Lovecraftian idiom is adaptable to a variety of literary modes, as Borges's "There Are More Things" and Pynchon's *Against the Day* are alone sufficient to testify. Even those tales that seem to adhere most closely to their Lovecraftian originals are distinguished by innovations in approach and outlook. Nicholas Royle has made use of the setting of Lovecraft's "The Hound" in his story "Rotterdam," but there is little else in this subtle and atmospheric tale that recalls the over-the-top pulpishness of its putative source.

The sense of place that was so integral a feature of Lovecraft's personal and literary vision, and that has caused such imaginary realms as Arkham or Innsmouth to seem so throbbingly real, is similarly reflected in many of the tales in this volume. The San Francisco of Michael Shea's "Copping Squid," the Southwest in the tales of Donald R. and Mollie L. Burleson, the Pacific Northwest of Laird Barron's and Philip Haldeman's stories are all as vivid as the New England milieu of Lovecraft's most representative tales, and as firmly based upon the authors' experience. It would, indeed, be misleading to suggest that these writers were seeking merely to transport Lovecraft's topographical verisimilitude into their own chosen regions; rather may it be said that the vitality of these settings is a product of their authors' awareness of the degree to which Lovecraft's historical and topographical richness allows—perhaps paradoxically—for an even more breathtaking cosmicism than the never-never-land of Poe.

One of the most interesting phenomena of recent years—although it may perhaps be traced all the way back to Edith Miniter's piquant parody, "Falco Ossifracus: By Mr. Goodguile" (1921)—is the way in which Lovecraft himself has taken on the role of a fictional character. Even during his lifetime he was regarded by his fans as a larger-than-life figure—the gaunt, lantern-jawed recluse who only wrote at night and who haunted the streets of Providence in solitary state just as his idol Poe had done nearly a century before. There are serious errors in some facets of this characterization (anyone who studies Lovecraft's two years in New York will know how gregarious he was in his meetings with the Kalem Club), but this image has worked in tandem with Lovecraft's stories to fashion an imaginative portrait of what a horror writer should be. The materialistic and atheistic Lovecraft might not have appreciated his resurrection as a ghost in such a story as Jonathan Thomas's "Tempting Providence," but he would certainly have echoed the devotion to his native city that the Lovecraftian specter in this tale exhibits. Jason Van Hollander's "Susie" brings Lovecraft's mentally disturbed mother to life as a means of accounting, at least in part, for the particular form that Lovecraft's imagination took in later years. And Sam Gafford's unclassifiable "Passing Spirits" breaks down the barrier between psychological horror and supernatural horror, and perhaps even between fiction and reality, in a tale whose poignancy and sense of inexorable doom dimly echo the fate of Lovecraft's cadre of hapless protagonists.

Cumulatively, it may at first glance appear that the stories in this volume are so diverse in tone, style, mood, and atmosphere as to be a kind of nuclear chaos. But if so, it is only a testament to the breadth of imaginative scope presented by the Lovecraftian corpus of fiction. It is also, perhaps, a testament to the starkly contrasting ways in which contemporary writers can draw upon Lovecraft to express their own conceptions and their own visions by using his work as a touchstone. If this is the case, then it augurs well for Lovecraft's endurance among both readers and writers throughout the twenty-first century.

S. T. Joshi

"The one test of the really weird is simply this—whether or not there be excited in the reader a profound sense of dread, and of contact with unknown spheres and powers; a subtle attitude of awed listening, as if for the beating of black wings or the scratching of outside shapes and entities on the known universe's utmost rim."

H. P. Lovecraft, "Supernatural Horror in Literature"

Pickman's Other Model (1929)

CAITLIN R. KIERNAN

Caitlín R. Kiernan is one of the most popular and critically acclaimed writers in contemporary horror fiction. She is the author of the story collections To Charles Fort, with Love *(Subterranean Press, 2005) and* Tales of Pain and Wonder *(Subterranean Press, 2000; rev. ed. 2008) and the novels* Silk *(Penguin/Roc, 1998; winner of the Barnes & Noble Maiden Voyage Award for best first novel),* Threshold *(Penguin/Roc, 2001),* Low Red Moon *(Penguin/Roc, 2003),* Murder of Angels *(Penguin/Roc, 2004), and* Daughter of Hounds *(Penguin/Roc, 2007). She has also novelized the recent film* Beowulf *(HarperEntertainment, 2007). She is a four-time winner of the International Horror Guild Award.*

 HAVE NEVER BEEN MUCH FOR THE MOVIES, PREFERRING, instead, to take my entertainment in the theater, always favoring living actors over those flickering, garish ghosts magnified and splashed across the walls of dark and smoky rooms at twenty-four frames per second. I've never seemed able to get past the knowledge that the apparent motion is merely an optical illusion, a clever procession of still images streaming past my eye at such a rate of speed that I only perceive motion where none actually exists. But in the months before I finally met Vera Endecott, I found myself drawn with increasing regularity to the Boston movie houses, despite this long-standing reservation.

I had been shocked to my core by Thurber's suicide, though, with the unavailing curse of hindsight, it's something I should certainly have had the presence of mind to have seen coming. Thurber was an infantryman during the war—*La Guerre pour la Civilisation*, as he so often called it. He was at the Battle of Saint-Mihiel when Pershing failed in his campaign to seize Metz from the Germans, and he survived only to see the atrocities at the Battle of the Argonne Forest less than two weeks later. When he returned home from France early in 1919, Thurber was hardly more than a fading, nervous echo of the man I'd first met during our college years at the Rhode Island School of Design, and, on those increasingly rare occasions when we met and spoke, more often than not our conversations turned from painting and sculpture and matters of aesthetics to the things he'd seen in the muddy trenches and ruined cities of Europe.

And then there was his dogged fascination with that sick bastard Richard Upton Pickman, an obsession that would lead quickly to what I took to be no less than a sort of psychoneurotic fixation on the man and the blasphemies he committed to canvas. When, two years ago, Pickman vanished from the squalor of his North End "studio," never to be seen again, this fixation only worsened, until Thurber finally came to me with an incredible, nightmarish tale which, at the time, I could only dismiss as the ravings of a mind left unhinged by the bloodshed and madness and countless wartime horrors he'd witnessed along the banks of the Meuse River and then in the wilds of the Argonne Forest.

But I am not the man I was then, that evening we sat together in a dingy tavern near Faneuil Hall (I don't recall the name of the place, as it wasn't one of my usual haunts). Even as William Thurber was changed by the war and by whatever it is he may have experienced in the company of Pickman, so too have I been changed, and changed *utterly*, first by Thurber's sudden death at his own hands and then by a film actress named Vera Endecott. I do not believe that I have yet lost possession of my mental faculties, and if asked, I would attest before a judge of law that my mind remains sound, if quite shaken. But I cannot now see the world around me the way I once did, for having beheld certain things there can be no return to the unprofaned state of innocence or grace that prevailed before those sights. There can be no return to the sacred cradle of Eden, for the gates are guarded by the flaming swords of cherubim, and the mind may not—excepting in merciful cases of shock and hysterical amnesia—simply forget the weird and dismaying revelations visited upon men and women who choose to ask forbidden questions. And I would be lying if I were to claim that I failed to comprehend, to suspect, that the path I was setting myself upon when I began my investigations following

Thurber's inquest and funeral would lead me where they have. I knew, or I knew well enough. I am not yet so degraded that I am beyond taking responsibility for my own actions and the consequences of those actions.

Thurber and I used to argue about the validity of first-person narration as an effective literary device, him defending it and me calling into question the believability of such stories, doubting both the motivation of their fictional authors and the ability of those character narrators to accurately recall with such perfect clarity and detail specific conversations and the order of events during times of great stress and even personal danger. This is probably not so very different from my difficulty appreciating a moving picture because I am aware it is *not*, in fact, a moving picture. I suspect it points to some conscious unwillingness or unconscious inability, on my part, to effect what Coleridge dubbed the "suspension of disbelief." And now I sit down to write my own account, though I attest there is not a word of *intentional* fiction to it, and I certainly have no plans of ever seeking its publication. Nonetheless, it will undoubtedly be filled with inaccuracies following from the objections to a first-person recital that I have already belabored above. What I am putting down here is my best attempt to recall the events preceding and surrounding the murder of Vera Endecott, and it should be read as such.

It is my story, presented with such meager corroborative documentation as I am here able to provide. It is some small part of her story, as well, and over it hang the phantoms of Pickman and Thurber. In all honesty, already I begin to doubt that setting any of it down will achieve the remedy which I so desperately desire—the dampening of damnable memory, the lessening of the hold that those memories have upon me, and, if I am most lucky, the ability to sleep in dark rooms once again and an end to any number of phobias which have come to plague me. Too late do I understand poor Thurber's morbid fear of cellars and subway tunnels, and to that I can add my own fears, whether they might ever be proven rational or not. "I guess you won't wonder now why I have to steer clear of subways and cellars," he said to me that day in the tavern. I *did* wonder, of course, at that and at the sanity of a dear and trusted friend. But, in this matter, at least, I have long since ceased to wonder.

The first time I saw Vera Endecott on the "big screen," it was only a supporting part in Josef von Sternberg's *A Woman of the Sea*, at the Exeter Street Theater. But that was not the first time I saw Vera Endecott.

I FIRST ENCOUNTERED THE NAME AND FACE OF THE actress while sorting through William's papers, which I'd been asked to do by the only surviving member of his immediate family, Ellen Thurber, an older sister. I found myself faced with no small or simple task, as the close, rather shabby room he'd taken on Hope Street in Providence after leaving Boston was littered with a veritable bedlam of correspondence, typescripts, journals, and unfinished compositions, including the monograph on weird art that had played such a considerable role in his taking up with Richard Pickman three years prior. I was only mildly surprised to discover, in the midst of this disarray, a number of Pickman's sketches, all of them either charcoal or pen and ink. Their presence among Thurber's effects seemed rather incongruous, given how completely terrified of the man he'd professed to having become. And even more so given his claim to have destroyed the one piece of evidence that could support the incredible tale of what he purported to have heard and seen and taken away from Pickman's cellar studio.

It was a hot day, so late into July that it was very nearly August. When I came across the sketches, seven of them tucked inside a cardboard portfolio case, I carried them across the room and spread the lot out upon the narrow, swaybacked bed occupying one corner. I had a decent enough familiarity with the man's work, and I must confess that what I'd seen of it had never struck me quiet so profoundly as it had Thurber. Yes, to be sure, Pickman was possessed of a great and singular talent, and I suppose someone unaccustomed to images of the diabolic, the alien or monstrous, would find them disturbing and unpleasant to look upon. I always credited his success at capturing the weird largely to his intentional juxtaposition of phantasmagoric subject matter with a starkly, painstakingly realistic style. Thurber also noted this and, indeed, had devoted almost a full chapter of his unfinished monograph to an examination of Pickman's technique.

I sat down on the bed to study the sketches, and the mattress springs complained loudly beneath my weight, leading me to wonder yet again why my friend had taken such mean accommodations when he certainly could have afforded better. At any rate, glancing over the drawings, they struck me, for the most part, as nothing particularly remarkable, and I assumed that they must have been gifts from Pickman, or that Thurber might even have paid him some small sum for them. Two I recognized as studies for one of the paintings mentioned that day in the Chatham Street tavern, the one titled "The Lesson," in which the artist had sought to depict a number of his subhuman, dog-like ghouls instructing a young child (a *changeling*, Thurber had supposed) in their practice of necrophagy. Another was a rather hasty sketch of what I took to be some of the statelier monuments in Copp's Hill Burying Ground, and there were also a couple of rather slapdash renderings of hunched gargoyle-like creatures.

But it was the last two pieces from the folio that caught and held my attention. Both were very accomplished nudes, more finished than any of the other sketches, and given the subject matter, I might have doubted they had come from Pickman's hand had it not been for his signature at the bottom of each. There was nothing that could have been deemed pornographic about either, and considering their provenance, this surprised me, as well. Of the portion of Richard Pickman's *oeuvre* that I'd seen for myself, I'd not once found any testament to an interest in the female form, and there had even been whispers in the Art Club that he was a homosexual. But there were so many rumors traded about the man in the days leading up to his disappearance, many of them plainly spurious, that I'd never given the subject much thought. Regardless of his own sexual inclinations, these two studies were imbued with an appreciation and familiarity with a woman's body that seemed unlikely to have been gleaned entirely from academic exercises or mooched from the work of other, less eccentric artists.

As I inspected the nudes, thinking that these two pieces, at least, might bring a few dollars to help Thurber's sister cover the unexpected expenses incurred by her brother's death, as well as his outstanding debts, my eyes were drawn to a bundle of magazine and newspaper clippings that had also been stored inside the portfolio. There were a goodly number of them, and I guessed then, and still suppose, that Thurber had employed a clipping bureau. About half of them were writeups of gallery showings that had included Pickman's work, mostly spanning the years from 1921 to 1925, before he'd been so ostracized that opportunities for public showings had dried up. But the remainder appeared to have been culled largely from tabloids, sheetlets, and magazines such as *Photoplay* and the *New York Evening Graphic*, and every one of the articles was either devoted to or made mention of a Massachusetts-born actress named Vera Marie Endecott. There were, among these clippings, a number of photographs of the woman, and her likeness to the woman who'd modeled for the two Pickman nudes was unmistakable.

There was something quite distinct about her high cheekbones, the angle of her nose, an undeniable hardness to her countenance despite her starlet's beauty and "sex appeal." Later, I would come to recognize some commonality between her face and those of such movie "vamps" and *femme fatales* as Theda Bara, Eva Galli, Musidora, and, in particular, Pola Negri. But, as best as I can now recollect, my first impression of Vera Endecott, untainted by film personae (though undoubtedly colored by the association of the clippings with the work of Richard Pickman, there among the belongings of a suicide), was of a woman whose loveliness might merely be a glamour concealing some truer, feral face. It was an admittedly odd impression, and I sat in the sweltering boardinghouse room, as the sun slid slowly toward dusk, reading each of the articles, and then reading some over again. I suspected they must surely contain, somewhere, evidence that the woman in the sketches was, indeed, the same woman who'd gotten her start in the movie studios of Long Island and New Jersey, before the industry moved west to California.

For the most part, the clippings were no more than the usual sort of picture-show gossip, innuendo, and sensationalism. But, here and there, someone, presumably Thurber himself, had underlined various passages with a red pencil, and when those lines were considered together, removed from the context of their accompanying articles, a curious pattern could be discerned. At least, such a pattern might be imagined by a reader who was either *searching* for it, and so predisposed to discovering it whether it truly existed or not, or by someone, like myself, coming to these collected scraps of yellow journalism under such circumstances and such an atmosphere of dread as may urge the reader to draw parallels where, objectively, there are none to be found. I believed, that summer afternoon, that Thurber's *idée fixe* with Richard Pickman had led him to piece together an absurdly macabre set of notions regarding this woman, and that I, still grieving the loss of a close friend and surrounded as I was by the disorder of that friend's unfulfilled life's work, had done nothing but uncover another of Thurber's delusions.

The woman known to moviegoers as Vera Endecott had been sired into an admittedly peculiar family from the North Shore region of Massachusetts, and she'd undoubtedly taken steps to hide her heritage, adopting a stage name shortly after her arrival in Fort Lee in February of 1922. She'd also invented a new history for herself, claiming to hail not from rural Essex County, but from Boston's Beacon Hill. However, as early as '24, shortly after landing her first substantial role—an appearance in Biograph Studios' *Sky Below the Lake*—a number of popular columnists had begun printing their suspicions about her professed background. The banker she'd claimed as her father could not be found, and it proved a straightforward enough matter to demonstrate that she'd never attended the Winsor School for girls. By '25, after starring in Robert G. Vignola's *The Horse Winter*, a reporter for the *New York Evening Graphic* claimed Endecott's actual father was a man named Iscariot Howard Snow, the owner of several Cape Anne granite quarries. His wife, Make-peace, had come either from Salem or Marblehead, and had died in 1902 while giving birth to their only daughter, whose name was not Vera, but Lillian Margaret. There was no evidence in any of the clippings that the actress had ever denied or even responded to any of these allegations, despite the fact that the Snows, and Iscariot Snow in particular, had a distinctly unsavory reputation in and around Ipswich. Despite the family's wealth and prominence in local business, it was notoriously secretive, and there was no want for back-fence talk concerning sorcery and witchcraft, incest, and even cannibalism. In 1899, Make-peace Snow had also borne twin sons, Aldous and Edward, though Edward had been a stillbirth.

But it was a clipping from *Kidder's Weekly Art News* (March 27, 1925), a publication I was well enough acquainted with, that first tied the actress to Richard Pickman. A "Miss Vera Endecott of Manhattan" was listed among those in attendance at the premiere of an exhibition that had included a couple of Pickman's less provocative paintings, though no mention was made of her celebrity. Thurber had circled her name with his red pencil and drawn two exclamation points beside it. By the time I came across the article, twilight had descended upon Hope Street, and I was having trouble reading. I briefly considered the old gas lamp near the bed, but then, staring into the shadows gathering amongst the clutter and threadbare furniture of the seedy little room, I was gripped by a sudden, vague apprehension—by what, even now, I am reluctant to name *fear*. I returned the clippings and the seven sketches to the folio, tucked it under my arm, and quickly retrieved my hat from a table buried beneath a typewriter, an assortment of paper and library books, unwashed dishes and empty soda bottles. A few minutes later, I was outside again and clear of the building, standing beneath a streetlight, staring up at the two darkened windows opening into the room where, a week before, William Thurber had put the barrel of a revolver in his mouth and pulled the trigger.

I HAVE JUST AWAKENED FROM ANOTHER OF MY nightmares, which become ever more vivid and frequent, ever more appalling, often permitting me no more than one or two hours sleep each night. I'm sitting at my writing desk, watching as the sky begins to go the grey-violet of false dawn, listening to the clock ticking like some giant wind-up insect perched upon the mantle. But my mind is still lodged firmly in a dream of the musty private screening room near Harvard Square, operated by a small circle of aficionados of grotesque cinema, the room where first I saw "moving" images of the daughter of Iscariot Snow.

I'd learned of the group from an acquaintance in acquisitions at the Museum of Fine Arts, who'd told me it met irregularly, rarely more than once every three months, to view and discuss such fanciful and morbid fare as Benjamin Christensen's *Häxen*, Rupert Julian's *The Phantom of the Opera*, Murnau's *Nosferatu—Eine Symphonie des Grauens*, and Todd Browning's *London After Midnight*. These titles and the names of their directors meant very little to me, since, as I have already noted, I've never been much for the movies. This was in August, only a couple of weeks after I'd returned to Boston from Providence, having set Thurber's affairs in order as best I could. I still prefer not to consider what unfortunate caprice of fate aligned my discovery of Pickman's sketches of Vera Endecott and Thurber's interest in her with the group's screening of what, in my opinion, was a profane and a deservedly unheard-of film. Made sometime in 1923 or '24, I was informed that it had achieved infamy following the director's death (another suicide). All the film's financiers remained unknown, and it seemed that production had never proceeded beyond the incomplete rough cut I saw that night.

However, I did not sit down here to write out a dry account of my discovery of this untitled, unfinished film, but rather to try and capture something of the dream that is already breaking into hazy scraps and shreds. Like Perseus, who dared to view the face of the Gorgon Medusa only indirectly, as a reflection in his bronze shield, so I seem bound and determined to reflect upon these events, and even my own nightmares, as obliquely as I may. I have always despised cowardice, and yet, looking back over these pages, there seems in it something undeniably cowardly. It does not matter that I intend that no one else shall ever read this. Unless I write honestly, there is hardly any reason in writing it at all. If this is a ghost story (and, increasingly, it feels that way to me), then let it *be* a ghost story, and not this rambling reminiscence.

In the dream, I am sitting in a wooden folding chair in that dark room, lit only by the single shaft of light spilling forth from the projectionist's booth. And the wall in front of me has become a window, looking out upon or into another world, one devoid of sound and almost all color, its palette limited to a spectrum of somber blacks and dazzling whites and innumerable shades of grey. Around me, the others who have come to see smoke their cigars and cigarettes, and they mutter among themselves. I cannot make out anything they say, but, then, I'm not trying particularly hard. I cannot look away from that that silent, grisaille scene, and little else truly occupies my mind.

"Now, do you understand?" Thurber asks from his seat next to mine, and maybe I nod, and maybe I even whisper some hushed affirmation or another. But I do not take my eyes from the screen long enough to glimpse his face. There is too much there I might miss, were I to dare look away, even for an instant, and, moreover, I have no desire to gaze upon the face of a dead man. Thurber says nothing else for a time, apparently content that I have found my way to this place, to witness for myself some fraction of what drove him, at last, to the very end of madness.

She is there on the screen—Vera Endecott, Lillian Margaret Snow—standing at the edge of a rocky pool. She is as naked as in Pickman's sketches of her, and is positioned, at first, with her back to the camera. The gnarled roots and branches of what might be ancient willow trees bend low over the pool, their whiplike branches brushing the surface and moving gracefully too and fro, disturbed by the same breeze that ruffles the actress' short, bob-cut hair. And though there appears to be nothing the least bit sinister about this scene, it at once inspires in me the same sort of awe and uneasiness as Doré's engravings for *Orlando Furioso* and the *Divine Comedy*. There is about the tableau a sense of intense foreboding and anticipation, and I wonder what subtle, clever cues have been placed just so that this seemingly idyllic view would be interpreted with such grim expectancy.

And then I realize that the actress is holding in her right hand some manner of phial, and she tilts it just enough that the contents, a thick and pitchy liquid, drips into the pool. Concentric ripples spread slowly across the water, much *too* slowly, I'm convinced, to have followed from any earthly physics, and so I dismiss it as merely trick photography. When the phial is empty, or has, at least, ceased to taint the pool (and I am quite sure that it *has* been tainted), the woman kneels in the mud and weeds at the water's edge. From somewhere overhead, there in the room with me, comes a sound like the wings of startled pigeons taking flight, and the actress half turns toward the audience, as if she has also somehow heard the commotion. The fluttering racket quickly subsides, and once more there is only the mechanical noise from the projector and the whispering of the men and women crowded into the musty room. Onscreen, the actress turns back to the pool, but not before I am certain that her face is the same one from the clippings I found in Thurber's room, the same one sketched by the hand of Richard Upton Pickman. The phial slips from her fingers, falling into the water, and this time there are no ripples whatsoever. No splash. Nothing.

Here, the image flickers before the screen goes blinding white, and I think, for a moment, that the filmstrip has, mercifully, jumped one sprocket or another, so maybe I'll not have to see the rest. But then she's back, the woman and the pool and the willows, playing out frame by frame by frame. She kneels at the edge of the pool, and I think of Narcissus pining for Echo or his lost twin, of jealous Circe poisoning the spring where Scylla bathed, and of Tennyson's cursed Shalott, and, too, again I think of Perseus and Medusa. I am not seeing the thing itself, but only some dim, misguiding counterpart, and my mind grasps for analogies and signification and points of reference.

On the screen, Vera Endecott, or Lillian Margaret Snow—one or the other, the two who were always only one—leans forward and dips her hand into the pool. And again, there are no ripples to mar its smooth obsidian surface. The woman in the film is speaking now, her lips moving deliberately, making no sound whatsoever, and I can hear nothing but the mumbling, smoky room and the sputtering projector. And this is when I realize that the willows are not precisely willows at all, but that those twisted trunks and limbs and roots are actually the entwined human bodies of both sexes, their skin perfectly mimicking the scaly bark of a willow. I understand that these are no wood nymphs, no daughters of Hamadryas and Oxylus. These are prisoners, or condemned souls bound eternally for their sins, and for a time I can only stare in wonder at the confusion of arms and legs, hips and breasts and faces marked by untold ages of the ceaseless agony of this contortion and transformation. I want to turn and ask the others if they see what I see, and how the deception has been accomplished, for surely these people know more of the prosaic magic of filmmaking that do I. Worst of all, the bodies have not been rendered entirely inert, but writhe ever so slightly, helping the wind to stir the long, leafy branches first this way, then that.

Then my eye is drawn back to the pool, which has begun to steam, a grey-white mist rising languidly from off the water (if it *is* still water). The actress leans yet farther out over the strangely quiescent mere, and I find myself eager to look away. Whatever being the cameraman has caught her in the act of summoning or appeasing, I do not want to *see*, do not want to *know* its daemonic physiognomy. Her lips continue to move, and her hands stir the waters that remain smooth as glass, betraying no evidence that they have been disturbed in any way.

At Rhegium she arrives; the ocean braves,
And treads with unwet feet the boiling waves...

But desire is not enough, nor trepidation, and I do *not* look away, either because I have been bewitched along with all those others who have come to see her, or because some deeper, more disquisitive facet of my being has taken command and is willing to risk damnation in the seeking into this mystery.

"It is only a moving picture," dead Thurber reminds me from his seat beside mine. "Whatever else she would say, you must never forget it is only a dream."

And I want to reply, "Is that what happened to you, dear William? Did you forget it was never anything more than a dream and find yourself unable to waken to lucidity and life?" But I do not say a word, and Thurber does not say anything more.

But yet she knows not, who it is she fears;
In vain she offers from herself to run,
And drags about her what she strives to shun.

"Brilliant," whispers a woman in the darkness at my back, and "Sublime," mumbles what sounds like a very old man. My eyes do not stray from the screen. The actress has stopped stirring the pool, has withdrawn her hand from the water, but still she kneels there, staring at the sooty stain it has left on her fingers and palm and wrist. *Maybe*, I think, *that is what she came for, that mark, that she will be known*, though my dreaming mind does not presume to guess what or whom she would have recognize her by such a bruise or blotch. She reaches into the reeds and moss and produces a black-handled dagger, which she then holds high above her head, as though making an offering to unseen gods, before she uses the glinting blade to slice open the hand she previously offered to the waters. And I think perhaps I understand, finally, and the phial and the stirring of the pool were only some preparatory wizardry before presenting this far more precious alms or expiation. As her blood drips to spatter and *roll* across the surface of the pool like drops of mercury striking a solid tabletop, something has begun to take shape, assembling itself from those concealed depths, and, even without sound, it is plain enough that the willows have begun to scream and to sway as though in the grip of a hurricane wind. I think, perhaps, it is a mouth, of sorts, coalescing before the prostrate form of Vera Endecott or Lillian Margaret Snow, a mouth or a vagina or a blind and lidless eye, or some organ that may serve as all three. I debate each of these possibilities, in turn.

Five minutes ago, almost, I lay my pen aside, and I have just finished reading back over, aloud, what I have written, as false dawn gave way to sunrise and the first uncomforting light of a new October day. But before I return these pages to the folio containing Pickman's sketches and Thurber's clippings and go on about the business that the morning demands of me, I would confess that what I have dreamed and what I have recorded here are not what I saw that afternoon in the screening room near Harvard Square. Neither is it entirely the nightmare that woke me and sent me stumbling to my desk. Too much of the dream deserted me, even as I rushed to get it all down, and the dreams are never exactly, and sometimes not even remotely, what I saw projected on that wall, that deceiving stream of still images conspiring to suggest animation. This is another point I always tried to make with Thurber, and which he never would accept, the fact of the inevitability of unreliable narrators. I have not lied; I would not say that. But none of this is any nearer to the truth than any other fairy tale.

AFTER THE DAYS I SPENT IN THE BOARDING-HOUSE IN Providence, trying to bring some semblance of order to the chaos of Thurber's interrupted life, I began accumulating my own files on Vera Endecott, spending several days in August drawing upon the holdings of the Boston Athenaeum, Public Library, and the Widener Library at Harvard. It was not difficult to piece together the story of the actress' rise to stardom and the scandal that led to her descent into obscurity and alcoholism late in 1927, not so very long before Thurber came to me with his wild tale of Pickman and subterranean ghouls. What was much more difficult to trace was her movement through certain theosophical and occult societies, from Manhattan to Los Angeles, circles to which Richard Upton Pickman was, himself, no stranger.

In January '27, after being placed under contract to Paramount Pictures the previous spring, and during production of a film adaptation of Margaret Kennedy's novel, *The Constant Nymph*, rumors began surfacing in the tabloids that Vera Endecott was drinking heavily and, possibly, using heroin. However, these allegations appear at first to have caused her no more alarm or damage to her film career than the earlier discovery that she was, in fact, Lillian Snow, or the public airing of her disreputable North Shore roots. Then, on May 3rd, she was arrested in what was, at first, reported as merely a raid on a speakeasy somewhere along Durand Drive, at an address in the steep, scrubby canyons above Los Angeles, nor far from the Lake Hollywood Reservoir and Mulholland Highway. A few days later, after Endecott's release on bail, queerer accounts of the events of that night began to surface, and by the 7th, articles in the

Van Nuys Call, *Los Angeles Times*, and the *Herald-Express* were describing the gathering on Durand Drive not as a speakeasy, but as everything from a "witches' Sabbat" to "a decadent, sacrilegious, orgiastic rite of witchcraft and homosexuality."

But the final, damning development came when reporters discovered that one of the many women found that night in the company of Vera Endecott, a Mexican prostitute named Ariadna Delgado, had been taken immediately to Queen of Angels–Hollywood Presbyterian, comatose and suffering from multiple stab wounds to her torso, breasts, and face. Delgado died on the morning of May 4th, without ever having regained consciousness. A second "victim" or "participant" (depending on the newspaper), a young and unsuccessful screenwriter listed only as Joseph E. Chapman, was placed in the psychopathic ward of LA County General Hospital following the arrests.

Though there appear to have been attempts to keep the incident quiet by both studio lawyers and also, perhaps, members of the Los Angeles Police Department, Endecott was arrested a second time on May 10th and charged with multiple counts of rape, sodomy, second-degree murder, kidnapping, and solicitation. Accounts of the specific charges brought vary from one source to another, but regardless, Endecott was granted and made bail a second time on May 11th, and four days later, the office of Los Angeles District Attorney Asa Keyes abruptly and rather inexplicably asked for a dismissal of all charges against the actress, a motion granted in an equally inexplicable move by the Superior Court of California, Los Angeles County (it bears mentioning, of course, that District Attorney Keyes was, himself, soon thereafter indicted for conspiracy to receive bribes and is presently awaiting trial). So, eight days after her initial arrest at the residence on Durand Drive, Vera Endecott was a free woman, and by late May she had returned to Manhattan, after her contract with Paramount was terminated.

Scattered throughout the newspaper and tabloid coverage of the affair are numerous details that take on a greater significance in light of her connection with Richard Pickman. For one, some reporters made mention of "an obscene idol" and "a repellent statuette carved from something like greenish soapstone" recovered from the crime scene, a statue which one of the arresting officer's is purported to have described as a "crouching, doglike beast." One article listed the item as having been examined by a local (unnamed) archeologist, who was supposedly baffled at its origins and cultural affinities. The house on Durand Drive was, and may still be, owned by a man named Beauchamp who had spent time in the company of Aleister Crowley during his four-year visit to America (1914–1918), and who had connections with a number of hermetic and theurgical organizations. And finally, the screenwriter Joseph Chapman drowned himself in the Pacific somewhere near Malibu only a few months ago, shortly after being discharged from the hospital. The one short article I could locate regarding his death made mention of his part in the "notorious Durand Drive incident" and printed a short passage reputed to have come from the suicide note. It reads, in part, as follows:

Oh God, how does a man forget, deliberately and wholly and forever, once he has glimpsed such sights as I have had the misfortune to have seen? The awful things we did and permitted to be done that night, the events we set in motion, how do I lay my culpability aside? Truthfully, I cannot and am no longer able to fight through day after day of trying. The Endecotte [sic] woman is back East somewhere, I hear, and I hope to hell she gets what's coming to her. I burned the abominable painting she gave me, but I feel no cleaner, no less foul, for having done so. There is nothing left of me but the putrescence we invited. I cannot do this anymore.

Am I correct in surmising, then, that Vera Endecott made a gift of one of Pickman's paintings to the unfortunate Joseph

Chapman, and that it played some role in his madness and death? If so, how many others received such gifts from her, and how many of those canvases yet survive so many thousands of miles from the dank cellar studio near Battery Street where Pickman created them? It's not something I like to dwell upon.

After Endecott's reported return to Manhattan, I failed to find any printed record of her whereabouts or doings until October of that year, shortly after Pickman's disappearance and my meeting with Thurber in the tavern near Faneuil Hall. It's only a passing mention from a society column in the *New York Herald Tribune*, that "the actress Vera Endecott" was among those in attendance at the unveiling of a new display of Sumerian, Hittite, and Babylonian antiquities at the Metropolitan Museum of Art.

What is it I am trying to accomplish with this catalogue of dates and death and misfortune, calamity and crime? Among Thurber's books, I found a copy of Charles Hoyt Fort's *The Book of the Damned* (New York: Boni & Liveright, December 1, 1919). I'm not even sure why I took it away with me, and having read it, I find the man's writings almost hysterically belligerant and constantly prone to intentional obfuscation and misdirection. Oh, and wouldn't that contentious bastard love to have a go at this tryst with "the damned"? My point here is that I'm forced to admit that these last few pages bear a marked and annoying similarity to much of Fort's first book (I have not read his second, *New Lands*, nor do I propose ever to do so). Fort wrote of his intention to present a collection of data that had been excluded by science (*id est*, "damned"):

Battalions of the accursed, captained by pallid data that I have exhumed, will march. You'll read them—or they'll march. Some of them livid and some of them fiery and some of them rotten.

Some of them are corpses, skeletons, mummies, twitching, tottering, animated by companions that have been damned alive. There are giants that will walk by, though sound asleep. There are things that are theorems and things that are rags: they'll go by like Euclid arm in arm with the spirit of anarchy. Here and there will flit little harlots. Many are clowns. But many are of the highest respectability. Some are assassins. There are pale stenches and gaunt superstitions and mere shadows and lively malices: whims and amiabilities. The naïve and the pedantic and the bizarre and the grotesque and the sincere and the insincere, the profound and the puerile.

And I think I have accomplished nothing more than this, in my recounting of Endecott's rise and fall, drawing attention to some of the more melodramatic and vulgar parts of a story that is, in the main, hardly more remarkable than numerous other Hollywood scandals. But also, Fort would laugh at my own "pallid data," I am sure, my pathetic grasping at straws, as though I might make this all seem perfectly reasonable by selectively quoting newspapers and police reports, straining to preserve the fraying infrastructure of my rational mind. It's time to lay these dubious, slipshod attempts at scholarship aside. There are enough Forts in the world already, enough crackpots and provocateurs and intellectual heretics without my joining their ranks. The files I have assembled will be attached to this document, all my "Battalions of the accursed," and if anyone should ever have cause to read this, they may make of those appendices what they will. It's time to tell the truth, as best I am able, and be done with this.

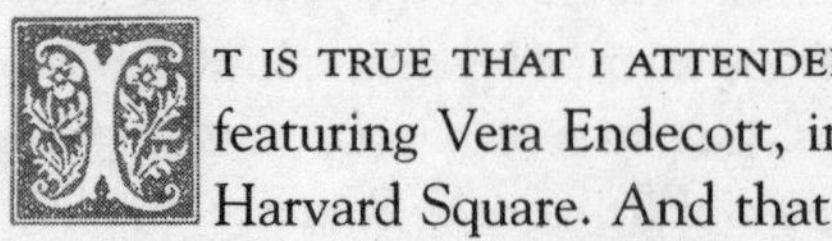

T IS TRUE THAT I ATTENDED A SCREENING OF A FILM, featuring Vera Endecott, in a musty little room near Harvard Square. And that it still haunts my dreams. But as noted above, the dreams rarely are anything like an accurate replaying of what I saw that night. There was no black pool, no willow trees stitched together from human bodies, no venomous phial emptied upon the waters. Those are the embellishments of my dreaming, subconscious mind. I could fill several journals with such nightmares.

What I *did* see, only two months ago now, and one month before I finally met the woman for myself, was little more than a grisly, but strangely mundane, scene. It might have only been a test reel, or perhaps 17,000 or so frames, some twelve minutes, give or take, excised from a far longer film. All in all, it was little more than a blatantly pornographic pastiche of the widely circulated 1918 publicity stills of Theda Bara lying in various risqué poses with a human skeleton (for J. Edward Gordon's *Salomé*).

The print was in very poor condition, and the projectionist had to stop twice to splice the film back together after it broke. The daughter of Iscariot Snow, known to most of the world as Vera Endecott, lay naked upon a stone floor with a skeleton. However, the human skull had been replaced with what I assumed then (and still believe) to have been a plaster or papier-mâché "skull" that more closely resembled that of some malformed, macrocephalic dog. The wall or backdrop behind her was a stark matte-grey, and the scene seemed to me purposefully under-lit in an attempt to bring more atmosphere to a shoddy production. The skeleton (and its ersatz skull) were wired together, and Endecott caressed all the osseous angles of its arms and legs and lavished kisses upon it lipless mouth, before masturbating, first with the bones of its right hand, and then by rubbing herself against the crest of an ilium.

The reactions from the others who'd come to see the film that night ranged from bored silence to rapt attention to laughter. My own reaction was, for the most part, merely disgust and embarrassment to be counted among that audience. I overheard, when the lights came back up, that the can containing the reel bore two titles, *The Necrophile* and *The Hound's Daughter*, and also bore two dates—1923 and 1924. Later, from someone who had a passing acquaintance with Richard Pickman, I would hear a rumor that he'd worked on scenarios for a filmmaker, possibly Bernard Natan, the prominent Franco-Romanian director of "blue movies," who recently acquired Pathé and merged it with his own studio, Rapid Film. I cannot confirm or deny this, but certainly, I imagine what I saw that evening would have delighted Pickman no end.

However, what has lodged that night so firmly in my mind, and what I believe is the genuine author of those among my nightmares featuring Endecott in an endless parade of nonexistent horrific films, transpired only in the final few seconds of the film. Indeed, it came and went so quickly, the projectionist was asked by a number of those present to rewind and play the ending over four times, in an effort to ascertain whether we'd seen what we *thought* we had seen.

Her lust apparently satiated, the actress lay down with her skeletal lover, one arm about its empty ribcage, and closed her kohl-smudged eyes. And in that last instant, before the film ended, a shadow appeared, something passing slowly between the set and the camera's light source. Even after five viewings, I can only describe that shade as having put me in mind of some hulking figure, something considerably farther down the evolutionary ladder than Piltdown or Java man. And it was generally agreed among those seated in that close and musty room that the shadow was possessed of an odd sort of snout or muzzle, suggestive of the prognathous jaw and face of the fake skull wired to the skeleton.

There, then. *That* is what I actually saw that evening, as best I now can remember it. Which leaves me with only a single piece of this story left to tell, the night I finally met the woman who called herself Vera Endecott.

"ISAPPOINTED? NOT QUITE WHAT YOU WERE EXPECTING?" she asked, smiling a distasteful, wry sort of smile, and I think I might have nodded in reply. She appeared at least a decade older than her twenty-seven years, looking like a woman who had survived one rather tumultuous life already and had, perhaps, started in upon a second. There were fine lines at the corners of her eyes and mouth, the bruised circles below her eyes that spoke of chronic insomnia and drug abuse, and, if I'm not mistaken, a premature hint of silver in her bobbed black hair. What *had* I anticipated? It's hard to say now, after the fact, but I was surprised by her height, and by her irises, which were a striking shade of grey. At once, they reminded me of the sea, of fog and breakers and granite cobbles polished perfectly smooth by ages in the surf. The Greeks said that the goddess Athena had "sea-grey" eyes, and I wonder what they would have thought of the eyes of Lillian Snow.

"I have not been well," she confided, making the divulgence sound almost like a *mea culpa*, and those stony eyes glanced toward a chair in the foyer of my flat. I apologized for not having already asked her in, for having kept her standing in the hallway. I led her to the davenport sofa in the tiny parlor off my studio, and she thanked me. She asked for whiskey or gin, and then laughed at me when I told her I was a teetotaler. When I offered her tea, she declined.

"A painter who doesn't *drink?*" she asked. "No wonder I've never heard of you."

I believe that I mumbled something then about the Eighteenth Amendment and the Volstead Act, which earned from her an expression of commingled disbelief and contempt. She told me that was strike two, and if it turned out that I didn't smoke, either, she was leaving, as my claim to be an artist would have been proven a bald-faced lie, and she'd know I'd lured her to my apartment under false pretenses. But I offered her a cigarette, one of the *brun* Gitanes I first developed a taste for in college, and at that she seemed to relax somewhat. I lit her cigarette, and she leaned back on the sofa, still smiling that wry smile, watching me with her sea-grey eyes, her thin face wreathed in gauzy veils of smoke. She wore a yellow felt cloche that didn't exactly match her burgundy silk chemise, and I noticed there was a run in her left stocking.

"You knew Richard Upton Pickman," I said, blundering much too quickly to the point, and, immediately, her expression turned somewhat suspicious. She said nothing for almost a full minute, just sat there smoking and staring back at me, and I silently cursed my impatience and lack of tact. But then the smile returned, and she laughed softly and nodded.

"Wow," she said. "There's a name I haven't heard in a while. But, yeah, sure, I knew the son of a bitch. So, what are you? Another of his protégés, or maybe just one of the three-letter-men he liked to keep handy?"

"Then it's true Pickman was light on his feet?" I asked.

She laughed again, and this time there was an unmistakable edge of derision there. She took another long drag on her cigarette, exhaled, and squinted at me through the smoke.

"Mister, I have yet to meet the beast—male, female, or anything in between—that degenerate fuck wouldn't have screwed, given half a chance." She paused, here, tapping ash onto the floorboards. "So, if you're *not* a fag, just what *are* you? A kike, maybe? You sort of *look* like a kike."

"No," I replied. "I'm not Jewish. My parents were Roman Catholic, but me, I'm not much of anything, I'm afraid, but a painter you've never heard of."

"Are you?"

"Am I what, Miss Endecott?"

"Afraid," she said, smoke leaking from her nostrils. "And do *not* dare start in calling me 'Miss Endecott.' It makes me sound like a goddamned schoolteacher or something equally wretched."

"So, these days, do you prefer Vera?" I asked, pushing my luck. "Or Lillian?"

"How about Lily?" she smiled, completely nonplussed, so far as I could tell, as though these were all only lines from some script she'd spent the last week rehearsing.

"Very well, Lily," I said, moving the glass ashtray on the table closer to her. She scowled at it, as though I were offering her a platter of some perfectly odious foodstuff and expecting her to eat, but she stopped tapping her ash on my floor.

"Why am I here?" she demanded, commanding an answer without raising her voice. "Why have you gone to so much trouble to see me?"

"It wasn't as difficult as all that," I replied, not yet ready to answer her question, wanting to stretch this meeting out a little longer and understanding, expecting, that she'd likely leave as soon as she had what I'd invited her there to give her. In truth, it had been quite a lot of trouble, beginning with a telephone call to her former agent, and then proceeding through half a dozen increasingly disreputable and uncooperative contacts. Two I'd had to bribe, and one I'd had to coerce with a number of hollow threats involving nonexistent contacts in the Boston Police Department. But, when all was said and done, my diligence had paid off, because here she sat before me, the two of us, alone, just me and the woman who'd been a movie star and who had played some role in Thurber's breakdown, who'd posed for Pickman and almost certainly done murder on a spring night in Hollywood. Here was the woman who could answer questions I did not have the nerve to ask, who knew what had cast the shadow I'd seen in that dingy pornographic film. Or, at least, here was all that remained of her.

"There aren't many left who would have bothered," she said, gazing down at the smoldering tip-end of her Gitane.

"Well, I have always been a somewhat persistent sort of fellow," I told her, and she smiled again. It was an oddly bestial smile that reminded me of one of my earliest impressions of her—that oppressive summer's day, now more than two months past, studying a handful of old clippings in the Hope Street boarding house. That her human face was nothing more than a mask or fairy glamour conjured to hide the truth of her from the world.

"How did you meet him?" I asked, and she stubbed out her cigarette in the ashtray.

"Who? How did I meet *who?*" She furrowed her brow and glanced nervously toward the parlor window, which faces east, toward the harbor.

"I'm sorry," I replied. "Pickman. How is it that you came to know Richard Pickman?"

"Some people would say that you have very unhealthy interests, Mr. Blackman," she said, her peculiarly carnivorous smile quickly fading, taking with it any implied menace. In its stead, there was only this destitute, used-up husk of a woman.

"And surely they've said the same of you, many, many times, Lily. I've read all about Durand Drive and the Delgado woman."

"Of course, you have," she sighed, not taking her eyes from the window. "I'd have expected nothing less from a persistent fellow such as you."

"How did you meet Richard Pickman?" I asked for the third time.

"Does it make a difference? That was so very long ago. Years and *years* ago. He's dead—"

"No body was ever found."

And, here, she looked from the window to me, and all those unexpected lines on her face seemed to have abruptly deepened; she might well have been twenty-seven, by birth, but no one would have argued if she laid claim to forty.

"The man is dead," she said flatly. "And if by chance he's *not*, well, we should all be fortunate enough to find our heart's desire, whatever it might be." Then she went back to staring at the window, and, for a minute or two, neither of us said anything more.

"You told me that you have the sketches," she said, finally. "Was that a lie, just to get me up here?"

"No, I have them. Two of them, anyway," and I reached for the folio beside my chair and untied the string holding it closed. "I don't know, of course, how many you might have posed for. There were more?"

"More than two," she replied, almost whispering now.

"Lily, you still haven't answered my question."

"And you *are* a persistent fellow."

"Yes," I assured her, taking the two nudes from the stack and holding them up for her to see, but not yet touch. She studied them a moment, her face remaining slack and dispassionate, as if the sight of them elicited no memories at all.

"He needed a model," she said, turning back to the window and the blue October sky. "I was up from New York, staying with a friend who'd met him at a gallery or lecture or something of the sort. My friend knew that he was looking for models, and I needed the money."

I glanced at the two charcoal sketches again, at the curve of those full hips, the round, firm buttocks, and the tail—a crooked, malformed thing sprouting from the base of the coccyx and reaching halfway to the bend of the subject's knees. As I have said, Pickman had a flare for realism, and his eye for human anatomy was almost as uncanny as the ghouls and demons he painted. I pointed to one of the sketches, to the tail.

"That isn't artistic license, is it?"

She did not look back to the two drawings, but simply,

slowly, shook her head. "I had the surgery done in Jersey, back in '21," she said.

"Why did you wait so long, Lily? It's my understanding that such a defect is usually corrected at birth, or shortly thereafter."

And she almost smiled that smile again, that hungry, savage smile, but it died, incomplete, on her lips.

"My father, he has his own ideas about such things," she said quietly. "He was always so proud, you see, that his daughter's body was blessed with evidence of her heritage. It made him very happy."

"Your heritage…" I began, but Lily Snow held up her left hand, silencing me.

"I believe, sir, I've answered enough questions for one afternoon. Especially given that you have only the pair, and that you did not tell me that was the case when we spoke."

Reluctantly, I nodded and passed both the sketches to her. She took them, thanked me, and stood up, brushing at a bit of lint or dust on her burgundy chemise. I told her that I regretted that the others were not in my possession, that it had not even occurred to me she would have posed for more than these two. The last part was a lie, of course, as I knew Pickman would surely have made as many studies as possible when presented with so unusual a body.

"I can show myself out," she informed me when I started to get up from my chair. "And you will not disturb me again, not ever."

"No," I agreed. "Not ever. You have my word."

"You're lying sons of bitches, the whole lot of you," she said, and with that, the living ghost of Vera Endecott turned and left the parlor. A few seconds later, I heard the door open and slam shut again, and I sat there in the wan light of a fading day, looking at what grim traces remained in Thurber's folio.

OCTOBER 24, 1929.

This is the last of it. Just a few more words, and I will be done. I know now that having attempted to trap these terrible events, I have not managed to trap them at all, but merely given them some new, clearer focus.

Four days ago, on the morning of October 20th, a body was discovered dangling from the trunk of an oak growing near the center of King's Chapel Burial Ground. According to newspaper accounts, the corpse was suspended a full seventeen feet off the ground, bound round about the waist and chest with interwoven lengths of jute rope and baling wire. The woman was identified as a former actress, Vera Endecott, *née* Lillian Margaret Snow, and much was made of her notoriety and her unsuccessful attempt to conceal connections to the wealthy but secretive and ill-rumored Snows of Ipswich, Massachusetts. Her body had been stripped of all clothing, disemboweled, her throat cut, and her tongue removed. He lips had been sewn shut with cat-gut stitches. About her neck hung a wooden placard, on which one word had been written in what is believed to be the dead woman's own blood: *apostate*.

This morning, I almost burned Thurber's folio, along with all my files. I went so far as to carry them to the hearth, but then my resolve faltered, and I just sat on the floor, staring at the clippings and Pickman's sketches. I'm not sure what stayed my hand, beyond the suspicion that destroying these papers would not save my life. If they want me dead, then dead I'll be. I've gone too far down this road to spare myself by trying to annihilate the physical evidence of my investigation.

I will place this manuscript, and all the related documents I have gathered, in my safety deposit box, and then I will try to return to the life I was living before Thurber's death. But I cannot forget a line from the suicide note of the screenwriter, Joseph Chapman—*how does a man forget, deliberately and wholly and forever, once he has glimpsed such sights*. How, indeed. And, too, I cannot forget that woman's eyes, that stony, sea-tumbled shade of grey. Or a rough shadow glimpsed in the final moments of a film that might have been made in 1923 or 1924, that may have been titled *The Hound's Daughter* or *The Necrophile*.

I know the dreams will not desert me, not now nor at some future time, but I pray for such fortune as to have seen the last of the waking horrors that my foolish, prying mind has called forth.

Desert Dreams

DONALD R. BURLESON

Donald R. Burleson's short stories have appeared in Twilight Zone, Fantasy and Science Fiction, Terminal Fright, Cemetery Dance, Deathrealm, Inhuman, *and other magazines, and in many anthologies. He is the author of three novels, including* Flute Song *(Black Mesa Press, 1996) and* Arroyo *(Black Mesa Press, 1999), and of the short story collection* Beyond the Lamplight *(Jack o'Lantern Press, 1996). He is a leading authority on H. P. Lovecraft. Among his critical works are* H.P. Lovecraft: A Critical Study *(Greenwood Press, 1983) and* Lovecraft: Disturbing the Universe *(University Press of Kentucky, 1990).*

E DWELL FOREVER IN REALMS OF SHADOW. STRANGELY complacent, we wander through our weary days as if we understood the texture of our world; yet in all truth we see with the eye of the worm and hear with the ear of the stone, and comprehend nothing. Our understanding is a skimming water-bug that tastes only the surface of a fathomless black sea, while reality, a frightful abyss of ocean-bottom horror, moves silently and darkly through depths beyond our reach, inscrutable, and mocks our ignorance.

Dreams try to tell us things of which we otherwise would know little, purporting to lend a semblance of clarity to our minds, yet I cannot even say when my own dreams, my strange and ever-recurrent night visions, began. "Dreams," I have said, but these visions, I now realize, have constituted one single pervasive dream running like an insane but oddly persistent thread through my life.

I recall waking in childhood with a sense of some striking impression that I could not quite remember, though when the dream came again and again over time I gradually managed to retain more of what I had seen. There seemed to be a consistent pattern to these dreams, but as the vision slowly gathered form it was not relief I felt at being able to remember, but rather a puzzlement as to what these still elusive fragments might mean. It had to do with some forsaken spot in a vast and sun-baked desert, but beyond that I could not be sure of much.

For a time during my adolescence the dreams became less frequent, and in fact I thought I was outgrowing them, too busy with life to concern myself with insubstantial matters. In time the dreams seemed to cease altogether. Growing to manhood in my native Providence, Rhode Island, I settled into mundane but adequate employment at an insurance company and bought a pleasant old house in Benefit Street, expecting to spend my days in simple contentment. I whiled away my evenings reading Proust and Baudelaire and Shakespeare and sometimes strolling along the ancient streets of the city and thinking quiet thoughts. I was at peace, satisfied with my life.

But then the dreams began anew.

I awoke very late one autumn night and struggled to retain a grasp on the ebbing tide of memory as the dream started to slip away. What had it been? Undeniably, it was essentially the vision of my childhood years, though rather more detailed this time. I remembered now a vista of vast and sprawling desert, where great brittle tumbleweeds, like aimless creatures on some distant planet, careened across the arid sand, and spiky yucca leaves and cactus blades pointed skyward in the blinding sun. Behind the scene there seemed to be a kind of subtle rumbling or humming, but I could scarcely be sure; and soon these half-remembered impressions faded, and I fell asleep again.

The next evening the dream was back, and when I woke I lay in the dark thinking about what I had seen. And heard, or almost heard.

Again, the sun-blistered sand had stretched away in all directions, dotted with standing sentries of cholla cactus and great angular yuccas and ragged bunches of mesquite. A warm wind had stirred the yellow earth, and a grumbling suggestion of sound seemed to hover just too low to be heard clearly. But for a moment it had resembled a low-pitched voice, a voice that seemed to be saying something like "G*wai-ti*." I could recall no more than that.

Unable this time to sleep again, I walked for hours in the

silent streets and felt oddly disoriented. The familiar façades of colonial New England houses with their fanlighted doors and small-paned windows only seemed to make me feel more oddly displaced, as if it were unclear which was reality, the well-known sights of Benefit and Jenckes and College Streets or the windswept desertland of my dream landscape.

I had lived in Providence all my life. I had never seen a desert, except occasionally in photographs. What did I know of cholla cactus or yucca plants or mesquite, or of boundless purple skies—the memory of them came back to me—skies unobstructed by city buildings, vast skies overlooking colossal oceans of sand? Yet I did seem to know of these things.

At work I sometimes found myself staring off into space, preoccupied with the enigma of my dream visions. I began to wonder *where* this desertland really was, if indeed it really was anywhere. Then when a work associate returned one day from a vacation in Albuquerque, and when I listened to his accounts of the region, it was suddenly and inexplicably clear to me that the desert vistas of my dreams were real, and were to be found somewhere in New Mexico. I really had no way to know that, yet I felt sure I knew.

As time went on, the setting of my dreams became more focused, but I found that this made the dreams more rather than less disturbing, as I could scarcely imagine how I came to know ever more particular detail about a locale of which I should have been wholly uninformed. I had never traveled any further west than Columbus, Ohio, and the American Southwest was only patches of color on a map to me; yet these desert visions were unsettlingly familiar in some surreal way.

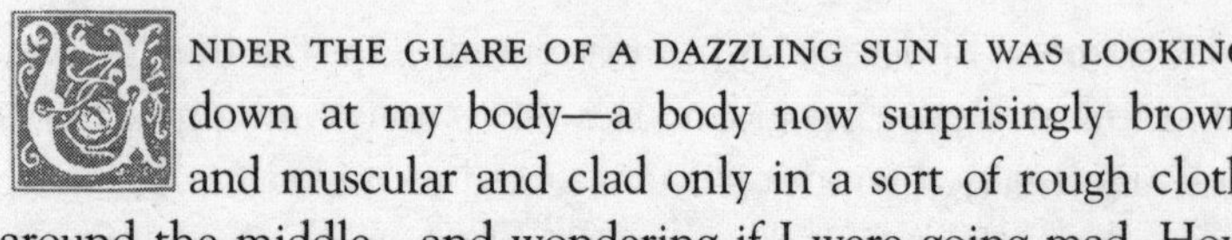

UNDER THE GLARE OF A DAZZLING SUN I WAS LOOKING down at my body—a body now surprisingly brown and muscular and clad only in a sort of rough cloth around the middle—and wondering if I were going mad. How could this be me? As I bent forward to see myself better, locks of long, silky, raven-black hair fell across my eyes, and it was only when I brushed these locks from my face that I glanced up to see the unfamiliar yet somehow oddly familiar figure standing near me on the warm, cactus-dotted sand. He was a medicine man, with a wizened face nearly hidden among a nest of lizard-like wrinkles out of which peered two dark eyes that seemed to hold the secrets of centuries. He was puffing at a great long clay pipe, sending jittery little clouds of gray smoke out upon the warm air, and as he puffed the pipe he shook a turtle-shell ceremonial rattle and intoned the words—incomprehensible to me on one level of consciousness, but faintly familiar on some other level—the words of an ancient ritual song. He turned as he chanted, sending the smoke and the cryptic words first in one direction and then another, finally coming all the way back around to face me, and as his timeless face turned again in my direction, the final words of the song took form in my mind: "G*wai-ti*, G*wai-ti*." I awoke with these impressions still fresh in my memory and walked far into the night hours trying either to understand the sounds I had heard or to dispel their memory. I paused among the great black gravestones in St. John's churchyard off Benefit Street and tried to collect my thoughts, finally rousing myself and making my weary way back home with no desire to sleep again. After reading awhile I feel asleep nonetheless, and, so far as I can remember, did not dream.

Taking the next day off from work, I made an appointment to speak with someone who I suspected might possibly be able to tell me something about my mystery: Professor Carlos Armijo at Brown University. His field was the anthropology of the Southwest, and I had heard him lecture once. I doubted that my nocturnal visions would mean anything to him, but it was worth a try.

I found Professor Armijo to be a soft-spoken and pensive-looking man of middle age, comfortably ensconced in a nest of books and professional journals in his office at Brown. Describing the overall nature of my dreams, I felt increasingly foolish having allowed myself to think there might be any real point in taking up his time with my account, and I barely mustered the courage to mention the nonsense syllables that had become part of my nocturnal visions of the desert, so that I was mightily surprised at his response.

"I have heard these syllables before," he said in a soft Spanish accent, "in connections that make them difficult to account for in the dreams of someone unacquainted with the cultures of the Southwest. Even scholars conversant with those cultures would for the most part find the words unknown to them. I only know of them myself because I am a specialist in, let us say, some of the darker aspects of Southwestern lore."

I was intrigued, though in a way unsure how much I really wanted to know about the origins of an expression having arisen for no discernible reason in my dreams; perhaps Carl Jung was right in theorizing that we all possess a Collective Unconscious capable of tapping into profound shared realms of being, archetypal realms, unknown to our conscious mind yet at some level connected to a sort of reality. "Please go on."

Professor Armijo looked out his window for a moment, evidently collecting his thoughts. "For centuries there was a kind of obscure cult among certain Native American shamans of Arizona and New Mexico," he said, "involving what seems to have been the worship of an ancient god unknown in the mainstream of American Indian tradition." He paused, rather dramatically, and not without cause, it seemed to me. "That god was apparently known as Gwai-ti."

I felt my breath catch at this revelation. What did I know of this? What did I really *want* to know of this? Nothing—yet I had undeniably dreamed the name.

"Very little is known," the professor went on, "about this cult or its god, as the whole subject has always been shunned among such few American Indians as have ever even heard of it. Even at places in New Mexico like Nambé Pueblo, where there are very dark and long-standing traditions of Southwest-style witchcraft, in my researches I have found only one shaman who admitted to knowing of the god Gwai-ti, and he spoke of the matter only with reluctance and, I might add, with obvious distaste.

"I gather from his disjointed accounts that Gwai-ti is supposed to have existed from the beginning of time, and to have come to dwell under the earth, showing itself only on rare occasions to hapless souls. There are stories of human sacrifices made from time to time by renegade Indian priests having no standing with the proper spiritual leaders in the region, most of whom, however, regard the supposed activities of the renegade priests as fabrications."

I was struggling to make some sense of all this. "And the name? Frankly, I thought it sounded Chinese."

Professor Armijo nodded. "I have had some interesting discussions with people in comparative linguistics here about the name Gwai-ti. Indeed there are words within the phonology of Chinese that sound like these syllables. I am given to understand that there is a word *gwai* that means something like 'strange' or 'monstrous.' There is a word *ti* that means 'body' or 'form.' And of course ethnologists theorize that Asian peoples migrated in prehistoric times across the Bering Strait into North America, but on the other hand there are virtually no discernible linguistic traces of Asian vocabulary in the languages of Native Americans."

"How do I know the name?" I asked.

The professor shrugged. "Perhaps you have heard it somewhere and have simply forgotten."

I made ready to leave, thanking the man for his time. "You're right, I must have heard the name somewhere."

But of course I knew that I had not. Except in my dreams.

A FEW NIGHTS LATER THE DREAMS BEGAN TO TAKE ON AN even more anomalous character.

One night I seemed to crouch in shadows watching some vile convocation in which a semicircle of strangely painted priests chanted: "*M'warrh* G*wai-ti*, *h'nah m'warrh* G*wai-ti*, *ph'nglui w'gah* G*wai-ti*." Another time I thought I was looking across a great desert plain in a wash of moonlight, with a distant ring of mountains in the background almost beyond the limits of vision, and watching what at first I took to be a swirl of blowing sand. Before long, though, this impression resolved itself into a young Indian girl running, screaming, flailing her arms in terror. In the inconsistent fashion of dreams, my view of her was suddenly closer than before, so close in fact that she filled my entire field of view. Somewhere I could hear a deep thrumming sound, like the bass tones on a pipe organ, and a voice—it was like the old shaman of my earlier visions—a voice that chanted, in some language known to me in the dream: "She was chosen, we had to send her." And in the next instant a great hungry darkness seemed to close around the screaming girl, and she was gone, and the thrumming died away. I awoke drenched in perspiration, and fancied I could still smell the pungent aroma of sagebrush. I was afraid to go back to sleep.

But of course the next night I did have to sleep again, and saw this time a tall, narrow stone in the sand, with ancient petroglyphs carved upon it like runic inscriptions from a bygone age, and I heard again the somber thrumming in the ground, and glimpsed unclear suggestions of movement in the wan moonlight, and only just made out a murmur of the name G*wai-ti* before the scene grew grainy and faded away altogether.

It was only a matter of time before I could no longer resist the nameless urge actually to visit New Mexico. I must long since have decided, unconsciously, that whatever unthinkable confluence of realities might have brought me into an awareness of that other world so unlike the waking world of my mundane life, I had to see, in objective truth, the setting of my dreams. I had no idea, of course, where exactly in those vast desertlands my visions might have originated.

Nevertheless, I found myself on an airplane one day, landing in Albuquerque with that odd sense of the unreal that one feels upon first visiting a place about which one has only read. Or dreamed.

I rented a four-wheel-drive vehicle at the airport and drove east and then south. While I had no notion where I should be going, I felt no reluctance just to let my instincts guide me. Threading my way through the foothills of the Sandia Mountains and finding my eyes charmed by occasional glimpses of earth-colored adobe walls and coyote fences, I made my way out into open desert, where distant, majestic mesas stood timeless beyond endless plains of waving prairie grass and nodding islands of mesquite and sagebrush and spikes of yucca. Given my motivations for visiting this land so different from my native New England, I had rather expected the desert to be redolent of subtle dread and unease, but I found myself gathering altogether different impressions.

The place was beautiful. There was nothing sinister about the dizzyingly vast expanse of turquoise sky, the stretches of chaparral, the blue-gray mountains in the distance, the great deep arroyos snaking across the land, the tranquil mesas stretched upon the sandy plain like serene grazing beasts. I scarcely knew now what I had expected, but what I had found was a land of enchanting beauty and peace.

As I drove through this desert pageantry, I wondered aloud that I had ever allowed myself to think that there could be anything spectral or bizarre about this region. I felt more at ease than I had felt for quite a long time, and I reflected that I had been foolish to be disturbed by my odd but essentially harmless dreams. Even those nonsense syllables, so coincidentally similar to some name from obscure Southwestern folklore, were surely something about which I had no need to concern myself.

The sun was beginning to go down behind the purple mountain ranges in the west, and I marveled at the beauty of the desert sunset, wherein the sky exploded in a riotous display of color that would surely challenge the brushwork of even the most gifted artist. Somewhere south of Corona I found myself on a smaller, more crudely paved road, and continued to delight in the incredible vistas of cholla cactus and undulating stretches of sandy earth, where the pointed shadows of yucca and mesquite began to splay themselves out upon the plain in the waning light of the sun. I reminded myself that soon it would be getting dark, and I would need either to return to Corona or go on to Roswell or Artesia to find a room for the night.

But first I felt in the mood for some more exploration; there was something addictive about this landscape.

I turned off onto an even smaller road and bounced along in a cloud of dust, feeling, with a certain pleasure, that I was further from human habitation than I could ever recall having been. After a while the road became a rock-strewn, primitive path where even the rugged vehicle I had chosen found it tricky to proceed. A darkening expanse of chaparral lay all around me, and now for the first time since my arrival I began to feel, in spite of the thrill that the newness of the place imparted to me, a certain suspicion that there could be something a little spectral about this land after all. But still I felt fascinated, and a little disinclined to head back to populated areas just yet.

At length the passable road, at this point merely a vague predominance of rock over cactus and mesquite, played out altogether, and I stopped the car and got out and walked ahead into the twilight, picking my way carefully and once pausing to watch the dusky form of a rattlesnake sidle off into the gloom, its warning rattles reaching me as a paper-dry burring on the evening air. Clearly, one had to be careful here, and the sight of this reptilian reminder was sufficient to suggest to me that indeed it might be time to turn back.

But I thought I saw something in the distance that I wanted to examine at closer range. It was something vaguely familiar, though the light was very uncertain now.

Stepping carefully over snake holes and prickly clusters of cactus, I made my way to a large standing stone that protruded from the sandy soil like a somber finger pointing at the darkening sky.

And I could not believe what I was seeing, in stark actuality now, rather than in the vagaries of dream. This simply could not be, but it was. Its ancient Indian petroglyphs still faintly visible in the dwindling remnants of light, the stone was undeniably the sinister monolith of my dream-visions back in Providence.

Providence, now infinitely far away in another, saner world.

Heaven help me, this was the place of my dreams.

I have no idea how long I stood there, unable to wrest my gaze from the dreadful stone, before my mind registered something else.

A sound. A low, insistent thrumming in the ground, like the bass notes of a great pipe organ.

And then—that other sound.

Two syllables, in some voice of the mind or some real

physical vibration, I could not tell which—two syllables upon which I must refuse to dwell.

The impressions that followed are what I must especially resist thinking too steadily upon, if I am to retain what sanity remains to me.

In the uneven light of a chalky moon beginning to spread its radiance from between black, scudding clouds, I thought somehow that the sandy plain on which I stood became—what shall I say?—lower, indented, subtly concave, while the shadowy line of the horizon rose slightly in contrast. Perhaps my unconscious mind understood before my reasoning self could do so, for I broke and ran, hoping that I was headed back toward the car, which was invisible from here. Stumbling and falling headlong, I scarcely felt the cactus and the stony soil rend my clothing as I fell and ran and fell and ran again, trying to block from my ears those reverberant tones that must have been rising in pitch all along, those notes that murmured "*Gwai-ti, Gwai-ti,*" from subterraneous regions of which I dared not allow myself to think.

I had the sensation that a great chasm was opening to receive me, and that in another moment it would be too late, and I would be gone, and no one would ever know what had happened to me. The whole scene seemed to churn itself up into a kaleidoscope of nightmare impressions, a blur of sand and tumbleweed and stone and muttering sound and frowning sky, and I ran and ran, choking on clouds of dust and terrified to look back over my shoulder. It was only when I was driving frantically back up the dusty, rocky road that some corner of my mind registered that I must have reached the car after all, before whatever came for me had time to close upon its prey.

I spent the rest of my trip moodily walking the populous and well-lighted streets of Albuquerque and Santa Fe, and I took an airplane back to Providence, Rhode Island.

Now when I walk down Benefit Street and stop to look at a fanlighted doorway or watch a sleek gray cat make its serene way along the ancient brick walkways, I realize that it is possible for consciousnesses beyond the common grasp to reach across unthinkable gulfs of time and space and fasten upon the unwary dreamer. I know now that, whatever some may say of dreams or of imagination or of the fanciful nature of such mythic creatures as the vile cannibal-god Gwai-ti, I came within seconds, one night in the desertlands of New Mexico, of dropping into the primal ravenous mouth of that horror from my dreams.

Engravings

JOSEPH S. PULVER, SR.

Joseph S. Pulver, Sr. is the author of the acclaimed Cthulhu Mythos novel Nightmare's Disciple *(Chaosium, 1999) as well as a strikingly original short story collection,* Blood Will Have Its Season *(Hippocampus Press, 2009), that nonetheless features homages to Lovecraft, Robert W. Chambers, and other classic authors of weird fiction.*

STRAIGHT RAIN. MEAN AND MURDEROUS. ITS EYES screaming for blood.

Denver faded 300 miles back. 300 miles of wet asphalt back... It could have been 1,000...

Rain. Mean and murderous—engraving the world with sheets of thorns. Rain. Screaming like the Old Man on a gin bender. Screaming like the Old Man before the belt and the fists.

Thirty years back...or it could have been yesterday.

This run was supposed to end in the desert, not in a ditch. But the clock pressed. Tick-tock/tick-tock. Like a boss with eyes that only said FASTER.

He needed coffee and a pack of smokes. Maybe some eggs and toast...and something other than this Bible-thumping Forever that poured out of the radio. A nice sexy waitress—not some upper-class package with radar eyes searching for money, but earthy—knowing, with blue eyes and a big butt that swayed. Not unkempt and worn, but nice and maybe with a little extra. And she would wink all-sexy-like when she refilled his coffee.

Rain—full throttle, carrying violence with each slap. Like the Old Man crossing the hardwood floor.

For the last 50 miles or every step he'd ever taken.

Broken. The knobs wouldn't work. He couldn't turn the fuckin' radio off or down. The wipers working overtime, fighting off this wallop of darkness.

He should pull over and wait it out. But he needed a smoke and needed to be warm. Wanted...wanted something to look at that didn't hurt his strained eyes. Wanted to hear something—

someone other than Rev. James Theodore Ellison's promise to heal you if you sent him money. To be healed by money. That's what got him here. Got him on this road. Got him out this night… With The Package in the trunk.

He should pull over and check The Package. When he did that 365 miles back, almost running off the road, he heard it slam into the side of the trunk. Heard it thud. Jittery balljoints, shitty tires, and bad shocks—shitty-ass Pontiac junkbucket, new this thing never purred along Nirvana Road like a hot kiss; a Chevy would, "Ain't nothin' like a fine-ass Chevy glidin' top down in the sun. A fine candy-apple red one, not this black piece of crap." And that timetable. He was screwed if The Package was damaged. That's what Mr. Phoenix said. Promised. Stark as bloody murder with one look and few words.

But that wasn't his fault. Wasn't his fault Mr. Phoenix gave him this car. Made him drive on thin tires. Not in this shit. This was Mr. Phoenix's fault. Not that he could tell him that and live.

Mr. Phoenix and his red tie and his red stickpin! and the red cufflinks… Red. It stared right into your eyes. Drilling. Burning, hungry venom. Mr. Phoenix and his cats—five of them, four black as midnight, one smoke and fog grey. Licking his hands. Staring at you, right into your eyes. Drilling.

He hated cats. His Old Man had moved like a cat, slinky and graceful, even when he was oiled. Then the claws came out. Blood. Red. Red was everywhere.

Then…and now. Red.

All his life driving away from it. Fast. And here it was again. Waiting. If he wasn't on time. If The Package was damaged. Red. Waiting to let its claws out.

"Fuck all this rain. Pissin' like someone in Hell drank all the fuckin' beer in every shithole bar this side of the Mississippi."

If he had time he'd pull over and yank the fuse for the radio out. At least he could stop Rev. Set-aside-your-sins-and-ask-God-for-forgiveness' moral deluge. But Mr. Phoenix said 11:30 sharp. Said he'd be waiting. Waiting. Red tie, tight and just so. Red stickpin! and the red cufflinks. And probably those fuckin' cats. Licking his hands. *Sick-shit lettin' animals lick ya. All those fuckin' germs. Germs from licking their assholes. Might dress like old time money—all uptown, but he was fuckin' nasty. Nasty ass cats lickin' shit.*

"Fuckin' treacherous cats. Yeowlin' like saxophones. Ballin' like that nigger music set 'em on fire." *Should kill all the cats like they did back in Europe when they was burnin' the fuckin' witches.*

He looks at the clock on the dash. 100 miles and less than an hour to make it there.

Raining. Harder. And Rev. James Theodore Ellison blatherin' like he knew it all.

And the Old Man, tellin' ya he knew it all.

And Mr. Phoenix actin' like he knew it all.

And this rain comin' down like the end of it all.

And those fuckin' cats and their hungry eyes, lookin' atcha like they wanted it all.

"Fuck-it-all! Gonna take my cash and hit some Mexican beach and score some nice Mexican pussy. Gonna leave all these wounded motherfuckers to their wounded neighbors and just lay there. No more in a hurry to get there. Fuck that." *Outta the flame and into the wine. Bye-bye bullshit. I'm spendin' my days and nights in the shade. On my soft cushion—blue or green like the color of the water. Starin' at some sweet shang-a-bang-bang that don't wanna bring me down. Tomorrow there'll be sunrise and I'm gonna hit Sugartown without a problem in sight... Might even have a little garden where I can grow some of that sweet Mexican shit.*

Sixteen hours of drivin' rain and barely a moment where it let up so he could pull over and take a piss. Sixteen hours behind the wheel with the clock following him. Pulling. Pushing. Mile after mile. Pushing. Prodding. Poking. Mile after mile. Minute by minute. Not even 50 minutes left and the clock wanting it to be over. And him wanting to be gone. And that bastard Rev. James Theodore Ellison sayin' The End is near—Bet the only thing he ever got near was the pink little backside of an altar boy. And the mean, murderous rain not letting up…

The flat ten hours back really put a dent in his plan, laid out all nice and straight. Fucked plans. Now all banged up and hollow. It seemed like it was last week and it killed any hope of stopping for dinner—some eggs and toast and hot black coffee would be nice, but… The rain and the clock and the flat killed at that. Left the day a victim. Roadkill, that got ran over and nicked and flattened and ran over again and again 'til it was pulp. Red. A red mess no one would stop for. No one would miss. Not even the clock.

He had a headache. Starin' through wipers killing themselves to beat off the rain hour after hour with no coffee and something filling his belly. He had a headache. Wanted to sleep. Wanted to eat. Wanted to wake up beside something warm and nice. And willing. Wanted this shit to be over. Now.

Wanted it to stop fucking raining. Let Mr. Phoenix build an ark and him and his fuckin' cats could sail off to one of those places like Babaluma or Zanzibar. He wanted this chapter closed and he wanted his money. Now.

If it would just let up and he could find a 7-Eleven or a gas station that hadn't dozed off into goodnight. Just one cup of java and a pack of smokes and he could make it 'til The End.

There'd be Mr. Phoenix at The End. Standin' there. With that stone, spider smile turnin' to poison and asking for The Package.

Bet if it was still rainin' the rain wouldn't touch him. Bet he had red eyes under those thick black sunglasses. Come to think of it he'd never seen him, day or pitch black, without them. Albinos had reddish eyes, and Mr. Phoenix could—maybe?, even if he was as black as the ace of spades, black as any old Mississippi bluesman with broken eyes filled with sorrow. Yeah. He had red eyes. Just like one of those hellfire demons in those creepy old movies.

And that wasn't all that wasn't right with Mr. Phoenix. Always decked out in that stupid scarlet robe. Did he think he was some pope or old pharaoh? All that Egyptian stuff layin' around his office—the place looked like some creepy-assed museum. And that time down by the trains on Hennepin St. when the dogs ran from him bawlin' like he beat them with an ugly stick and he had his back to 'em and was at least twenty feet away. And those clove cigarettes, red tip burnin' like hellfire—smelled like they was rolled in Hell too. And his voice, sounded as if it came from deep in a well and it boomed, those old Bible prophets must have sounded like that to fill people with doom and damnation. Sounded pitch black and wise. Wise in things That Were.

But he had to get there first. Had to beat this clock ticking, pulling its load into some unknowable future. Had to get outta this rain.

Highbeams trying to read the snake-curve of the road. The rain confusing the context of space and time. Rain. Here now. Here then. Like a plague.

A sign—*The Sign*. The sign said just ahead. On the left. Almost here. All those hours almost free. Almost free to go to Mexico. With all that money. He'd have eggs and toast and smokes and sweet Mexican pussy with that money. He'd have every day on the beach—with no rain. Never a fuckin' drop! And he'd never have to deal with Mr. Phoenix again. Never look at that stone grin that froze yer bones. Never have to hear the fuckin' cats yeowlin'. He was gonna buy two dogs—wasn't gonna let any cats near his beach house in Mexico. The sign said just ahead.

$50,000. Just ahead. Long afternoons alone with a cold beer—drunk and ready for a nap if he wanted, unless he wanted her around. Everything he wanted, just ahead.

Hours and hours in the dark. No sky, no horizon. Now—wet and repeated endlessly. No shore. Minute by minute. No clouds. Minute after minute. No moon. Hour after hour. Rain. Leviathan.

Out of it. Hot summer complaining. Cactus. Sand. Moon—low and somehow energetic, smiling in satisfaction. Rev. James Theodore Ellison's sermon instantly ended, cut off. Joshua trees, bent old crones, twisted and passing for dead. The yellow spine down the middle of the road, dry, untouched by the merciless storm. Everything here in this exhibition of midnight and the small hours of morning bone-dry.

The hill off to his left. What passes for a road leading to it. Brakes. Left at the big boulder, just where he was told it would be. The tires quieter in the sand. Slow, not wanting to kick up dust. Three minutes late, not wanting to face Mr. Phoenix.

The Pontiac stops in front of three large rocks, sentinels, white as bones. They have no eyes, arms, hands. Still he sees them as dangerous. Something about them pulses. They don't belong here. His finger touches his mother's crucifix under his shirt before passing between them.

He steps from the deep black shadows of the sentinels on to white sand. *Ground from bone*, he thinks. *An ocean of bones*.

Two more steps—ghost steps. He feels he's walking up a long hill toward a great dark house, carrying something obscene and unwanted. He feels slight. Stops. He doesn't know if he should get The Package out of the trunk. Doesn't remember his instructions. Was there a script that disappeared? He'd like to turn back. But he doesn't know the way.

The flash of a match, a scar burning this cell of night. Mr. Phoenix without his dark-brimmed hat, face under it, glowing black edge to black edge. Mr. Phoenix carved out of sharp moonlight. Smiling. Smiling that blasted, open-faced, silent smile that soured his stomach, that could hit you like a shot to the ribs. Mr. Phoenix seated at a table under a canvas pavilion. Saxophones—a pair?—coming from a tape recorder by his feet, playing blind, surging, interstellar meditations, the lost music of some vertical invader awakened from slumber, hungry, hunting. Saxophones screeching and yeowlin' like those fuckin' black-souled cats had their tails on fire. And his cats, pushing each other aside to lick his hands. Mr. Phoenix singing, "In the Outer Nothingness, Heavenly things dancing in the sun… They Dwell on Other Planes." Empty well-deep voice—thin, stone lips hardly moving—reflecting yesterdays gone with the wind.

Not a drug deal. Not a delivery of some hijacked old shit. Devil worship? He turns his head and looks back at the Pontiac. At the trunk. The trunk he'd never looked in.

"Hello, Johnny."

"Sorry I'm late, but the rain—"

"Rain?"

"It stopped just over there. Freaky. Like there was a barrier it couldn't pass through."

"Rarely does the rain hunt in the Halls of Fire." With a hand, thin wisps of curling smoke rising off it, he removed his sunglasses.

Red eyes leveled at him. Unblinking. Stabbing red eyes, bare of all except contempt.

Fuck, that's…unholy! His mouth open—language flattened out with a bang, the burning air rushing into it.

The dark man has not moved. As cursed shadows tethered to forgotten riddles his cats sit at the edges of the table.

"Heavenly things dancing in the sun… They Dwell on Other

Planes." Empty well-deep voice. Thin, stone lips hardly moving.

How does he do that? His hand moves to his left for comfort—no gun. He has a gun, but it's on the seat of the car. Forgotten in haste; to get this over and get out of here, to get his money.

The moon falls between cracks in the clouds. The air smells of light-devouring blackness. And the black man has not moved. And the scarring pattern of the swelling music boils on.

All he can do—simple and terrified—is stare. At the loud red eyes. He wants The End. Wants the money—*his money*. Wants to leave, to be on his way to Mexico. Wants Now to be over. But all he can do is stare.

The song the black man sings ends. The red eyes grow cold, the smile widens. "So we have arrived. Dark and light in shadows on this hill. Dark and light, one to take and one to give."

Shit, the package. It's still in the trunk. "Right. Sorry. I'll get the package."

Low laughter dancing. "I've no need for it. I know the way."

"But I have it. It's in the trunk. Right where your man said it was. I've never touched it. Never even looked at it... Could I get my money? And go?"

"Money? Oh, yes, that. Calm yourself, my boy, you'll have no need for money—not that there ever was any. Not where you are going."

The stone smile.

Bait. Tricked.

Going? I'm going to get my fuckin' gun. He'll give me my money, then...and I'll put two in his head for fuckin' with me. Shoot his fuckin' cats too.

"Johnny, I can see by your face you think to do me violence and leave. That will not happen. I control the opening of every door. I've a few moments to fill, so allow me to amuse you with a detail or two about you and the road traveled.

"Your dear mother was a drunkard and a whore, not that

she took money for her wanton rutting, mind you, but for a few cheap drinks she would spread her legs wide. And I had a need, a need that required a vessel to carry a drop of my essence. A need for an act to occur under a star engraved in times ancient. A little song in her ear followed by a several glasses of gin and she...how would you put it? She fucked like a rabbit—climbed on top and took to my lust as if she were a maggot to an apple. I left her sleeping and dripping with my seed."

Black laughter brands him.

"I never saw her again, yet I've kept an eye on you. The night you were born the moon was fire-red—did she never tell you of The Burning? My pets were there, watching, walking in your first dream. After engraving you they came and reported to me. As the years found themselves whitened by the teeth of time, I've sent one of my servants to check on you from time to time. You'll recall the attorney who suddenly showed up to rid you of your legal entanglements when that girl died. He was a servant I employ on occasion. And Pitt—even the worm fears the scent of what he sends to the soil, did you ever wonder why a cold-blooded monster like that befriended and protected you in jail? Again, my handiwork. Remember the evening your father fell down the stairs to his death, consumed by the spleen of a hard drunk?"

Mr. Phoenix's finger strokes the neck of the cat sitting at his right hand. "*Mesah* was there watching that night and made certain the coarse mite flew to the Labyrinth Where the Damned Howl. I could not, after all, have you damaged. Every time some loose extreme put you at risk I cut it back to nothing."

Assaulted by the life sprawling in his telescope of memory, his skin crawls. He wants out of the bullring, wants the weathervane to turn. Wants something sane. Wants his life to be another life, one not framed in the shipwreck of 100 sabbaths, not washed away by the teeth of 1,000 drinks. He is too stunned to cry. All capacity for speech is stitched shut.

"Though your life has been dark and violent, have you never taken note of the fact that in 32 years no scar has been born upon your body?"

His mind weak, beaten down. He is desperate for words. For some key to freedom.

"I see you wish you could trade the empty box in the trunk for your liberty. Yes, Johnny, the box contains *nothing*." The word a grave.

"You see, for this, what shall we call it? Prelude To Windfall, perhaps… You needed to come here freely. The package was merely a vehicle for you to do so. I can see you're searching for a reason for all this… I'll be plain. I am called by many names. Tonight the verse of stone and wind call me, The Opener of the Way. You and I are here to open a door. A door opened by the harvest."

Harvest? Like in dead?

He would run—the keys are still in the Pontiac's ignition, but finds himself bound, held knee-deep in sand.

Mr. Phoenix's hands glow. Tendrils of jet-black smoke curl from his spider-fingers. There is a blade in his hand.

The black man stands. His stone smile widens.

He finds his tongue, hisses, "A door to what?"

"To something you'll never see, nor would you understand."

Lost and overwhelmed. "I don't—"

"The only thing you need understand is there will be blood spilled."

Copping Squid

MICHAEL SHEA

Michael Shea has written the Lovecraftian novel The Color out of Time *(DAW, 1984). He is the author of the short story collection* Polyphemus *(Arkham House, 1987). His Cthulhu Mythos story "Fat Face" has been widely reprinted, notably in* Cthulhu 2000 *(Arkham House, 1995). Among his many other works are a four-volume series of novels chronicling the adventures of* Nifft the Lean *(1982–2000), the first of which won the World Fantasy Award. Shea has also worked in science fiction and has been nominated for a Hugo Award.*

ICKY DEUCE, TWENTY-EIGHT AND THREE YEARS SOBER, was the night clerk at Mahmoud's Mom and Pop Market. He was a small, leanly muscled guy, and as he sat there, the darkness outside deepening toward midnight, his tight little Irish face looked pleased with where he was. Behind Ricky on his stool, the whole wall was bottles of every kind of Hard known to man.

This job was easy money—a sit-down after his day forklifting at the warehouse. He already owned an awesomely restored '64 Mustang and had near ten K saved, and by rights he ought to be casting around for where he might take off to next. But the fact was, he got a kick out of clerking here till two a.m. each night.

A kick that was not powder nor pill nor smoke nor booze, that was not needing any of them, especially not booze, which could shine and glint in its bottles and surround him all night long, and he not give a shit. He never got tired of sitting here immune, savoring the unadorned adventure of being alive.

Not that the job lacked irritants. There were obnoxious clientele, and these preponderated toward the deep of night.

Ricky thought he heard one even now.

Single cars shushed past outside, long silences falling between, and a scuffy tread advanced along the sidewalk. A purposeful tread that nonetheless staggered now and then. It reminded Ricky that he was It, the only island of comfort and light for a half a mile in all directions, in a big city, in the dead of night.

Then, there in Mahmoud's Mom and Pop Market's entryway,

stood a big gaunt black guy. Youngish, but with a strange, outdated look, his hair growing weedily out toward a 'fro. His torso and half his legs were engulfed in an oversize nylon athletic jacket that looked like it might have slept in an alley or two, and which revealed the chest of a dark T-shirt that said something indecipherable RULES. The man had a drugged look, but he also had wide-arched, inquiring brows. His glossy black eyes checked you out, as if maybe the real him was somewhere back in there, smarter than he looked.

But then, as he lurched inside the store, and into the light, he just looked drunk.

"Evening," Ricky said smiling. He always opened by giving all his clientele the benefit of the doubt.

The man came and planted his hands of the counter, not aggressively, it seemed, but in the manner of someone tipsily presenting a formal proposition.

"Hi. I'm Andre. I need your money, man."

Ricky couldn't help laughing. "What a coincidence! So do I!"

"OK, Bro," Andre said calmly, agreeably. As if he was shaping a counter-proposal, he straightened and stepped back from the counter. "Then I'ma cut your fuckin ass to *ribbons* till you *give* me your fuckin money!"

The odd picture this plan of action presented almost made Ricky laugh again, but then the guy whipped out and flipped open—with great expertise—a very large-gravity knife, which he then swept around by way of threat, though still out of striking range. Ricky was so startled that he half fell off his stool.

Getting his legs under him, furious at having been galvanized like that, Ricky shrieked, "A knife? You're gonna to rob me with a fucking *knife? I've* got a fucking knife!"

And he unpocketed his lock-back Buck knife and snapped it open. All this while he found himself once again trying to decipher the big, uncouthly lettered word on the guy's T-shirt above the word RULES.

Andre didn't seem drunk at all now. He swept a slash over the counter at Ricky's head, from which Ricky had to recoil right smartly.

"You shit! You do that again and I'm gonna slice your—"

Here came the gravity knife again, as quick as a shark, and, snapping his head back out of the way, Ricky counter-slashed at the sweeping arm and felt the rubbery tug of flesh unzipped by the tip of his Buck's steel.

Andre abruptly stepped back and relaxed. He put his knife away and held up his arm. It had a nice bloody slash across the inner forearm. He stood there letting it bleed for Ricky. Ricky had seen himself and others bleed, but not a black man. On black skin, he found, blood looked more opulent, a richer red, and so did the meat underneath the skin. That cut would take at least a dozen stitches. They both watched the blood soak the elastic cuff of Andre's jacket.

"So here's what it is," said Andre, and dipped his free hand in the jacket and pulled out a teensy, elegant little silver cellphone. "Ima call the oinkers, and say I need an ambulance because this mad whacked white shrimp—that's you—slashed me when I just axed him for some spare change, and then Ima ditch the shit outta this knife before they show up, and it won't matter if they believe me or not, when they see me bleedin like this they gonna take us both down for questioning and statements. How's your rap sheet, Chief, hey? So look. Just give me a little money and I'm totally outta your face. It don't have to be much. Ten dollars would do it!"

This took Ricky aback. "Ten dollars? You make me cut you for ten dollars?"

"You wanna give me a hundred, give me a hundred! Ten's all you gotta give me—and a ride. A short ride, over to the Hood."

"You want money and a ride! You think I'm outta my mind? You wanna ride to your connection to score, and when we get there, you're gonna try an get more money out of me. And that's the *best* case scenario." Ricky was dismayed to hear a hint of negotiation in his own words. It was true, he'd had a number of contacts with the San Francisco Police Department, as the result of alcohol-enhanced conflicts here and there. But also, he felt intrigued by the guy. Something fascinating burned in this Andre whack. Intensity came off him in waves, along with his faint scent of street-funk. The man was consumed by a passion. In the deformed letters on his t-shirt, Ricky thought he could make out a T_H_U.

"What could I be coppin for ten bucks?" crowed Andre. "I'm not out to harm you! This just has to do with *me*. See, it's *required*. I have to get these two things from someone else, the money and the ride."

"Explain that. Explain why you *have* to get these two things from someone else."

Andre didn't answer for a moment. He stared and stared, not exactly at Ricky, but at something he seemed to see in Ricky. He seemed to be weighing this thing he detected. He had eyes like black opals, and strange slow thoughts seemed to move within their shiny hemispheres…

"The reason is," he said at last, "that's the *procedure*. There are these particular rules for seeing the one I want to see."

"And who is that?"

"I can't tell you. I'm not allowed."

It was almost time to close up anyway. Ricky became aware of a powerful tug of curiosity, and aware of the fact that Andre saw it in his eyes. This put Ricky's back up.

"No. You gotta give me something. You gotta tell me at least—"

"Thassit! Fuck you!" And Andre flipped open the cellphone.

His big spatulate fingertips made quick dainty movements on the minute keys. Ricky heard the bleep, minuscule but crystal clear, of the digits, and then a micro-voice saying, "Nine One One Emergency."

"I been stabbed by a punk in a liquor store! I been stabbed!"

Ricky violently shook his head, and held up his hands in surrender. With a bleep, Andre clicked off. "Believe me! You're not makin a mistake. It's something I can't talk about, but you can *see* it. You can see it yourself. But the thing is, it's got to be now. We can't hem an haw. And Ima tell you now, now that you're in, that there's something *in* it for you, something good as gold. Trust me, you'll see. Help me with this knot," he said, pulling a surprisingly clean-looking handkerchief from his jacket pocket. He folded it—rather expertly, Ricky thought—into a bandage. Ricky wrapped it round the wound and tied the ends in a neat, tight square-knot, feeling as his fingers pressed against flesh that he was forming a bond with this whack by stanching his blood. He was accepting a dangerous complicity with his whack aims, whatever they might be…

Bandaged, Andre held out his hand. Ricky put a ten in it.

"Thanks," said Andre. "So. Where's your ride?"

THE BLUE MUSTANG BOOMED DOWN SIXTEENTH through the Mission. All the signals were on blink. Here and there under the streetlights, there was a wino or two, or someone walking fast, shoulders hunched against the emptiness, but mostly the Mustang rolled through pure naked City, a vacant concrete stage.

Ricky liked driving around at this hour, and often did it on his own for fun. When he was a kid, he'd always felt sorcery in the midnight streets, in the mosaic of their lights, and he'd never lost the sense of unearthly shapes stirring beneath their web, stirring till they almost cohered, as the stars did for the ancients into constellations. Tonight, with mad, bleeding Andre riding shotgun, the lights glittered wilder possibilities, and a sinister grandeur seemed to lurk in them.

They passed under the freeway and down to the Bayside, hanging south on Third. After long blocks of big blank buildings, Third took a snaky turn, and they were rolling through the Hood.

Pawn shops and thrift stores and liquor stores. A whiff of Mad Dog hung over it, Mad Dog with every other drug laced through it. The Hood was lit, was like a long jewel. The signals were working here.

The signals stretched out of sight ahead, like a python with scales of red and green, their radiance haloed in a light fog that was drifting in off the Bay. And people were out, little knots of them near the corners. They formed isolated clots of gaudy life, like tidepools, all of them dressed in baggy clothes of bright-colored nylon, panelled and logoed with surreal pastels under the emerald-and-ruby signal glare. And as they stood and talked together, they moved in a way both fitful and languid, like sealife bannering in a restless sea.

The signals changed in pattern to a slow tidal rhythm. It seemed a rhythm meant to accommodate rush-hour traffic. You got a green for two blocks max, and then you got a red. A long, long red. Ricky's blue Mustang was almost the only car on the road in this phantom rushhour, creeping down the long bright python two blocks at a time and then idling, idling interminably, while the sealife on the corners seemed astir with interest and attention.

Ricky had no qualms about running red lights on deserted streets, but here it seemed dangerous, a declaration of unease.

"Fuck this!" he said at their fourth red light, slipping the brake and rolling forward. At a stroll though, under twenty.

The Mustang lounged along, taking green and red alike, as if upon a scenic country road. The bright languid people on the corners threw laughter at them now, a shout or two, and it seemed as if the whole great submarine python stirred to quicker currents. Ricky felt a ripple of hallucination, and saw here, for just a moment, a vast inked mural, the ink not dry, themselves and all around them still half-liquid entities billowing in an aqueous universe…

Out of nowhere, for the first time in three years, Ricky had the thought that he would like a drink. He was amazed at this thought. He was frightened. Then he was angry.

"I'm not drivin much farther, Andre. Spit out where we're going, and it better be nearby, or you can call 911 and I'll take my chances. I'll bet you got a longer past with the SFPD than I do."

"*Damn* you! Whip in here, then."

This cross street was mostly houses—some abandoned—with a liquor store on the next corner, and a lot of sealife lounging out in front of it. "Pull up into some light where you can see this."

They idled at the curb. The people on the main drag were two-thirds of a block behind them, the liquor store tidepool much closer ahead of them. Andre leaned his fanatic's face close to Ricky. The intensity of the man was an almost tactile experience; Ricky seemed to feel the muffled crackling of his will through the inches of air that separated them. "Here," hissed Andre. "I'm gonna give you *this*, just to drive me another coupla miles up into these hills. Look at it. Count it. Take it." He shoved a thick roll of bills into Ricky's ribs.

It was in twenties and fifties and hundreds… It was over five thousand dollars.

"You're…you're batshit, Andre! You make me cut you to get ten bucks, and now you—"

"Just listen." Some people from the liquor store tide pool were drifting their way, and Ricky saw similar movement from Third Street in his rearview mirror. "What I needed," said Andre, "was money that blood was spilt for—it didn't matter how much blood, it didn't matter how much money. Your ten-spot? It's worth that much to me there in your hand. Your ten-spot and another couple miles in your car."

The locals were flowing closer to the Mustang at both ends. Ricky fingered the money. The gist of it was, he decided, that if he didn't follow this waking dream to its end, he would never forgive himself. "OK," he said.

"Another couple miles in your car," said Andre, "an one more thing. You gotta come in."

"You fuck! You shit! Where does it *end* with you? You just keep—"

"You come in, you watch me connect, and you go out again, scot-free, no harm, no strings attached! I gotta bring blood money, and I gotta bring a *witness*. I lied to you. It wasn't the ride I needed. It was a *witness*."

A huge shape in lavender running-sweats, and a gaunt one wearing a lime-green jumpsuit, stood beside the Mustang, smiling and making roll-down-the-window gestures. Behind the car, shapes from the main drag were moving laterally out into the street to come up to the driver's side...

But in that poised moment what Ricky saw most vividly was Andre's face, his taut narrow face within its weedy 'fro. This man was in the visionary's trance. His eyes, his soul were locked upon something that filled him with awe. What he pursued had nothing to do with Ricky, nor with anything Ricky could imagine, and Ricky wanted to know what that thing was.

Andre said, "Ima show you—what's your name again?"

"Ricky."

"Ima show you, Richie, the power and the glory. They are

right here *among* you, man, an you don't even see it! Hell, even these fools out here can *see* it!"

The Mustang was surrounded now. From behind it sprouted shapes in crimson hoods, with fists bulging inside gold velvet jacket pockets. Up to Ricky's door (its window already open, his elbow thrust out, and five K in cash on his lap) stepped two men with thundercloud hair, wearing shades, their cheeks and brows all whorled with Maori tatooing like ink-black flames. A trio of gaudy nylon scarecrows leaned on his hood, conferring, the side-thrust bills of their caps switching like blades. But Ricky also noted that all this audience, every one of them, had eyes strictly for Andre sitting there at his side. Ricky was free to scan all those exotic, piratical faces as though he were invisible…

All their eyes were grave. They showed awe, and they showed loathing too, as if they abhorred something Andre had done, but just as piercingly, longed for his nerve to do it. Ricky realized he had embarked on a longer journey than he'd thought.

Andre scanned all these buccaneer faces, his fellow mariners of the Hood. A remote little grin was hanging slantwise across his jaw. "Check this out Rocky," he growled, "an learn from these fools. Learn their *awe*, man, cause what I'ma show you, up in those hills, is *awe*."

He shouldered his door open and thrust himself up onto the sidewalk. He towered just as tall as the giant in lavender sweats, but he was narrow as a reed. Yet his voice fairly boomed:

"Yo! Alla you! Listen up! Looka here! Looka me! You all wanna see something? Wanna see something *about* something besides *shit*!? See something *real*, just for a *change*? See the ice-cold, spine-crawlin, hair-stirrin *truth*? Looka here! Looka here, at the power! Looka here! Looka here, at the glory!"

Ricky scanned all the dark faces that ringed them round, and every eye was locked upon that wild gaunt man in his rapture, who now, with a powerful shrug, shouldered off his nylon jacket. It flopped down on the sidewalk with a slither and a sigh, and lay there on the concrete like a sloughed cocoon. He stretched the fabric of his T-shirt, displaying it to every locked-on eye.

Rickey's angle was still too acute to let him decipher exactly who it was who "ruled." But all these encircling faces, *they* seemed to know. They shared a vision of awe and terror and...something like hope. A frosty hope, endlessly remote... but hope. Ricky realized that there prevailed on these mean streets a consensus of vision. He clearly saw that all these eyes had seen, and understood, a catastrophic spectacle beyond his own imagining.

Andre barked, hoarse and brutish as a sea-lion, "Jus *look* at me here! I have gone up to see Him, and I have looked through His eyes, and I have *been* where He *is*, time without end! An I'm here to tell you, all you dearly beloved mongrel dogs of mine, I'm here to tell you that it's *consumed* me! My flesh, and my time, have been blown off my bones, by the searing winds of His breath! I'm not far off now from eternity! Not far off from infinity now!"

The raving seer then hiked up his T-shirt to his chest. What Ricky, from behind, saw there was like a blow to his own chest, an impact of terror and dizziness, for Andre's thorax on its left side was normal, gauntly fleshed and sinewed, but along its right side, his spine was denuded bone, and midriff was there none, and just below his hoisted shirt-hem, a lathed bracket looped down: a fleshless rib, as clean and bare as sculpture...

His rapt audience recoiled like a single person, some lifting their arms convulsively, as in a reflex of self-protection, or acclaim...

Ricky dropped the Mustang into gear and launched it from the curb, but in that selfsame instant Andre dropped into his seat again and slammed his door, and so he was snatched deftly away, as if he were a prize that Ricky treasured, and not a horror that Ricky had been trying to flee.

Moon-silvered, lightless blocks floated past, yet Ricky never took his eyes from the gaunt shape whose T-shirt he could now, uncomprehending, read: *CTHULHU RULES*.

Somehow he drove and, shortly, pulled again to a more deserted curb, and killed the engine. On this block, a sole dim streetlight shone. Half the houses were doorless, windowless…

He sat with only silence between himself and a man who had, at the least, submitted to a grave surgical mutilation in the service of his deity. Ricky looked into Andre's eyes.

That was the first challenge, to establish that he dared to look into Andre's eyes—and he found that he did dare.

"For all you've lost," Ricky said, queasily referencing the gruesome marvel, " …you seem very…alive."

"I'm more alive than you will ever be, and when I'm all consumed, I'll be far *more* alive, and I will live forever!"

Ricky fingered the little bale of cash in his hand. "If you want me to go on, you have to tell me this. *Why* do you have to have a witness?"

"Because the One I'm gonna see wants someone new to see Him. He doesn't wanna know you. He wants *you* to know *Him*." In the darkness, Andre's polished eyes seemed to burn with this thing that he knew, and Ricky did not.

"He wants me to know him. And then?"

"And then it's up to you. To walk away, or to see him like I do."

"And how is that? How do you see him?"

"All the way."

Ricky's hand absently stroked the gearshift knob. "The choice is absolutely mine?"

"Your will is your own! Only your knowledge will be changed!"

Ricky slipped the Mustang into gear, and once more the blue beast growled onward. "Take a right here," purred Andre. "We going up to the top of the hills."

It was the longest "couple miles" that Ricky had ever driven. The road poured down past the Mustang like time itself, a slow stream of old, and older houses, on steepening blocks gapped by vacant lots, or by derelict cottages whose windows and doors were coffined in grafittied plywood.

They began to wind, and a rising sense of peril woke in Ricky. He was charging up into the sinister unknown! There was just too much missing from this man's body! You couldn't lose all that and still walk around, still fight with knives... could you?

But you could. Just look at him.

The houses thinned out even more, big old trees half-shrouding them. Dead cars slept under drifts of leaves, and dim bedroom lights showed life just barely hanging on, here in the hungry heights.

As they mounted this shoulder of the hills, Ricky saw glimpses of other ridges to the right and left, rooftop-and-tree-encrusted like this one. All these crestlines converged toward the same summit, and when Ricky looked behind, it seemed that these ridges poured down like a spill of titanic tentacles. They plunged far below into a thick, surprisingly deep fog that drowned and dimmed the jeweled python of the Hood.

Near the summit, their road entered a deepening gully. At the apex stood a municipal watertank, the dull gloss of its squat cylinder half-sunk in trees and houses.

"We goin to that house there right upside the tank. See that big gray roof pokin from the trees? The driveway goes down through the trees, it's steep an dark. Just roll down slow and easy, kill the engine, an let me get out first an talk to her."

"Her?"

Andre didn't answer. The road briefly crested before plunging, and Ricky had a last glimpse below of the tentacular hills rooted in the fogbank—and rooted beyond that, he imagined, more deeply still into the black floor of the Bay, as if the tentacles rummaged there for their deep-sunk food...

"Right there," said Andre, pointing ahead. "See the gap in the bushes?"

The Mustang crept muttering down the dark leafy tunnel, just as a wind rose, rattling dry oak foliage all around them.

A dim grotto of grassy ground opened below. There was a squat house on it, so dark it was almost a shadow-house. It showed one dim yellow light on the floor of its porch. A lantern, it looked like. A large dark shape loomed on one side of this lantern, and a smaller dark shape lay on the other.

Ricky cut his engine. Andre drew a long, slow breath and got out. Leaves whispered in the silence. Andre's feet crackled across the yard. Ricky could hear the creak of his weight on the porch steps as he climbed them, halfway up to the two dark shapes and their dim shared light. And Ricky could also hear...a growly breathing, wasn't it? Yes...a slow, phlegmy purr of big lungs.

Andre's voice was a new one to Ricky: low and implacable. "I'm back again, Mamma Hagg. I got the toll. I got the witness." Then he looked back and said, "Stand on out here...what's your name again?"

Ricky got out. How dangerous it suddenly seemed to declare himself in this silence, this place! Well, shit. He was here. He might as well say who he was. Loudly: "Ricky Deuce."

When he'd said it, he found his eyes could suddenly decipher the smaller dark shape by the lantern: it was a seated black dog, a big one, with the hint of aging frost on his lower jaw, and with his red tongue hanging and gently pulsing by that frosted jaw. The dog was looking steadily back at him, its tongue a bright spoon of greedy tissue scooping up the taste of the night...

It was not the brute's breathing Ricky had heard. It was Momma Hagg's, her voice deep now from the vault of her cave-like lungs:

"Then show the toll, fool."

Andre bent slightly to hold something toward the hound. And above his bent back, the woman in her turn became visible to Ricky. Within a briar-patch of dreads as pale as mushrooms, her monolithic black face melted in its age, her eyes two tarpools in this terrain of gnarled ebony. The shadowy bulk of her body eclipsed the mighty chair she sat in, though its armrests jutted into view, dark wood intricately carven into the coils and claws and thews of two heraldic monsters. Ricky couldn't make out what they were, but they seemed to snarl beneath the fingers of Momma Hagg's immense hands.

The dog's tongue was licking what Andre held up to it—Ricky's ten-spot. The mastiff sniffed and sniffed, then snorted, and licked the bill again, and licked his chops.

"Come on up," said Momma. "The two of you." The big woman's voice had a strange kind of pull to it. Like surf at your legs, its growl dragged you toward her. Ricky approached. Andre mounted to the porch, and Ricky climbed after him. He had the sensation with each step up that he entered a bigger and emptier kind of space. When he stood on the porch, Momma Hagg seemed farther off than he had expected. From her distance wafted the smell of her—an ashen scent like the drenched coals of a bonfire that had included flesh and bones in its fuel. The dog rose.

The porch took too long to cross as they followed the hound. His bright tongue lolling like a casually held torch, with just one back-glance of one crimson eye, the brute led them through a wide, doorless doorframe, and into a high dark interior that gusted out dank salty breath in their faces.

A cold gray light leaked in here, as if the fog that had

swallowed the Hood had now climbed the hills, and its glow was seeping into this gaunt house. They trod a rambling, unpartitioned space, the interior all wall-less, while the outer walls were irregularly recessed in alcoves, nooks, and grottos. In some of these stood furniture, oddly forlorn, bulky antique pieces—an armchair, a settee, an escritoire crusted with ancient papers. These stranded little settings—like fossils of foregone transactions whose participants had blown to dust long since—seemed to mark the passage of generations through this rambling gloom.

Ricky had the disorienting sense they had been trekking for a long, long time. He realized that the stranded furniture had a delicately furred and crusted profile in the gray light, like tidepool rocks, and a cold tidal scent touched his nostrils. Realized too, that here and there in those recesses, there were windows. Beyond their panes lay a different shade of darkness, where weedy and barnacled shadows stirred and glinted wetly…

And throughout this shadowy passage, Ricky noted, on every stretch of wall he could discern, wooden wainscottings densely carven. The misty glow put a sheen on the sinuous saliences of this dark chiselwork, which seemed to depict bulbous, serpentine knots of tail and claw and thew—or perhaps woven cephalopodia, braided greedy tentacles, and writhing prey in ragged beaks…

But now the walls had narrowed in, and here were stairs, and up these steep, worn stairs the hound, not pausing, led them. The air of this stairwell was slightly dizzying. The labor of the black beast climbing before them seemed to pull the two men after, as if the beast drew them in an executioner's tumbril. They were lifted, Ricky suddenly felt, by a might far greater than theirs, and Andre, ahead of him, seemed to shiver and quake in the flux of that dire energy. It gave Ricky the sensation of walking in Andre's lee, and being sheltered by his body from a terror that streamed around him like a solar wind.

From the head of the stairs, a great moldy vacancy breathed down on them. They emerged into what seemed a simpler and far older structure. High-beamed ceiling, carven walls…it was no more than a grand passage ending at a high dark archway. The floorplanks faintly drummed, as if this was a bridgeway, unfoundationed. That great black arch ahead…it was inset in a wall that bowed. A metallic wall.

"The tank!" said Ricky. It jumped out of him. "That's that big water tank!"

The hound halted and turned. Andre too turned, gave him eyes of wild reproof, but the hound, raising to Ricky his crimson eyes, gave him a red-tongued leer, gave him the glinty-pupiled mockery of a knowing demon. This look set the carven walls to seething, set the sculpted thews rippling, limbs lacing, beaks butchering, all brutally busy beneath their fur of dust…

The hound turned again and led them on. Now they could smell the water in the great tank—an odor both metallic and marine—and the hound's breathing began to echo, to grow as cavernous as Mamma Hagg's had been. Within that archway was a blackness absolute, a darkness far more perfect than the gloom that housed them. As they closed with it, the hound's nails echoed as on a great oaken drum above a jungle wilderness. The beast dropped to its belly, lay panting, whining softly. The two men stood behind.

Within the portal, a huge glossy black surface confronted them, a great shield of glass, a mirror as big as a house. There they were in it: Ricky, Andre, the hound. The brightest feature of their tiny, distorted reflection was the bright red dot of the hound's tongue.

Andre paused for a few heartbeats only. Then he stepped through the arch, with an odd ceremonial straightness to his posture. He gestured and Ricky followed him, seeing, as he did so, that the aperture was cut through a double metal wall that showed a cross-section of struts between.

They stood on a narrow balcony just within the tank and felt a huge damp breath of the steel-clad lake below them, and gazed into the immense glass that was to afford them their Revelation of the Power and the Glory…

Andre stared some moments at his reflection, then turned to Ricky. "Now I tell you what it is…you say your name was Rocky?"

"Ricky."

"Ricky, now Ima tell you what it is. I came to see, and be seen by Him. When He really sees *you*, you can see through *His* eyes, and you can live His mind."

"But what if I don't want to live his mind?"

"You can't! You didn't pay the toll! You'll *see* some shit, though! You'll see enough, you'll know that if you got any adventure in your soul, you got to *pay* that toll! But that's up to you! Now look, an learn!"

He faced the mirror again, and in a cracked voice he cried, "Iä! Iä! Iä fhtagn!"

And the mirror, ever so slightly, contracted, and the faintest circumference of white showed round its great rim, and encompassing that ring of pallor, something black and scaly like a sea-beast's hide crinkled into view…and Ricky realized that they stood before the pupil of an immense eye.

And Ricky found his feet were rooted, and he could not turn to flee.

And he beheld a dizzying mosaic of lights flashing to life within the mighty pupil. A grand midnight vision crystallized: the whole of San Francisco Bay lay within the black orb, bordered by the whole bright oroboros of coastal lights…

He and Andre gazed on the vista, on the bridges' glittering spines transecting it, all their lengths corpuscled with fleeing lights red and white. The two men gazed on the panorama and it drank their minds. Rooted, they inhabited its grandeur, even as it began a subtle distortion. The vista seemed tugged awry, torqued toward the very center of the giant's pupil. And within that grand, slow distortion, Ricky saw strange movements. Across the Bay Bridge, near its eastern end, the cargo cranes of West Oakland—tracked monsters, each on four mighty legs—raised and bowed their cabled booms in a dinosaurian salute—obeisance, or acclaim…while to their left, the giant tanks on Benecia's tarry hills, and the Richmond tanks too in the west, began a ponderous rotation on their bases, a slow spin like planets obeying the pupil's gathering vortex.

Andre cried out, to Ricky, or just to the world he was about to leave, "I see it all coming apart! In detail! Behold!"

This last word reverberated in a brazen basso far larger than the lean man's lungs could shape. And the knell of that voice awoke winds in the night, and the winds buffeted Ricky as though he hung in the night sky within the eye, and Ricky *knew*. He knew this being into whose view he'd come! Knew this monster was the King of a vast migration of titans across the eons of the countless Space-Times! Over the gale-swept universe they moved, these Great Old Ones. Across the cracked continents they trawled, they plundered! Worlds were the pastures that they grazed, and the broken bodies of whole races were the pavement that they trod!

It astonished him, the threshold to which this Andre, night-walking zealot, had brought him. He looked at Andre now, saw the man utterly alone at the brink of his apotheosis. How high he seemed to hang in the night winds! Look at the frailty of that skinny frame! The mad greed of his adventure!

Andre seemed to shudder, to gather himself. He looked back at Ricky. He looked like he was seeing in Ricky some foreigner in a far, quaint land, some backward Innocent, unknowing of the very world he stood in.

"On squid, man," he said, "...on squid, *Ricky*, you get big! All hell breaks loose in the back of your brain, and you can *hold* it, you can *contain* it! And then you get to watch Him *feed.* And now *you'll* see. Just a little! Not too much! But you going to *know*."

Andre turned and faced the eye. He gathered himself, gathered his voice for a great shout:

"Here's my witness! Here I come!"

And he vaulted from the balcony, out into the pupil—impacted it for an instant, seemed to freeze in mid-leap as if he had struck glass—but in the instant after, was within the vast inverted cone of light-starred night, and hung high, tiny but distinct, above the slowly twisting panorama of the great black Bay all shoaled and shored and spanned with light. That galactic metropolis, round its core of abyss, was—less slowly now—still contorting, twisting toward the center of the pupil...

And Ricky found that he too hung within it, he stood on the wide cold air in the night sky, he felt against his face the winds' slow torque toward the the center of the Old One's sight.

And now all hell, with relentless slow acceleration, broke loose. The City's blazing, architected crown began to discohere, brick fleeing brick in perfect pattern, in widening pattern, till they all became pointilist buildings snatched away in the whirlwind, and from the buildings, all the people too like flung seed swirled up into the night, their evaporating arms raised as in horror, or salute, crying out their being from clouding faces that the black winds sucked to tatters...

He saw the great bridges braided with—and crumpling within—barnacle-crusted tentacles as thick as freeway tunnels, saw the freeways themselves—pillared rivers of light—unraveling, their traffic like red and white stars fleeing into the air, into the cyclone of the Great Old One's attention.

And an inward vision was given to Ricky, simultaneous

with this meteoric overview. For he also knew the Why of it. He knew the hunger of the nomad titans, their unappeasable will to consume each bright busy outpost they could find in the universal Black and Cold. Knew that many another world had fled, as this one fled, draining into the maw of the grim cold giants, each world's collapsing roofs and walls bleeding a smoke of souls, all sucked like spume into the mossy curvature of His colossal jaws...

T WAS PERFECTLY DARK. IT WAS ALMOST SILENT, EXCEPT for a rattle of leaves. The cold against his face had the wet bite of fog...

Ricky shook his head, and the dark grew imperfect. He put out his hand and touched rough wooden siding. He was alone on the porch, no lantern now, no armchair, no one else. Just dead leaves in crackly little drifts on the floorboards as—slowly and unsteadily—he started across them.

He had *seen* some shit. Stone cold sober, he had *seen*. And now the question was, who was he?

He crossed the leaf-starred grass, on legs that felt increasingly familiar. Yes...here was this Ricky-body that he knew, light and quick. And here was his Mustang, blown oak leaves chittering across its polished hood. And still the question was, who was he?

He was this car, for one thing, had worked long to buy it and then to perfect it. He got behind the wheel and fired it up, felt his perfect fit in this machine. Flawlessly it answered to his touch, and the blue beast purred up through the leaf-tunnel as the house—a doorless, glassless derelict—fell away behind him. But this Ricky Deuce...who was he now?

He emerged from the foliage and dove down the winding highway. There was the fog-banked Bay below, the jeweled snake of the Hood glinting within its gray wet shroud, and Ricky took the curves just like his old self, riding one of the hills' great tentacles down, down toward the sea they rooted in…

There was something Ricky had to do. Because in spite of his body, his nerves being his, he didn't *know* who he was now, had just had a big chunk torn out of him. And there was something terrible he had to do, to locate, by desperate means, the man he had lost, to find at least a piece of him he was sure of.

His hands and arms knew the way, it seemed. Diving down into the thicker fog, he smoothly threw the turns required… and slid up to the curb before the liquor store they'd parked near…when? A universe ago. Parked and jumped out.

Ricky was terrified of what he was going to do, and so he moved swiftly to have it done with, just nodding to his recent companions as he hastened into the store—nodding to the Maoris in shades, to the guys with the switchblade cap-bills, to the guys with the crimson hoods and the golden pockets. But rushed though he was, it struck him that they were all looking at him with a kind of fascination…

At the counter he said, "Fifth of Jack." He didn't even look to see what he peeled off his wad to pay for it, but there were a lot of twenties in his change. The Arab bagged him his bottle, his eyes fixed almost raptly on Ricky's, so Ricky was moved to ask in simple curiosity, "Do I look strange?"

"No," the man said, and then said something else, but Ricky had already turned, in haste to get outside where he could take a hit. Had the man said *no, not yet*?

Ricky got outside, cracked the cap, and hammered back a stiff, two-gurgle jolt.

He scarcely could wait to let it roll down and impact him. He felt the hot collision in his body's center, the roil of potential energy glowing there, then poked down a long, three-gurgle chaser. Stood reeling inwardly, and outwardly showing some impact as well…

And there it was: a heat, a turmoil, a slight numbing. No more. No magic. No rising trumpets. No wheels of light… The half-pint of Jack he'd just downed had no marvel to show like the one he'd just seen.

And so Ricky knew that he was someone else now, someone he had not yet fully met.

"'Sup?" It was the immense guy in the lavender sweats. He had a solemn Toltec-statue face, but an incongruously merry little smile.

"'S happnin," said Ricky. "Hey. You want this?"

"That Jack?"

"Take the rest. Keep it. Here's the cap."

"No thanks." This to the cap. The man drank. As he chugged, he slanted Ricky an eye with something knowing, something *I thought so* in it. Ricky just stood watching him. He had no idea at all of what would come next in his life, and for the moment, this bibulous giant was as interesting a thing as any to stand watching…

The man smacked his lips. "It ain't the same, is it?" he grinned at Ricky, gesturing the bottle. "It just don't matter any more. I mean, so I *understand.* I like the glow just fine myself. But you…see, you widdat Andre. You've been a *witness.*"

"Yeah. I have. So…tell me what that means."

"You the one could tell me. Alls I know is *I'd* never do it, and a whole lotta folks around here *they'd* never do it—but you didn't know that, did you?"

"So tell me what it *means.*"

"It means what you make of it! And speakin of which, man, of what you might make of it, I wanna show you something right now. May I?"

"Sure. Show me."

"Let's step round here to the side of the building…just round here…" Now they stood in the shadowy weed-tufted parking lot, where others lounged, but moved away when they appeared.

"I'm gonna show you somethin," said the man, drawing out his wallet and opening it.

But opening it for himself at first, for he brought it close to his face as he looked in, and a pleased, proprietary glow seemed to beam from his Olmec features. For a moment, he gloated over the contents of his billfold.

Then he extended and spread the wallet open before Ricky. There was a fat sheaf of bills in it, hand-worn bills with a skinlike crinkle. It seemed the money, here and there, was stained.

Reverently, Olmec said, "I bought this from the guy that capped the guy it came from. This is as pure as it gets. Blood money with the blood right on it! An you can have a bill of it for five hundred dollars! I *know* that Andre put way more than that in your hand. I *know* you know what a great deal this is!"

Ricky…had to smile. He saw an opportunity at least to *gauge* how dangerously he'd erred. "Look here," he told Olmec. "Suppose I did buy blood money. I'd still need a witness. So what about *that*, man? Will *you* be my witness for…almost five grand?"

Olmec did let the sum hang in the air for a moment or two, but then said, quite decisively, "Not for twice that."

"So Andre got me cheap?"

"Just by my book. You could buy witnesses round here for half that!"

"I guess I need to think it over."

"You know where I hang. Thanks for the drink."

And Ricky stood there for the longest time, thinking it over…

Passing Spirits

SAM GAFFORD

Sam Gafford grew up on a steady diet of comic books, television, old horror movies, and the fiction of H. P. Lovecraft. Small wonder that he would want to become a writer. His stories and essays have appeared in a variety of small-press publications and magazines. Gafford has also helped to advance the critical study of the fiction of William Hope Hodgson. He is working on a novel about Jack the Ripper.

"...THULHU NEVER EXISTED. AZATHOTH NEVER EXISTED... Nyarlathotep, Shub-Niggurath, Nug, Yeb, none of them. I made them all up."

I was sitting in H. P. Lovecraft's small study, listening to him rant. It was 1937. In barely under a year he would be dead of stomach cancer. I felt a need to try to tell him this. To let him know that the pain in his abdomen was not just "grippe" but a serious medical problem that he should seek treatment for immediately. When I tried to explain that I knew all about those types of things, he refused to listen and went on ranting.

"But you know what is the worst thing about all of this?" he continued in his nasal voice. "This is what I'll be remembered for...if I'm remembered by anyone. For making up a pantheon of monster-gods. Basically, for stealing from Dunsany."

I tried to explain that that wasn't the truth. That he had added much more to it than just the idea of a cosmic mythology, but he wouldn't listen. It was very strange and not at all the type of conversation I had envisioned having. I wouldn't say that the man was bitter, but he certainly wasn't happy about a lot of things.

Looking at him, I felt that there were so many things that I should be saying but I didn't. My time was too short for that and the memory was already fading.

HEN I AWOKE, I WAS IN MY APARTMENT AND THERE WAS a ribbon of spit on the pillow next to me. I checked it for blood, but it was clear. My head throbbed as usual and I felt the familiar dull ache behind my eyes. I crawled out of bed and turned the TV on as I dressed. CNN was going on about some flareup in the Middle East (I had long ago stopped caring about such things, there was always a flareup somewhere or other) and I flipped it over to *Scooby-Doo* on the Cartoon Network. It was one of my favorites from the first year (the best year before they got into all that guest-star nonsense and then brought in Scrappy-Doo—who the hell ever thought that was a good idea?) with the space ghost that had the glowing, laughing head. I remember how that scared the piss out of me as a kid. A lot of things scared me back then, before I learned that the only real scary thing in life was stuff like cancer and brain tumors. There weren't any gods or monsters. Not in the real world. Here we had sickness and disease instead of vampires and ghosts.

I brushed my teeth and took my medicine. Looking at the clock, I had about an hour to get to work, so I knew I'd have enough time. I sat down and watched the rest of the show, waiting for that great *Scooby-Doo* ending where they unmask the villain. I always loved that.

T WORK, I TRIED TO PRETEND THAT I CARED ABOUT what I was doing, but it didn't really matter. I was just another clerk in just another bookstore. Nothing special. Nothing unique. I had "Help Desk" duty, which everyone knew was the worst. Listening to blue-haired old ladies trying to describe what they wanted. "I don't know the name but I saw it on *Oprah*. It had a black cover."

The other clerks tried not to look at me too closely. My hair had grown back, more or less, but there's still something about a cancer patient that sets you off from everyone else. Maybe it's a smell or some invisible "early-warning" system, but no one looks at you the same way afterward. That didn't bother me too much. Most of them weren't worth knowing anyway. Weird, trendy people of questionable sexuality. I'd never had much in common with them nor they with me.

Lovecraft's ghost followed me through the reference section, pointing out books with errors in them. I hate it when he does that.

"HE TUMOR'S GETTING LARGER," INTONED DR. LYONS with all the seriousness of a hanging judge. He held up two CAT scans. "As you can see from the earlier one, it was only about the size of a grape. Now it's getting close to a plum."

I'd never eaten a plum, so had no idea about its size. I figured that it wasn't a good comparison.

"So none of the treatments have done anything?"

Dr. Lyons sighed. "No. The radiation treatments barely seemed to hold its growth. Since we stopped doing those, it's gotten bigger. The medication doesn't seem to be working either. Surgery, although not recommended, is still an option."

"You told me before that it was too dangerous."

"It is. But I don't really see any other way." He got up from behind his desk. "Michael, you have to understand that without surgery this is going to continue to grow."

Apparently I wasn't impressed enough by this.

"Michael, you will die without this operation."

I thought about this. Dying wasn't necessarily the worst thing. Chemo was certainly on an equal footing. Poverty was right up there too.

"How long?"

"If the tumor continues to grow at this size, maybe four to six months, on the outside. But, Michael, they won't be comfortable months."

He went on to describe how, as the tumor grows, I would begin to lose brain functions. My speech and sight would be affected. My coordination would deteriorate. In short, it would be a living death.

I thanked him and left. Dr. Lyons was confused and followed me out into the hall. He wanted to know why I didn't want to schedule the operation immediately. I looked at him.

"Because I can't afford it." I turned away. He didn't stop me.

ROBERT E. HOWARD MADE A WRITING CAREER OUT OF stories of strong rugged men who tamed their worlds and bent others to their will. It was a universe of barbarians with strong sword arms and evil sorcerers who plotted magic schemes of conquest. Not once do I recall an REH character dying of cancer or an illness. Of course, that probably would have been too personal a thing considering how his mother died.

"Don't forget," Lovecraft said, "Two-Gun Bob killed himself."

"Yeah, well, there's plenty of ways to do that. Sometimes doing nothing works just as well." I replied.

THERE HAD BEEN AN ARTICLE IN THE PAPER NOT TOO long ago about a doctor doing work on cancer treatment. It wasn't one of those peach-pit things, but it was an herbal remedy. Supposedly some type of combination of herbs and diets. I'd read a lot of those books, including the one by Norman Cousins. Sometimes they seemed to work, most times they didn't. I'd never had the discipline to see them all through but, considering the alternatives, I didn't have a lot of choices.

At work, I looked up the doctor's book. To my surprise, we actually had a copy. Glancing through it, it looked more like a cookbook than anything else. The medicine was a blend of herbs and vitamins (supposedly available at any health food store), and there was a special diet that focused on macrobiotics and avoided things like meat and oils. It seemed to be typical stuff, but the doctor's photo had a kind and gentle face, so I bought it. I enjoyed making my manager nervous when she rang it up. It was obvious why I was buying it, but no one dared to mention it.

"You know," Lovecraft said to me in a horrified whisper, "someone once said that my Shub-Niggurath was a representation of sexual disease. Can you believe that?"

I heard this at least once a day. It was one of the things that really bothered him, given his upbringing and personality.

"Yeah, I can believe it," I replied. My manager didn't even look at me. She had gotten used to me talking like this.

On the way home, I bought the herbs listed in the book at the only local health food store. I didn't recognize most of the names and the clerk wasn't much help either. Several of the ingredients weren't there, so I had to substitute. The clerk thought that the other herbs and vitamins were just as good and, even though I didn't believe him, didn't have anything else to go on.

I stopped at a local restaurant and had a big steak meal with a plateful of french fries. My farewell to meat. I avoided the seafood platter out of deference to Lovecraft who, as always, kept looking around and exclaiming, "Gad, how these birds do eat!"

At home later, I read through the book some more. The doctor believed that the steady use of his herb/vitamin combination, along with the diet, was able to curb the growth of cancer. In a few instances he described, the cancer had disappeared completely. I laid the pill bottles on the counter. I mixed the herbs together. There was a specific pattern on what to take, how much, and when. I took the first dose and followed it with Dr. Lyons's medication. It had a long clinical name that I couldn't pronounce but it was "the latest in cancer treatment." Couldn't hurt to keep taking it. I'd paid for it, after all, and it hadn't been cheap. The cost of being poor and sick in America.

HAT NIGHT, THERE WASN'T MUCH ON TV. THE CABLE channels were all boring so I put an old *Night Stalker* tape on and read for a while. Out of habit, I picked up *The Dunwich Horror* and started reading "The Shadow over Innsmouth" again. It had always been one of my favorites, but Lovecraft wouldn't give me any peace.

"Disease, disease, disease. That's all they keep talking about. According to some critics, everything I wrote came from a fear of disease, either sexual or mental. Why couldn't it just be a story? Why did it have to be *about* something?"

"You think that's bad," I replied, "you should read Hodgson. Now *there's* a man who had a real problem with disease."

That piqued his interest and he settled down with a volume of Hodgson's short stories. One of the small-press books, of course, I would never have been able to afford a first edition and he wasn't reprinted often.

Lovecraft read quickly and quietly. Reading was one of the few things that kept him calm. Every so often he would chuckle to himself or make a satisfied sound after reading a particularly good section.

In this wise, I eventually fell asleep.

WAS WALKING THROUGH THE STREETS OF INNSMOUTH past the Esoteric Order of Dagon church (with its sinister shadow in the basement), along the streets of houses that, though habitable, showed no signs of life. I walked by the supermarket and waved to the stock clerk who, as normal, bore a striking resemblance to Frank Long. (I hoped he'd had an easier life than the real Long.) Zadok Allen was wandering about, of course, and we exchanged laughs and old stories.

"Well, ya know, death's funny. It comes when ya don't call and never answers when ya do!" Zadok laughed without the trademark Yankee accent.

Lovecraft the narrator came lumbering down the street from the supermarket and Zadok staggered off to meet him, practicing his Yankee-speak as he walked. They had an appointment to keep.

I sat on the beach and looked out at Devil's Reef. It was an ugly thing. A piece of rock jutting out of the water. Beyond it, I knew, the ocean floor fell away and the Deep Ones swam not far beyond.

Several fishermen with the "Innsmouth look" stopped by and encouraged me to swim out. "G'wan," they said, "why not?"

Why not, indeed? I took off my clothes (never self-conscious in dreams… I had never had the "waking up in school naked" dream) and entered the water. Though I had done it a few times before, I'd never swum out very far. This time felt different. The water was warmer, heavier than before, and it enveloped me like nothing I had ever felt. I swam out to the rock and climbed on top of it.

From there, I could see Zadok and Lovecraft talking on the beach as Zadok gave his little speech. And then it struck me. Every other time I'd been here, I had only seen and experienced what Lovecraft had written in the story. I'd never been out to Devil's Reef before and, remembering the story, neither had the narrator. Oh sure, he described planning on *going* to Devil's Reef with his cousin and diving off the deep end, but it wasn't an actual place he visited in the story. Yet I was there. I could feel the rough stone beneath my fingers and, looking over the other end, could swear that I could see other things beneath the surface, beckoning to me.

Slowly, I dipped into the water and followed.

WHEN I WOKE UP THIS TIME, THERE WAS BLOOD ON THE pillow. That wasn't good. I touched my nose and my fingers came away bloody. Suddenly, my head was shoved into an invisible vise and I collapsed back into my pillow, barely able to keep from screaming.

In his chair, stroking an invisible cat that wasn't there but was anyway, Lovecraft sat silently.

After a few minutes, the pain subsided and I was able to sit up. The front of my undershirt was covered in blood. This hadn't been the first attack, but it was definitely the worst.

"Dr. Lyons said it would only get worse," Lovecraft added unnecessarily.

I ignored him and went to clean myself up.

Sometime later, I made myself some breakfast. I didn't have any of the macrobiotic stuff the book doctor recommended, so I made do with eggs and bacon. I'd give up the bad stuff later, although I had begun to think that there wasn't any point in giving anything up and that I should just surrender to excesses. Spend the last months of my life carousing from one bar to another, drinking too much, eating bad food, sleeping with anonymous women (assuming I could find any who were willing) and just give myself up to the extremes.

Lovecraft looked disapprovingly at me. "I know," I said, "you'd probably prefer if I just sat there quietly and suffered like you did while I eat a can of cold beans and some crackers."

"You could do worse," he said, but I didn't see how.

"I could do a lot better," I said and started mentally counting up the money in my bank account. Just enough for a real large splurge or six months of diminishing capacity. Yeah. Life's great.

"What about the dream?" Lovecraft asked.

I looked at him. I'd grown used to him asking questions at the most inappropriate time for a spirit who shouldn't even be here ("Why are you haunting me anyway? What'd I do to you?") but this was unexpected.

"What dream?"

He looked at me. I knew perfectly well what he meant and he had this habit of looking at me a certain way when I was avoiding a subject. I expected him to hand me a business card someday with *H. P. Lovecraft, conscience* printed on it. Jiminy Cricket had nothing on him.

"It was a dream, that's all."

He just glared at me. "Here," he finally said, "read this. It might help you understand." He threw a copy of Hodgson's *The Ghost Pirates* at me. I still hadn't figured out how he was able to manipulate objects but my head was hurting too much to wonder about it.

I looked at the book. "I read it already."

"Read it again. You obviously didn't get the connection." He went back and starting petting the cat again. It was an all-black kitten whose name, if you dared to mention it in today's PC climate, could get you into a lot of trouble. "*All the pigeons come home to roost*," I thought.

I took the herb/vitamin potion and chased it with one of Dr. Lyons's Miracle Cure. "*Good for what ails ya!*" I got dressed and left for work. On the way, I found the Hodgson buried deep into my coat pocket. *He* put it there. *I* put it there. Didn't matter. It was still there anyway.

When I got to work, I saw Keziah Mason in the occult section, chuckling to herself as she read one of the New Age witchcraft books. She certainly didn't look like the young, trendy/sexy girls that are witches in today's movies and TV shows. Brown Jenkin was curling around her feet, looking up at her from time to time with a very hungry shine in his eyes. This was something new. Usually it's just Lovecraft, now other characters were coming to visit.

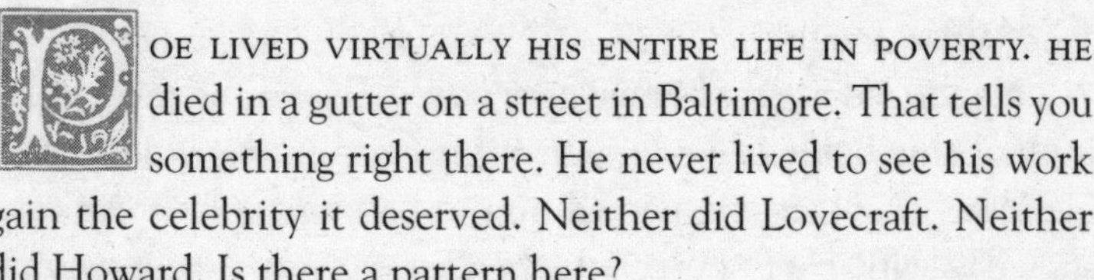

POE LIVED VIRTUALLY HIS ENTIRE LIFE IN POVERTY. HE died in a gutter on a street in Baltimore. That tells you something right there. He never lived to see his work gain the celebrity it deserved. Neither did Lovecraft. Neither did Howard. Is there a pattern here?

THE LAST CLEAR THING I REMEMBER FROM THAT afternoon at work was waiting on Nyarlathotep. I suppose it was only inevitable. With Keziah and Jenkin about, the Dark Man couldn't be far away. I was running the register when he came up. He put a couple of self-help books on the counter (two of those *I'm Okay, You're Okay* self-affirmation kind of things) and started fumbling for his wallet. This struck me as kind of funny as I couldn't imagine Nyarlathotep having a wallet. I wondered what would be inside it. Would he have a driver's license? From where? Kadath maybe? Snapshots of Keziah and Azathoth? Who did he want contacted in case of an emergency? And what was the wallet made out of? I started laughing which made him look up at me. The man was dark. I don't mean just your normal black man. Nyarlathotep was the antithesis of light. Then he smiled and I could smell his breath. It wasn't the stagnating breath of decay as I'd been expecting. It was sweet and cloying. It made you think of hot summer nights when the heat sticks to your skin and you can peel your sweat away in layers. My eyes closed and I went away.

WAS IN THE MISKATONIC LIBRARY WITH LOVECRAFT AS Henry Armitage. We were looking at the dead thing that lay on the floor where the guard dog had killed it. The upper body was strange enough but it was below the torso that "sheer phantasy began." Wilbur Whateley had died in his attempt to steal the *Necronomicon*. "Why didn't he just buy a copy from a book dealer or something?" I said. Armitage glared at me.

The game was afoot and I was standing in the open fields of Dunwich. Before me was the farmhouse of the Fryes, the poor, doomed Fryes. It was 3 a.m. but I could see everything as if it was high noon. Even from a distance I could hear their terrified conversation on the party-line phone. I saw the trees near the house bend apart as the invisible thing came closer. I had expected it to be something like Godzilla rampaging through downtown Tokyo. That's what happens when you're a child of the media and you grow up watching a genre that consumes itself with such gusto.

I heard the splintering of wood and looked up to see the top of the farmhouse cave in the middle. The screams were horrible. Within seconds, the house was gone and the thing continued walking through the forest. "The Elmer Fryes had been erased from Dunwich."

I made my way up to Sentinel Hill where the final confrontation would take place. I had walked this route before with Lovecraft/Armitage but this time felt different. I could feel the wind on my face. My body had form and substance where before it was only dust and mist. Sometimes I was Rice. Sometimes I was Morgan. And once, just once, there was a brief time when I could have sworn I was Armitage and I was spraying the spawn of Azathoth with the powder.

Above me there was the usual half-face squirming in torment except, this time, it stopped. It looked straight at me, ignoring the other two. "And what do you think you're looking at?" it said before it went back to its part and obligingly disappeared. I almost expected it to say "*I'm gonna keep my eye on you*" before it left, but it didn't. Afterwards we went back to the circle of terrified townsfolk and Armitage went into his speech. "*Watch the skies!*" I mouthed behind him. "*Watch the skies!*" The townspeople looked at me as if perhaps the wrong thing had been sprayed with the powder on the hill.

I regretted not seeing Old Wizard Whateley this trip. He was always a lot of fun to talk to, particularly if you got a few drinks into him.

HEN I AWOKE, I WAS IN A HOSPITAL BED.

I'd been in them before, of course, so this was no real strange thing to me, but it still wasn't a good sign. There was a strong coppery taste in my mouth. I knew that wasn't a good sign either. My finger was hooked into one of those machines and I could hear the heartbeat monitor behind me, happily beeping away. (I've always wondered why they put those things just out of your sight. As if watching your heartbeat might make it stop.) I felt weak and worn out. My clothes were gone and I was in the hospital gown. Lovecraft was sitting in the chair nearby.

"Can you believe what they've done to my city?" he asked when he saw I was finally awake. "They tore up the bridge. Tore up that historic bridge to make room for more traffic and make the downtown more *scenic*." He pronounced scenic with an extra flourish of sarcasm.

"Where am I?" My bed was encircled by one of those curtains but, because of the lack of noise, I could tell I wasn't in an emergency ward. It was still somewhat light out, so I knew it was daytime but I didn't know what day.

"You're in Rhode Island Hospital. It's attached to Jane Brown, you know. I went and looked in at the room where I died. There's a nurses' station there now. Everything changes."

I pulled the cord and buzzed for the nurse.

A large woman in a white uniform came a few minutes later. She explained that I had been unconscious for the last few days after I'd come into the emergency room by ambulance. "You've had an attack," she said and Dr. Lyons had me admitted. She'd alert him that I was awake and left the room after giving me some more medication. "Painkillers," she said, but she didn't bother to tell me what kind.

Inspector Legrasse walked by my door and waved at Lovecraft. He was dragging along some half-crazed swamp dweller behind him.

A little while later, Dr. Lyons came in but he looked an awful lot like Jeffrey Coombs from *Re-Animator*.

"Mike," he said.

"Dr. Lyons," I replied in my best Jack Webb voice. "Where's Bill Gannon? I heard he got arrested for wife beating."

He looked at me as if I was some sort of test bug. "What?"

"Nothing. Just a bad TV reference. What am I doing here?"

Dr. Lyons pulled up a chair. "You had an attack."

"What kind of an attack?"

He sat there for a moment, searching for the right words. "You were at work. Do you remember that?"

I nodded yes.

"You were waiting on a customer. He was a black gentleman.

In the middle of the transaction you began screaming and yelling for him to leave you alone. In fact, I'm told that you actually said that the man should 'take his old witch away and stop haunting you.' Sound familiar?"

"No. Not at all. I really did that?"

"I'm afraid so. A few of your co-workers tried to get you to calm down, but you went into a spasm and blacked out. You've been here for two days."

I tried to concentrate on what he was saying, but all I could see were those weird dimensional things from *From Beyond* circling his head.

"What happened?"

"The tumor is growing. It's pressing on the part of your brain that covers motor functions and memory. I don't know what's happening to it. It almost seems as if something is making it grow faster." He paused for a moment. "Michael, you're experiencing hallucinations."

"Oh?"

"It's not unusual, given the tumor's location. But I admit that I didn't think this would happen so quickly."

Dr. Lyons/Herbert West stood up so he would appear more impressive.

"Michael, you need to have the operation."

"We've gone over that before."

"I know. You don't have the money or insurance. But we'll find a way, Michael. You've got to do this."

I looked at him. It was easier to just go along.

"Okay. Sure."

"Good. I've got you set up for the operation in two days. We'll keep you here and keep an eye on you until then. Okay?"

I nodded.

"All right. Just rest easy. I'll be back later."

After he left, I lay there for about ten minutes. Then I got up, got dressed, and left. Lovecraft followed me out. No one stopped me. It seemed that no one took any notice of me, and I wondered if they saw me at all or if it was just the way things are in Rhode Island.

I took the bus home.

There was only one message on my machine. It was from my boss. "Michael…um, I'm sorry to have to say this but we're going to have to let you go. I hope you understand. We just can't have any more scenes like today. I know you have problems but, legally, we can't afford the risk. Sorry. We'll mail you your last paycheck. Um…so you don't really need to come back. Okay? Hope everything works out for you. Bye."

I took an extra dose of the herb/vitamin potion and laid down in bed.

"So now what are you going to do?" asked Lovecraft.

I didn't say anything.

Lovecraft was standing near the window. There wasn't much of a view to see. He had on one of his father's old suits. It fitted him pretty well but was still a little loose in the shoulders. I wasn't sure if it was one of the suits that got stolen while he was in New York.

"You know," I finally said, "I've read both of the biographies. Joshi's and de Camp's."

He grimaced.

"At least Joshi took the time to try and understand the era," he responded. "De Camp lived through some of it and he still couldn't understand how it affected me."

"They never said much about your death. About how you felt as you lay there in that bed at Jane Brown."

He turned to look at me. For some reason, his lantern jaw looked more solid. I could almost swear that his chin was reflecting the light.

"Go to sleep, Michael." It was the first time I had heard

him refer to me by name.

I went to sleep.

Professor Wilmarth/Lovecraft was talking about the black stone. Akeley had sent it through the mail and it had disappeared. I took out the stone from Machen's "Novel of the Black Seal" and showed it to him. He was interested but disappointed. "Yes, but it's not quite what we're looking for." He played the record for me and I listened to that strange otherworldly voice.

"To Nyarlathotep, Mighty Messenger, must all things be told. And He shall put on the semblance of men, the waxen mask and the robe that hides, and come down from the world of Seven Suns to mock…"

It was not surprising that it was my voice speaking on the record.

Wilmarth/Lovecraft took no notice.

Suddenly, we jumped forward and I was in Akeley's cabin. Wilmarth/Lovecraft was talking to Akeley, who was sitting in the opposite chair and covered in his huge robe. Akeley was describing Yuggoth with its great cities of black stone. After awhile, Wilmarth/Lovecraft went to bed and I took his place.

"So," Akeley said in that queer, disjointed voice, "what are *you* looking for?"

"Not much," I answered. "It's just that I've always wondered—a *lot* of us have wondered—who are you really? Under that mask. Who are you? Are you one of the Fungi? Are you Nyarlathotep?"

"Why don't you see for yourself?"

I reached over and took off the mask. It was Lovecraft. "Of course," he said, "who *else* would it be?"

I NEVER DEVELOPED A TASTE FOR CLARK ASHTON Smith. I knew he was a good writer, but just something about his work never clicked with me. Lovecraft, Howard, and Smith were touted as *Weird Tales*' "three musketeers." And yet it was often said that Seabury Quinn was more popular with the readers than any of them. Lovecraft never got a cover. Guess Margaret Brundage just couldn't bring herself to paint Cthulhu and, after all, there were no half-naked damsels in distress in Lovecraft. Maybe he would have been more successful if there had been.

THE NEXT FEW DAYS PASSED STRANGELY.

I don't need to say that I didn't show up for the operation. Dr. Lyons called once, demanding to know where I was and why I didn't come in. He didn't call again. In fact, nobody called after a while. I got to the point where I had to pick up the phone and check it regularly to make sure it was still working.

I stopped doing that when a thick, guttural voice came on the empty line and said, "*YOU FOOL, WARREN IS DEAD!*"

The dreams went back and forth then. Sometimes I'd have them when I was sleeping. Sometimes I'd have them when I was awake. I'd be walking down Thayer Street and suddenly I'd be walking down a street in Arkham, heading for the Witch House.

Were they real? Was anything real at this point? I remember all those stories where everyone knows that the dreams are real except for the dreamer. In *Pet Sematary*, the main character (whose name escapes me but he was played by Dale Midkiff in the movie, which wasn't a bad adaptation—King had suffered far worse) goes for a midnight walk with the spirit of the dead student. The student leads him down the path to the Pet

Sematary and then tells him not to go beyond the wall. He might as well have put a big neon sign saying, "This way to the Wendigo's Zombie grounds." When he wakes up, he's stunned to find his feet covered with mud and sticks. When I read that, I wasn't overcome with fear. Of course the dream was real. Aren't they always? My first thought was, "Damn, that's gonna be hard to clean up."

The dreams. Eventually the dreams are the only things that are real. In the dreams there's no cancer, only monsters, gods, demons, ghouls, and things you can grab and hold with your hands. Something you can fight and batter into submission. Ever try to grab a cancer?

I STOPPED EATING AFTER A WHILE. DIDN'T KNOW WHY I was bothering anyway. Everything tasted the same and had that metallic, coppery taste to it. Lovecraft approved of that. We talked a long time about things and only occasionally would something creep through the woods or the walls. I kept taking the herb/vitamin potion along with Dr. Lyons's medication until it ran out. The Hounds of Tindalos ran through every once in a while but stopped coming when I ran out of food to give them. The cats of Ulthar never bothered to come at all, preferring to stay on the moon until everything was over.

"Am I dying?" I asked Lovecraft.

"Maybe. Who knows? What is death? Don't ask me."

"But *you're* dead."

"Am I?"

I FINALLY FOUND THE SECTION IN *THE GHOST PIRATES* that Lovecraft was talking about.

The good ship had been plagued by the appearance of ghost pirates who are making away with the sailors. There were ghost ships following them through the mist. The narrator tries to explain what's happening:

"Well, if we were in what I might call a healthy atmosphere, they would be quite beyond our power to see or feel, or anything. And the same with them; but the more we're like *this*, the more *real* and actual they could grow to *us*. See? That is, the more we should become able to appreciate their form of materialness. That's all. I can't make it any clearer."

I was spending more time away. I couldn't remember what day it was or what month. The cable was shut off eventually, which was okay because the electricity followed shortly after. I lay in bed, fumbling through my mind. Things and places wandered through me until, eventually, I found myself spending less and less time in that small room in Rhode Island. When I was there, my head was one large hurt. I had begun to think of my brain as a big black stain. If I could lift my head and look in the mirror, I felt sure that my eyes would be completely black.

Lovecraft accompanied me most of the time, but sometimes I was alone walking through the worlds. I was solid, with form and substance. Here, I was thin and ghostly. The people there welcomed me. They grabbed my hand, slapped me on the back, and brought me along. Here, only Lovecraft stayed at my side and, eventually, I woke up and even he wasn't there anymore. He had moved beyond and to see him, I'd have to let myself drift away.

I didn't float off like you hear in those near-death shows. I fell away from myself, sinking through the earth. I was going beyond and following old Joe Slater to that strange place that was a star far away that shone upon Olathoë aeons ago.

The ground below me became a solid deck of a ship. I felt it move through the water as we raced forward into the strange and forbidding water where an island had suddenly appeared.

Asenath looked at me through Edward Derby's eyes. I sent six bullets into his brain.

I reached for the smooth surface of polished glass.

I thrilled to the sound of Erich Zann's music as the dead, mute man called to something outside the window.

I tore through Capt. Norrys's body while the sounds of the rats ran off in the distance.

I unfurled the photo at the corner of Pickman's painting.

I cringed in Nahum Gardner's farmhouse as the colour sprang free.

I…had become…fiction.

The Broadsword

LAIRD BARRON

Laird Barron is the author of the acclaimed short story collection The Imago Sequence and Other Stories *(Night Shade, 2007). His stories have appeared in* Sci Fiction *and* Fantasy & Science Fiction *and have been reprinted in* The Year's Best Fantasy and Horror, The Year's Best Fantasy, *and* Best New Fantasy 2005. *He is now at work on his first novel.*

LATELY, PERSHING DREAMED OF HIS LONG LOST FRIEND Terry Walker. Terry himself was seldom actually present; the dreams were soundless and gray as surveillance videos, and devoid of actors. There were trees and fog, and moving shapes like shadow puppets against a wall. On several occasions he'd surfaced from these fitful dreams to muted whispering—he momentarily formed the odd notion a figure stood in the shadows of the doorway. And in that moment his addled brain gave the form substance: his father, his brother, his dead wife, but none of them, of course, for as the fog cleared from his mind, the shadows were erased by morning light, and the whispers receded into the rush and hum of the laboring fan. He wondered if these visions were a sign of impending heat stroke, or worse.

September had proved killingly hot. The air conditioning went offline and would remain so for God knew how long. This was announced by Superintendent Frame after a small mob of irate tenants finally cornered him sneaking from his office, hat in hand. He claimed ignorance of the root cause of their misery. "I've men working on it!" he said as he made his escape; for that day, at least. By the more sour observers' best estimates, "men working on it" meant Hopkins the sole custodian. Hopkins was even better than Superintendent Frame at finding a dark hole and pulling it in after himself. Nobody had seen him in days.

Pershing Dennard did what all veteran tenants of the Broadsword Hotel had done over the years to survive these too-frequent travails: he effected emergency adaptations to his habitat. Out came the made-in-China box fan across which he draped damp wash cloths. He shuttered the windows and snugged heavy drapes to keep his apartment dim. Of course he maintained a ready supply of vodka in the freezer. The sweltering hours of daylight were for hibernation; dozing on the sofa, a chilled pitcher of lemonade and booze at his elbow. These maneuvers rendered the insufferable slightly bearable, but only by inches.

He wilted in his recliner and stared at the blades of the ceiling fan cutting through the blue-streaked shadows while television static beamed between the toes of his propped-up feet. He listened. Mice scratched behind plaster. Water knocked through the pipes with deep-sea groans and soundings. Vents whistled, transferring dim clangs and screeches from the lower floors, the basement, and lower still, the subterranean depths beneath the building itself.

The hissing ducts occasionally lulled him into a state of semi-hypnosis. He imagined lost caverns and inverted forests of roosting bats, a primordial river that tumbled through midnight grottos until it plunged so deep the stygian black acquired a red nimbus, a vast throbbing heart of brimstone and magma. Beyond the falls, abyssal winds howled and shrieked and called his name. Such images inevitably gave him more of a chill than he preferred and he shook them off, concentrated on baseball scores, the creak and grind of his joints. He'd shoveled plenty of dirt and jogged over many a hill in his career as a state surveyor. Every swing of the spade, every machete chop through temperate jungle had left its mark on muscle and bone.

Mostly, and with an intensity of grief he'd not felt in thirty-six years, more than half his lifetime, he thought about Terry Walker. It probably wasn't healthy to brood. That's what the grief counselor had said. The books said that, too. Yet how could a man *not* gnaw on that bone sometimes?

Anyone who's lived beyond the walls of a cloister has had at least one bad moment, an experience that becomes the proverbial dark secret. In this Pershing was the same as everyone. His own dark moment had occurred many years prior; a tragic event he'd dwelled upon for weeks and months with manic obsession, until he learned to let go, to acknowledge his survivor's guilt and move on with his life. He'd done well to box the memory, to shove it in a dusty corner of his subconscious. He distanced himself from the event until it seemed like a cautionary tale based on a stranger's experiences.

He was an aging agnostic and it occurred to him that, as he marched ever closer to his personal gloaming, the ghosts of Christmases Past had queued up to take him to task, that this heat wave had fostered a delirium appropriate to second-guessing his dismissal of ecclesiastical concerns, and penitence.

In 1973 he and Walker got lost during a remote surveying operation and wound up spending thirty-six hours wandering the wilderness. He'd been doing field work for six or seven years and should have known better than to hike away from the base camp that morning.

At first they'd only gone far enough to relieve themselves. Then, he'd seen something—someone—watching him from the shadow of a tree and thought it was one of the guys screwing around. This was an isolated stretch of high country in the wilds of the Olympic Peninsula. There were homesteads and ranches along its fringes, but not within ten miles. The person, apparently a man, judging from his build, was half-crouched, studying the ground. He waved to Pershing; a casual, friendly gesture. The man's features were indistinct, but at that moment Pershing convinced himself it was Morris Miller or Pete Cabellos, both of whom were rabid outdoorsmen and constantly nattering on about the ecological wonderland in which the crew currently labored. The man straightened and beckoned, sweeping his hand in a come-on gesture. He walked into the trees.

Terry zipped up, shook his head and trudged that direction. Pershing thought nothing of it and tagged along. They went to where the man had stood and discovered what he'd been staring at—an expensive backpack of the variety popular with suburbanite campers. The pack was battered, its shiny yellow and green material shredded. Pershing got the bad feeling it was brand new.

Oh, shit, Terry said. *Maybe a bear got somebody. We better get back to camp and tell Higgins*. Higgins was the crew leader; surely he'd put together a search and rescue operation to find the missing owner of the pack. That would have been the sensible course, except, exactly as they turned to go, Pete Cabellos called to them from the woods. His voice echoed and bounced from the cliffs and boulders. Immediately, the men headed in the direction of the yell.

They soon got thoroughly lost. Every tree is the same tree in a forest. Clouds rolled in and it became impossible to navigate by sun or stars. Pershing's compass was back at camp with the rest of his gear, and Terry's was malfunctioning—condensation clouded the glass internally, rendered the needle useless. After a few hours of stumbling around yelling for their colleagues, they decided to follow the downhill slope of the land and promptly found themselves in mysterious hollows and thickets. It was a grave situation, although, that evening as the two camped in a steady downpour, embarrassment figured more prominently than fear of imminent peril.

Terry brought out some jerky and Pershing always carried waterproof matches in his vest pocket, so they got a fire going from the dried moss and dead twigs beneath the boughs of a massive old fir, munched on jerky, and lamented their predicament. The two argued halfheartedly about whether they'd actually heard Pete or Morris calling that morning, or a mysterious third party.

Pershing fell asleep with his back against the mossy bole and was plunged into nightmares of stumbling through the foggy woods. A malevolent presence lurked in the mist and shadows. Figures emerged from behind trees and stood silently. Their wickedness and malice were palpable. He knew with the inexplicable logic of dreams that these phantoms delighted in his terror, that they were eager to inflict unimaginable torments upon him.

Terry woke him and said he'd seen someone moving around just beyond the light of the dying fire. Rain pattering on the leaves made it impossible to hear if anyone was moving around in the bushes, so Terry threw more branches on the fire and they warmed their hands and theorized that the person who'd beckoned them into the woods was the owner of the pack. Terry, ever the pragmatist, suspected the man had struck his head and was now in a raving delirium, possibly even circling their camp.

Meanwhile, Pershing was preoccupied with more unpleasant possibilities. Suppose the person they'd seen had actually killed a hiker and successfully lured them into the wild? Another thought insinuated itself; his grandmother had belonged to a long line of superstitious Appalachian folk. She'd told him and his brother ghost stories and of legends such as the Manitou, and lesser-known tales about creatures who haunted the woods and spied on men and disappeared when a person spun to catch them. He'd thrilled to her stories while snug before the family hearth with a mug of cocoa and the company of loved ones. The stories took on a different note here in the tall trees.

It rained hard all the next day and the clouds descended into the forest. Emergency protocol dictated staying put and awaiting the inevitable rescue, rather than blindly groping in circles through the fog. About midday, Terry went to get a drink from a spring roughly fifty feet from their campsite. Pershing never saw him again. Well, not quite true: he saw him twice more.

PERSHING MOVED INTO THE BROADSWORD HOTEL IN 1979, a few months after his first wife, Ethel, unexpectedly passed away. He met second wife, Constance, at a hotel mixer. They were married in 1983, had Lisa Anne and Jimmy within two years, and were divorced by 1989. She said the relationship was been doomed from the start because he'd never really finished mourning Ethel. Connie grew impatient of his mooning over old dusty photo albums and playing old moldy tunes on the antique record player he stashed in the closet along with several ill-concealed bottles of scotch. Despite his fondness for liquor, Pershing didn't consider himself a heavy drinker, but rather a steady one.

During their courtship, Pershing talked often of leaving the Broadsword. Oh, she was queenly in her time, a seven-floor art deco complex on the West Side of Olympia on a wooded hill with a view of the water, the marina, and downtown. No one living knew how she'd acquired her bellicose name. She was built in 1918 as a posh hotel, complete with a four-star restaurant, swanky nightclub-cum-gambling hall, and a grand ballroom; the kind of place that attracted not only the local gentry, but visiting Hollywood celebrities, sports figures, and politicians. After passing through the hands of several owners, the Broadsword was purchased by a Midwest corporation and converted to a middle-income apartment complex in 1958. The old girl suffered a number of renovations to wedge in more rooms, but she maintained a fair bit of charm and historical gravitas even five decades and several facelifts later.

Nonetheless, Pershing and Connie had always agreed the cramped quarters were no substitute for a real house with a yard and a fence. Definitely a tough place to raise children—unfortunately, the recession had killed the geophysical company he'd worked for in those days and money was tight.

Connie was the one who eventually got out—she moved to Cleveland and married a banker. The last Pershing heard, she lived in a three-story mansion and had metamorphosed into a white-gloved, garden party-throwing socialite who routinely got her name in the lifestyle section of the papers. He was happy for her and the kids, and a little relieved for himself. That tiny single bedroom flat had been crowded!

He moved up as well. Up to the sixth floor into 119; what the old superintendent (in those days it was Anderson Heck) sardonically referred to as an executive suite. According to the super, only two other people had ever occupied the apartment—the so-called executive suites were spacious enough that tenants held onto them until they died. The previous resident was a bibliophile who'd retired from a post at the Smithsonian. The fellow left many books and photographs when he died and his heirs hadn't seen fit to come around and pack up his estate. As it happened, the freight elevator was usually on the fritz in those days and the regular elevator wasn't particularly reliable either. So the superintendent offered Pershing three months' free rent if he personally dealt with the daunting task of organizing and then lugging crates of books and assorted memorabilia down six steep flights to the curb.

Pershing put his muscles to good use. It took him three days' hard labor to clear out the apartment and roughly three hours to move his embarrassingly meager belongings in. The rest, as they say, was history.

ERSHING WOULD TURN SIXTY-SEVEN IN OCTOBER. Wanda Blankenship, his current girlfriend of nine months and counting, was forty-something—she played it coy, careful not to say, and he hadn't managed a peek at her driver license. He guessed she was pushing fifty, although she took care of herself, hit the Pilates circuit with her chums, and thus passed for a few years on the uphill side. "Grave robber!" he said when she goosed him, or made a half-hearted swipe at his testicles, which was often, and usually in public. She was a librarian too; a fantasy cliché ironically fulfilled during this, his second or third boyhood when he needed regular doses of the little blue pill to do either of them any justice.

Nine months meant their relationship had edged from the danger zone and perilously near the edge of no return. He'd gotten comfortable with her sleeping over a couple of nights a week, like a lobster getting cozy in a kettle of warm water. He'd casually mentioned her to Lisa Anne and Jimmy during one of their monthly phone conferences, which was information he usually kept close to his vest. More danger signals: she installed a toothbrush in the medicine cabinet and shampoo in the bath. He couldn't find his extra key one night after coming home late from the Red Room and realized he'd given it to her weeks before in a moment of weakness. As the robot used to say, *Danger, Will Robinson! Danger! Danger!* He was cooked, all right, which was apropos, considering the weather.

"Oh, ye gods! Like hell I'm coming up there!" she said during their latest phone conversation. "My air conditioner is tip top. *You* come over here." She paused to snicker. "Where I can get my hands on you!"

He wanted to argue, to resist, but was too busy melting into the couch, and knew if he refused she'd come flying on her broom to chivvy him away most unceremoniously. Defeated, he put on one of his classier ties, all of which Constance had chosen, and made the pilgrimage—on foot in the savage glare of late afternoon because he walked everywhere, hadn't owned a car since he sold his El Camino in 1982. Walking generally suited him; he'd acquired a taste for it during his years of toil in the wilderness. He took a meager bit of pride in noting that his comfortable "traveling" pace left most men a quarter his age gasping and winded after a short distance.

He disliked visiting her place, a small cottage-style house in a quiet neighborhood near downtown. Not that there was anything wrong with the house itself, aside from the fact it was too tidy, too orderly, and she insisted on china dishes for breakfast, lunch, supper, and tea. He lived in constant fear of dropping something, spilling something, breaking something with his large, clumsy hands. She cheerily dismissed such concerns, remarking that her cups and dishes were relics passed down through the generations—"They gotta go sometime. Don't be so uptight." Obviously, this served to heighten his paranoia.

Wanda made dinner; fried chicken and honeydew, and wine for dessert. Wine disagreed with his insides and gave him a headache. When she broke out the after-dinner merlot, he smiled and drank up like a good soldier. It was the gentlemanly course—also, he was loath to give her any inkling regarding his penchant for the hard stuff. Her husband had drunk himself to death. Pershing figured he could save his own incipient alcoholism as an escape route. If things got too heavy, he could simply crack a bottle of Absolut and guzzle it like soda pop, which would doubtless give him a heart attack. Freedom either way! Meanwhile, the deceit must perforce continue.

They were snuggling on the loveseat, buzzed by wine and luxuriating in the blessed coolness of her living room, when she casually said, "So, who's the girl?"

Pershing's heart fluttered, his skin went clammy. Such questions never boded well. He affected nonchalance. "Ah, sweetie, I'm a dashing fellow. Which girl are you talking about?" That heart attack he sometimes dreamt of seemed a real possibility.

Wanda smiled. "The girl I saw leaving your apartment the other morning, silly."

The fact he didn't know any girls besides a few cocktail waitresses didn't make him feel any better. He certainly was guilty of *looking* at lots of girls and couldn't help but wonder if that was enough to bury him. Then, instead of reassuring her that no such person existed, or that there must be some innocent mistake, he idiotically said, "Oh. What were you doing coming over in the morning?" In short order, he found himself on the porch. The sky was purple and orange with sunset. It was a long, sticky walk back to the hotel.

HE NEXT DAY HE ASKED AROUND THE BROADSWORD. Nobody had seen a girl and nobody cared. Nobody had seen Hopkins either. *Him* they cared about. Even Bobby Silver—Sly to his friends—didn't seem interested in the girl, and Sly was the worst lecher Pershing had ever met. Sly managed a dry cackle and a nudge to the ribs when Pershing described the mystery girl who'd allegedly come from his apartment. Young (relatively speaking), dark-haired, voluptuous, short black dress, lipstick.

"Heard anything about when they're gonna fix the cooling system? It's hotter than the hobs of Hell in here!" Sly sprawled on a bench just off the columned hotel entrance. He fanned himself with a crinkled Panama hat.

Mark Ordbecker, a high-school math teacher who lived in the apartment directly below Pershing's with his wife Harriet and two children, suggested a call to the police. "Maybe one of them should come over and look around." They made this exchange at Ordbecker's door. The teacher leaned against the doorframe, trying in vain to feed the shrieking baby a bottle of milk. His face was red and sweaty. He remarked that the start of the school year would actually be a relief from acting as a househusband. His wife had gone east for a funeral. "The wife flies out and all hell breaks loose. She's going to come home to *my* funeral if the weather doesn't change."

Ordbecker's other child, a five-year-old boy named Eric, stood behind his father. His hair was matted with sweat and his face gleamed, but it was too pale.

"Hi, Eric," Pershing said. "I didn't see you there. How you doing, kiddo?"

Little Eric was normally rambunctious or, as Wanda put it, obstreperous, as in *an obstreperous hellion*. Today he shrank farther back and wrapped an arm around his father's leg.

"Don't mind him. Misses his mom." Mark leaned closer and murmured, "Separation anxiety. He won't sleep by himself while she's gone. You know how kids are." He reached down awkwardly and ruffled the boy's hair. "About your weirdo visitor—call the cops. At least file a report so if this woman's crazy and she comes at you with a pair of shears in the middle of the night and you clock her with a golf club, there's a prior record."

Pershing thanked him. He remained unconvinced this was anything other than a coincidence or possibly Wanda's imagination, what with her sudden attack of jealousy. He almost knocked on Phil Wesley's door across the hall. The fellow moved in a few years back; a former stage magician, or so went the tales, and a decade Pershing's senior. Well-dressed and amiable, Wesley nonetheless possessed a certain aloofness; also, he conducted a psychic medium service out of his apartment. Tarot readings, hypnosis, séances, all kinds of crackpot business. They said hello in passing, had waited outside Superintendent Frame's office, and that was the extent of their relationship.

Pershing preferred the status quo in this case.

"Cripes, this is all nonsense anyway." He always locked his apartment with a deadbolt; he'd become security-conscious in his advancing years, not at all sure he could handle a robber, what with his bad knees and weak back. Thankfully, there'd been no sign of forced entry, no one other than his girlfriend had seen anything, thus he suspected his time schlepping about the hotel in this beastly heat playing amateur investigator was a colossal waste of energy.

Wanda didn't call, which wasn't surprising considering her stubbornness. Dignity prohibited *him* ringing her. Nonetheless, her silence rankled; his constant clock watching annoyed him, too. It wasn't like him to fret over a woman, which meant he missed her more than he'd have guessed.

As the sun became an orange blob in the west, the temperature peaked. The apartment was suffocating. He dragged himself to the refrigerator and stood before its open door, straddle-legged in his boxers, bathed in the stark white glow. Tepid relief was better than nothing.

Someone whispered behind him and giggled. He turned quickly. The laughter originated in the living area, between the coffee table and a bookshelf. Because the curtains were tightly closed the room lay in a blue-tinged gloom that played tricks on his eyes. He sidled to the sink and swept his arm around until he flicked the switch for the overhead light. This illuminated a sufficient area that he felt confident to venture forth. Frankie Walton's suite abutted his own—and old Frankie's hearing was shot. He had to crank the volume on his radio for the ballgames. Once in a while Pershing heard the tinny exclamations of the play-by-play guys, the roar of the crowd. This, however, sounded like a person was almost on top of him, sneering behind his back.

What, you think someone's hiding under the table? Don't be a fool, Percy. Good thing your girl isn't here to see you shaking in the knees like a wimp.

Closer inspection revealed the sounds had emanated from a vent near the window. He chuckled ruefully as his muscles relaxed. Ordbecker was talking to the baby and the sound carried upstairs. Not unusual; the hotel's acoustics were peculiar, as he well knew. He knelt and cocked his head toward the vent, slightly guilty at eavesdropping, yet in the full grip of curiosity. People were definitely in conversation, yet, he gradually realized, not the Ordbeckers. These voices were strange and breathy, and came from farther off, fading in and out with a static susurration.

Intestines. Kidneys.

Ohh, either is delectable.

And sweetbreads. As long as they're from a young one.

Ganglia, for me. Or brain. Scoop it out quivering.

Enough! Let's start tonight. We'll take one from—

They tittered and their words degenerated into garble, then stopped.

Shh, shh! Wait!... Someone's listening.

Don't be foolish.

They are. There's a spy hanging on our every word.

How can you tell?

I can hear them breathing.

He clapped his hand over his mouth. His hair stood on end.

I hear you, spy. Which room could you be in? First floor? No, no. The fifth or the sixth.

His heart labored. What was this?

We'll figure it out where you are, dear listener. Pay you a visit. While you sleep. Whoever it was laughed like a child, or someone pretending to be one. *You could always come down here where the mome wraths outgrabe...* Deep in the bowels of the building, the furnace rumbled to life as it did every four hours to push air circulation through the vents. The hiss muffled the crooning threats, which ceased altogether a few minutes later when the system shut down.

Pershing was stunned and nauseated. Kidneys? Sweetbreads? He picked up the phone to punch in 911 before he got hold of his senses. What on earth would he say to the dispatcher? He could guess what they'd tell him: *Stop watching so many late night thrillers, Mr. Dennard.* He waited, eyeing the vent as if a snake might slither forth, but nothing happened. First the phantom girl, now this. Pretty soon he'd be jumping at his own shadow. *First-stage dementia, just like dear old Dad.* Mom and Uncle Mike put Ernest Dennard in a home for his seventieth birthday. He'd become paranoid and delusional prior to that step. At the home Pop's faculties degenerated until he didn't know if he was coming or going. He hallucinated his sons were the ghosts of war buddies and screamed and tried to leap through his window when they visited. Thankfully, long before this turn of events, Mom had the foresight to hide the forty-five caliber pistol he kept in the dresser drawer. Allegedly Grandma went through a similar experience with Gramps. Pershing didn't find his own prospects very cheery.

But you don't have dementia yet, and you don't knock back enough booze to be hallucinating. You heard them, clear as day. Jeezus C., who are they?

Pershing walked around the apartment and flicked on some lights; he checked his watch and decided getting the hell out for a few hours might be the best remedy for his jangled nerves. He put on a suit—nothing fancy, just a habit he'd acquired from his uncle who'd worked as a professor—and felt hat and left. He managed to catch the last bus going downtown. The bus was an oven; empty except for himself, a pair of teens, and the driver. Even so, it reeked from the day's accumulation; a miasma of sweat and armpit stench.

The depot had attracted its customary throng of weary seniors and the younger working poor, and a smattering of fancifully coiffed, tattooed, and pierced students from Evergreen; the former headed home or to the late shift, the latter off to house parties, or bonfires along the inlet beaches. Then there were the human barnacles—a half-dozen toughs decked out in parkas and baggy sports warm-up suits despite the crushing heat; the hard, edgy kind who watched everyone else, who appraised the herd. Olympia was by no means a big town, but it hosted more than its share of beatings and stabbings, especially in the northerly quarter inward from the marina and docks. One didn't hang around the old cannery district at night unless one wanted to get mugged.

Tonight none of the ruffians paid him any heed. From the depot he quickly walked through several blocks of semi-deserted industrial buildings and warehouses, made a right and continued past darkened sporting good stores, bookshops, and tattoo parlors until he hooked onto a narrow side lane and reached the subtly lighted wooden shingle of the Manticore Lounge. The Manticore was a hole in the wall that catered to a slightly more reserved set of clientele than was typical of the nightclubs and sports bars on the main thoroughfares. Inside was an oasis of coolness, scents of lemon and beer.

Weeknights were slow—two young couples occupied tables near the darkened dais that served as a stage for the four-piece bands that played on weekends; two beefy gentlemen in tailored suits sat at the bar. Lobbyists in town to siege the legislature; one could tell by their Rolexes and how the soft lighting from the bar made their power haircuts glisten.

Mel Clayton and Elgin Bane waved him over to their window booth. Mel, an engineering consultant who favored blue button-up shirts, heavy on the starch, and Elgin, a social worker who dressed in black turtlenecks and wore Buddy

Holly-style glasses and sometimes lied to women at parties by pretending to be a beat poet; he even stashed a ratty pack of cloves in his pocket for such occasions. He quoted Kerouac and Ginsberg chapter and verse regardless how many rounds of Johnny Walker he'd put away. Pershing figured his friend's jaded posturing, his affected cynicism, was influenced by the depressing nature of his job: he dealt with emotional basket cases, battered wives, and abused children sixty to seventy hours a week. What did they say? At the heart of every cynic lurked an idealist. That fit Elgin quite neatly.

Elgin owned a house in Yelm, and Mel lived on the second floor of the Broadsword—they and Pershing and three or four other guys from the neighborhood got together for drinks at the Manticore or The Red Room at least once a month; more frequently now as the others slipped closer to retirement and their kids graduated college. Truth be told, he was much closer to these two than he was to his younger brother Carl, who lived in Denver and whom he hadn't spoken with in several months.

Every autumn, the three of them, sometimes with their significant others, drove up into the Black Hills outside Olympia to a hunting cabin Elgin's grandfather owned. None of them hunted; they enjoyed lounging on the rustic porch, roasting marshmallows, and sipping hot rum around the campfire. Pershing enjoyed these excursions—no one ever wanted to go hiking or wander far from the cabin, and thus his suppressed dread of wilderness perils remained quiescent, except for the occasional stab of nervousness when the coyotes barked, or the wind crashed in the trees, or his unease at how perfectly dark the woods became at night.

Mel bought him a whiskey sour—Mel invariably insisted on covering the tab. *It's you boys or my ex-wife, so drink up!* Pershing had never met the infamous Nancy Clayton; she was the inimitable force behind Mel's unceremonious arrival at the Broadsword fifteen years back, although judging from his flirtatious behavior with the ladies, his ouster was doubtless warranted. Nancy lived in Seattle with her new husband in the Lake Washington townhouse Mel toiled through many a late night and weekend to secure. He'd done better with Regina, his second wife. Regina owned a bakery in Tumwater and she routinely made cookies for Pershing and company. A kindly woman and large-hearted; she'd immediately adopted Mel's cast of misfit friends and associates.

After the trio had chatted for a few minutes, griping about the "damnable" weather, mainly, Elgin said, "What's eating you? You haven't touched your drink."

Pershing winced at *eating*. He hesitated, then chided himself. What sense to play coy? Obviously he wished to talk about what happened. Why else had he come scuttling in from the dark, tail between his legs? "I…heard something at home earlier tonight. People whispering in the vent. Weird, I know. But it really scared me. The stuff they said…"

Mel and Elgin exchanged glances. Elgin said, "Like what?"

Pershing told them. Then he briefly described what Wanda said about the mystery girl. "The other thing that bothers me is…this isn't the first time. The last couple of weeks I've been hearing stuff. Whispers. I wrote those off. Now, I'm not so sure."

Mel stared into his glass. Elgin frowned and set his palm against his chin in apparently unconscious imitation of *The Thinker*. He said, "Hmm. That's bizarre. Kinda screwed up, in fact. It almost makes me wonder—"

"—if your place is bugged," Mel said.

"Bugged?"

"This from the man with a lifetime subscription to the *Fortean Times*," Elgin said. "Damn, but sometimes I think you and Freeman would make a great couple." Randy Freeman being an old school radical who'd done too much Purple Haze in the sixties and dialed into the diatribes of a few too many Che Guevara-loving hippie chicks for his own good. He was another of The Red Room set.

Mel took Elgin's needling in stride. "Hey, I'm dead serious. Two and two, baby. I'll lay odds somebody miked Percy's apartment."

"For the love of—" Elgin waved him off, settling into his mode of dismissive impatience. "Who on God's green earth would do something crazy like that? *No-freaking-body*, that's who."

"It is a bit farfetched," Pershing said. "On the other hand, if you'd heard this crap. I dunno."

"Oh, hell." Elgin took a sip of his drink, patently incredulous.

"Jeez, guys—I'm not saying Homeland Security wired it for sound…maybe another tenant is playing games. People do wacko things."

"No forced entry." Pershing pointed at Mel. "And don't even say it might be Wanda. I'll have to slug you."

"Nah, Wanda's not sneaky. Who else has got a key?"

Elgin said, "The super would have one. I mean, if you're determined to go there, then that's the most reasonable suspect. Gotta tell you, though—you're going to feel like how Mel looks when it turns out to be television noise—which is to say, an idiot."

"Ha, ha. Question is, what to do?"

"Elgin's right. Let's not make a bigger deal of this than it is…I got spooked."

"And the light of reason shines through. I'm going to the head." Elgin stood and made his way across the room and disappeared around a big potted fern.

Pershing said, "Do you mind if I sleep on your couch? If I'm not intruding, that is."

Mel smiled. "No problem. Gina doesn't care. Just be warned she goes to work at four in the morning, so she'll be stumbling around the apartment." He glanced over to make certain Elgin was still safely out of sight. "Tomorrow I'll come up and help you scope your pad. A while back Freeman introduced me to a guy in Tacoma who runs one of those spy shops with the mini-cameras and microphones. I'll get some tools and we'll see what's what."

After another round Elgin drove them back to the Broadsword. Just before he pulled away, he stuck his head out the window and called, "Don't do anything crazy."

"Which one of us is he talking to?" Mel said, glaring over his shoulder.

"I'm talking to both of you," Elgin said. He gunned the engine and zipped into the night.

EGINA HAD ALREADY GONE TO BED. MEL TIPTOED around his darkened apartment getting a blanket and a pillow for Pershing, cursing softly as he bumped into furniture. Two box fans blasted, but the room was muggy as a greenhouse. Once the sleeping arrangements were made, he got a six-pack of Heineken from the refrigerator and handed one to Pershing. They kicked back and watched a repeat of the Mariners game with the volume turned most of the way down. The seventh-inning stretch did Mel in. His face had a droopy, hangdog quality that meant he was loaded and ready to crash. He said goodnight and sneaked unsteadily toward the bedroom.

Pershing watched the rest of the game, too lethargic to reach for the remote. Eventually he killed the television and lay on the coach, sweat molding his clothes to him like a second skin. His heart felt sluggish. A night light in the kitchen cast ghostly radiance upon the wall, illuminating bits of Regina's Ansel Adams prints, the glittery mica eyes of her menagerie of animal figurines on the mantel. Despite his misery, he fell asleep right away.

A woman gasped in pleasure. That brought him up from the depths. The cry repeated, muffled by the wall of Mel and Gina's bedroom. He stared at the ceiling, mortified, thinking that Mel certainly was one hell of a randy bastard after he got a few drinks under his belt. Then someone whispered, perhaps five feet to his left where the light didn't penetrate. The voice chanted: *This old man, this old man…*

The syrupy tone wicked away the heat as if he'd fallen into a cold, black lake. He sat upright so quickly pains sparked in his neck and back. His only consolation lay in the recognition of the slight echoing quality, which suggested the person was elsewhere. Whistling emanated from the shadows, its falsetto muted by the background noise. He clumsily sprang from the couch, his fear transformed to a more useful sense of anger, and crab-walked until he reached the proper vent. "Hey, jerk!" he said, placing his face within kissing distance of the grill. "I'm gonna break your knees with my baseball bat if you don't shut your damn mouth!" His bravado was thin—he did keep a Louisville slugger, signed by Ken Griffey Jr., no less, in the bedroom closet in case a burglar broke in at night. Whether he'd be able to break anyone's knees was open to question.

The whistling broke off mid-tune. Silence followed. Pershing listened so hard his skull ached. He said to himself with grudging satisfaction, "That's right, creepos, you *better* stuff a sock in it." His sense of accomplishment was marred by the creeping dread that the reason his tormentors (or was it Mel's since this was his place?) had desisted was because they even now prowled the stairwells and halls of the old building, patiently searching for him.

He finally went and poured a glass of water and huddled at the kitchen table until dawn lighted the windows and Gina stumbled in to make coffee.

HE TEMPERATURE SPIKED TO ONE HUNDRED AND three degrees by two p.m. the following afternoon. He bought Wanda two dozen roses with a card and chocolates, and arranged to have them delivered to her house. Mission accomplished, he went directly to an air-conditioned coffee shop, found a dark corner, and ordered half a dozen consecutive frozen frappucinos. That killed time until his rendezvous with Mel at the Broadsword.

Mel grinned like a mischievous schoolboy when he showed off his fiber-optic snooper cable, a meter for measuring electromagnetic fluctuations, and his battered steel toolbox. Pershing asked if he'd done this before and Mel replied that he'd learned a trick or two in the Navy.

"Just don't destroy anything," Pershing said. At least a dozen times he'd started to tell Mel about the previous night's visitation, the laughter; after all, if this was occurring in different apartments on separate floors, the scope of such a prank would be improbable. He couldn't devise a way to break it to his friend and still remain credible, and so kept his peace, miserably observing the operation unfold.

After lugging the equipment upstairs, Mel spread a dropcloth to protect the hardwood floor and arrayed his various tools with the affected studiousness of a surgeon preparing to perform open-heart surgery. Within five minutes he'd unscrewed the antique brass grillwork plate and was rooting around inside the guts of the duct with a flashlight and a big screwdriver. Next, he took a reading with the voltmeter, then, finding nothing suspicious, made a laborious circuit of the entire apartment, running the meter over the other vents, the molding, and outlets. Pershing supplied him with glasses of lemonade to diffuse his own sense of helplessness.

Mel switched off the meter, wiping his face and neck with a damp cloth. He gulped the remainder of the pitcher of lemonade and shook his head with disappointment. "Damn. Place is clean. Well, except for some roaches."

"I'll make Frame gas them later. So, nothing, eh? It's funny acoustics. Or my imagination."

"Yeah, could be. Ask your neighbors if they heard anything odd lately."

"I dunno. They already gave me the fishy eye after I made the rounds checking on Wanda's girl. Maybe I should leave it alone for now. See what happens."

"That's fine as long as whatever happens isn't bad." Mel packed his tools with a disconsolate expression.

The phone rang. "I love you, baby," Wanda said on the other end.

"Me too," Pershing said. "I hope you liked the flowers." Meanwhile, Mel gave him a thumbs up and let himself out. Wanda asked if he wanted to come over and it was all Pershing could do to sound composed. "It's a date. I'll stop and grab a bottle of vino."

"No way, Jose; you don't know Jack about wine. I'll take care of that—you just bring yourself on over."

After they disconnected he said, "Thank God." Partly because a peace treaty with Wanda was a relief. The other portion, the much larger portion, frankly, was that he could spend the night well away from the Broadsword. *Yeah, that's fine, girly man. How about tomorrow night? How about the one after that?*

For twenty years he'd chewed on the idea of moving; every time the furnace broke in the winter, the cooling system died in the summer, or when the elevators went offline sans explanation from management for weeks on end, he'd joined the crowd of malcontents who wrote letters to the absentee landlord, threatened to call the state, to sue, to breach the rental contract and disappear. Maybe the moment had come to make good on that. Yet in his heart he despaired of escaping; he was a part of the hotel now. It surrounded him like a living tomb.

HE DREAMED THAT HE WOKE AND DRESSED AND RETURNED to the Broadsword. In this dream he was a passenger inside his own body, an automaton following its clockwork track. The apartment smelled stale from days of neglect. Something was wrong, however; off kilter, almost as if it wasn't his home at all, but a clever recreation, a stage set. Certain objects assumed hyper-reality, while others submerged into a murky background. The sugar in the glass bowl glowed and dimmed and brightened, like a pulse. Through the window, leaden clouds scraped the tops of buildings and radio antennas vibrated, transmitting a signal that he felt in his skull, his teeth fillings, as a squeal of metal on metal. His nose bled.

He opened the bathroom door and stopped, confronted by a cavern. The darkness roiled humid and rank, as if the cave was an abscess in the heart of some organic mass. Waves of purple radiation undulated at a distance of feet, or miles, and from those depths resonated the metallic clash of titanic ice flows colliding.

"It's not a cave," Bobby Silver said. He stood inside the door, surrounded by shadows so that his wrinkled face shone like the sugar bowl. It was suspended in the blackness. "This is the surface. And it's around noon, local time. We do, however, spend most of our lives underground. We like the dark."

"Where?" He couldn't manage more than a dry whisper.

"Oh, you *know*," Sly said, and laughed. "C'mon, bucko—we've been beaming this into your brain for months—"

"No. Not possible. I've worn my tinfoil hat every day."

"—our system orbits a brown star, and it's cold, so we nestle in heaps and mounds that rise in ziggurats and pyramids. We swim in blood to stay warm, wring it from the weak the way you might squeeze juice from an orange."

Pershing recognized the voice from the vent. "You're a fake. Why are you pretending to be Bobby Silver?"

"Oh. If I didn't wear this, you wouldn't comprehend me. Should I remove it?" Sly grinned, seized his own cheek, and pulled. His flesh stretched like taffy accompanied by a squelching sound. He winked and allowed it to deform to a human shape. "It's what's underneath that counts. You'll see. When we come to stay with you."

Pershing said, "I don't want to see anything." He tried to flee, to run shrieking, but this being a dream, he was rooted, trapped, unable to do more than mumble protestations.

"Yes, Percy, you do," Ethel said from behind him. "We love you." As he twisted his head to gape at her, she gave him the soft, tender smile he remembered, the one that haunted his waking dreams, and then put her hand against his face and shoved him into the dark.

HE STAYED OVER AT HER PLACE FOR A WEEK—HID OUT, like a criminal seeking sanctuary from the Church. Unhappily, this doubtless gave Wanda the wrong impression (although at this point even Pershing wasn't certain what impression she *should* have), but at all costs he needed a vacation from his suddenly creep-infested heat trap of an apartment. Prior to this he'd stayed overnight fewer than a dozen times. His encampment at her house was noted without comment.

Jimmy's twenty-sixth birthday fell on a Sunday. After morning services at Wanda's Lutheran church, a handsome brick building only five minutes from the Broadsword, Pershing went outside to the quiet employee parking lot and called him.

Jimmy had wanted to be an architect since elementary school. He went into construction, which Pershing thought was close enough despite the nagging suspicion his son wouldn't agree. Jimmy lived in California at the moment—he migrated seasonally along the West Coast, chasing jobs. Pershing wished him a happy birthday and explained a card was in the mail. He hoped the kid wouldn't check the postmark as he'd only remembered yesterday and rushed to get it sent before the post office closed.

Normally he was on top of the family things: the cards, the phone calls, the occasional visit to Lisa Anne when she attended Berkeley. Her stepfather, Barton Ingles III, funded college, which simultaneously indebted and infuriated Pershing, whose fixed income allowed little more than his periodic visits and a small check here and there. Now graduated, she worked for a temp agency in San Francisco and, embarrassingly, her meager base salary surpassed his retirement.

Toward the end of their conversation, after Pershing's best wishes and obligatory questions about the fine California weather and the job, Jimmy said, "Well, Pop, I hate to ask this..."

"Uh, oh. What have I done now? Don't tell me you need money."

Jimmy chuckled uneasily. "Nah, if I needed cash I'd ask Bart. He's a tightwad, but he'll do anything to impress Mom, you know? No, it's...how do I put this? Are you, um, drinking? Or smoking the ganja, or something? I hate to be rude, but I gotta ask."

"Are you kidding?"

There was a long, long pause. "Okay. Maybe I'm... Pop, you called me at like two in the morning. Wednesday. You tried to disguise your voice—"

"*Whaat?*" Pershing couldn't wrap his mind around what he was hearing. "I did no such thing, James." He breathed heavily, perspiring more than even the weather called for.

"Pop, calm down, you're hyperventilating. Look, I'm not pissed—I just figured you got hammered and hit the speed dial. It would've been kinda funny if it hadn't been so creepy. Singing, no less."

"But it wasn't me! I've been with Wanda all week. She sure as hell would've noticed if I got drunk and started prank calling my family. I'll get her on the phone—"

"Really? Then is somebody sharing your pad? This is the twenty-first century, Pop. I got star sixty-nine. Your number."

"Oh." Pershing's blood drained into his belly. He covered his eyes with his free hand because the glare from the sidewalk made him dizzy. "What did I—this person—sing, exactly?"

"'This Old Man,' or whatever it's called. Although you, or they, added some unpleasant lyrics. They slurred…falsetto. When I called back, whoever it was answered. I asked what gave and they laughed. Pretty nasty laugh, too. I admit, I can't recall you ever making that kinda sound."

"It wasn't me. Sober, drunk, whatever. Better believe I'm going to find the bastard. There's been an incident or three around here. Wanda saw a prowler."

"All right, all right. If that's true, then maybe you should get the cops involved."

"Yeah."

"And Pop—let me explain it to Mom and Lisa before you get on the horn with them. Better yet, don't even bother with Mom. She's pretty much freaked outta her mind."

"They were called."

"Yeah. Same night. A real spree."

Pershing could only stammer and mumble when his son said he had to run, and then the line was dead. Wanda appeared from nowhere and touched his arm and he nearly swung on her. She looked shocked and her gaze fastened on his fist. He said, "Jesus, honey, you scared me."

"I noticed," she said. She remained stiff when he hugged her. The tension was purely reflexive, or so he hoped. His batting average with her just kept sinking. He couldn't do a much better job of damaging their relationship if he tried.

"I am so, so sorry," he said, and it was true. He hadn't told her about the trouble at the Broadsword. It was one thing to confide in his male friends, and quite another to reveal the source of his anxiety to a girlfriend, or any vulnerability for that matter. He'd inherited his secretiveness from Pop who in turn had hidden his own fears behind a mask of stoicism; this personality trait was simply a fact of life for Dennard men.

She relented and kissed his cheek. "You're jumpy. Is everything all right?"

"Sure, sure. I saw a couple of the choir kids flashing gang signs and thought one of the little jerks was sneaking up on me to go for my wallet."

Thankfully, she accepted this and held his hand as they walked to her car.

STORM ROLLED IN. HE AND WANDA SAT ON HER BACK porch, which commanded a view of the distant Black Hills. Clouds swallowed the mountains. A damp breeze fluttered the cocktail napkins under their half-empty Corona bottles, rattled the burnt yellow leaves of the maple tree branches overhead.

"Oh, my," Wanda said. "There goes the drought."

"We better hurry and clear the table." Pershing estimated at the rate the front was coming they'd be slammed inside of five minutes. He helped her grab the dishes and table settings. Between trips the breeze stiffened dramatically. Leaves tore from the maple, from trees in neighboring yards, went swirling in small technicolor cyclones. He dashed in with the salad bowl as the vanguard of rain pelted the deck. Lightning flared somewhere over the Waddel Valley; the boom came eight seconds later. The next thunderclap was five seconds. They stood in her window, watching the show until he snapped out his daze and suggested they retreat to the middle of the living room to be safe.

They cuddled on the sofa, half watching the news while the lights flickered. Wind roared around the house and shook its frame as if a freight train slammed along tracks within spitting distance of the window, or a passenger jet winding its turbines for takeoff. The weather signaled a change in their static routine of the past week. Each knew without saying it that Pershing would return to the Broadsword in the morning, and their relationship would revert to its more nebulous aspect. Pershing also understood from her melancholy glance, the measured casualness in her acceptance, that matters between them would remain undefined, that a line had been crossed.

He thought about this in the deepest, blackest hours of night while they lay in bed, she lying gently snoring, her arm draped across his chest. How much easier his life would be if his mock comment to Elgin and Mel proved true—that Wanda was a lunatic; a split personality type who was behind the stalking incidents. *God, I miss you, Ethel.*

"HOUSTON, WE HAVE A PROBLEM," MEL SAID. HE'D BROUGHT ham sandwiches and coffee to Pershing's apartment for an early supper. He was rattled. "I checked around. Not just you hearing things. Odd, odd stuff going on, man."

Pershing didn't want to hear, not after the normalcy of staying with Wanda. And the dreams… "You don't say." He really wished Mel wouldn't.

"The cops have been by a couple of times. Turns out other tenants have seen that chick prowling the halls, trying doorknobs. There's a strange dude, as well—dresses in a robe, like a priest. Betsy Tremblay says the pair knocked on her door one night. The man asked if he could borrow a cup of sugar. Betsy was watching them through the peephole—she says the lady snickered and the man grinned and shushed her by putting his finger over his lips. Scared the hell out of Betsy; she told them to scram and called the cops."

"A cup of sugar," Pershing said. He glanced out at the clouds. It was raining.

"Yeah, the old meet-your-cute-neighbor standby. Then I was talking to Fred Nilson; he's pissed because somebody below him is talking all night. 'Whispering,' he said. Only problem is, the apartment below his belongs to a guy named Brad Cox. Cox is overseas. His kids come by every few days to water the plants and feed the guppies. Anyway, no matter how you slice it, something peculiar is going on around here. Doncha feel better?"

"I never thought I was insane."

Mel chuckled uneasily. "I was chatting with Gina about the whole thing, and she said she'd heard someone singing while she was in the bath. It came up through the vent. Another time, somebody giggled in the closet while she dressed. She screamed and threw her shoe. This was broad daylight, mind you—no one in there, of course."

"Why would there be?"

"Right. Gina thought she was imagining things; she didn't want to tell me in case I decided she was a nut. Makes me wonder how many other people are having these...experiences and just keeping it to themselves."

The thought should have given Pershing comfort, but it didn't. His feelings of dread only intensified. *I'm almost seventy, damn it. I've lived in the woods, surrounded by grizzlies and wolves;*

spent months hiking the ass end of nowhere with a compass and an entrenchment spade. What the hell do I have to be scared of after all that? And the little voice in the back of his mind was quick to supply Sly's answer from the nightmare, *Oh, you know*. He said, "Food for thought. I guess the police will sort through it."

"Sure they will. Maybe if somebody gets their throat slashed, or is beaten to death in a home invasion. Otherwise, I bet they just write us off as a bunch of kooks and go back to staking out the doughnut shop. Looks like a police convention some mornings at Gina's store."

"Wanda wants me to move in with her. I mean, I think she does."

"That's a sign. You should get while the getting's good."

They finished the sandwiches and the beer. Mel left to meet Gina when she got home from work. Pershing shut the door and slipped the bolt. The story about the strange couple had gotten to him. He needed a stiff drink.

The lights blinked rapidly and failed. The room darkened to a cloudy twilight and the windows became opaque smudges. Sounds of rain and wind dwindled and ceased. "Gracious, I thought he'd *never* leave." Terry Walker peeked at him from the upper jamb of the bedroom door, attached by unknown means, neck extended with a contortionist's ease so his body remained obscured. His face was very white. He slurred as if he hadn't used his vocal chords in a while, as if he spoke through a mouthful of mush. Then Pershing saw why. Black yolks of blood spooled from his lips in strands and splattered on the carpet. "Hello, Percy."

"You're alive," Pershing said, amazed at the calmness of his own voice. Meanwhile, his brain churned with full-blown panic, reminding him he was talking to an apparition or an imposter.

"So it seems." Terry was unchanged from youth—clean-shaven, red hair curling below his ears, and impressive mutton chop sideburns in the style that had been vogue during the seventies.

"It was you in the vents?" Then, as an afterthought, "How could you terrorize my family?"

"I got bored waiting all week for you to come back. Don't be mad—none of them ever cared for you anyway. Who knows—perhaps we'll get a chance to visit each and every one; make them understand what a special person you are." Terry grinned an unpleasant, puckered grin and dropped to the floor, limber as an eel. He dressed in a cassock the color of blackened rust.

"Holy crap. You look like you've come from a black mass." He chuckled nervously, skating along the fine line of hysteria. There was something wrong with his friend's appearance—his fingers and wrists had too many joints and his neck was slightly overlong by a vertebra or two. This wasn't quite the Terry Walker he knew, and yet, to some degree it *was*, and thus intensified Pershing's fear, his sense of utter dislocation from reality. "Why *are* you here? Why have you come back?" he said, and regretted it when Terry's smile bloomed with Satanic joy.

"Surveying."

"Surveying?" Pershing felt a new appreciation for the depths of meaning in that word, the inherent coldness. Surveying preceded the destruction of one order to make way for another, stronger, more adaptable order.

"What else would I do? A man's got to have a niche in the universe."

"Who are you working for?" *Oh Lord, let it be the FBI, Homeland Security, anybody*. Still trying for levity, he said, "Fairly sure I paid my taxes, and I don't subscribe to *American Jihadist*. You're not here to ship me to Guantánamo, or wherever, are you? Trust me, I don't know jack squat about anything."

"There's a migration in progress. A diaspora, if you will. It's been going on…well, when numbers grow to a certain proportion, they lose relevance. We creep like mold." Terry's grin showed that the inside of his mouth was composed of blackened ridges, and indeed toothless. His tongue pulsed; a sundew expanding and contracting in its puddle of gore. "Don't worry, though, Earthman. We come in peace." He laughed and his timbre ascended to the sickly-sweet tones of a demented child. "Besides, we're happy to live in the cracks; your sun is too bright for now. Maybe after it burns down a bit…"

The bathroom door creaked open and the woman in the black dress emerged. She said, "Hullo there, love. I'm Gloria. A pleasure to meet you." Her flesh glowed like milk in a glass, like the sugar bowl in his visions. To Terry, she said, "He's older than I thought."

"But younger than he appears." Terry studied Pershing, his eyes inscrutable. "City life hasn't softened you, has it, pal?" He nodded at the woman. "I'm going to take him. It's my turn to choose."

"Okay, dear." The woman leaned her hip against the counter. She appeared exquisitely bored. "At least there'll be screaming."

"Isn't there always?"

Pershing said, "Terry…I'm sorry. There was a massive search. I spent two weeks scouring the hills. Two hundred men and dogs. You should've seen it." The secret wound opened in him and all the buried guilt and shame spilled forth. "Man, I wanted to save you. It destroyed me."

"You think I'm a ghost? That's depressingly provincial of you, friend."

"I don't know what to think. Maybe I'm not even awake." He was nearly in tears.

"Rest assured, you will soon make amazing discoveries," Terry said. "Your mind will shatter if we aren't careful. In any event, I haven't come to exact vengeance upon you for abandoning me in the mountains."

The woman smirked. "He'll wish you were here for that, won't he?"

"Damn you, you're not my friend," Pershing said. "And lady, you aren't Gloria, whoever she was—poor girl's probably on a milk carton. You wear faces so we will understand, so you can blend in, isn't that right? Who are you people, really?"

"*Who are you people?*" Gloria mimicked. "The Children of Old Leech. Your betters."

"Us?" Terry said. "Why, we're kin. Older and wiser, of course. Our tastes are more refined. We prefer the dark, but you will too. I promise." He moved to a shelf of Pershing's keepsakes—snapshots from the field, family photos in silver frames, and odd pieces of bric-a-brac—and picked up Ethel's rosary and rattled it. "As I recall, you weren't a man of any particular faith. I don't blame you, really. The New Testament God is so nebulous, so much of the ether. You'll find my civilization's gods to be quite tangible. One of them, a minor deity, dwells in this very system in the caverns of an outer moon. Spiritual life is infinitely more satisfying when you can meet the great ones, touch them, and, if you're fortunate, be touched..."

Pershing decided to go through the woman and get a knife from the butcher block. He didn't relish the notion of punching a girl, but Terry was bigger than him, had played safety for his high school football team. He gathered himself to move—

Gloria said, "Percy, want me to show you something? You should see what Terry saw...when you left him alone with us." She bowed her neck and cupped her face. There came the cracking as of an eggshell; blood oozed through her fingers as she lifted the hemisphere of her face away from its bed. It made a viscid, sucking sound; the sound of bones scraping together through jelly. Something writhed in the hollow. While Pershing was transfixed in sublime horror, Terry slid over and patted his shoulder.

"She's got a cruel sense of humor. Maybe you better not watch the rest." He smiled paternally and raised what appeared to be a bouquet of mushrooms, except these were crystalline and twinkled like Christmas lights.

Violet fire lashed Pershing.

N UFO ABDUCTION STORIES, HAPLESS VICTIMS ARE usually paralyzed and then sucked up in a beam of bright light. Pershing was taken through a hole in the sub-basement foundation into darkness so thick and sticky it flowed across his skin. They *did* use tools on him, and, as the woman predicted, he screamed, although not much came through his lips, which had been sealed with epoxy.

An eternal purple-black night ruled the fleshy coomb of an alien realm. Gargantuan tendrils slithered in the dark, coiling and uncoiling, and the denizens of the underworld arrived in an interminable procession through vermiculate tubes and tunnels, and gathered, chuckling and sighing, in appreciation of his agonies. In the great and abiding darkness, a sea of dead white faces brightened and glimmered like porcelain masks at a grotesque ball. He couldn't discern their forms, only the luminescent faces, their plastic, drooling joy.

We love you, Percy, the Terry-creature whispered right before he rammed a needle into Pershing's left eye.

IS CAPTORS DUG IN HIS BRAIN FOR MEMORIES AND made him relive them. The one they enjoyed best was the day of Pershing's greatest anguish:

When Terry hadn't returned to their impromptu campsite after ten minutes, Pershing went looking for him. The rain slashed through the woods, accompanied by gusts that snapped the foliage, caused treetops to clash. He tramped around the spring and saw Terry's hat pinned and flapping in some bushes. Pershing began to panic. Night came early in the mountains, and if sundown found him alone and isolated… Now he was drenched as well. Hypothermia was a real danger.

He caught movement from the corner of his eye. A figure walked across a small clearing a few yards away and vanished into the underbrush. Pershing's heart thrilled and he shouted Terry's name, actually took several steps toward the clearing, then stopped. What if it wasn't his friend? The gait had seemed wrong. Cripes, what if, what if? What if someone truly was stalking them? Farfetched; the stuff of late-night fright movies. But the primeval ruled in this place. His senses were tuned to a much older frequency than he'd ever encountered. The ape in him, the lizard, hissed warnings until his hackles rose. He lifted a stone from the muck and hefted it, and moved forward.

He tracked a set of muddy footprints into a narrow ravine. Rock outcroppings and brush interlaced to give the ravine a roof. Toadstools and fungi grew in clusters among beds of moss and mold. Water dripped steadily and formed shallow pools of primordial slime. There was Terry's jacket in a wad; and ten yards further in, his pants and shirt hanging from a dead tree that had uprooted and tumbled down into the gulley. A left hiking shoe had been dropped nearby. The trail ended in a jumble of rocks piled some four or five yards high. A stream, orange and alkaline, dribbled over shale and granite. There was something about this wall of stone that accentuated his fear; this was a timeless grotto, and it radiated an ineffable aura of wickedness, of malign sentience. Pershing stood there in its presence, feeling like a Neanderthal with a torch in hand, trembling at the threshold of the lair of a nameless beast.

Two figures in filthy robes stood over a third, mostly naked man, his body caked in mud and leaves. The moment elongated, stretched from its bloom in September 1973 across three and a half decades, embedded like a cyst in Pershing's brain. The strangers grasped Terry's ankles with hands so pale they shone in the gloom. They wore deep cowls that hid their faces…yet, in Pershing's nightmares, that inner darkness squirmed with vile intent.

The robed figures regarded him; one crooked a long, oddly jointed finger and beckoned him. Then the strangers laughed—that sickening, diabolic laughter of a man mimicking a child—and dragged Terry away. Terry lay supine, eyes open, mouth slack, head softly bumping over the slimy rocks, arms trailing, limp, an inverted Jesus hauled toward his gruesome fate. They walked into the shadows, through a sudden fissure in the rocks, and were gone forever.

HE ONE THAT IMITATED TERRY RELEASED HIM FROM the rack and carried him, drifting with the ungainly coordination of a punctured float, through a stygian wasteland. This one murmured to him in the fashion of a physician, a historian, a tour guide, the histories and customs of its race. His captor tittered, hideously amused at Pershing's perception of having been cast into a subterranean hell.

Not hell or any of its pits. You have crossed the axis of time and space by means of technologies that were old when your kind yet oozed in brine. You, sweet man, are in the black forest of cosmic night.

Pershing imagined passing over a colossal reef of flesh and bone, its coils and ridges populated by incalculable numbers of horridly intelligent beings that had flown from their original planets, long since gone cold and dead, and spread implacably across the infinite cosmos. This people traveled in a cloud of seeping darkness. Their living darkness was a cancerous thing, a mindless, organic suspension fluid that protected them from the noxious light of foreign stars and magnified their psychic screams of murder and lust. It was their oxygen and their blood. They suckled upon it, and in turn, it fed upon them.

We eat our children, Terry had said. Immortals have no need for offspring. We're gourmands, you see; and we do love our sport. We devour the children of every sentient race we metastasize to...we've quite enjoyed our visit here. The amenities are exquisite.

He also learned their true forms, while humanoid, were soft and wet and squirming. The human physiognomies they preferred for brief field excursions were organic shells grown in vats, exoskeletons that served as temporary camouflage and insulation from the hostile environments of terrestrial worlds. In their own starless demesne they hopped and crawled and slithered as was traditional.

Without warning, he was dropped from a great height into a body of water that bore him to its surface and buoyed him with its density, its syrupy thickness. He was overcome with the searing stench of rot and sewage. From above, someone grasped his hair and dragged him to an invisible shore.

There came a long, blind crawl through what felt like a tunnel of raw meat, an endless loop of intestine that squeezed him along its tract. He went forward, chivvied by unseen devils who whispered obscenities in his ear and caressed him with pincers and stinging tendrils, who dripped acid on the back of his neck and laughed as he screamed and thrashed in the amniotic soup, the quaking entrails. Eventually, a light appeared and he wormed his way to it, gibbering mindless prayers to whatever gods might be interested.

"It is always hot as hell down here," Hopkins the custodian said. He perched on a tall box, his grimy coveralls and grimy face lighted by the red glow that flared from the furnace window. "There's a metaphor for ya. Me stoking the boiler in Hell."

Pershing realized the custodian had been chatting at him for a while. He was wedged in the corner of the concrete wall. His clothes stuck to him with sweat, the drying juices of a slaughterhouse. He smelled his own rank ammonia odor. Hopkins grinned and struck a match and lighted a cigarette. The brief illumination revealed a nearly done-in bottle of Wild Turkey leaning against his thigh. Pershing croaked and held out his hand. Hopkins chuckled. He jumped down and gave Pershing the bottle.

"Finish it off. I've got three more hid in my crib, yonder." He gestured into the gloom. "Mr. 119, isn't it? Yeah, Mr. 119. You been to hell, now ain't you? You're hurtin' for certain."

Pershing drank, choking as the liquor burned away the rust and foulness. He gasped and managed to ask, "What day is it?"

Hopkins held his arm near the furnace grate and checked his watch. "Thursday, 2:15 p.m., and all is well. Not really, but nobody knows the trouble we see, do they?"

Thursday afternoon? He'd been with *them* for seventy-two hours, give or take. Had anyone noticed? He dropped the bottle and it clinked and rolled away. He gained his feet and followed the sooty wall toward the stairs. Behind him, Hopkins started singing "Black Hole Sun."

AS IT HAPPENED, HE SPENT THE REST OF THE AFTERNOON and much of the evening in an interrogation room at the police station on Perry Street. When he reached his apartment, he found Superintendent Frame had left a note on the door saying he was to contact the authorities immediately. There were frantic messages from Mel and Wanda on the answering machine wondering where he'd gone, and one from an Officer Klecko politely asking that he report to the precinct as soon as possible.

He stripped his ruined clothes and stared at his soft, wrinkled body in the mirror. There were no marks, but the memory of unspeakable indignities caused his hands to shake, his gorge to rise. Recalling the savagery and pain visited upon him, it was inconceivable his skin, albeit soiled with dirt and unidentifiable stains, showed no bruises or blemishes. He showered in water so hot it nearly scalded him. Finally, he dressed in a fresh suit and fixed a drink. Halfway through the glass he dialed the police and told his name to the lady who answered and that he'd be coming in shortly. He called Wanda's house and left a message informing her of his situation.

The station was largely deserted. An officer on the opposite side of bulletproof glass recorded his information and asked him to take a seat. Pershing slumped in a plastic chair near a pair of soda machines. There were a few empty desks and cubicles in a large room to his left. Periodically a uniformed officer passed by and gave him an uninterested glance.

Eventually, Detective Klecko appeared and shook his hand and ushered him into a small office. The office was papered with memos and photographs of wanted criminals. Brown water stains marred the ceiling tiles and the room smelled moldy. Detective Klecko poured orange soda into a Styrofoam cup and gave it to Pershing and left the can on the edge of the desk. The detective was a large man, with a bushy mustache and powerful hands. He dressed in a white shirt and black suspenders, and his bulk caused the swivel chair to wobble precariously. He smiled broadly and asked if it was all right to turn on a tape recorder—Pershing wasn't being charged, wasn't a suspect, this was just department policy.

They exchanged pleasantries regarding the cooler weather, the Seattle Mariners' disappointing season, and how the city police department was woefully understaffed due to the recession, and segued right into questions about Pershing's tenancy at the Broadsword. How long had he lived there? Who did he know? Who were his friends? Was he friendly with the Ordbeckers, their children? Especially little Eric. Eric was missing, and Mr. Dennard could you please tell me where you've been the last three days?

Pershing couldn't. He sat across from the detective and stared at the recorder and sweated. At last he said, "I drink. I blacked out."

Detective Klecko said, "Really? That might come as a surprise to your friends. They described you as a moderate drinker."

"I'm not saying I'm a lush, only that I down a bit more in private than anybody knows. I hit it pretty hard Monday night and sort of recovered this afternoon."

"That happen often?"

"No."

Detective Klecko nodded and scribbled on a notepad. "Did you happen to see Eric Ordbecker on Monday…before you became inebriated?"

"No, sir. I spent the day in my apartment. You can talk to Melvin Clayton. He lives in 93. We had dinner about five p.m. or so."

The phone on the desk rang. Detective Klecko shut off the recorder and listened, then told whoever was on the other end the interview was almost concluded. "Your wife, Wanda. She's waiting outside. We'll be done in a minute."

"Oh, she's not my wife—"

Detective Klecko started the recorder again. "Continuing interview with Mr. Pershing Dennard… So, Mr. Dennard, you claim not to have seen Eric Ordbecker on Monday, September 24? When was the last time you did see Eric?"

"I'm not claiming anything. I didn't see the kid that day. Last time I saw him? I don't know—two weeks ago, maybe. I was talking to his dad. Let me tell you, you're questioning the wrong person. Don't you have the reports we've made about weirdoes sneaking around the building? You should be chatting them up. The weirdoes, I mean."

"Well, let's not worry about them. Let's talk about you a bit more, shall we?"

And so it went for another two hours. Finally, the detective killed the recorder and thanked him for his cooperation. He didn't think there would be any more questions. Wanda met Pershing in the reception area. She wore one of her serious work dresses and no glasses; her eyes were puffy from crying. Wrestling with his irritation at seeing her before he'd prepared his explanations, he hugged her and inhaled the perfume in her hair. He noted how dark the station had become. Illumination came from the vending machines and a reading lamp at the desk sergeant's post. The sergeant himself was absent.

"Mr. Dennard?" Detective Klecko stood silhouetted in the office doorway, backlit by his flickering computer monitor.

"Yes, Detective?" *What now? Here come the cuffs, I bet.*

"Thank you again. Don't worry yourself over…what we discussed. We'll take care of everything." His face was hidden, but his eyes gleamed.

The detective's words didn't fully hit Pershing until he'd climbed into Wanda's car and they were driving to Anthony's, an expensive restaurant near the marina. She declared a couple of glasses of wine and a fancy lobster dinner were called for. Not to celebrate, but to restore some semblance of order, some measure of normalcy. She seemed equally, if not more, shaken than he was. That she hadn't summoned the courage to demand where he'd been for three days told him everything about her state of mind.

We'll take care of everything.

ANDA PARKED IN THE SIDE LOT OF A DARKENED BANK and went to withdraw cash from the ATM. Pershing watched her from the car, keeping an eye out for lurking muggers. The thought of dinner made his stomach tighten. He didn't feel well. His head ached and chills knotted the muscles along his spine. Exhaustion caused his eyelids to droop.

"Know what I ask myself?" Terry whispered from the vent under the dash. "I ask myself why you never told the cops about the two 'men' who took me away. In all these years, you've not told the whole truth to anyone."

Pershing put his hand over his mouth. "Jesus!"

"Don't weasel. *Answer the question.*"

In a gesture he dimly acknowledged as absurd, he almost broke the lever in his haste to close the vent. "Because they didn't exist," he said, more to convince himself. "When the search parties got to me, I was half dead from exposure, ranting and raving. You got lost. You just got lost and we couldn't find you." He wiped his eyes and breathed heavily.

"You think your visit with us was unpleasant? It was a gift. Pull yourself together. We kept the bad parts from you, Percy my boy. For now, at least. No sniveling; it's unbecoming in a man your age."

Pershing composed himself sufficiently to say, "That kid! What did you bastards do? Are you trying to hang me? Haven't I suffered enough to please you sickos?"

"Like I said; you don't know the first thing about suffering. Your little friend Eric does, though."

Wanda faced the car, folding money into her wallet. A shadow detached from the bushes at the edge of the building. Terry rose behind her, his bone-white hand spread like a catcher's mitt above her head. His fingers tapered to needles. He grinned evilly at Pershing, and made a shushing gesture.

From the vent by some diabolical ventriloquism: "We'll be around. If you need us. Be good."

Wanda slung open the door and climbed in. She started the engine and kissed Pershing's cheek. He scarcely noticed; his attention was riveted upon Terry waving as he melted into the shrubbery.

He didn't touch a thing at dinner. His nerves were shot—a child cried, a couple bickered with a waiter, and boisterous laughter from a neighboring table set his teeth on edge. The dim lighting was provided by candles in bowls and lamps in sconces. He couldn't even see his own feet through the shadows when he glanced under the table while Wanda had her head turned. The bottle of wine came in handy. She watched in wordless amazement as he downed several consecutive glasses.

That night his dreams were smooth and black as the void.

HE CALENDAR TICKED OVER INTO OCTOBER. ELGIN proposed a long weekend at his grandfather's cabin. He'd bring his latest girlfriend, an Evergreen graduate student named Sarah; Mel and Gina, and Pershing and Wanda would round out the expedition. "We all could use a day or two away from the bright lights," Elgin said. "Drink some booze, play some cards, tell a few tales around the bonfire. It'll be a hoot."

Pershing would have happily begged off. He was irritable as a badger. More than ever he wanted to curl into a ball and make his apartment a den, no trespassers allowed. On the other hand, he'd grown twitchier by the day. Shadows spooked him. Being alone spooked him. There'd been no news about the missing child and he constantly waited for the other shoe to drop. The idea of running into Mark Ordbecker gave him acid. He prayed the Ordbeckers had focused their suspicion on the real culprits and would continue to leave him in peace.

Ultimately he consented to the getaway for Wanda's sake. She'd lit up at the mention of being included on this most sacred of annual events. It made her feel that she'd been accepted as a member of the inner circle.

Late Friday afternoon, the six of them loaded food, extra clothes, and sleeping bags into two cars and headed for the hills. It was an hour's drive that wound from Olympia through the nearby pastureland of the Waddell Valley toward the Black Hills. Elgin paced them as they climbed a series of gravel and dirt access roads into the high country. Even after all these years, Pershing was impressed how quickly the trappings of civilization were erased as the forest closed in. Few people came this far—mainly hunters and hikers passing through. Several logging camps were located in the region, but none within earshot.

Elgin's cabin lay at the end of an overgrown track atop a ridge. Below, the valley spread in a misty gulf. At night, Olympia's skyline burned orange in the middle distance. No phone, no television, no electricity. Water came from a hand pump. There was an outhouse in the woods behind the cabin. While everyone else unpacked the cars, Pershing and Mel fetched wood from the shed and made a big fire in the pit near the porch, and a second fire in the massive stone hearth inside the cabin. By then it was dark.

Wanda and Gina turned the tables on the men and demonstrated their superior barbequing skills. Everyone ate hot dogs and drank Löwenbräu and avoided gloomy conversation until Elgin's girlfriend Sarah commented that his cabin would be "a great place to wait out the apocalypse" and received nervous chuckles in response.

Pershing smiled to cover the prickle along the back of his neck. He stared into the night and wondered what kind of apocalypse a kid like Sarah imagined when she used that word. Probably she visualized the polar icecaps melting, or the world as a desert. Pershing's generation had lived in fear of the Reds, nuclear holocaust, and being invaded by little green men from Mars.

Wind sighed in the trees and sent a swirl of sparks tumbling skyward. He trembled. *God, I hate the woods. Who thought the day would come?* Star fields twinkled across the millions of light years. He didn't like the looks of them either. Wanda patted his arm and laid her head against his shoulder while Elgin told an old story about the time he and his college dorm mates replaced the school flag with a pair of giant pink bloomers.

Pershing didn't find the story amusing this time. The laughter sounded canned and made him consider the artificiality of the entire situation, man's supposed mastery of nature and darkness. Beyond this feeble bubble of light yawned a chasm. He'd drunk more than his share these past few days; had helped himself to Wanda's Valium. None of these measures did the trick of allowing him to forget where he'd gone or what he'd seen; it hadn't convinced him that his worst memories were the products of nightmare. Wanda's touch repulsed him, confined him. He wanted nothing more than to crawl into bed and hide beneath the covers until everything bad went away.

It grew chilly and the bonfire died to coals. The others drifted off to sleep. The cabin had two bedrooms—Elgin claimed one, and as the other married couple, Mel and Gina were awarded the second. Pershing and Wanda settled for an air mattress near the fireplace. When the last of the beer was gone, he extricated himself from her and rose to stretch. "I'm going inside," he said. She smiled and said she'd be along soon. She wanted to watch the stars a bit longer.

Pershing stripped to his boxers and lay on the air mattress. He pulled the blanket to his chin and stared blankly at the rafters. His skin was clammy and it itched fiercely. Sharp, throbbing pains radiated from his knees and shoulders. Tears formed in the corners of his eyes. He remembered the day he'd talked to Mark Ordbecker, the incredible heat, young Eric's terrified expression as he skulked behind his father. Little pitchers and big ears. The boy heard the voices crooning from below, hadn't he?

A purple ring of light flickered on the rough-hewn beam directly overhead. It pulsed and blurred with each thud of his heart. The ring shivered like water and changed. His face was damp, but not from tears, not from sweat. He felt his knuckle joints split, the skin and meat popping and peeling like an overripe banana. What had Terry said about eating the young and immortality?

How does our species propagate, you may ask. Cultural assimilation, my friend. We chop out the things that make you lesser life forms weak and then pump you full of love. You'll be part of the family soon; you'll understand everything.

A mental switch clicked and he smiled at the memory of creeping into Eric's room and plucking him from his bed; later, the child's hands fluttering, nerveless, the approving croaks and cries of his new kin. He shuddered in ecstasy and burst crude seams in a dozen places. He threw off the blanket and stood, swaying, drunk with revelation. His flesh was a chrysalis, leaking gore.

Terry and Gloria watched him from the doorways of the bedrooms—naked and ghostly, and smiling like devils. Behind them, the rooms were silent. He looked at their bodies, contemptuous that anyone could be fooled for two seconds by these distorted forms, or by his own.

Then he was outside under the cold, cold stars.

Wanda huddled in her shawl, wan and small in the firelight. Finally she noticed him, tilting her head so she could meet his eyes. "Sweetie, are you waiting for me?" She gave him a concerned smile. The recent days of worry and doubt had deepened the lines of her brow.

He regarded her from the shadows, speechless as his mouth filled with blood. He touched his face, probing a moist delineation just beneath the hairline; a fissure, a fleshy zipper. Near his elbow, Terry said, "The first time, it's easier if you just snatch it off."

Pershing gripped a flap of skin. He swept his hand down and ripped away all the frailties of humanity.

Usurped

WILLIAM BROWNING SPENCER

William Browning Spencer is the author of the innovative Lovecraftian novel Résumé with Monsters *(White Wolf, 1995) as well as the novels* Maybe I'll Call Anna *(Permanent Press, 1990),* Zod Wallop *(St. Martin's Press, 1995), and* Irrational Fears *(White Wolf, 1998) and the short story collections* The Return of Count Electric and Other Stories *(Permanent Press, 1993) and* The Ocean and All Its Devices *(Subterranean Press, 2006).*

HEY WERE DRIVING BACK FROM EL PASO, WHERE THEY had been visiting Meta's parents, when Brad saw something shimmering on the road, a heat mirage or, perhaps, some internal aberration, those writhing, silver amoebae that were the harbingers of one of his murderous migraines.

Meta had insisted that they turn the air off and roll the windows down. "I love this desert air," she had said, inhaling dramatically.

"Nothing like the smell of diesel fumes at dusk," Brad had responded, only he hadn't. He was thirty-six years old, and he had been married for almost half his life, and he loved his wife, loved her enthusiasm for the flawed world, and understood how easily, how unthinkingly, he could curdle her good mood with his reflexive cynicism. Besides, the trucks that had heaved by earlier were gone, as was their stink, and the two-lane highway he presently followed was devoid of all vehicles and had been ever since he'd abandoned the more straightforward eastbound path.

Having satisfied himself that the cloud was illusion, a trick of nature or his mind, he no longer saw it. Such is the power of reason.

And then, like that, the wasps filled the cab. Incredibly, amid the pandemonium and his panic, he knew them instantly for what they were, saw one, red-black and vile, arc its abdomen and plunge its stinger into his bare forearm, a revolting, indelible mental snapshot. A whirring of wings, wind buffeting his ears, thwack of bodies, one crawling on his neck, another igniting his cheek with bright pain, and Meta shrieking—and he made a sound of his own, an *aaaaaaaghaaah* of disgust—as he wrenched the steering wheel, and the Ford Ranger leapt up, surprised by his urgency, and twisted, exploded, a series of jolting explosions, with the sky and the earth tumbling in ungainly combat.

HE BLINKED AND A HUNDRED THOUSAND STARS regarded him. He lay on his back, unable to summon full consciousness, resistant to what its return might mean. Breathing was not easy; the air was full of razors. He rolled onto his side, slowly. Mesquite and cacti and unruly juniper threw tortured shadows across a flat, moonlit expanse that stretched toward distant mountains.

He raised himself on his elbows; a knife-thrust of pain took his breath away, and he was still, waiting, as a deer might freeze at the sound of a predator. He slid his right hand under his T-shirt, and he found the source of the pain, more than he wanted to find, ragged bloody flesh and the broken spike of a rib.

He stood and might have thought to rejoice that he had no greater injuries, that he had, miraculously, survived the wreck, but he couldn't imagine more pain; he had a plenitude of pain, a surfeit. Meta might say—

Meta!

He saw the Ranger then, lying on its side, the passenger door gone and the windshield gone, a bright spume of pebbled glass vomited into the sand in front of its sprung hood. "Meta!" he shouted. "Meta!"

He limped toward the vehicle. There was something wrong with his left knee, too, as though his knee cap had been replaced with a water-filled balloon.

She wasn't in the Ranger, wasn't under it either.

Moonlight painted everything in pale silver, revealing detail in every shadow, a hallucinatory world, too precisely rendered to be real. Brad moved in slow, widening circles, calling her name. Finally, he turned toward the road, approaching a thick-trunked live oak, solitary and massive, its thousand gnarled branches festooned with small, glittering leaves. The tree, he saw, had claimed the passenger door, which lay, like a fallen warrior's shield, close to the oak's gashed trunk.

And here, Brad thought, *is where she was thrown.*

Maybe he would discover her on the other side of that thick trunk, her body hidden in some declivity, invisible until you stumbled on its very edge.

But there was no hollow to hide her body, nothing. And after he had climbed to the road, looked up and down it, and crossed to gaze at another stark vista that revealed no trace of her, he accepted what he'd already known. She wasn't here. He would have known if she were nearby—because he was connected to her, more than ever since the onset of her illness. He had always had this psychic compass, this inexplicable but inarguable ability to know just where she was in the world.

In their house in Austin, he always knew what room she was in. If she was down the street visiting a neighbor, Brad knew that, too—and knew *which* neighbor. If her car was gone, he knew where she had driven to (the library, the grocery store, the YMCA at Town Lake, wherever), and he realized, one day, that he knew this whether or not she had told him.

Once, when they were kids, nine-year-olds, Meta had gone missing. It was dark outside, and Meta had failed to come home.

The neighborhood went looking. Brad set off on his own. Under the luminous summer moon, he ran past the elementary school, past the creek where they hunted frogs and crayfish, across old man Halder's field. He found her at the abandoned barn. She lay next to a rusted-out wheelbarrow, one of her legs crimped oddly under her. That she was alive filled him with wild relief and the terrible knowledge that he could have lost her forever, that the world was a monstrous machine, and anyone in its path could come to mortal grief. She frowned at him, pale blue eyes under tangled red hair, and said, "You were right about that rope," and they both gazed at the tire, on its side in the dust. Until recently, the tire had been an integral part of a swing.

"Why did you do something so stupid?" he had shouted, and she had begun to cry, silently, tears falling from her eyes, her lips parted, lower lip trembling, and he thought, *I'm an idiot*, and he realized that he would marry her one day, if only to keep an eye on her, to protect her (from evil, which ranged across the world, and from his own desperate love, half-mad and hiding in his heart).

Standing on the road, he remembered that he had a cell phone and, after retrieving it from his pocket and turning it on, he remembered why the cell phone was no cause for rejoicing: no signal, no help.

He turned away from the empty road and studied the mountains. They were purple and black and seemed closer now. Could she have walked to the mountains? And why would she do such a thing? Surely the road was more likely to bring rescue.

He thought of Meta, conjured her, carefully visualizing her blue eyes, curly red hair, and high cheekbones (sown with a constellation of freckles that refused to fade, a last vestige of her tomboy childhood). Ordinarily, imagining her calmed him, relieved the stress of a bad day at the office, an unhappy client, the black dog of depression, of fear, but now, with Meta missing, her image failed to console, only exacerbated his dread. Her face shimmered, faded, was gone, and he realized that the mountains were glowing, exuding a pulsing light, a mottled purple hue that filled him with inexplicable disgust and panic and despair.

He felt consciousness receding like a tide. He leaned into oblivion, seeking refuge from the horror that assaulted him.

E WOKE TO WHITE LIGHT IN A WHITE ROOM. HE WAS propped up in a hospital bed, his left leg encased in an elaborate cast and suspended artfully from stainless steel scaffolding. A large, ridiculous bolt pierced the cast in the vicinity of his knee, like an elaborate magic trick. Breathing, he discovered, was difficult—although not, he decided, impossible, not worthy of panic—and gazing down at his chest, he saw what looked like duct tape, yards of it, binding swathes of surgical gauze and cotton around his ribs.

He remembered the damage then, remembered the wasps.

A woman stepped into the room and said, "Where's Meta?"

It was Gladys, Meta's mother, dressed in khaki pants and a white blouse, filling the room with willed energy.

Where is—Before Brad could speak, someone to his right spoke.

"She went to the cafeteria to get some coffee." It was Buddy, Gladys's husband. He had been sitting silently in a chair, dozing perhaps. He was a stern, formal old man (much older than his wife), bald with tufts of grey hair sprouting above each ear. Querulous, nobody's buddy: Buddy.

Before Brad could assimilate Buddy's statement, Meta appeared in the doorway, behind her mother. She was holding a cardboard carton containing three styrofoam cups with plastic lids. Her eyes widened. "Oh," she said. "Brad."

Gladys turned. "Oh my," she said.

Meta put the carton down on a dresser top and came to him. There were tears in her eyes, and she was smiling. Brad felt as light as dust, mystified, out of context. Wasn't Meta the one in hospital beds? Wasn't he her visitor, her caretaker, her terrified lover?

"Where have you been?" she said, laughing, running her hand through his hair.

And wasn't that *his* question?

META TOLD HIM HE HAD BEEN UNCONSCIOUS FOR TWO days. They sorted it out, or rather, they did their best to make sense of what had happened. Wayne County's sheriff came by the hospital, and Brad and Meta told him what they could remember.

The sheriff was a big man with a broad face and a mournful mustache. He was slow, his bearing solemn and stoical, as though he'd seen too much that ended badly. He introduced himself by taking his hat off and saying, "Mr. and Mrs. Phelps, my name is Dale Winslow, and I'm the sheriff in these parts, and I'm sorry for your misadventure," and he pulled up a chair and produced a small notebook and a ball-point pen from his breast pocket.

He told them what he already knew. A local named Gary Birch had been driving back from a visit to his ex in Owl Creek when he'd seen a woman out on the road. He stopped and got out of his car. He could see she was bleeding, blood on her face, her blouse, and, when he came up to her, he could see the Ford Ranger on its side maybe fifty yards from the road. It didn't take any great deductive powers to figure out what had happened. Here was a woman who had flipped her truck; she was in shock, couldn't make a sound. Gary told her to hang on, and he went down and looked at the Ranger, checked to see that there wasn't a gas leak, took the keys out of the ignition. He didn't see anyone else, but he wasn't looking. A fool thing, not to look, but it didn't even enter his mind. He wanted to get her over to the hospital in Silo. For all he knew she might already be as good as dead and just not know it. That happened sometimes. Gary had heard about such things from his dad, a Nam vet. A fellow could say, "I'm okay," when he was nothing but a disembodied head, although maybe that one was just a story.

Meta, it turned out, had sustained no serious injuries. She didn't remember anything about the accident. She didn't remember the wasps in the truck, didn't remember Gary stopping for her and taking her to the hospital. At some point, in the ER, she'd started screaming for Brad, and a nurse, Eunice Wells, who'd worked the ER for twenty-some years, put two and two together, got Sheriff Winslow on the phone, and hollered Gary Birch out of the waiting room. "This is Eunice Wells," she told Winslow. "Gary Birch just brought a woman in here for treatment. He found her on Old Nine where she'd flipped her truck. Sounds like there's someone still out there. I'm gonna give the phone to Gary, and he's gonna tell you just where you gotta go."

Which Gary did. Sheriff Winslow found Brad lying by the side of the highway, as inert as yesterday's roadkill, a dark lump next to a creosote bush. He might have been a sideswiped deer or a sack of trash that fell off someone's pickup on the way out to the Owl Creek dump. Likely Winslow wouldn't have noticed him if he hadn't known where to look.

Brad asked about the wasp swarm. Was that sort of thing common around here?

Brad thought he saw something flicker in Winslow's eyes, something furtive. The sheriff closed his eyes, and when he opened them, whatever had been there was gone. The man just looked tired. He said, "It's hard to say what an insect will do. I haven't heard of anyone running through a patch of wasps, but termites will swarm. And you can get locusts out of nowhere, like a judgment." He shrugged. "I'd thank the good Lord you're alive and put it behind you."

Good advice, but not easy to follow. He was in the hospital four more days, foggy time, nurses in and out of the room, Meta sitting in a chair, sometimes holding his hand in hers. He would wake as though falling into freezing water, his heart clenching like a fist, nightmares leaving a coppery sediment in the back of his throat. He had no memory of the dreams, only a sense of diminishment and hopelessness. He would look down and see his hand resting in that other's hand, and his eyes would trace the route of that hand to arm, to shoulder, to neck, to that lovely face, and slow seconds would fill with disquiet before he realized he was looking at his wife, at Meta. He, who had always been able to find her wherever she was in the world, could no longer sense her presence when she sat beside him holding his hand. He said nothing of this to Meta; it frightened him too much. This disoriented state might, he reasoned, be the result of the pain medications they gave him, and as he tapered off, his sense of his darling's spiritual weight, her certainty in his world, would return.

The day before Brad was to leave the hospital, a wizened man with a close-cropped gray beard came to visit him. The man wore a light blue shirt, tan slacks, and a brown sports jacket. He was pale and sickly looking, wearing glasses with thick black frames, glasses that a younger man would have worn for comic or ironic effect. He introduced himself, and Brad said, "So, how am I doing? Do I still get to leave tomorrow?"

The man frowned, perplexed. "I don't—" He realized his mistake then and said, "I'm sorry. I'm not a medical doctor. That's what I get for calling myself a doctor in a hospital. I'm a Ph.D. I taught at Baylor but I'm retired now."

It was Brad's turn to look stumped. Dr. Michael Parkington introduced himself again. He said that he was writing a book on the desert and was particularly interested in unusual anecdotal material. He'd heard about Brad's encounter with a swarm of wasps, and he wondered if Brad would mind telling him about it.

Brad had nothing better to do—Meta was seeing her parents off at the airport and wouldn't be back for hours—and he was interested in what this man could tell him.

Parkington asked if it would be all right if he recorded Brad's recollections of the accident, and Brad almost said no, which was irrational, of course, but he would have preferred an undocumented chat. He'd heard his voice on a recorder once, and his voice sounded thin and full of complaint. But he said, "Sure," and the professor turned on a small, cell-phone-sized recorder, and Brad told him everything he could remember, ending with, "I got woozy standing out there on the road, and I just passed out, I guess."

"How many times were you stung?" Parkington asked.

Brad shrugged. "Maybe half a dozen times. I don't know. It's hard to keep count when you're flying through a windshield."

Parkington smiled ruefully. "Any welts? Any swellings or discolorations?"

Brad looked down at his forearm where he'd seen the wasp sting him. Nothing. His skin was smooth, unblemished. He lifted his hand to touch his cheek. No soreness there, and, shaving for the first time that morning, he hadn't noticed any redness or swelling.

"No," he said, slightly puzzled. "I didn't even think to look."

Parkington turned the recorder off and put it in his pocket. "I want to thank you for your time, Mr. Phelps." He stood up.

"Sure. How many people have you interviewed?" Brad asked.

The professor sat down again. He took his glasses off, rubbed his forehead, and put the glasses back on. "I'd appreciate it if you wouldn't say anything to Sheriff Winslow about my coming by."

"Why's that?" Brad was starting to feel a little miffed. He

hadn't wanted that recorder running, and he should have trusted his intuition, because...well, here was this guy getting all circumspect, enlisting him in some local intrigue.

"Winslow thinks I'm trying to stir things up. Truth is, he thinks I'm a crackpot," Parkington said. "He'd be pissed if he knew I'd come out here." He looked at the doorway, as though expecting the sheriff to come walking through it on cue. He made a decision then. Brad could see it in the way he straightened his spine and narrowed his eyes. "I haven't been entirely candid with you."

The man leaned over and fumbled in his briefcase. "I've already written a book," he said. He retrieved a book and handed it to Brad. Brad knew a self-published book when he saw one. The title was set in a lurid, old-English typeface: *Haunted Mountains: Atlantis in the Desert* by Michael Parkington, Ph.D. Translucent ocean waves were superimposed over a photograph of a desert panorama, mountains in the background. This computer-manipulated image, murky and lurid, offended Brad's artistic sensibility while managing to instill a queasy sense of dislocation.

Brad looked up from the book in his hands and said, "And what, exactly, haven't you told me?"

Parkington nodded his head. "I didn't tell you that after interviewing some other people who encountered hostile swarm phenomena, I've come to the conclusion that these people were *not* attacked, not physically, in any event. I believe they all experienced a psychic derangement. I'm telling you that I don't think you were attacked by wasps, Mr. Phelps. I think you were the victim of an induced hallucination."

Brad sighed, disgusted. "The last week hasn't been one of my best, but I think I know what I saw." Brad held out the book, but Parkington smiled and shook his head.

"You keep the book. Maybe you'll want to read it sometime.

You know, not a single wasp was found in your vehicle, which is what I expected. I've documented *five* other cases of people being attacked by swarms, all within a half-mile of where you were found."

Brad was silent.

Parkington held his hand up, fingers wide, and lowered each successive finger as he ticked off an attack: "Birds, bats, rattlesnakes, ants, and—my favorite menace—moths. In all but one case, the subjects were driving down Route 9 when they were attacked. The drivers were all forced to abandon their vehicles as a result of an onslaught of bats or flying ants or sparrows or moths, and all the attack victims seem to have lost consciousness for some period of time. Your adventure was the only life-threatening encounter, although any of the attacks could have resulted in a fatal accident.

"I might add that I know about *these* attacks because other travelers along that lonely stretch spotted the abandoned vehicles or the confused, semi-conscious owners and stopped to offer assistance. It seems reasonable to assume that some other drivers suffered swarm attacks during times when traffic was sparse, came to their senses, shrugged off their weird adventures, and drove on."

Parkington said that there was one man who was *not* in a car when attacked. A man named Charlie Musgrove was on foot when he found himself surrounded by rattlesnakes. Musgrove maintained that he was bitten by five or six of the creatures, but a sample of his blood revealed no toxins, other than the alcohol he habitually imbibed.

"He's a local, a homeless alcoholic," Parkington said, "and not a credible witness, but I'm inclined to believe him, because he was in the vicinity of the other reported incidents, and his account is consistent with them."

Parkington said that, in every single one of these reported

attacks, no sign of the attacking creatures was found, no birds, bats, rattlesnakes, ants, or moths. And in the case of the birds, the driver was adamant in her description of their thrashing and banging around in the car, feathers flying everywhere, much avian carnage, so one would think that the most cursory forensic examination would have produced some corroborating evidence. Nothing could be found. "I'm guessing Sheriff Winslow hasn't told you any of this."

"He hasn't," Brad said. "Probably because he is a professional and understands that it is not his job to share bizarre theories with someone who has just been traumatized by a near-fatal accident. Now my meds are kicking in, and I'm going to close my eyes and get some sleep. Thanks for the book."

And Brad closed his eyes, and when he opened them again, it was dark outside his window, and Meta was sitting in a chair with the book on her lap. She looked up, smiled, and said, "It says here that during the Permian age this whole area was under an ocean. That was 250 million years ago. Who gave you this book?"

"The ancient mariner," Brad said.

THEY DROVE BACK TO AUSTIN IN A RENTED HONDA Accord. Meta did all the driving. Brad remained bundled in a semi-fog of pain meds, and a substantial cast girded his left leg. He'd been instructed in the use of crutches, but they were of limited utility thanks to his ravaged rib cage. A folded wheelchair, which would be his primary mode of transportation for the next six weeks, lay in the car's trunk.

Once home, Brad called friends and family, quickly wearied of telling his story, and cast a forlorn eye on the upcoming weeks of recuperation.

On the positive side, he accompanied Meta to an appointment with her oncologist, who was pleased to tell them that all tests were negative; there was no trace of the cancer that had short-circuited their lives for the last year and a half. They had celebrated that night, with champagne and sex.

The sex had not been entirely successful. Brad had been struck with the intense conviction that, should he experience an orgasm, it would kill him; something vital to sustaining his life would be seized and devoured by his partner's need. This thought robbed him of an erection, but his failure to achieve orgasm was, paradoxically, a great relief, as though he had survived a brush with death, so it wasn't the *worst* sex he'd ever had, but it didn't bode well for his erotic future.

Brad called work and had to talk to the insufferable Kent, a completely insincere creature, ambitious and feral, who assured Brad that he could avail himself of as much time off as his recuperation required. "I got your back, Brad-O," he said, which didn't cheer Brad at all. And yet, Brad felt no urgency about returning to work. Work felt like some remote, arcane endeavor, the rituals of some strange religion in which he had long ago ceased to believe.

Having plenty of time on his hands, Brad read Parkington's book, *Haunted Mountains: Atlantis in the Desert*. The bulk of the book, after its author had argued unconvincingly for a sunken Atlantis near the town of Silo, presented the usual lost civilization stories. The only part of the book that was interesting (and poignant for the insights it offered) was Parkington's revelation that his own father, a lawyer and amateur paleontologist, had encountered an Entity (his father's word) while camping in the mountains outside of Silo. Parkington's father referred to this alien visitation as a "remnant manifestation" and had embarked on a book about this visitation. He believed that there was an alien enclave established under the mountains in a "waiting configuration" that would transform the world when its time came round.

The author's father disappeared in 1977 after a sudden decline in his mental state, characterized by paranoia, hallucinations, and a fervid hatred and fear of Christian doctrine. On more than one occasion, the man had entered one of Silo's numerous churches during a Sunday service, wild-eyed and disheveled, and beseeched the minister and his congregation to "be silent and know that the only thing that hears you is monstrous and indifferent to prayers." Much of the man's rant was in an unknown tongue, and he was committed to private mental asylums on two occasions, but he was never at such places for long, because he grew remarkably calm and rational after a brief period of confinement. When he disappeared, he left a note for his son, which, Parkington writes, "I destroyed after reading, or, rather, after I had read as much as my sanity could bear."

It was this last part of the book that spoke most directly to Brad, because it explained the author's attempt to find some explanation for his father's last years. The book Brad held in his hands was an artifact of two generations of pathology, and, as such, it was sadder and more profound than its clichéd, sensational subject initially suggested.

There was no mention of the swarm attacks, and Brad assumed that such attacks were a more recent phenomenon.

BRAD'S HEALTH IMPROVED, AND HE CEASED TO RELY on the wheelchair. The cast came off his leg, and his ribs were protected by a more flexible, shower-friendly fiberglass cage. With the help of a cane—he'd never had any success with the crutches, which promoted a form of locomotion too unnatural to be taken seriously—he was able to hobble to the kitchen and back to the bedroom, exhausted at first but slowly regaining his stamina, reclaiming his will.

He had much time for solitary reflection, because Meta, on his urging, had returned to her job at the UT library. In the evenings, she'd talk to him about her day, her voice his only window on a larger world.

Brad found his attention straying from her words. His mind, his heart was otherwise occupied: he was waiting (every day, every hour, every second) to feel, again, her presence. Since the accident, she had turned invisible...*and* opaque. Both words described her, despite their warring definitions. She was a ghost in his mind when out of his sight. His psychic compass could no longer find her. She could be anywhere, pursuing any activity—and he imagined her in the strangest places: curled amid warm towels in a clothes dryer; hanging upside down in a closet; smiling with her eyes open while underwater in the upstairs bathtub—and when she was in front of him, he did not know her. She seemed to study him with cool interest and an absence of any binding emotion. Even her voice had altered, and he found himself marveling at how skillfully this woman reproduced his wife's sounds, failing only in recreating certain resonances that were within the province of her soul.

He should have been afraid, but he was not—not, that is, until he received a call from Sheriff Winslow, who informed Brad that Michael Parkington had left Silo, abruptly and without notice. The date of his departure was uncertain, since he kept to himself. Only when Parkington failed to show up on the first with the rent check did anyone (i.e., his landlord) evince interest in his whereabouts.

Brad was wondering why he had been called, since he had only met the man once, but the sheriff must have been anticipating this question, because he answered it before Brad asked.

"I called because we don't know whether the man is dead or alive, and he may be dangerous." Winslow explained that, on entering Parkington's apartment, they had immediately been confronted with a wall of photographs and newspaper clippings, and while the bulk of these items had yet to suggest anything relevant to the man's disappearance, the investigation had discovered an interesting and disturbing connection between four people (one woman and three men). These people were all the subjects of hometown newspaper articles (newspapers in Newark, El Paso, Phoenix, and Santa Fe) and had all, prior to the appearance of these articles, been interviewed by Dr. Parkington.

"We also discovered a small digital recorder and listened to your interview," Winslow said.

"I still don't understand why you called me," Brad said, mildly irked, again, for having allowed Parkington to record him.

"Those newspaper articles are about people who have disappeared. They are the people Parkington interviewed. Since they all disappeared between one and four months after he interviewed them, and since he took the trouble to track those clippings down and stick them on his wall, it is likely those vanished folks are connected, in some way, to Parkington. I wanted to call and give you a heads up, in case he comes knocking on your door. You might not want to open it."

"You think he killed those people?" Brad had difficulty envisioning a homicidal Parkington.

"I don't know what to think. Do you?"

Brad didn't, and he promised to call if Parkington showed up in Austin.

After he replaced the phone in its cradle, he went to the refrigerator and got a beer. He drank half of it and decided to call Meta at work.

"She left early today," someone told him. "A couple of hours ago, I guess."

Brad sat in a kitchen chair and drank the rest of his beer. He had no idea where she was.

But he did. He realized he did know. Not in the way he had always known, not with that magical (gone and now precious) lost sense but with the new cold logic that had replaced it. She was on her way to Silo, the town where it had all unraveled and where, now, some accursed force awaited her.

He set off at once, driving toward Silo, stopping every hundred miles or so to empty his bladder and take on gas and supplies (which consisted primarily of beer and snacks). He wasn't up for such a trip, not fully recovered from the accident and emotionally exhausted by Meta's betrayal, her retreat from his love and protection into the arms of some monstrous Casanova from Atlantis—and, yes, he admitted that he now swallowed Parkington's nutcase scenarios, and they went down easy; there was something out there in the mountains—*under the mountains*—that had reached out and wrecked his marriage and was now dragging Meta toward its lair.

But he was exhausted and would be no good at all unless he rested. So, on the far side of midnight, miles away from morning, he pulled into a rest stop and turned the engine off and slept.

The sun was up when he woke, and it was late afternoon when he drove down Silo's Main Street. It was a lean town, not given to airs, saturated with the sun's weight, sidewalks cracked by time, two old men on a bench in front of Roy's Restaurant, the Silo Library next door, then a barbershop called Curly's Quick Hair. Brad parked in front of a bar, B&G (which he knew, having eaten lunch there with Meta on a therapeutic outing from the hospital, stood for Bar & Grill, minimalist humor or the lack of it).

Brad wasn't a drinker, and his overindulgence of the day before was now taking its toll. So he went into B&G and sat at the bar counter. He ordered a beer and a fried egg sandwich from the barmaid, a middle-aged woman of undecided hair color with a tattoo on her shoulder that said "Dwayne" over a heart. Under the heart, clearly the work of a less skilled artist, it read: "Stinks." It made Brad sad, that tattoo. He thought of the entropy inherent in all relationships, and he ordered another beer. He considered a plan of action.

He didn't have one, he realized. The certainty that had brought him here had drained out over the miles, and he was left with a panicky sense of abandonment. Who did he know in town? No one. Well, Sheriff Winslow, but what could he say to him? Nothing relevant. He'd sound like a madman.

Am I? he wondered. But it was the truth itself that was mad, and how could it help but irradiate him, taint his own sanity?

His musings were interrupted by the barmaid, shouting "Musky! Hey Musky! Wake up! Come on. I got a couple of beers for you if you take out the trash."

She was leaning over a man and shaking his shoulder. He stirred, raised his head like an ancient bloodhound scenting a rabbit, and said, "Trash." He was a bearded man with a pocked face and heavy-lidded eyes stained yellow, the same color as the bar's smoke-saturated walls, and he had been sleeping in a corner booth, the only other patrons an elderly couple who were dancing to tinny sounds from the jukebox, the sort of music you could make with a comb and a piece of wax paper.

Brad watched the man lumber past the bar counter and through a door that must have led to the alley in back. Brad called to the barmaid, and when she came over, he asked her who she'd just been talking to.

"You mean old Musky?" She looked a little incredulous, a little suspicious. "Musky?"

"That's his name?"

"It's what he answers to, yeah. Why you want to know?"

Brad hesitated. “I thought he might be somebody I heard of recently. But I believe that person’s name was Charlie.”

“Ain’t nobody calls him that anymore. But that’s what he was born. Born Charlie Musgrove, the light of his momma’s eye, and as full of promise…you won’t credit this, ’cause he looks about a hundred years old now, but we were in high school together.”

“What happened?” Brad said.

“Shit,” the woman said. “Ain’t that what the bumper sticker says? Shit happens. He drank up all his opportunities ’cept the opportunity to drink more.” She backed up and narrowed her eyes. “Why you want to know about Musky? What makes him any of your business?”

Brad explained, starting with the wasps that had attacked him and his wife in the desert. He did not mention Atlantis under the mountains or the alien theft of his wife’s soul, however. He did tell her how Charlie Musgrove figured in the narrative.

“Rattlesnakes!” she said. “You want old Musky to tell you about them rattlesnakes that tried to get him!”

“Yes,” Brad said, not wishing to explain, in detail, what he really wanted.

“Hell, he’s been hard to shut up on that subject. You won’t have any trouble there. If you say the magic words, you’ll get an earful. I guarantee it.”

“What are the magic words?”

“Can I buy you a beer?” she said.

“TURN HERE,” MUSKY SAID. THEY FOLLOWED A WINDING road into the mountains. The car leaned upward, as though the stars above were their destination. Musky took a swig from the beer bottle and lurched into song again:

"Away in a manager no crib for his bed, the little Lord Jesus was wishin' he's dead. No..."

It hadn't been hard to elicit the rattlesnake story from Musky—who hadn't responded to Brad's initial *Charles Musgrove?* query—and Musky had a few things to say about Michael Parkington. "That fellow told me I didn't see no rattlesnakes, said I *lucinated* them. I didn't tell him I'd read that fool book he wrote. Yep, found a copy in a dumpster, autographed to Cindy Lou with his cell phone number, but I guess that didn't work out. That book was a lot of crap, all that Atlantis stuff."

"You don't believe there is some alien force in these mountains?"

Musky finished the beer and threw the empty bottle out the window, which made the Austin-environmentalist in Brad cringe when he heard the shattering glass. "Oh, there's something awful and ancient in these mountains. My grandfather knew all about it, said he'd seen it eat a goat by turning the goat inside out and sort of licking it until it was gone. He said it was a god from another world, older than this one. He called it Toth. A lot of people in these parts know about it, but it ain't a popular subject."

He opened another beer and drank it. "Anyway, I think those rattlesnakes were real."

They bumped along the road, flanked by ragged outcroppings, shapes that defied gravity, everything black and jagged or half erased by the brightness of the car's rollicking headlights.

"Okay! Stop 'er!" Musky said. Brad stopped the car. Musky was out of the car immediately, tumbling to the ground but quickly staggering upright with the beer bottle clutched in his hand. Brad turned the ignition off, put the key in his pocket, and got out.

Brad followed the man, who was moving quickly, invigorated, perhaps, by this adventure. The incline grew steeper, the terrain devoid of all vegetation, a moonscape, and Brad thought he'd soon be crawling on his hands and knees. Abruptly, the ground leveled, and he saw Musky, stopped in front of him, back hunched, dirty gray hair shivered by the breeze.

"There's people who would pay a pretty penny to see this," he said, without turning around. Brad reached the man and looked down from the rocky shelf on which they stood. Beneath them, a great dazzling bowl stretched out and down, a curving mother-of-pearl expanse, a skateboarder's idea of heaven—or imagine a giant satellite dish, its diameter measured in miles, pressed into the stone. No, it was nothing *like* anything. He knew he would never be able to describe it.

He felt a sharp, hot ember sear into the flesh immediately above his right eyebrow, brought his hand up quickly, and slapped the insect, crushing it. He opened his fist and looked at the wasp within. Its crumpled body trembled, and it began to vibrate faster and faster, emitting a high-pitched *whirrrrr*. It exploded in a purple flash that left an after-image in Brad's mind so that, when he turned toward the sound of Musky's voice, part of the man's face was eclipsed by a purple cloud.

"I always bring them up here," he said. "Toth calls 'em and I bring 'em the last lap."

"You brought my wife here?" Brad asked.

"Nope. Just you. She wasn't savory somehow. She had the chemicals in her, and it changed her somehow. Wouldn't do. Mind you, I ain't privy to every decision, I just get a notion sometimes. I think she was poison to it, so it didn't fool with her."

"But it changed her," Brad shouted, filled with fury, intent on killing this traitor to his race.

"It wasn't interested."

Brad's cell phone rang.

"You get good reception up here," Musky said.

Brad tugged the phone out of his pocket, flipped it open.

"Hello?"

"Brad?"

"Meta?"

"Where are you, honey? I've been trying to call you. I've been going crazy. I called the police. I even called Sheriff Winslow, although why—"

Brad could see her standing in the kitchen, holding the wall phone's receiver up to her ear, her eyes red and puffy from crying. He could see her clearly, as though she stood right in front of him; he could count the freckles on her cheeks.

Her tears, the flush in her cheeks, the acceleration of her heart, he saw these things, saw the untenable vascular system, the ephemeral ever-failing creature, designed by the accidents of time.

He was aware that the cell phone had slipped from his fingers and tumbled to the stony ledge and bounced into the bright abyss. He leaned over and watched its descent. Something was moving at the bottom of the glowing pit, a black, twitching insectile something, and as it writhed it grew larger, more spectacularly alive in a way the eye could not map, appendages appearing and disappearing, and always the creature grew larger and its fierce intelligence, its outrageous will and alien, implacable desires, rose in Brad's mind.

He felt a monstrous joy, a dark enlightenment, and wild to embrace his destiny, he flung himself from the ledge and fell toward the father of all universes, where nothing was ever lost, and everything devoured.

Denker's Book

DAVID J. SCHOW

David J. Schow began publishing short stories in Rod Serling's The Twilight Zone *magazine in the 1980s. His first novel,* The Kill Riff *(Tor), appeared in 1988. In 1990 he published three books: the novel* The Shaft *(Macdonald) and the story collections* Seeing Red *(Tor) and* Lost Angels *(New American Library/ Onyx). He has gone on to publish several further collections–* Black Leather Required *(Ziesing, 1994),* Crypt Orchids *(Subterranean Press, 1998),* Eye *(Subterranean Press, 2001),* Zombie Jam *(Subterranean Press, 2005), and* Havoc Swims Jaded *(Subterranean Press, 2006), and the novels* Bullets of Rain *(Morrow, 2003)–and* Rock Breaks Scissors Cut *(Subterranean Press, 2003). Schow is also the author of* The Outer Limits Companion *(Ace, 1986; rev. ed. GNP Crescendo Records, 1999) and the editor of the anthology* Silver Scream *(Dark Harvest, 1988).*

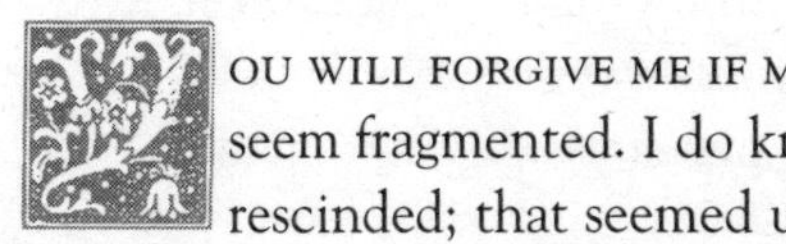

OU WILL FORGIVE ME IF MY RECOLLECTIONS OF DENKER seem fragmented. I do know that his Nobel Prize was rescinded; that seemed unfair to me, but at the same time I understand the thinking behind it, the dull necessity of the counter-arguments, all the disparate points of view that had to swim together into a public accord in an attempt to salve the outrage.

It used to be held as common superstition that if you paint an interior door in your home with a certain kind of paint, the door might open into another time. The paint was lead-based and long-prohibited. In 1934, there were doors like this all over the place. The doors generally had to be facing south. People have forgotten this now.

Chinese horticulturalists discovered that dead pets, buried in a specific pattern around the entryways to houses and gardens, not only seemed to restrict access by spirits, but lengthen daylight by as much as half an hour. Type of animal, number of burials, interment pattern, and even the sexual history of the pet owner all seemed to have modulating effects.

I cite these stories as examples among thousands—the kind of revelations that seem to defy not only physical laws thought to be immutable, but logic itself.

Nevertheless, they took Langford Meyer Denker's Nobel Prize away from him. They—the big, faceless "they" responsible for everything—probably should not have. Denker made the discovery and fathered the breakthrough. "They" claimed Denker cheated; that is, he did not play by strict rules of science. But there are no such things as rules in science; merely observations that are regularly displaced by new, more consolidated observations.

Some said that the dimensional warp door Denker created was real, that it worked. Others held that it was a flashy deception; sleight-of-hand rather than science. Still others maintained that Denker's demonstration was inconclusive. By the time the furor settled, all of them said Denker had cheated. Denker had used the book.

Denker's machine was a gigantic, Gothic clockwork; an Expressionist maze of gears, liquid reservoirs, lasers, and lenses. Lathed brass bins held clumps of humid earth. Common stones were vised by hydraulics in that peculiar way you can squeeze an egg between your palms with all your might and not break it. Particle-emitters were gloved in ancient lead. Imagine a medieval clepsydra wirelessly married to countless yottabytes of computing power and stage-managed by a designer who had been seduced by every mad scientist movie ever made. The containment chamber was made of pitted bronze shot through with rods of chemically pure glass; it weighed several tons and was completely non-aerodynamic, yet Denker claimed that once the whole package was transposed into a realm where earthly physics were irrelevant its properties recombined according to perverse rules to render the device as safe as a pressurized bathysphere or commercial space capsule.

Of course the earliest naysayers called him mad.

I remind you at this point in the story that without a totally arbitrary baseline of normalcy, "insanity" is not possible. (It has been said that normalcy is the majority's form of lunacy, which I suppose explains Christianity.)

Colors can drive people mad. It follows that there are spectra yet unknown to us, flavors and timbres that might catalyze our air, our light, in new and unpredictable ways. "Sounds that were not wholly sounds"—that sort of thing. The scientific community's rebuke of Denker was a denial of the most commonplace protocols of experimentation, but by that time the point was to demonize the man, not disprove the theory.

A portal to another universe different from our own perceived reality? Something that functioned so far out there that what we thought of as our physical laws seemed irrelevant? Fine.

A glimpse into the unutterable? Also fine.

But Denker had used the book. Not fine.

I ask you to stop right now and consider the purpose of a book that was *never intended to be read*. What is the point?

Consider this: You take an ordinary bible, which credits supernatural forces for all the bloodshed and horror in the world. They still make people swear on this book in courts of law; its symbolism has become part of ritual.

Denker's book was no mere opposite pole or gainsaying counter-dogma, although many people tried to discredit it that way. That's an irony: the arrogance to assume you can neutralize something that will not be denied.

Where Denker found the book, if he ever truly possessed it, I do not know.

Scholars claimed the book was a repository of forbidden knowledge, therefore much sought or shunned through millennia. Bait for fanatics. A grail for obsessives; a self-destructive prize for the foolhardy. Unless it was akin to a key or a storage battery—a necessary link in a logic chain—it was still a dead end, because in the end (as one story went) you wound up dead too. Denker's philologists rapidly proved that trickle-down translations of the book (about 400 years' worth) were virtually worthless because there was no way to reconcile different languages to the concept of the unnameable. Latin held many of the book's conceits in polar opposition to the Greek interpretation, and so on. In many ways the book was like a tesseract, partially unfolded into a yet-undiscovered realm.

But Denker did not stop at etymology. His scheme advantaged the top skim of curious geniuses all over the world. He used crypto experts to translate partial photo plates from Arabic—an iteration long thought lost forever. No one ever saw more than an eighth of a full page. Then he used colloquialists to defang the language piecemeal, in order to render down the simple sense of highly convoluted and frequently unpronounceable arcana. The resultant text was presented to a hand-picked and highly elite international group preselected by Denker for the interests he knew he could arouse.

When he had exhausted one scholar, Denker moved to the next, and you have probably already heard the story about how Rademacher Asylum gradually filled up with his depleted former colleagues.

These were not dazzled hayseeds or the easily swoggled rustics of a fictive Red America, nor were they the deluded zealotry of one improbable religion or other. These were minds capable of the most labyrinthine extrapolations—the first, second, and third strings of pawns to fall to Denker's inquiry.

Denker followed his instincts, and in the hope of discovering an anti-linear correlation presented his findings to a physicist who was then in the grip of Alzheimer's. He consulted South Seas tribal elders with no word for "insane" in their lexicon. Then philosophers, wizards, the deranged and the disenfranchised. With a brilliant kind of counter-intuitiveness, he allowed children to interpret some of his findings. Then autistics. The man with Alzheimer's was said to have "lost his mind completely" prior to his death. But as I've told you, the mad are always safe to expose. The mad enjoy hermetic protections unavailable to the mentalities that judge them unfit for normal human congress. "Normal humans" were the last thing Denker wanted.

Darwin pondered natural selection for twenty years before going into print; Denker did not have that kind of leisure. Our science these days is competitive; cut-throat; the sixties-era model of the Space Race has overrun all rational strategy. There are very few scientific rock stars and most of our millionaires are invisible. Resources may be accessed at the fierce cost of corporate sponsorship, which often mandates blood sacrifice or the occasional bitterly humbling obeisance: while the former can be a mental snap point, the latter is often a more serious derailment of any kind of exploratory enthusiasm, crushing instinct and logic into the box of fast, visible progress. Expediency becomes cardinal. This was the bind in which Denker found himself, in both senses—he embraced the delirious possibilities of risk and, using stress as a motivator, discovered his own interior limitations.

Coleridge wrote that "we do not feel horror because we are haunted by a sphinx, we dream a sphinx in order to explain the horror that we feel." Borges, after Coleridge, wrote, "If that is true, how might a mere chronicling of its forms transmit the stupor, the exultation, the alarms, the dread, and the joy that wove together that night's dream?" This was in essence the chicken-and-egg riddle that governed Denker's inquiries. Possessed of a fanciful mind, he did not believe the most transporting inspirations to be reduceable to mere mathematical schemata, yet that was the task set before him. Others had failed. Replacements waited hungrily. More tempting, to Denker, was that capacity which Apollonius Rhodius coined as "the poetics of uncertainty," itself reducible to the twentieth-century argot of doing a wrong thing for the right reason.

All this citation makes Denker sound stuffy or cloistered or pretentiously intellectual, so I need to give you an example of the man's humor. He referred to the book as his "ultra-tome-bo"—at once conflating the Spanish *ultratumba* (literally, "from beyond the grave") with the Latin *ultima Thule* (i.e., "the northernmost part of the habitable ancient world")—thereby hinting with a wink that his quest aimed beyond both death and the world as we know it. Knew it, rather.

(He further corrupted *ultra* into *el otro*—"the other." The other book, the other tomb. He was very witty as well as smart.)

I hope you can follow this without too much trouble. Sometimes my memory itself is like a book with stuck-together pages; huge chunks of missing narrative followed by short sections of over-detail. If I have learned one thing, it is that harmonics are important. You may sense contradictions in some of what I am telling you, and I would urge you to look past them—try to see them with new eyes.

Denker's so-called scientific fraud was revealed when his device was taken from his stewardship and disassembled. The machinery held a bit of nuclear credibility, but the heart of the drive was an iron particle accelerator that resembled a World War Two-era sea mine, a heart fed by cables and hoses and fluid.

Empty inside.

Because Denker had removed his fundamental component —the book.

Having spent three-quarters of a billion dollars in corporate seed money and suffering the deep stresses of delivery-to-schedule that such funds can mandate, Denker cheated the curve. Science failed him, but when he combined science with sorcery, he was able to give his backers what they thought they wanted. All he had to do then was word his interviews precisely enough to feature that hint of arched-eyebrow evasion as to method. Money was already coming at him from all sides.

Most people don't know exactly how an internal combustion engine functions, but they drive automobiles. In kind, Denker's device could transcend space-time boundaries; the point was that it worked. Never mind that on the other side of the boundary might be a group of surly cosmic Vastators, or the displaced First Gods of our entire existence, itching for a rematch now that we have evolved, devised technology, and gotten ourselves so damned civilized.

A long time ago, I used to have a lit-crit friend who was enchanted by the idea of haunts—in particular, living quarters in which resonant works of literature were conceived, the way that James M. Cain wrote *Double Indemnity* while resident in his "Upside-Down House" in the Hollywood Hills. If it was true that the most dedicated writers "lived, ate, slept, drank and shat" their way through their most lasting works, might not some of that ectoplasmic effluvia generate a mood or lingering charge of unsettled energy, the sort of thing ordinary people might classify as a ghost?

My interest was not in Denker's book. That seemed too risky. So I sought out the place where Denker's book was not so much *written* as assembled, collated.

The locale, you might have guessed. It is dead now. The structures engird no whispers. The "charge" was long gone, if it ever existed. No negative energy. No ghosts.

Because it had *all* gone into the book.

By then, naturally, the world was dealing with other problems. Disequilibration was, in many ways, the most predictable outcome.

Throughout history, certain individuals had sought to destroy the book, not realizing the futility of the attempt. In the state Denker used it, it could not be destroyed. It could only be discomponentialized—taken apart the same way it had been put together. Except now that it was whole, it could only be handled in certain limited ways, and none of those would permit its possible destruction. Again, as I have said—contradictions. Did Denker have the book, whole and entire, in a single place? We may never know. Thus, when I reference "the book," we are speaking of whatever grand assembly Denker managed, which stays in my mind as his true achievement.

One mishandling of the book caused peculiar incipient radiations—or new colors and sounds, if you will. Unfathomable byproducts and side-effects. This was one reason Denker insisted his cumbersome bronze-and-cast-iron device had to be tested in outer space.

This achieved two important goals: It removed the book briefly from the physical surface of the Earth, and it guaranteed Denker's deception would be a long time unraveling.

I saw in Denker's journals that he noted, early in the experiment, that animals were profoundly affected by the proximity of the book. Animals lack the ameliorative intellect by which humans justify insanity.

If one is inflexible and devoted to an illusion of normalcy—stability, permanence, reality—then the break is always harsher. The more rules there are to violate, the more violations there will be, because what we call reality is an interpretative construct of the human mind; a reality we re-make every day to deny the howling nothingness of existence and the meaningless tragedy of life. Bacilli have no such concerns. They just are. They can't be horrified or elated.

Denker's two safety margins were time and space. Many of his translations—the words from the book—were not meant to be in the same place at the same time, not even as ones and zeros in a database. The whole of it, as I have said, was tricky to handle. There was no manual for this sort of thing. This was completely new, untried, unsaid, undone.

In the end, Denker realized that ultimately all his equipment was not needed. The physical hardware briefly won him that fickle Nobel Prize, but all he had really needed was the book. He had already achieved what we have agreed to call a break from reality, but in the end people are more comfortable saying that he just snapped.

I think it is overreachingly grandiloquent and silly to blame Denker for the downslide of the entire planet. Haven't you noticed that long before the incident, we had already become so biosensitive that we could not even travel without getting sick? I think the Earth is simply evolving, and it is not *for* us anymore.

In the midst of all that I have told you, it might be said that Denker himself fragmented. His mind went elsewhere.

And if you could find me, you could probably find Denker too, but it's not really Denker you're interested in, is it? You're after the book, just like the ones before you.

Now, of course, the fashion is to impugn Denker for the way the sky looks at night. For the night itself, since I have heard that the sun no longer rises. I have not been able to bear witness to the other stories I have heard about the freezing cold or the sounds of beasts feeding.

But once I find a way to free myself from this room, I am going to seek out Denker and ask him to explain it to me.

Inhabitants of Wraithwood

W. H. PUGMIRE

W. H. Pugmire is a widely published and popular author of Lovecraftian stories, including the volumes Dreams of Lovecraftian Horror *(Mythos Books, 1999),* Sesqua Valley and Other Haunts *(Delirium Books, 2003), and* The Fungal Stain *(Hippocampus Press, 2006). An omnibus of his collected weird fiction is forthcoming from Centipede Press.*

 AWAKENED TO THE RAUCOUS CRY OF CROWS AND pushed my torso away from the tree beneath which I had fallen asleep. Where the hell was I? I remembered deciding not to return to the halfway house where I was completing my time for three counts of bank robbery, after doing two years in federal prison. I think the prison officials let me out early because they were impressed with my intellect and good manners. I had been the first inmate on record who had requested a one-volume *Complete Works of Shakespeare*. I ain't no intellectual, but I've been raised by a woman who taught literature and art in college. One of my fondest memories was of my seventh birthday, when Mom took me to a thrilling production of *Cymbeline*, a play with which I was familiar from bedtime readings of Shakespeare since infancy. When I listen to or read Shakespeare, I hear my mother's voice. Loving the plays is loving her.

Yes, I screwed up. After her early death, I didn't care about anything, fell in with "bad types" and learned to enjoy petty crime. Drug addiction heightened my criminal tendencies, and I got hooked on danger. Doing time was no hassle. I read a lot of good books and improved my education. But the goons and clueless "therapists" in the halfway house were too insulting to be endured, and so I didn't return one day from job hunting, robbed a store from which I stole a couple of bottles of choice whiskey, hijacked a weakling's car and drove until the petrol ran out. After that things get a bit blurry, thanks to the booze. I sort of remember hoofing it for quite a while, and then stopping to rest after climbing a hill and entering a woodland. I guess I passed out beneath the oak tree.

It must have been early dusk when at last I came to my senses. The sky still held a quality of violet, and a low orange moon hung like some gigantic disc in heaven. I've never liked the way the moon looks at me, and so I threw my empty bottle at it; and then I noticed the other glow, the moving lamplight that slowly approached and became a lantern held by Jesus. This Christ was a tall red-headed dude with dark, penetrating eyes, attired in what looked like a suit from the 1920s. He stopped a few feet from me, and the moon directly behind his head looked like some illuminated halo as one sees in the works of Cimabue or Giotto. Moaning, I made an effort to stand up, becoming aware of the dampness at my crotch and the stink of urine. I began to laugh. "Drink, sir, is a great provoker, of sleeping and piss," I told Jesus, paraphrasing the Immortal Bard.

"Are you in need of shelter?" asked my savior.

"Shelter would be cool, good fellow," says me, struggling to my feet and working diligently to steady my sense of balance. The gentleman turned and walked away. Guessing that I was meant to follow, I stumbled through the growing darkness, passing a large sunken pond as I moved beneath and out of the mass of oak trees. We crossed a wide dirt roadway and approached a two-story building situated on the crest of a mammoth hill. Looking down the hill I saw a small town twinkling its lights as day expired. The building looked of the same era as the silent man's dress. Perhaps it had been some kind of hotel-cum-speakeasy in the Prohibition era. Why else would it be situated up here, so far from the rest of town?

Jesus led me into an anteroom that contained a couple of chairs and bureau on top of which were delicate bits of *objet d'art*. A stairway led to the second floor. We stepped through double doors into a charming sitting room filled with what looked like choice antiques. A brass chandelier softly illuminated the room, and one of the several small sofas looked especially inviting. I sat in it and sank into its comfortable depths. I saw that Jesus had abandoned me, and I assumed he had gone to fetch me a change of clothing. Leaning toward the low coffee table in front of the sofa, I grabbed hold of the large album of red leather that lay there, which turned out to be a heavy photo album.

My mother had taught art and literature to university brats, and so our home had been packed with quality books. I had delighted in pouring over those picture books when I was a kid, long before the text explaining the artwork was of interest. Mom had always encouraged me to be imaginative, and many of our games together, after father had left us, consisted of trying our hand at copying great works of art, our tools being color crayons, watercolor, and children's modeling clay. (My Play-do Pietà had been a deliciously somber affair.) Because I am by nature lazy, I never advanced in art or literature, although I had a modicum of talent. I was a curious and tragic combination of intellect and debauchery, and my high priest was Oscar Wilde. I was equally comfortable in either a museum of classical art or in the lowest mire of Malebolge. Art was one of my sanest obsessions. And thus, when I opened this oversized leather binder and began to study the photographs within, I was instantly mesmerized.

I recognized the first photograph as a kind of take on Caspar David Friedrich's *Raven Tree*; but instead of an actual tree the main focus in the print was an outrageously lean old guy with long hair and beard, who had contorted himself to mimic the shape of Friedrich's tree. The sky above the fellow was crowded with crows, one of which had perched on his scrawny shoulder. The photo's sepia tone suggested that it was an extremely old print.

Turning the leaf, I saw that the next photo was a wicked

parody of the *Mona Lisa.* The ancient woman pictured, old and haggard though she be, still contained a degree of facial beauty. She had been a seductress in her day. The diabolic smile unnerved me, as did the hand that clutched one wrist, digging a talon into thin flesh. A single drop of blood upon that talon was the photo's one touch of vivid color.

The next photo was Jesus, posing with his lantern and attired with a gown of what looked like silken gold. Over the gown he wore an embroidered cloak, and a curious crown of metallic thorns adorned his dome. He was standing within the grove of oaks, knocking upon one tree. Unlike the two previous images, this one was new and full of color.

Ah, how I sighed when I turned the leaf and beheld the next image, for it copied my favorite painting, Fuseli's *The Nightmare*, and this photographic representation was superb. Where they had found a creature who so resembled Fuseli's incubus was beyond conjecture. There were, however, unnerving anomalies. The gremlin in the photograph was tragically incomplete, missing both legs and all its fingers. One stunted paw leaned against the thing's chin, near its mouth, and one could not escape the suggestion that the beast had been supping on its corporeal tissue.

The woman on whom the daemon squatted was dressed in white, as in the original painting, but her hair was dark and fell in such a way as to conceal most of her face. Unlike the original, her mouth did not frown. Above the woman and her incubus, to the viewer's left, an equine skull peeked through an opening in the curtain behind the bed.

I shifted in my seat, and the smell of my soiled pants drifted to me. Feeling restless, I shut the album and got up to investigate the room. Upon one wall was a large painting of an oak grove at night-time. Arching over the trees was what looked like a pale lunar rainbow, and I seemed to remember some such effect in a painting by Friedrich. It certainly produced an eerie effect. Dim winged specks, which I took to be night birds, spotted the darkened dimension.

Sensing company, I turned to face the beings who were watching me. The woman, tall and slender, was dressed in a long black gown of antique silk, its tight brocade collar decorated with raised patterns in gold and silver. Gloves of black lace covered dainty hands, and a veil concealed the details of an emaciated face. I could just make out the pale and colorless eyes that observed me. She stood behind a ramshackle wheelchair that was occupied by the incubus from the photograph I had earlier been admiring. I stared at that impish visage with its sickly hue, at the yellow eyes and bulbous nose, at the blue veins that lined the grotesque face.

"Welcome to Wraithwood," the gnome sighed, in a high child-like voice. "Philippe has gone to find you clothing. You could benefit from a bath. Pera has a wee bathroom adjoining her room. Follow her, please."

"Thank you, uh..." I hesitated, not knowing how to address him, not wanting to shake the malformed hand. When I studied the right hand, I saw that it differed from the photograph, having two stunted fingers where in the photograph there were none.

"Eblis Mauran," he offered, bowing his head.

"Hank Foster," I said, smiling. The silent woman held a hand to me, then turned to a door near a corner. I followed her into a hallway and through another door that entered on a spacious boudoir. Undoing my shirt buttons, I watched as she went into a small bathroom and began to run a bath, sprinkling various salts from antique jars into the running water. I thanked her, but she said nothing as she ushered me into the bathroom and shut the door. I tested the water for heat, then undressed and stepped into the tub. The effect was instantaneous. My groans of pleasure rose with the steam as sore limbs and soiled flesh relaxed. I barely noticed when Jesus quietly entered with an armful of clean clothing, which he placed atop the closed toilet seat. I momentarily froze as he bent and placed a hand into the water, joined to it his other hand, then brought the hands above my head and let the cupped water drop over my hair. Smiling, he turned off the running water, rose, and vacated the room.

Okay, I thought as a scrubbed myself, I've entered into a house full of loonies and queers. Pulling the plug, I listened as the water drained, then stepped out of the tub and reached for a nearby towel. Examining the clothes, I saw that they were from an earlier decade; but they fit well enough, and I rather liked the way I looked in the full-length mirror, nothing like the alcoholic drug addict I had become since Mother's death.

I opened the door and entered Pera's dusky room. The place was semi-lit by various wall fixtures that resembled candles in holders, each candle topped by an electric flame. The furnishings were all dark, with long blue-purple drapery at the windows. A black bedspread covered the commodious bed. The young woman rested upon the bed, very still, resembling a lifeless husk on its deathbed. Her frail arms clutched a length of sturdy rope. I stepped to the bed and knelt next to it, as if I were preparing to pray for the soul of a departed loved one. I touched the rope, and her head moved so that the pale eyes behind the veil gazed into my own.

She then began to sing; and as I watched the vague impression of her mouth behind its curtain of lace, I felt a chill. The song was from my mother's favorite play.

"He is dead and gone, lady,
He is dead and gone;
At his head a grass-green turf,
At his heels a stone."

I was uncertain of what line actually followed, and thus I recited the line I knew. "How do you, pretty lady?"

Pera smiled and blew at the veil, and some of her soft sweet air lightly touched my face. Then she turned away from me and stared at the ceiling. I moved my vision to the painting on the wall above the bed. It, too, had been one of Mother's favorite works of art, John Everett Millais's *Ophelia.* This somewhat explained the strange girl's song. Looking at her again, I saw that her eyes were closed. Mutely, I vacated the room.

I was uncertain what way led to the main room, for there were doors on either end of the hallway. But then the sound of someone playing music in the room next to Pera's caught my attention. Through the partially parted doorway came a smell of incense. Gingerly, I pushed at the door with the toe of my shoe. A small man sat on the floor, playing a kind of Egyptian music on a short-necked lute. I laughed silently, for the tiny guy closely resembled the Hungarian film actor Peter Lorre. The piece he played was simple yet expressive, and to its cadence danced the creature named Eblis. Dance, of course, is a generous verb, given that the fellow had no legs. And yet he was not clumsy as he stood upon his stumps and moved with a kind of nimbleness, now and then smacking together the palms of his fragmentary hands. The dancer noticed me and wickedly smirked, his ochrous eyes twinkling.

The music ceased, and Eblis moved to his wheelchair as swiftly as a scuttling insect. The other fellow observed me from his position on the floor. "Ah, the new guest."

"Yes," I answered, and then quickly corrected myself. "No, actually. I've had some trouble with my car a ways back. One of your compatriots found me sleeping in that grove of oaks and brought me here to clean up. So, what is this place, a hotel or something?"

"Or something. Just a collection of lost souls, you might say, gathered accidentally—fatefully." He shrugged and laughed. "So, the old crone hasn't had you sign yet?"

"Sorry?" He shrugged again and got to his feet, throwing his instrument onto the narrow bed. Seeing the painting above that bed I went to it and touched a finger to its surface. It was a painting rather than a print, although it had not been varnished. The image seemed familiar, but I couldn't place it. What interested me was that the sitter was almost a dead ringer for the small man who now sat upon the bed. "Wow, this could be you."

"Eventually it will be. I've already lost three inches of height." I gave him a troubled look, which moved him to more laughter.

"I've seen it somewhere before, but I can't remember the artist."

"Kokoschka. This is his portrait of a tubercular Count he met in, I believe, Switzerland. Once my face began to thin I took to parting my hair in the middle. My hands aren't quite as bad as his—yet."

What the fuck was he talking about? Yes, I had certainly stumbled onto a clutch of crazies. "The resemblance is quite uncanny," I continued.

"That's the very word. Come on," he said, standing and touching my arm. "We'll return you to the convening room."

I tried to smile as he loped to the wheelchair and guided it through the doorway. The door to Pera's room was partially open, as I had left it, and I caught a glimpse of her sleeping on the bed, the length of rope in her embrace. When I followed my new acquaintance into the drawing room, I found another person awaiting our arrival. She turned and smiled at me, and I saw that it was the woman in the *Mona Lisa* photo. Although ancient and vaguely sinister, yet was she anomalously lovely. Her streaked hair was long and smooth, and it was only her hands and face that bespoke of age. I saw that she held a book to her bosom, the crimson leather of which she tapped with a tapered fingernail. The woman walked toward me and examined my face with piercing blue eyes, and then she linked her arm with mine and guided me to the sofa. On the table before us, next to the photo album, was a small pot of ink and one of those quaint feather pens. Playfully, the elderly woman sat next to me and opened her book, which I saw was a registry with yellowed paper. A column of signatures filled one page.

"You seem down on your luck," the lady crooned.

Sardonically, I chuckled. "Hell, passing out and pissing myself ain't nothing new, if that's what you mean. As for luck, she's a lady I've never kissed."

Deeply, she sighed. "This edifice was built during the Prohibition era. It served as asylum for persons of fugitive nature." There was something funny about the way she spoke, as if from personal memory. "Asylum" was well chosen, I thought. I studied her face, and could believe that she had been a bonny lass in the 1920s. My kind of woman. Yet something in her words gave me pause.

"What makes you think of me as fugitive?"

"You wear a hunted aura. You are lost and hungry. We can give you shelter. You'll find it entertaining."

"I'm broke."

"Oh, we'll make use of you. Now," and she pointed to the column of names and picked up the feather pen. "I want you to sign your name here, and then we'll have Oskar find you a room. Hmm?" I looked at the Peter Lorre dude, who I supposed was Oskar, and he slyly winked at me. I paused. Everything seemed like some weird, crafty game. But the idea of a room sounded really nice. I was exhausted and hungry. This crazy pad would be far more comfortable and entertaining than anything I've been used to these past few years. What the hell? I moved my hand toward the pen, which the woman moved to my finger. Swiftly, the sharp point of the pen's tip nicked my flesh. I watched a drop of blood spill onto the feather pen's tip. With smooth dexterity the woman dipped the stained point into the wee container of ink, then placed the feather into my hand. My little drip of blood smeared her fingernail, which she tapped onto the yellowed paper.

"Your name, young man." I signed, then returned the pen to her. "Thank you…Hank," she said, examining my signature. "You won't mind if I call you Henry."

"That's cool," I told her, sensing that it wasn't a request. Suddenly quite weary, I yawned. The fellow named Oskar touched my shoulder. Rising, I followed him out into the antechamber and up the flight of stairs.

HE ROOM INTO WHICH I WAS LED WAS COSY, SMALL YET quite exquisitely furnished with antiques. Sitting on the bed, I found it quite comfortable, and I smiled as Oskar moved to an end table on which were various decanters of booze. Standing, I went to join him and poured some excellent corn whiskey into one of the small heavy tumblers. I held the bottle to my guest.

"No, thank you. I prefer a little of this." He took up a bottle of sherry and filled his glass, then sipped quietly. I examined the room once more, until my eyes fell upon the painting above the bedstead. Going to it, I touched the unfinished work. "Ah," Oskar sighed, "your painting."

"This is none of mine—it's revolting!" It was an original work by an artist with whom I was unfamiliar. Of moderate size, the majority was a background of etching and under-painting, dreary in tone and subject. The setting was a wood, and from the sturdy branch of one tree a woman's form hanged from a length of rope, its snug slipknot taut around her broken neck. A length of dark hair entoiled her face. Beneath there stood three dark forms, indistinct and faded, mere specters of ink and wash.

But it was the cacodemonic thing leering prominently in the foreground that riveted my eyes to the canvas. I had never known a work of art to produce a sense of fear, but when I gawked at the painted thing, I trembled with fright. I suppose what terrified me was the absolute realism with which the ghoul had been conveyed; one could feel in the pit of one's soul the unholy appetite that smoldered in the rapacious eyes. The wide face had a kind of leathery texture, and the scraggly hair was clotted with dirt. Beneath the green eyes flared a wide, flat nose. Thick lips twisted so to reveal strong square teeth. This was the only figure in the work that had been fully painted, with such lifelike detail that one could almost imagine it to be a study from life.

"It's one of his unfinished works," Oskar informed me.

"His?"

"Richard Upton Pickman, of Boston. An obscure artist, but one who has attained a spectacular underground reputation. A majority of his works were destroyed by his father, just before the old man's suicide in 1937. This is one of the incomplete pieces that were discovered in an old section of Boston that was razed and used as a site for warehouses. One of the antique dwellings was apparently used by Pickman as a secret studio." Draining his glass, Oskar set it on top of an antique dressing table that served as bedside stand, and opening the table's single drawer he took from it an old sketchbook. "I found these and the painting in a shop in Salem some years ago."

We sat on the bed and I took hold of the ratty sketchbook. "So you're one of his fans?" Oskar shrugged. I slowly flipped through the pages of sketchings. Pickman had a fine sense of line, but his subjects were nauseating, just as disturbing as the abhorrent painting. "Ugh," I moaned, "the guy was really obsessed with that image of the hanged woman. But it's weird, because in all these other sketches he's drawn a semicircle of jackal things that resemble the freak in the foreground. There's no working sketch showing the three, whatever they are."

Oskar took the booklet from me and spoke in a cautious kind of way. "Yes, I think the Three Sisters, as I call them, are original to this one unfinished painting. The one completed oil is hanging in a bookshop in a valley town in the Northwest, and it's magnificent. It shows the semicircle of that dingo brood."

I stood again and studied the painted ghoul. "I've never seen such nauseous colors in oil. They're ghastly. How the hell am I supposed to sleep with that thing drooling over me?"

"You must admit that it's unique, Hank. Pickman followed the now discarded tradition of composing his own pigments. The effects are startling, I agree."

He was flipping through the sketchbook when a photograph that had been wedged between two leaves escaped and fell to the floor. I picked it up and studied the cuss's ugly mug. "Is that him?"

My new friend nodded. "Taken just before he vanished."

I whistled. "Damn, he looks just as creepy as his artwork. He must have toyed with trick photography, no one could really look like that. What was his family background?"

Oskar took the photograph and admired it. "I once went to a showing of his work that was held at a disabled asylum in Arkham. The brochure mentioned that Pickman came from old Salem stock and supposedly had a witch ancestor hanged on Gallow's Hill in 1692."

"Ah, that explains his *idée fixe*. The hanged wretch is his great-great-granny." I watched as Oskar placed the photo back into the booklet and then return that volume to its drawer. Suddenly quite sleepy, I yawned.

"You're exhausted. You'll find some pajamas in that

chiffonier. Pleasant dreams." Mischief played upon his sickly face, and I lightly laughed as he turned to cross to the door. He hesitated for a moment, as if there was something else he wanted to express; but he must have thought better of it, for he quietly opened the door and slipped from the room.

I went to the high and narrow chest of drawers and found a pair of bright yellow sleepwear. Whistling nonchalantly, I undressed, threw my clothes over a chair, and put on the very comfortable cotton nightclothes. The song of windstorm drew me to the room's one window, and going to it I peered at an eerie sight. The grove across the roadway was bathed in tinted moonlight. High above it a pale band of illumination arched above the woodland, resembling the scene that had been crafted in the painting I had observed in the sitting room. I scratched at the window pane with fingernails, certain that the lunar bow had been painted onto the glass; but no flakes of paint rubbed off, nor was the surface rough with artistry. Wind raged just outside the window, and beneath its ululation I could just detect the irregular squawking of distant crows, such as I had heard earlier when Jesus had discovered me beneath the oak.

I yawned once more, found the switch that shut out the room's dim light, then climbed into bed. Looking up, I could just make out the dark shape of the ghoul in the feeble light that filtered through the window. "If I see you in my dreams I'll rip you to shreds," I promised the bogey, pulling the covers over me.

AWAKENED TO A SOUND THAT I TOOK TO BE THE moaning of the wind, until I realized that it was coming from the hallway outside my door. Had I in fact heard such a noise, or was it a revenant of dreaming? No matter. I had to piss, and so got out of bed and wandered into

the shadowed hallway, hoping that there was a toilet on this floor. Spying a pale light coming from one narrow door, I went to it and saw that it was indeed a water closet. The toilet was a relic, and to flush it one pulled a hanging chain. I ran cool water over my hands and wiped those hands on my face and through my hair. Feeling refreshed, I re-entered the hallway, and seeing another door that was partially ajar, I sneaked to it and paused to listen. Someone inside was happily humming, and a smacking sound suggested feeding. I was hungry, and so I pushed the door with my toe and gazed at the room beyond.

The chamber was smaller than my own, with a modicum of furniture. Most of the walls were covered with wallpaper designed in black and red squares, but I saw that the wall space directly behind the bed had been painted red, except for one large black rectangle just above the headboard, where in every other room I had seen had hung a painting. In one corner, standing before a credenza, stood a tall figure with a shock of wild gray hair. He was bent over what looked like an antique casserole dish, from which he was plating a repast. When he turned to smile at me, I saw that it was the guy from the photo that copied Friedrich's *Raven Tree*.

"Enter, Hank Foster," he sang in a high nasal tone. "You must be famished. Here, take this, and I'll fill another plate for myself."

"Thank you," I said, taking the plate and examining the webbed meat and potatoes smothered with a kind of bechamel. The funny old guy motioned to a small table and two chairs, where two settings of sterling silver and napkins had been assembled. When my host sat down to join me I saw that his wide eyes were lined with red. Either he was a lunatic or flying some delectable high. Or a combination of both. Taking up fork and knife, he sliced his food with dainty precision, in continental fashion. Lowering my nose to the food, I took in its rich aroma. Gingerly, I cut into a piece of meat and popped it into my mouth. It was delicious, and suddenly famished I began to chomp. "This is great."

"'Tis our daily staple, so it's a good thing you like it. You'll get little else during your stay."

I didn't feel the need to correct his presumption of my staying around. Truth to tell, I hadn't given the outside world much thought since I arrived at this cuckoo nest. As if to qualify my thoughts, a cuckoo clock across the room struck five. "Is that the time?"

"Almost dawn. Sleep well?"

"Like a log."

"No dreams? No? Ah, lovely oblivion." He happily goggled at me, and I couldn't refrain from asking:

"Dude, what are you on?"

He hooted laughter. "What exuberant light shines in your eyes. Ha, ha!" He raised a finger, floated out of his chair, and went to a small kitchenette with which his room had been equipped. Opening a cupboard, he took out a glass, which he filled with water at the small sink. "Rinse away your food, and then place this beneath your tongue." From his shirt pocket he produced a little tin, which he opened and from which he took out a small red tablet. Taking the glass, I did as he instructed. The tablet had no flavor, and I was amazed how quickly it dissolved.

"You'll want to catch a bit more sleep, I dare say. Do you like your room?"

"It's nice enough. That damn painting is a bit offensive." He merely smiled, not moving. I got up and went to investigate the wall behind his bed. The black rectangle kind of got to me. I thought I could detect subdued motion within its opacity. The little red pill was kicking in. "My Mom taught art at college. She died ten years ago."

"And you're all alone in the world."

"Yeah. It sucks," I bitterly replied. "I was so pissed at her dying on me that I rejected my fine upbringing, my stalwart tutelage. I thought I was so cool and daring, hanging with hoods and living on the edge." My voice grew quiet with self-pity. "I didn't know it would turn into this." I gazed into the blackness on the wall, at the liquid crimson that surrounded it. I could feel the wall drawing me forward. I tilted toward it and touched its surface, and laughed as my hand seemed to sink into the satanic shades. "Dude, this is some good shit."

"Let's return you to your chamber."

I took my hand from the wall and put my arm around his neck. "You freaks remind me of some of the cats that came to Mom's parties. You know, those eccentric arty types. Kind of makes me feel at home here."

He guided me to the door and out into the hallway. When we reached my room, I stopped and pushed my companion from me. "You should return to bed," he told me.

"No thanks. Don't want to look at that ugly mug in the painting."

"But it's your painting, Henry." I stopped and looked at him. My mother had been the only one to call me that name. To be so addressed by a stranger weirded me out. "What's your name, bud?"

"I am Pieter."

"Yeah. Well, listen, bro, I'm gonna go outside for a while and get some air. No, it's cool, I can see my own way out. Thanks for the grub." His face wore such a strange expression that, laughing, I patted it with my hand, then carefully found my way down the stairs, to the foyer or whatever the hell it was. Noticing that a light was on in the sitting room, I stepped into it to see if pretty Pera was there. Perhaps I could coax her into walking with me.

The room was vacant. I liked the way the dim light seemed to swim along the walls; but when I felt a sudden lightheadedness

I decided to sit down for a spell on the comfortable little sofa, and seeing the shiny red album on the table, I grabbed it and set it on my lap. I opened it at the middle and sighed at the sight before me. The image was one with which I was familiar, for my mother used to have a print of it on her writing desk. The ghostly photograph copied Gustav Klimt's allegorical drawing, *Tragedy*. I traced the woman's outline with my finger. The original work had been composed with black crayon and pencil, white chalk and gold. The figure in the photograph duplicated exactly the pose of the drawing, of a woman holding a macabre mask. Everything in the photo, however, had blanched to a muted mauve and pale gray, blurry in outline. The one exception was the woman's spectral face, its whiteness quite luminous. I could just make out the woman's bouffant hairstyle and languid demi-mode deportment.

Hearing a noise, I looked up and saw Pera wheeling Eblis into the room. The gnome wore a sleeveless shirt, and I cringed at the sight of his too-thin arms, limbs that resembled those of some gaunt Auschwitz survivor. Closing the album, I staggered to my feet and skipped toward them. The dwarf's eyes were sickly yellow and red-rimmed. Blue and purple veins lined his expanded face with its bulbous nose. Cradled in his lap was a small oblong box.

I fell to my knees before him. "Yo, what's your trip?" Blinking fevered eyes, he tapped the wooden box with the black stump of what should have been a left hand. I looked at his malformed flesh, at the nub that looked as if it had been melted in some combustion. Reaching to the box, I opened it and took out one of the brown-black joints with which the box was stuffed. From his shirt pocket the little man produced a wooden match, held tightly between two stubby fingers. Swiftly, he struck it against the box and held the flame to me. I placed the reefer into my mouth and tilted toward the amber flame. I sucked, holding the inhalation for a minute and then let it slip slowly through nose and mouth.

The light in the room took on a golden hue. Trying to stand straight, I suffered a moment's vertigo and stumbled backward, colliding with the veiled and silent Pera, to whom I clung and with whom I crashed onto the floor. My face nestled in her hair. My nostrils took in the scent of her etiolated flesh. She offered no resistance as I held her down, and I fancied that I could hear her purring. My mouth pressed against her delectable neck, and my hand reached to pull the veil from her face. Savagely, Eblis flew from his chair and landed on me. A ragged nail from one malformed, sullied finger pierced my face, just below the right eye, slicing downward.

Cursing, I swung at the dwarf and screamed in rage, then tried to raise myself on hands and knees. A smell of blood assailed my nostrils, and a coppery taste slipped into my mouth. My hands reached out and clutched the beast's wild hair, and with all the force that I could muster I hurled him off me. The sound of his whimpering made me laugh and spit. The room was spinning, and so was I. Trying to stand, I fell on my ass. A shadow loomed above me, a scented phantom. It pressed its veiled face nearer to my own until I could taste the fabric. Underneath that veil I could feel the probing tongue that investigated the substance with which my face was stained.

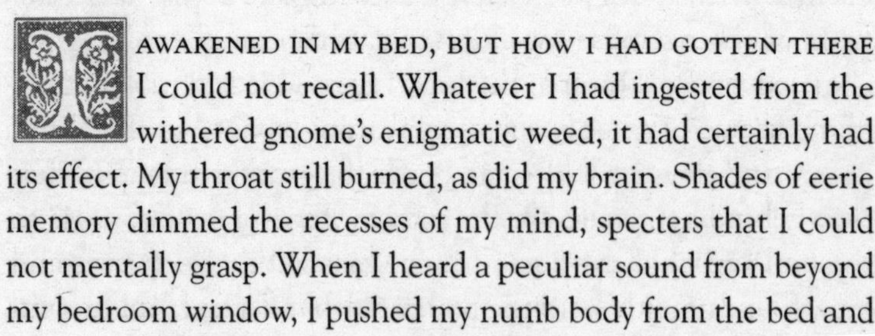

AWAKENED IN MY BED, BUT HOW I HAD GOTTEN THERE I could not recall. Whatever I had ingested from the withered gnome's enigmatic weed, it had certainly had its effect. My throat still burned, as did my brain. Shades of eerie memory dimmed the recesses of my mind, specters that I could not mentally grasp. When I heard a peculiar sound from beyond my bedroom window, I pushed my numb body from the bed and staggered to peer out the windowpane. I saw the dark oaks of the distant grove, and thought that I could just make out a portion of the moonlit pool. I saw a dancing shadow. It was attired in some black flowing gown, but the naked arms and face seemed somehow to drink in the drenching moonlight. Cool air pushed against the pane, and so I opened the window and leaned my head out of it, toward the grove. Coldness brushed my new-made scar, and on that wind I thought that I could just detect the dancing figure's lullaby. Was it Pera? Had she also partaken of the narcotic, and was she now out there in the chilly night, high and prancing recklessly in the growing storm? I felt drops of rain splash against my face, and so I found my jacket and went outside.

Crossing the quiet roadway, I walked into the grove and toward the dancing woman. At first I could not understand what was wrong with her face, and then I realized that she wore a mask, one that had been held by the woman in the photo I had seen based on Klimt's drawing, *Tragedy*. Gold encircled her throat and arms, flesh that was semi-transparent. Beneath the sound of wind and rain I could hear her soft chanting to a tune that reminded me of Mahler, one of Mother's favorite composers. Storm clouds occluded the earlier moonlight, and yet I could see amazingly well, and it struck me as odd that the woman's clothing had not grown sopping wet, nor did water drip from the death-white mask. Seeming to sense that I was watching her, the figure stopped moving and stood very still, facing me, her hands now clutching at her crotch.

I advanced toward her, my eyes glued to her mask, which seemed the only substantial thing about her. I did not understand how I could vaguely see the trees and bushes that were behind her, could see *through* her. I was now very close to her, and I reached out to touch the mask, its bulging eyes and wide round mouth. A smooth limpid hand joined mine and seemed to blend its texture with my skin. Together, we touched the edge of the mask and lifted. I shut my eyes as something firm yet fleshy encased my face.

A violent force pulled the mask from my face. Jesus stood before me, frowning, the mask in his left hand. "Philippe," I said, remembering his actual name, and then I looked about us. "Where's Pera?"

"Inside, where you should be. We do not enter the wooded place at night."

"Nonsense, she was just here, wearing that thing."

"No." He tossed the mask into the pool. It floated for a moment, and then was gone. "Come, take my hand."

"Uh, that's cool, dude."

"My hand," he commanded, holding it to me. I reached out and took hold of his hand, wincing as his fingers tightened like a clamp. I wanted to stop and look into the pool, but my captor forcefully yanked me after him, out of the grove, into rain, across the road and inside the old motel. We stood scowling at each other. "Go to bed, Henry."

"Aren't you going to go fetch Pera? She'll catch her death out there. You must have seen her, she was standing right in front of me, beside the pool."

"That was Alma. Now, to bed."

"Fuck you, you're not my mother. Who's Alma?" Ignoring me, he turned and went into the parlor. I followed. "Who is Alma? I want to meet her."

"She's faded. Now, go to bed."

"What do you mean, faded? Like her photograph?" I stomped to the table and picked up the photo album. Turning to the image that copied Klimt, I studied the girl pictured, that very young creature. "Are you telling me that I saw a ghost? Is that your game, freak boy? I didn't imagine that stupid mask. Take me to her room."

Philippe sighed. "You grow tedious."

"Yeah? Well, I don't like your little game. Okay, don't show me. I'll find it myself." Again he sighed, then held out his hand. "Forget it, Mary. Just show me the way."

Did he slightly smile? He shut his eyes for one moment, then turned and walked to the door that led to the hallway. I followed him to the end of the hallway, where he stopped before two doors, opened one of them, and entered a tiny room. I walked to the small bed and looked at the wall behind it. "There's no picture. Come on, I've figured a few things out. Every room I've been in has had a picture above the bed. Except this one. Where is Alma's picture, the copy of Klimt?"

"It's been taken to the catacombs, of course."

"Show me."

Again, his subtle smile. We exited the room and he opened the neighboring door. Crossing the threshold, we came to a flight of small stone steps. Philippe reached for a lantern that sat in a cavity cut into the wall, took a lighter from his pocket, and nonchalantly lit the wick. Saying nothing, he descended. The place to which he led me was like some ancient religious grotto, but here it was art that was divine. Framed pictures hung on walls like objects of adoration. As Philippe began to light various candles, I went to a stone pillar on which there sat a small framed copy of Klimt's piece, beautifully copied in full color.

I looked around me, and the place seemed to contract, as if eaten by spreading shadow. My breathing became labored, and I cringed as blackness seemed to seep hungrily toward me. Gasping, I hurried to the steps and scrambled up them. Philippe eventually joined me and shut the door behind him. Removing a handkerchief from a pocket, he patted at the perspiration on my brow. Annoyed, I took the piece of cloth from him and roughly wiped my face.

"Tight places," I explained. He nodded, with such a smug

expression on his face that I wanted to hit him. Instead, I strode across the hallway, past Pera's room and into the sitting room. Oskar was sitting on the sofa, placing a photograph into the leather album. Sitting next to him, I examined the photo, which was of him posed as the Count in Kokoschka's painting. I took the photograph, with which he was having difficulty, from his clumsy hands and slid it into one of the album's vacant sleeves. Then I took hold of the man's hand and examined its sulfur-yellow pigment. His face had also grown more discolored, and his sad hazel eyes had submerged within dark hollows.

"What the hell has happened to you?"

"The elder ones have worked their alchemy."

I was about to ask him more questions when he lifted his crippled hand and touched it to the scar on my face. My nostrils drank the sickened scent of his polluted flesh, the skin that reeked of death. Taking hold of that hand with both of mine, I pressed its fingers against my nose, my mouth. Something in its stench beguiled me.

"You look awful," he whispered as I touched his hand with my tongue. He took his hand from me. "Not sleeping well?"

Bitterly, I laughed. "Too many weird things are going on. Or so I imagine, although it could just be the freaky stuff that Eblis offered me last night. Or was it tonight? What day is it?"

He could not answer, for he suddenly jerked away, convulsed with hoarse coughing. Producing a piece of yellow cloth, he covered his mouth with it until the attack subsided. When he removed the rag from his mouth I saw that it had been sprinkled with beads of blood. "What the hell is wrong with you?"

Oskar waved away my inquiry. "You need not bother about me—take care of yourself." He stared into space, frowning, and I sensed that he was deciding whether or not to confide in me, to let me into his world. But then he stood and smiled down on me. "Get some sleep, Hank. You look half-dead."

"Not so fast," I yelled, grabbing his arm. "Damn it, explain what's going on in this godforsaken place. Look, I'm not an idiot. I can see the connections, the paintings in the rooms and the stills in that album. Now, I've just had a really freaky experience with Jesus." Oskar threw me an odd look. "With Philippe," I corrected myself. "I need to understand what I've stumbled on. Explain."

"Explanations are tedious. Understanding comes with the passage of time, but it won't really explicate anything. I'll tell you only this, that we have blurred the barrier betwixt art and nature, reality and dream. The outside world, the wretchedly bogus here and now, has no pertinence for us here. 'That bloody tyrant, Time,' scarcely touches us, and abhorrent modernity is utterly rejected. What was Pound's dull dictum concerning art, 'make it new'? Our aesthetic axiom is far more fascinating: 'Make it you'!" The reprehension that I felt deep within me must have been evident on my face, for Oskar began to laugh and shake his head. "Get some sleep, Hank."

I watched him leave the room. His coaxing seemed to have had an effect, for my eyelids were suddenly heavy. I stretched out on the sofa and closed my eyes. The man was clearly ill. TB was often regarded a quaint disease largely conquered by modern medicine, but I remembered having read of recent epidemics in various regions of the globe. It was an old contagion, for traces of tubercles had been discovered in mummies dating to 2000 B.C. Wanting to observe his photograph one more time, I reached for the album, propped it against my raised knees, and turned to Oskar's image. The original painting had been inspired by Kokoschka's stay at an institute in Switzerland, where the artist had painted the portraits of some tubercular patients. Although my eyes grew heavier and my mind hazy, I tried to study the photograph, to understand its connection to the original painting, to discern the relationship with Oskar's condition. My new friend had just hinted of a link, but what it was and how it existed was a mystery that I could not fathom.

I closed my eyes and began to sink toward slumber. As consciousness slipped from me, I remembered the sickly sweet aroma of Oskar's tainted skin, his delicious smell of moribund mortality. I felt the drool that lightly gathered in my mouth, that began to drip as wakefulness evaporated.

AWAKENED IN DARKNESS AND STRETCHED ON THE comfortable sofa, and then I noticed movement in the room. Looking up, I whispered her name. "Pera." She lit a candle that leaned within a sconce, and then picked up the flaming thing and held it before her veiled face.

"You're not sleeping in your bed. You need to do so. That's the way it works."

Rising, I went to her and took the candlestick from her gloved hand. "The way what works?" I listened to her hiss of laughter, a sound that was not sane. Lightly, I touched her hair. "Why do you hide your face?"

She began to rock slightly, and I put a gentle hand to her waist. "It shields me from the world, the bright reality. The envious dark drifts to kiss my drab face, and I'll be wedded to a death's-head, with a bone in my mouth."

"This is crazy talk," I mumbled.

She stopped rocking and leaned her body against mine. I could smell the cool breath that washed my face. "You name me mad? Is this lunacy?" She slid her hand toward the candle's flame and pinched the fire out, then knocked the holder to the floor. Funny, even without light I could see her clearly. The fabric of the veil tickled my face as she lifted it and smoothed it over her dark hair. I gazed at her face, with its skin that radiated like burnished porcelain. The unnatural pallor made me suspect that Pera was an arsenic eater, as society ladies were wont to be in distant eras. I had heard of dwellers in the mountains of southern Austria who consumed arsenic as a tonic, building up a tolerance for ingested amounts that would normally prove fatal. The world was filled with freaks, and I had stumbled into a realm of mutation, physical and mental. What worried me was that I was feeling more and more at home.

I pressed my nostrils against her temple and took in her mortal fragrance, never having smelled someone who aroused such odd longings within me. Her sudden deep laughter chilled me. "Pickman is a potent warlock. You're already altered." Ignoring her senseless prattle, I moved my face to her throat and raised my hands so as to fondle her breasts. Her sheathed hands took hold of my face and raised it to her own. Oh, how ghostly pale she was, so much so that I fancied I could vaguely see beneath her lucent hide to the bone of her delicate cranium. Her hands wound into my hair and tightened. Her mouth exhaled into my eyes, and vision fogged. I let her go and rubbed my face with hands that trembled. When again I looked at her, the veil had been dropped. Her hands took hold of mine. "To bed, to bed. Come, come, come, give me your hands. What's done cannot be undone. To bed."

I raised her hands to my mouth and kissed them. "Not yet. Show me some other rooms."

"Whatever for?" she asked, with an inflection that hinted of regained sanity. "Most of the rooms are vacant."

"Because their dwellers are faded?"

"Ah," she purred. She wouldn't move, and I suddenly began to feel like a cat's-paw. Disconnecting our hands, I walked into the foyer and up the stairs, the silent woman following me like some shadow. Reaching my floor, I went to try one of the many doors, but found it locked. The next door I tried yielded to my violence, and I entered an untenanted chamber. The painting over the bedstead was dimly lit by the rays of moonlight that drifted through the window. I went to it and touched the canvas. The dashingly handsome figure was familiar, and after a moment I remembered the original work that it copied, a Titian showing a young man in black, one hand naked, the other gloved and holding the glove that had been removed.

Pera stood beside me, then she quietly climbed onto the bed and placed her hand to the necklace worn by the painted figure. "They wanted to put him down in the catacombs, but I said nay. He'll not dwell in that darkened crypt, that place of death. Isn't he beautiful? So young." She reached for a varnished box that sat upon a stand. Opening it, she took out a red necklace identical to that worn by the lad in the painting. Kissing it, Pera clutched it to her chest as she lowered into the bed and curled into a fetal position.

Silently, I slipped out of the room and went to my own. I undressed and got into bed, kneeling on the mattress and studying the Pickman. The fellow's green canine eyes absurdly seemed to return my gaze. When at last I reclined, I saw those eyes in my dreams.

When my eyes opened to the glare of daylight streaming through the window, I heard from outside that window the song of laughter. Pushing the covers from me, I sat in bed and saw the plate of covered food on my bedside stand. I removed the cover and found some slices of the odd webbed meat that Pieter had offered me earlier. I wasn't very hungry, but I picked up a slice and began to eat. Standing, I wobbled to the window and looked out toward the oak grove, which was filled with moving figures. Were the freaks having a picnic? I found the idea slightly sinister, and that rather attracted me, for I was feeling bored. I dressed and went to join in the fun.

The light of day stung my eyes, and everything was thus a bit out of focus as I sauntered across the road toward the wooded place. Most of the faces were familiar, but there were three persons to whom I had not yet been introduced. The youngest, dressed in rather dandified Victorian garb, leaned against a tree, and something in her pose and the style in which she wore her flame red hair was familiar. A few yards from her, standing at an easel, a box of brushes and tubes of paint on the ground beside him, was Pieter. I went to study his canvas and saw pinned to its top left corner a small black and white picture.

"Isn't that Swinburne?" I ventured, watching the old guy copying the wee image in watercolor, blending the poet's facial features with those of the ascetic girl beside the tree. It was she who, frowning at me, spoke.

> *"Who hath known the ways of time*
> *Or trodden behind his feet?"*

"Whatever, babe," I threw at her, disliking her haughty attitude. "So, you're copying, um, Burne-Jones…?"

"Nope. Rossetti, painter and poet. Interesting, isn't it, how many artists have also been rhymers?" He worked his brush with dexterity and aptitude, and suddenly an idea flashed in my brain.

"Hey, those paintings above the beds…"

Mocking meekness, he bowed his head. "Most of them are mine own. The Pickman in your room is an original. I've touched it up a little, to bring out the beast."

"That explains it," I cheerfully replied. "I was wondering why the ones I was familiar with didn't look quite right. You've blended the original sitters with models of your own, as you're doing now. That's kind of cool." I did not mention that I thought it a dubious practice to "touch up" another artist's work.

Leaving him to his labor, I went to join Pera, who sat beside the pool of water, a petite parasol protecting her from sunlight.

Absentmindedly, she dipped her hand into the bunch of

pretty flowers in her lap. "Playing her part to the full," I thought, although when I saw the expression in her eyes beneath their veil I reconsidered. She gazed at me with eyes that were wide and lunatic, but also so sad that I grew quite melancholy. Tenderly, I took up a bloom and tossed it into the murky water.

Oskar came to join us, sitting next to the pool and staring into its depths with an odd expression shifting the features of his yellow face. When I asked if he was feeling well, he merely smiled and shrugged, then dipped his hand into the pool and raised a handful of cupped water to his crown. I watched the water dribble down his features. Pera reached out to his wet face and began to dry it with her glove. Oskar took her hand and kissed it, then turned to watch an approaching figure.

"The Mistress approaches," Oskar whispered.

I studied the crone as she stalked toward us, then smiled as she held a boxlike contraption and pointed its covered lens to us. Pera turned away, but Oskar stared, transfixed, as the witch removed the brass covering from the lens. I heard the squawking of crows in the trees above us and imagined that the light of day subtly subdued. Quickly, the cover was snapped back into place. The old hag's mirthless laughter unnerved me. I did not like the way she investigated my facial features as she placed her camera or whatever it was on the ground and untied the piece of black fabric that encircled her throat.

"It's time to play, my sprigs," she cackled. Slowly, steadily, everyone except Pera stopped what they were doing and walked to the elderly woman, encircling her. I was the last to stand and join their circle, standing next to Oskar and a woman I had not yet been introduced to. The ancient beldame stepped to Oskar and wrapped her ribbon so that it covered his eyes, tying it behind his head. She led him to the center of our circle, then joined our number.

We did not join hands, but everyone began to hum in a

low, nearly inaudible way, and our circle began to rotate slowly. As we moved around him, Oskar reached into the air as if ready to touch our faces. At last he reached out and touched the face of one of the women I did not know. He said her name, and she laughed as she untied the band from around his eyes. Above us, the cry of crows mingled with her laughter.

Oskar skipped to me and clapped. "My turn to choose, and you're it, Hank." I wanted to protest as he pulled me to the center of the circle and began to tie the ribbon 'round my head. "Do be a good sport, old boy," he requested, and so I stopped fidgeting and let him finish. My attention was focused on the smell of his jaundiced flesh and its effect on my appetite. He tied the knot and began to take his hands away, but I clasped mine over them and pressed them to my nose, my mouth. He allowed me to savor his mortality for a few moments, and then he sighed, "Do let go, there's a good lad."

I sensed him walk away from me, and then I heard the sound of humming encircling me. Feeling slightly foolish, I raised my hands and, although I couldn't see anything, shut my eyes. I thought that I could feel a faint and shifting radiance on my hands, as if globes of soft auras pirouetted before me. Pitching forward, I grasped a face. The atmosphere grew still and silent. My fingers investigated the invisible visage; they felt the thick nose and full lips, lips that flexed so that my fingertips played against large square teeth. Thick stubble, almost a beard, covered the chin. Was it Philippe? Had he shortened his beard and I not notice it? I moved my fingers along the face and felt the ragged scar beneath the right eye, and on my other hand I felt the heat that emitted from a mouth that mocked with easy laughter.

Cursing, I ripped the band of cloth from before my eyes, and then cried in fright as a winged shadow fluttered before me, squawking risibility. The crow's beady eyes stared directly into mine as I felt the wind of its flapping wings. And then it vanished to join its comrades in the boughs above us. I stood in the center of the circle, looking at the faces that were all too far away for me to have touched.

Thunder rumbled in the distance. The circle broke up and my companions moved away. Eblis, who had not been a part of the circle, jumped out of a tree, landing near Pera. She arose and held onto the handles of his wheelchair as he leaped into it, maneuvering his stunted torso with hands, like some malformed monkey. I stood beneath the trees and listened to the sound of birds moving among the branches. I heard the patter of rain on bark and leaves, drops that slipped between those leaves and fell into the nearby pool. I looked at the others, who had crossed the road and were entering the building as Oskar held its door open for them. He stood there alone for some time, gazing at me, and then he waved and went inside.

A loud clap of thunder shook me from my mental void. I leaned against a tree and closed my eyes. My sharp hearing took in the sounds of storm, of moving shadow. The world was alive with sound such as I had never experienced. Pushing away from the tree I passed the pond and peered into its water, not understanding the spheres beneath its surface, those pale globes that seemed almost to watch me.

I ran through the rain, into the building, and stepped into the drawing room. The tiny lights of the brass chandelier spread dim illumination through the room. Stopping before the painting of the oak grove, I examined it with interest. I saw that the "rainbow" was not actually white but rather a mixture of pale yellows and greens. The same wan green glowed among the numerous brown clouds. My eyesight oddly blurred as I stared at the thing, and that painted mass of nubilation seemed to billow and convulse, its patches of pale green reflecting a kind of alien light.

Turning away, I rubbed my eyes and listened to the frail

music that issued from some distant place. I stepped into the hallway and passed Pera's closed door, approached the door that opened onto the catacombs, and crossed its threshold. I needed no light as I held my hand against the rough-hewed wall and climbed down the small stone steps. Curiously, my discomfort for small dark places had deserted me. Glancing to where the whistling music was coming from, I noticed a doorway cut into the basalt, into which a squat round door had been fitted. Beside the wall leaned the dented wheelchair. Cracking open the door, I peered into an incommodious cell.

Eblis sat upon a squalid mat, looking like some troglodytic chimera, a plate of food before him. He watched me enter his domain as he put a slab of webbed meat to his mouth and tore into it with diseased teeth. Oskar stood in one corner, facing the wall as he played some flute-like instrument. Ignoring both of them, I went to examine the dark painting above the goblin's mat. Unlike the others, it did not represent another artist's work. Rather, it was a simple representation of Eblis Mauran in his wheelchair, the knobs that were his hands in his lap.

Oskar killed his music and turned to face me.

"Tell me about Pickman," I ordered.

"Not much to tell. He disappeared in September of 1926, after an unsuccessful career as an artist in Boston."

"Why did he paint his chosen subjects?"

"He was attracted to the macabre. Who can explain why? Tell me why Goya's mood so darkened that he ended his career with the so-called Black Paintings. What moods arrested Poe and Baudelaire so as to produce their diabolic lore? Hmm?"

"Stop being precious and tell me about Pickman."

"Henry, there's little to tell. Like Goya, his mood darkened near the end of his life, fueled perhaps by his lack of luck in being able to exhibit and sell his paintings. People were turned off by the image of the morbid changeling that kept appearing in his work, that became his whoreson theme. People felt abused when looking at his art."

"I'm sure they did."

"Look, I'm busy. Eblis has a session with the Mistress. Good day." So saying, he exited the room and picked up the old wheelchair, carrying it away.

I frowned at the goblin, then turned my attention once more to his painting. It was a large work in an ancient frame and seemed quite accomplished. And then I noticed the hands that nestled in the painted figure's lap, the nubs of which were both fingerless.

The gnome's plaintive voice spoke. "Master Pieter painted it just after I was woven."

I looked down at him. "I don't understand you."

"The Mistress grants me a new addition tonight." He held up his arms and smiled. "Will you carry me?"

I tilted to him and he scrambled into my embrace. His tiny arms wound around my neck, his large sad face fell onto my breast, and suddenly there were tears in my eyes. I could taste his loneliness. I carried him up the steps and into the hallway, then placed him into his wheelchair, which awaited him. He thanked me in his high and childlike voice, and I followed as he wheeled himself down the hallway and into the parlor. As I watched the tiny creature work his chair, something that Oskar had said about Pickman reverberated in my head. Oskar had described the creature in Pickman's painting as a changeling. Watching Eblis, I was certain that the word exactly described him: a secret child, unwanted in this world.

I followed Eblis to a door, which I opened for him. The crone sat at what looked like a prehistoric spinning wheel. In her left hand she held a moist mass of flesh, which she worked into the spindle and pulled through the outlandish device. I watched as the stringy meat was twisted and wound into a thread of glistening brawn. On a nearby table sat a shallow metal bidet in which a pile of the fibrous stuff had been tossed. Beside that mass of meat lay a large silver tray on which some of the flesh, woven together, was piled, ready to be eaten.

Seeing us, the old woman stopped her work and stood. "Ah, Henry, welcome. Will you have some opium?" Reaching for a pipe, she brought it to her mouth and lit the bowl. She sucked loudly and closed her eyes. "'Tis an old blend, from Burma. It will soothe your troubled mind."

Saying nothing, I took the pipe and drew on it. I watched as she sat in a chair next to the metal bowl, reaching for the gnome, who hastened to her lap. Deftly, she took up a pair of slender steel knitting needles, implements with which she worked a length of fibrous flesh into the hand on which Eblis wore two digits. My gut twisted as I watched her work, moving the needles into his flesh, her hands stained by spilling blood. Eblis neither screamed nor squirmed, and when at last he held to me his gory limb, I saw that the hand now wore a newly formed third finger. I sucked deeply on the pipe and held the smoke, and then I began to laugh, because I knew that I was dreaming.

UTSIDE, THE STORM HAD PASSED, AND THE SKY WAS fairly clear. I walked to the crest of the hill, my mind and soul at peace. Knowing that I was dreaming gave me a longing for adventure, and so I began to follow the road down the hill, walking toward the dark and silent town. Just on the periphery of the sleeping hamlet I came upon a small cemetery crowded with willow trees, a place that looked so peaceful that I decided to investigate its weathered stones. And then I was startled by what sounded like a low harmonious wailing. Beneath a willow, standing around a barrow of stones, were three women dressed in black. I could not understand why they looked familiar, but then I remembered that I was dreaming, and so I ceased trying to make sense of these new phantoms. Boldly, I went to them and picked up one large rock that sat atop the mound. It felt very real, cold, and heavy.

The woman nearest walked to and joined me in holding the rock. I sucked the air through my nose, hoping to smell her mortality, but no fragrance wafted to me. She was a phantom indeed. Softly, she began to sing, and as her beady eyes observed me, I fancied that her song was meant for me. Taking the rock from her, I stepped closer to the pile and returned the rock to its place on top.

"I've never seen anything like this. I suppose whoever lies beneath must have died long ago."

"Long, long ago," the woman sang. I did not move as she came nearer, as her hand raised and began to investigate my face. I did not flinch as her talon poked into my scar and reopened it. I could smell the wet red stuff that began to leak down my face. Funny, I'd never experienced a sense of smell when dreaming, or of touch. Roughly, I grabbed hold of the woman's hand. She was real enough.

"What's happening to me?"

"You were lost, and now are found," the woman sighed.

I pushed her from me and looked again at the mound of stones. "For whom do you warble?"

The woman motioned to the mound. "For our antecedent. For them who float in Wraithwood. For you."

I shut my eyes and began to laugh. I could feel my high wearing off, but I was high enough to imagine that I could hear the sound of beating wings, and the noise reminded me of a line from Poe:

> *"Flapping from out their Condor wings*
> *Invisible Wo!"*

When my eyes opened, I stood alone on the cemetery sod. Above me I could hear the crying of crows as they flew upward, toward Wraithwood.

I whistled loudly and sucked in necrophagous air, a hungry aether that sank beneath my pores and chilled my soul. How soft seemed the ground beneath my feet. Falling to my knees, I clawed into that earth and brought a handful of it to my nostrils. My mouth began to water. I felt an overwhelming intensity of hunger, and in some dark secluded mental place I dreamed an image of myself digging deep into this chilly sod in search of sustenance. A memory came to me of the weird webbed food I had been served at the hotel. I craved it now. Rising, I walked out of that place, following the road upward, toward home.

All lights inside had been extinguished, and yet I could see wonderfully well when I entered the building. I had planned on going straight to my chamber, but when I heard a low murmuring within the parlor, I went to its doors and crept inside. A figure paced the room, babbling to herself. A gloved hand, through which two pointed fingernails had ripped, madly clutched the face beneath a lacerated veil. How keenly I could smell the blood that stained her face! I went to her, unable to comprehend the thing that hung from her mouth until I was very close. The crimson necklace that was a copy of the one in the Titian painting was clenched between the teeth of a tightened jaw. And still she tried to babble.

I unfastened the torn veil and let it drift to the wooden floor. Her hand shot up to scratch her face, but I held it tight so as to block the nail from slicing once more into the emaciated skin. Touching my fingers to her mouth, I gently pulled the necklace from her teeth, catching a spill of drool with my cupped hand. When again she muttered, I understood her words.

"I know when one is dead and when one lives; he's dead as earth." She took the ruddy necklace from me and swung it before our eyes. "Why should a dog, a rat, a witch have life and he no breath at all?"

"Of whom do you speak, kind lady? I did not find his likeness in the album. Where is his photograph?"

The woman tilted her head and examined me with lunatic eyes. Raising her hands above me, she slipped the necklace over my head. With one hand, she tightened it around my neck. When I began to have trouble breathing, I clawed at her hands and pushed her from me. Tittering, she fled the room, and I followed to her bedchamber, where I found her lighting a candle on a bookshelf that she had littered with various bric-a-brac. I noticed the gilded frame before which she swayed. Going to her, I examined the glossy sheet of paper within the frame. At first I could discern no image, but the more I studied it in the flickering light, the more I could almost make out an imperceptible and spectral outline. "Is this your young man?" I asked, touching the frame. "Is he the young man in the Titian?"

"The Titian," she spat, in a voice that sounded coherent and sane. "He was young, wasn't he? Not yet nineteen. And so beautiful. I take flowers to him, to his shining face. I shall soon answer his summons." She shuddered and wrapped her arms around her shoulders. Turning to me, she tugged at her collar. "Pray you, undo this button."

I worked the buttons loose, then took the candle and led her to bed, setting the candle on the little bedside stand. Her face was smeared with dark blood that had seeped from her self-inflicted wounds. "I'll be right back," I promised, and then I went to her bathroom and threw a washcloth into the small porcelain basin. I turned one of the brass-spigots and let cold water flow onto the cloth, and as I waited I glanced at my reflection in the mirror. This reminded me that I was dreaming; for how could I see my face so clearly in an unlit room, and how could that reflection be mine own? I hadn't seen myself since my arrival to the motel, and so it should not have surprised me to see the growth of hair upon my face. But why was the bristle so thick, and how had my face grown so wide? Could those broad lips be mine, those large square teeth that almost protruded from the mouth?

No, this was all some mad hallucination, for only in a dream could my visage so alter as to resemble the ghoul in Pickman's painting. I thought of Oskar and his similarity to the figure in the painting above his bed. This was naught but mad delusion. And yet, when I reached for the cloth and wrung the excess water from it, I could feel the cold wetness so vividly. Returning to Pera, I washed the congealed blood from her face as she sat on the bed and stared at the flame. When I had finished, she took the rag from me and pressed it to the scar beneath my eye. Our mouths were very close, and I could smell her breath.

Dropping the washcloth to the floor, Pera picked up the candle and placed it between our mouths. "Put out the light," she whispered, "and then put out the light." My tongue, coated with saliva, licked out the tiny blaze. I took the candle from her and set it down, then reached to undo more buttons on her blouse. We sat in deep darkness, and yet I could see her, and even fancied that I could just make out the skull beneath her thin translucent skin. Together we reclined. She took hold of the necklace around my throat and spoke a stranger's name. I wrapped my hungry arms around her meat and shut my eyes. I dreamed within my dreaming, and those dreams were of dark cemetery sod, and of the carcasses beneath the earth. How piquant was the smell of that soil and its inhabitants! And mingled with their odor I took in the sweet fragrance of the lunatic in my arms.

But when the morning light fell on me from the window in her room, I was alone. And when I went to that window to seek the source of singing that I heard, I saw the figures that stood within the grove, encased by dawn's dim light. Crying, I fled the room and rushed outside, running across the road and into that grove. When I saw the figure hanging from a length of rope that had been fastened to a sturdy branch, I fell upon wet grass.

Someone called my name, and I turned to face the crone. She was pointing her camera device at me, nodding her head in approval. Cursing her, I turned once more to look at the woman hanging from the tree, at the three other women who stood underneath her and wailed harmoniously. Eblis was suddenly beside me, touching his three fingers to my face and nodding his happy head. I watched as he scampered to the tree and began to scuttle up it, like something in a Kafkaesque delirium. Oskar and Philippe now stood beneath the corpse and took hold of it as Eblis gnawed the rope around the branch. The body fell as the wailing trio blurred into one cloudy entity that rose to hidden branches, from which there came the squall of crows. I watched as the men took her body to the pool and gently tossed her into its water. In dream, I saw her dead hand gather a bunch of flowers that floated in the water next to her, and I sighed as she chose one lovely bloom and held it to me. Creeping to the edge of the pool, I reached for the flower that she offered me, and by chance I peered into the water, at the shining spheres that frolicked just beneath her. I saw the one pale globe that rose to kiss the back of her neck, that moved its mouth as if to name her. At the touch of his tender kiss, my lucent beauty smiled, closed her eyes, and sank into the water's depths.

The Dome

MOLLIE L. BURLESON

Mollie L. Burleson's short stories have appeared in the magazines Eldritch Tales, Crypt of Cthulhu, *and* Bare Bone, *and in a number of anthologies, including* 100 Creepy Little Creature Stories *(Barnes & Noble, 1994),* 100 Vicious Little Vampire Stories *(Barnes & Noble, 1995),* 100 Wicked Little Witch Stories *(Barnes & Noble, 1995),* Horrors! 365 Scary Stories *(Barnes & Noble, 1998),* Weird Tales *(Triad, 2002), and* Return to Lovecraft Country *(Triad, 1997).*

 CLOUD FORMED ATOP THE DISTANT MOUNTAIN AS he headed west on Second Street. Pretty sight, he thought. It had been a big decision, moving out here. Not at all like living in the northeast. Better. Much better.

The vast turquoise sky above and the clean air and the people were just some of the reasons he had chosen to move here. Squinting slightly as the hot desert sun beat down, making watery images across the road, Tom nosed his car onto Saltillo Road.

He really liked it in New Mexico and was reminded daily of the rightness of his choice by just enjoying the natural wonders he'd see. The small town of Sand Rock was ideal for someone who had retired and was looking for a place to escape the rigors of the northern winters.

It was a friendly place, even though he had to drive two hundred miles a few times a year to shop the big stores and malls in Albuquerque or Las Cruces, and even Midland and Lubbock in Texas. It was a life without hearing daily about crime, and the air was pure, if you didn't count the occasional smell of manure as a pecan rancher fertilized his orchards.

Yes, it was a good life, he thought, as he turned left onto his rocky driveway and parked his truck. Slamming the door, he smiled as he watched the antics of a jackrabbit scampering across the lawn and heard the raucous cry of the long-tailed grackle. Yes, a good place to live.

He thought then about the only eyesore to the place, the huge, silver-colored building on the east side. It was rumored to have once been a place for storing cotton seed, but he'd never in his life seen its like. A tall building, ominous-looking and mysterious as it squatted on its gravel lot. The great domed roof could be seen from almost everywhere in town. It now housed a motley assortment of junk—collectibles, the sign read, which consisted of broken-down furniture, faded drapes and curtains piled high in cardboard boxes, outmoded children's toys, rusty bikes, tarnished mirrors, and the like.

The building was immense. He had been told that it measured a good three hundred feet across and was over one hundred feet high. Somehow, when standing in its very center, he had the feeling of having been swallowed up by a gigantic and repellant bug.

The circular walls of the interior were painted black halfway up and at the very top, a thing, very much like an eye, could be opened to the sky. It had been open for ventilation the day he stopped in to look at the items for sale, and the view it afforded had not been inspiring, but gray, for the day had been threatening rain.

What *was* curious was the proprietor, a man of few words who spoke only when asked a direct question and then as concisely as possible. Tom didn't know his name and wondered if anyone in town did. The man was clad in tattered overalls, rundown boots, a plaid shirt with gray undershirt beneath, and the ubiquitous southwestern red kerchief at his neck. The kerchief appeared to have never been washed, as it was darkly stained and oily looking. Atop his rather large head, the old man wore a grimy straw hat, and the scraggly long beard upon his chin was as gray as his underwear. What little of his face that could be seen was a pair of reptilian-shaped eyes with lids that never seemed to close. They stared at you, unblinkingly. But of course, that was just Tom's imagination. The man appeared very old and that would make his eyes look like that. Wouldn't it?

Upon Tom's arrival in the town, the Dome had been pointed out to him as a good place to eke out his sparse assortment of furniture. Living on a set income from Social Security and a tiny pension, he was only too happy to give the building a try. He had purchased a rickety chest for twenty dollars that he could use in his shed to hold tools and whatnot, and it suited him admirably. Still, dealing with the taciturn, almost surly old man was no pleasure, and Tom was glad to escape into the sunshine.

He had been in Sand Rock for almost a year now, and fit well into the community. He had met some men his age at the senior center and played pinochle with them from time to time.

One afternoon, as the game ended, Tom's friend Phil hung around and offered to get Tom a cup of coffee. They sat at a table near the snack bar and talked of many things. In passing, Tom mentioned the chest he had bought at the Dome.

"That place?" Phil said. "Why, you couldn't get me closer than a mile to it, now."

"Why?" Tom looked astonished.

"Well, I went there a few years ago to pick up some tools I'd been needing, and when I walked in there, I saw the old man that runs the place crouched over some huge old book and mumbling to himself, and as I went closer, I could see strange figures and drawings on its pages and tried for a better look, but when I stumbled against one of the chairs, he looked up, wary-like, slammed the book shut and stuck it under the desk.

"You don't say."

"I do say! And the look he gave me with those bleary eyes was enough to kill! So I'd never go back there even if everything was free."

Tom thought about this and took a last swallow of his now-cold coffee.

They sat together in companionable silence for a while, then Phil took up the tale once more.

"And you know, my granddaddy once told me about that place and the story he'd heard about a strange cult that held its meetings at night under the Dome, usually about midnight around May Eve or Halloween. When granddaddy said that, he'd spit into the dust. It was the kind of thing that didn't set well with him, seeing that he was raised a Baptist."

Tom sat there, engrossed.

"'Course, that was after the seed was gone and they'd turned it into that junk store," Phil went on. "Don't think it's changed much, even to this day."

Tom had gone home then, stopping at the local country market. Being a fairly good cook, he enjoyed being able to buy freshly roasted chiles and local spices, and he produced some very tasty meals. Usually after dinner, coffee cup in hand, he would sit in his rocker on the cement patio and listen to the birds and locusts. Sometimes he'd walk back onto his property and survey his few pecan trees. In the distance, ever present, was the silver dome jutting into the sky. The structure seemed to him a blight on the town, a gigantic metallic blister, as it squatted there, silent and forbidding, and he'd turn his back on it and concentrate on the nearby beauty that surrounded him.

It was near the end of July that he received a note from his granddaughter telling him that she'd be passing through town soon and wondering if he could put her up for a night. He was overjoyed at the news, for he loved his pretty little granddaughter who had just graduated from high school and was heading west to a college near Phoenix.

But there was a problem. Although he had two bedrooms, only one was furnished. He'd have to go to town and find a bed for her. It wouldn't be too great an expense if he bought it second hand, and, he *could* use it for unexpected guests in the future.

So, the next morning after breakfast, he got into his truck and headed for the used furniture store in town, a real store without domed roof or surly proprietor. But, as luck would have it, there was no bed suitable for his granddaughter and none priced to fit his meager budget. He squared his shoulders. There was nothing for it but to try out the silver dome again. He seemed to recall a fairly good selection of used beds when he last was in the store, and what harm could an old building and a crusty owner do?

The building was the same as before, huge and unpleasantly warm and slightly humid, even though the humidity was in the teens. There seemed to be an indefinable odor to the place, something reminiscent of the salt flats near the east coast of Maine. As he wandered the uneven and cluttered aisles, his footsteps and the voices of two other customers speaking to each other, echoed eerily off the walls. Almost as if they were underground. Or under the sea.

Now where had that idea come from? Under the sea, in the desert southwest! Strangely enough, Tom had read a little about the area in which he lived and had been surprised to learn that the hundreds of miles that stretched from west Texas to where he now lived had once been the bottom of a great Permian sea. Shallow, but still a sea.

The other two customers left and it was oddly still, except for his own echoing footsteps. There was an eerie sense of being dwarfed by the immensity of the place, and an almost claustrophobic feeling even though it was so huge. A panicky feeling came over him and he wanted to run. To get out of the place. To reach safety. Foolish! He got control of himself and went on looking.

Finding the assortment of beds for sale, he bent over, examining closely the quality of one of them. It wasn't bad at all, white with pink flowers on the headboard, and the price was only one hundred dollars, including mattress and box spring. And best of all, it was clean.

He reared up in surprise then as he heard a terrific screeching from above and saw the "eye" of the dome slowly opening like the lens of a camera. The sky, seen from the interior of the dome was black, a roiling, churning fathomless black, and he imagined he could see something moving within the ropy coils of cloud. He knew that the sky couldn't be black. It was only eleven in the morning and the sky outside was its usual vivid blue.

He cried out then and as he did, the old man appeared out of nowhere and scuttled beetlelike to the wall, where he manipulated some dials or controls, thereby closing the aperture.

Tom, shaking and ashen, stood looking upwards at the now-closed opening when the old man sidled up to him, grinning a broken-toothed smile, and looking, for the first time, actually affable. And talkative. He told Tom that the bed was on sale for fifty dollars. Even shaken as he was, Tom knew a bargain when he saw one, and he hastily paid the man and with his help loaded the bed and mattress onto his truck. As he did so, he noticed the man's hands—or what appeared to be hands. Dark and leathery and webbed! Webbed! Surely that was a trick of his eye or a condition caused from a rare disease. Everything about the man appeared strange and *diseased*. Tom shuddered.

That evening, as Tom sat in his yard, he pondered what he had seen or *thought* he had seen at the top of the dome. It had probably been some aberration—the sun had been high and somehow the rays hit the silvery metal, blinding him for an instant. That's what it had been. He shivered and wrapped his arms around himself, though the temperature was in the nineties.

His granddaughter came on that Friday and they had a grand time together, enjoying some of his hot and spicy burritos and reminiscing on the patio. When she left the next morning he felt alone, more alone than he had ever felt before.

That night he had awful dreams, dreams about black skies, twisting snake-like arms, and the smell of the sea bottom. He awoke in a sweat and went to the refrigerator for a cold glass of water. Now why should he dream such dreams? It had to be that experience he'd had in the Dome. A mere trick of the eye and his subconscious had added the gory and frightening details.

The next day he spent puttering around in his shed, mending a few things and then watering his pecans. He went to the senior center and played a few hands of pinochle. Phil wasn't around. No one seemed to know where he was. Tom enjoyed the game, but still, at the back of his mind dwelled his experience and his terrible dreams.

He spent another fright-filled night, tossing and turning, dreaming of things ancient and horrible and of a writhing, twisting thing wrapping itself around his throat. He woke up screaming and found his sheet twined around his neck. In the morning he decided to put an end to the awful fears he had of the Dome and what he thought he saw there, high up in the eye. After dressing and downing a cup of coffee, he got into his truck and headed for that bloated sphere.

He parked his truck and noticed that though it was after nine a.m. there was no other vehicle in the lot. He climbed out and closed the door, being careful not to slam it. He quietly made his way to the doors of the building and walked inside. He had purposely worn his sneakers so that his footsteps wouldn't be heard. There appeared to be no one around, no customers, no old man. He went inside and looked upward toward the ceiling. The eye was closed. And then he heard some strange ululating sounds, as if from someone chanting in a strange language. Louder and louder the voice called, higher and higher in pitch. The language was some guttural tongue with impossible vowels and consonants. Along with the strident tones, the screeching that he had heard before began again—this time, ear-deafening in volume. He looked up to see the black and roiling sky above, the sky of his nightmares. And appearing through the inky darkness was something moving, something sinuous in motion, which seemed to come through the eye and snake downward toward the interior of the dome.

He could bear no more; he screamed and ran, stumbling through the masses of detritus, falling once, bloodying his face and then half running, half crawling to the doors. As he reached the safety of the threshold he turned around, just once, and that sight was enough to last him the rest of his days.

At last he reached his house, trembling and nauseous, and fell into bed. He dropped into a sort of stupor in which he had no dreams. He awakened at sunset and felt better and sat at his table pondering the events of the morning. Was what he saw real or did he imagine the whole thing? But why should he imagine something like this when he had never been a man of fancy, but a practical person who took each day as he found it? Then it must have been real, what he saw, and he shuddered as he recalled the vision. It was Tom's scream that alerted the old man in the domed building, that made him start the machinery in motion that caused the eye to close.

Tom's scream that stopped that monstrous thing from entering this world.

INTER HAD COME AND GONE. TOM KEPT TO HIS DAILY ritual of doing his chores and tending to the pecan trees. He had few dreams anymore, but at times during the day the whisper of a hated memory crept through and he felt afraid. Locals had told him that the Dome was closed. The day after Tom's visit, the place had been boarded up, and in time the signs that announced its wares had fallen into disrepair. Whenever he would pass the place, he couldn't help looking its way and he would notice that it now looked only squat and benign and somehow ludicrous. Its silver dome was turning rusty and no one came to its doors. What had happened to the old man remained a mystery.

But the fleeting memories Tom still had were enough to convince him that what he had seen that day had been real—that blackness, those bloated wormlike arms writhing and groping, and that sound, like waves breaking upon an unlit and unknown shore. And most of all, the smell, a rank and rotten smell of a sea bottom upturned. The smell of things better left alone. Yes, there *had* been something in that aperture, something gigantic and evil. Something ancient and grotesque, called there by the old man. Some *thing* whose entry into this world had been stopped by Tom's screams. And, before the eye had screeched shut, that nameless being had stretched ropy arms downward and enfolded the old caretaker into its embrace before the opening had closed forever.

Rotterdam

NICHOLAS ROYLE

Nicholas Royle is the author of the novels Counterparts *(Barrington, 1993; Penguin, 1995),* Saxophone Dreams *(Penguin, 1996),* The Matter of the Heart *(Abacus, 1997),* The Director's Cut *(Abacus, 2000), and* Antwerp *(Serpent's Tail, 2004), and the short story collection* Mortality *(Serpent's Tail, 2006). He has published more than 100 short stories in magazines and anthologies. His Lovecraftian tale "The Homecoming" appeared in Stephen Jones's* Shadows over Innsmouth *(Fedogan & Bremer, 1994).*

S SOON AS JOE ARRIVED IN ROTTERDAM, HE MADE FOR the river. He believed that a city without a river was like a computer without memory. A camera without film.

The river was wide and gray. A slice of the North Sea.

Joe was listening to "Rotterdam," a track on the Githead album, *Art Pop*. When he'd last been to Paris he'd played the Friendly Fires single of that name over and over. Earlier in the year, walking through the Neukölln district of Berlin, he'd selected Bowie's *Heroes* album and listened to one track, "Neukölln," on repeat.

He switched it off. It wasn't working. Sometimes it worked, sometimes it didn't. The chugging, wiry pop of Githead didn't fit this bleak riverscape. The breathy vocals were a distraction. Instrumentals worked better.

He didn't have long. A couple of days. The producer, Vos, wouldn't wait any longer. The American was a busy man and Joe knew he had already more than tried Vos's patience with repeated requests to have a shot at writing the screenplay, or have some input elsewhere on the movie. For now, at least, the script had John Mains's name on it and Joe knew he could count himself lucky to be scouting locations, albeit unpaid. He hoped that by showing his willingness and maybe coming up with some places that not only corresponded to what Vos wanted but also helped to back up his own vision of how the film could look, he might still get to gain some influence.

Joe turned back on himself and selected a cheap hotel

with a river view. His room, when he got up to the fourth floor, managed to reveal very little of the Nieuwe Maas, but if you craned your neck you could just make out the distinctive outline of the Erasmus Bridge. They called it the Swan; to Joe it looked more like a wishbone, picked clean. Did swans have wishbones?

The room itself was basic, and while you wouldn't necessarily pick up dirt with a trailing finger, there was a suggestion of ingrained grime, a patina of grease. Joe quickly unpacked his shoulder bag, placing his tattered Panther paperback of *The Lurking Fear and Other Stories* by the side of the bed. He checked his e-mails and sent one to Vos to let him know he had arrived in Rotterdam and was heading straight out to make a start.

He walked toward the center. The kind of places he was looking for were not likely to be found there, but he wanted to get a feel for the city. He'd known not to expect a replica of Amsterdam, or even Antwerp. Rotterdam had been flattened in the war and had arisen anew in the twentieth century's favorite materials of glass and steel. But really the commercial center could have been plucked from the English Midlands or the depressed Francophone cities of Wallonia.

A figure on top of an anonymous block of chrome and smoked glass caught his eye. It was either hubris or a remarkable achievement on the artist's part that Antony Gormley's cast of his own body had, by stealth, become a sort of Everyman figure. A split second's glance was all you needed to identify the facsimile as that of the London-born sculptor.

Only absently wondering why there might be an Antony Gormley figure standing on top of an office block in Rotterdam, Joe walked on. He stopped outside a bookshop and surveyed the contents of the window as an inevitable prelude to going inside: Joe couldn't walk past bookshops. It was their unpredictability that drew him in. They might not have his book in stock, but then again they might.

This one had the recently published Dutch edition of Joe's crime novel, *Amsterdam*. He stroked the cover, lost for a moment in the same reverie that always gripped him at this point. The thought that the novel was this far—*this far*—from reaching the screen.

Leaving the bookshop, Joe spotted another tall figure standing erect on the flat roof of a shiny anonymous building two hundred meters down the road.

When Vos had optioned the book, Joe had thought it was only a matter of time, but delay followed delay. Vos had a director attached, but couldn't find a writer the director would work with. Joe had asked his agent to show Vos the three unsold feature-length scripts he had written on spec, but the agent had explained that Vos and his director were looking for someone with a track record. Which was why Joe made a bid to write the adaptation of Lovecraft's "The Hound," Vos's other optioned property, but the response was the same. Hence the visit to Rotterdam to look for empty spaces and spooky graveyards.

On the Westzeedijk, a boulevard heading east away from the city center, Joe came upon the Kunsthal: a glass-and-steel construction, the art gallery had a protruding metal deck on which were scattered more Gormley figures in different positions. Lying flat, sitting down, bent double. Inside the gallery, visible through the sheet-glass walls, were more figures striking a variety of poses. Two faced each other through the plate glass, identical in all respects except height. The one inside looked taller, presumably an illusion.

Joe had missed the original Gormley exhibition in London, when cast-iron molds of the artist's body had popped up on rooftops across the capital. Leaving the Kunsthal in his wake, he caught sight of another figure at one corner of the roof of the Erasmus Medical Center. He realized he had started looking for them. This was Gormley's aim, he supposed, to alter the way you looked at the world. To get into your head and flick a switch. As public art, it was inescapable, insidious, invasive. Was that a good thing? Was his work really a "radical investigation of the body as a place of memory and transformation," as Joe remembered reading on the artist's own website? Or was it all about him? All about Gormley. And if it was, did that matter? Wasn't Joe's novel all about Joe? Who's to say Lovecraft's essays were the extent of his autobiographical work?

Joe was halfway to the top of the Euromast when his phone buzzed. The incoming text was from Vos. John Mains, the scriptwriter, was going to be in Rotterdam, arriving later that day. They should meet, compare notes, Vos advised.

Joe scowled. He reached the top landing of the structure and exited on to the viewing deck. The panorama of the city ought to have dominated, but Joe couldn't help but be aware of the ubiquitous figure perched on the railing above his head.

He tried to think of a way in which he could get out of meeting up with Mains. He'd lost his phone and not received Vos's text. Amateurish. Didn't have time. Even worse.

He checked his watch. He still had a few hours.

At the foot of the Euromast he found an empty fire station. He peered through the fogged windows. A red plastic chair sat upturned in the middle of a concrete floor. A single boot lay on its side. Joe took a couple of pictures and moved on. A kilometer or so north was Nieuwe Binnenweg. With its mix of independent music stores, designer boutiques, print centers, and sex shops, this long east-west street on the west side of the city would be useful for establishing shots. At the top end he photographed a pet grooming salon, Doggy Stijl, next door to a business calling itself, less ambiguously, the Fetish Store. There were a few empty shops, more cropping up the further out of town he walked, alongside ethnic food stores and tatty establishments selling cheap luggage and rolls of brightly colored vinyl floor coverings.

The port of Rotterdam had expanded since Lovecraft's day to become the largest in Europe. Why the late author had chosen to set his story here did not concern Joe; indeed, he had no reason to suspect Lovecraft had ever set foot on Dutch soil. The references to Holland and Rotterdam in particular were so general he could have been describing any port city. All credit to Vos, Joe conceded, that he had chosen to film here rather than in Hull or Harwich, or the eastern seaboard of the U.S., for that matter.

Joe's westward migration out of the city had taken him into one of the port areas. The cold hand of the North Sea poked its stubby fingers into waste ground crisscrossed by disused railway sidings. Ancient warehouses crumbled in the moist air. New buildings the size of football pitches constructed out of corrugated metal squatted amid coarse grass and hardy yellow flowering plants. Interposed between one of these nameless buildings and the end of a long narrow channel of slate-colored water was an abandoned Meccano set of rusty machinery—hawsers, articulated arms, winches, pulleys. Elsewhere in the city this would pass as contemporary art. Out here it was merely a relic of outmoded mechanization, with a possible afterlife as a prop in a twenty-first-century horror film.

There had been a few adaptations of Lovecraft's work, successful and otherwise, and they weren't *all* by Stuart Gordon. Just most of them. Joe wasn't sure where Vos's film was destined to play, arthouse or multiplex. As he lowered the camera from his eye, he caught sight of a dark shape behind the machinery.

Tasting a rush of adrenaline, he moved his head for a better view, but there was nothing—or nobody—there.

Disconcerted, he backed away. In the distance a container lorry crunched down through the gears as it negotiated a corner. A faint alarm could be heard as the driver of another vehicle reversed up to a loading bay.

Keileweg had been the center of the dockside red light district before the clean-up of 2005 that had driven prostitution off the streets. If he hadn't done his research, Joe wouldn't have guessed. He found Keileweg devoid of almost any signs of life. The street was lined with boxy gray warehouses and abandoned import/export businesses. A dirty scarf of sulphurous smoke trailed from a chimney at an industrial site near the main road end of Keileweg. On the opposite side, a little way down, a building clad in blue corrugated metal drew Joe's eye. Christian graffiti decorated the roadside wall: "JEZUS STIERF VOOR ONS TOEN Wij NOG ZONDAREN WAREN." The building's main entrance was tucked away behind high gates. High but not unscaleable. Approaching the dirty windows, Joe shielded his eyes to check out the interior. The usual story: upturned chairs, a table separated from its legs, a computer monitor with its screen kicked in, a venetian blind pulled down from the wall, its blue slats twisted and splayed like some kind of post-ecological vegetation.

The place had potential.

Likewise the waste ground and disused railway sidings running alongside Vier-Havens-Straat.

Slowly, Joe made his way back into town photographing likely sites, even throwing in the odd windmill in case Vos wanted to catch the heritage market.

He returned to the hotel to shower and pick up his e-mails, including one from Vos telling him where and when to meet John Mains. Joe studied the map. He left the hotel and walked north until he reached Nieuwe Binnenweg, where he turned left. At the junction with 's Gravendijkwal, where the traffic rattled beneath Nieuwe Binnenweg in an underpass, he entered the Dizzy Jazzcafé and ordered a Belgian brown beer. He drank it quickly, toying with his beermat, and ordered another. Checking his watch, he emptied his glass for the second time. As he stood up, his head span and he had to hold on to the back of the chair. Belgian brown beers were notoriously strong, he remembered, a little too late.

Two blocks down Nieuwe Binnenweg was Heemraadssingel, a wide boulevard with a canal running up the middle of it. Joe stood on a broad grassy bank facing the canal and beyond it the bar where he was due to meet Mains. He straightened his back and breathed in deeply. He needed a moment of calm.

A soft voice in his ear: "Joe!"

He whiled around. A figure stood on the grass behind him, legs slightly apart, arms by his side. The lights of the bars and the clubs on the near side of the street turned the figure into a silhouette; the lights from the far side of the canal were too distant to provide any illumination.

Joe stood his ground, straining his eyes to see.

The figure didn't move.

And then a shape ghosted out from behind it. A man.

"Joe," said the man in a gentle Scots accent. "Didn't mean to make you jump. Well, I guess I did, but you know… These are a laugh, aren't they?" He indicated the cast-iron mold as he moved away from it. "Easily recyclable, too. John Mains." He offered his hand.

"Joe," said Joe, still disoriented.

"I know," said Mains, smiling slyly.

He was about Joe's height with an uncertain cast to his slightly asymmetrical features that could go either way—charmingly vulnerable or deceptively untrustworthy.

"Busy day?" Mains asked, moving dark hair out of his eyes.

"Yeah."

"When did you get here?"

"This morning."

"*How* did you get here?"

"I flew."

"Shall we?" Mains gestured toward the far side of the canal.

They walked toward where the road crossed over the canal, and Joe was the first to enter the bar. Rock music played loudly from speakers bracketed to the walls. They sat on stools at a high table in a little booth, and a bartender brought them beers. Joe observed Mains while the scriptwriter was watching the lads in the next booth, and he wondered what anyone would think, looking at them. Would they be able to spot the difference between them? Was Mains's precious track record visible to the naked eye?

Mains looked back and it was Joe's turn to redirect his gaze.

Mains said something and Joe had to ask him to repeat it.

"I said I haven't booked into a hotel yet."

"It's not exactly high season."

"No." He took a sip of his beer. "Could you not have taken the train? Or the ferry?"

"What?"

"It's not very environmentally friendly to fly, especially such a short distance."

"It was cheaper."

"Not in the long run, Joe. You've got to take the long view."

Joe looked at the other man's dark eyes, small and round and glossy like a bird's. A half-smile.

"So what have you got for me?" Mains asked.

Joe hesitated. He wondered if it was worth making the point that he was working for Vos. He decided that since neither of them was paying him, it didn't make much difference. He was about to answer when Mains spoke again.

"Look, Joe, I know you pitched to write this script, but we do have to work together."

"I know, I know," Joe shouted into a sudden break between tracks. The boys in the next booth looked over at them. Joe returned their stare, then turned to look at Mains. "I know," he continued. "Here, have a look."

He handed Mains the camera phone on which he'd taken his pictures, and Mains flicked through them using his thumbs.

"Great," he said, not particularly sounding like he meant it. "I suppose I was expecting something more atmospheric."

Joe tried to keep the irritation out of his voice—"I guess the Germans weren't thinking about that when they bombed the place to fuck"—and failed.

Another group of young men entered the bar. Joe didn't consider himself an expert on the outward signifiers of particular social groupings, particularly in foreign countries, but he wondered if Mains had brought him to a gay bar. One of the newcomers glanced at Joe, then switched his attention to Mains, his eyes lingering on the tattoos on the Scot's forearms.

"Are you hungry?" said Mains.

"I haven't eaten all day."

"Let's go get something to eat."

As they got down from their stools, Joe felt his head spinning again. He really did need something to eat, and quick.

They ate in a Thai restaurant. Joe smiled at the waitress, but it was his dining partner she couldn't take her eyes off.

"You'd better write a decent script, that's all I can say," Joe said to Mains, argumentatively, as the waitress poured them each another Singha beer. "It better not be shit."

Mains laughed.

"I'm not fucking joking. When's it set, for example? Is it contemporary?"

'It's timeless, Joe. It's a timeless story, after all. I'm sure you agree. Grave-robbing—it's never a good idea."

"Tell me you're not writing it as a fucking period piece."

"Like I say, it's timeless."

"Fuck's sake."

As they left, Mains slipped the tip directly into the waitress's hand. Joe thought he saw her fingers momentarily close over his.

Out on the street, Joe wanted nothing more than to drink several glasses of water and get his head down, but Mains wasn't done yet, insisting that they go to a club he'd read about near Centraal Station.

"I'm fucked," Joe said, pulling a face.

"Ah come on, man. It's new. I want to check it out and I can't go on my own."

Why not? Joe wanted to yell at him. *Why the fuck not?*

But instead he allowed his shoulders to slump in a gesture of acquiescence.

"Good man!" Mains clapped him on the back. "Good man! Let's go."

They walked together through the city streets, dodging bicycles. Joe knew he was making a mistake. He just didn't know how big.

They reached West-Kruiskade. The nightclub—WATT—was located between a public park and an Asian fast food restaurant. Dozens of bikes were parked outside. Bouncers looked over a steady stream of clubbers as they entered. Joe and Mains joined them.

They waited to be served at the bar.

"The glasses are made from recycled materials," Mains said.

"Right," said Joe.

A bartender cracked open two brown bottles and poured the contents into two plastic glasses.

"They have a rainwater-flush system for the loos," Mains went on.

"Brilliant," Joe said in a deliberately flat voice.

"The lighting is all LEDs. Renewable energy sources."

"This is why you wanted to come here?" A disgusted grimace had settled on Joe's face.

"The best part is over there." Mains turned and pointed toward the dance floor, accidentally brushing the shoulder of the girl next to him, who turned and stared at the two men. "It's a brand new concept," he continued, ignoring the girl, who eventually looked away. "Sustainable Dance Club. Energy from people's feet powers the lights in the dance floor."

Joe concentrated on trying to remain upright. He drank some beer from his recycled plastic glass. Something Mains had said in the restaurant came back to him.

"You know you said grave-robbing is never a good idea?" Joe looked at Mains, whose face was unreadable. "Surely what we're doing is a form of grave-robbing? Adapting the work of a dead man without his approval." Joe finished his beer. "I'm not saying I wouldn't have done the adaptation, offered the chance, but still, eh?"

Mains stared back into Joe's eyes and for a moment Joe thought he had outwitted the scriptwriter.

"I prefer to think of it," Mains said eventually, "as recycling."

Joe held his beady gaze for a second or two, then, with an air about him of someone conceding defeat but slipping a card up his sleeve at the same time, said, "I have some ideas."

"Uh-huh?"

"Mike Nelson."

"The installation artist?"

"Works a lot with abandoned buildings, something Vos told me to keep an eye out for. Plus, he's a fan of Lovecraft. He entitled one of his works *To the Memory of H. P. Lovecraft*. Admittedly he's quoting a dedication from a short story by Borges, but why would he do that if he wasn't a fan?"

"So what about him?" Mains asked.

"Get him on board as production designer. I suggested it to Vos. Do you know what he said? 'Production design's not art, it's craft.'"

Mains appeared to alter the direction of the conversation. "Vos optioned your novel, didn't he?"

Joe nodded.

"You realize if the Lovecraft adaptation gets made it increases the chances of yours going into development?"

Joe nodded again.

"It would make a good movie," Mains added.

"You've read it?" Joe asked before he could stop himself.

"Vos gave me a copy."

Joe felt more conflicted than ever. If Vos had given Mains a copy of his book it could mean he wanted him to adapt it, and whereas Joe would rather write any script himself, the ultimate goal was seeing a film version on the big screen, whoever got the writer's credit.

Joe saw himself buying more beers, which was madness, given how seriously drunk he was by now. He turned around to pass one to Mains, but the writer was not there. The back of his jacket could be seen threading its way between the crowds toward the dance floor.

Joe looked at the beers in his hands.

The rest of the evening was a maelstrom of pounding music, throbbing temples, flashing lights. Grabbed hands, shouted remarks, glimpsed figures. Time became elastic, sense fragmentary, perception unreliable. Joe was aware, while staggering back to the hotel, of feeling so utterly isolated from the rest of the world that he felt alternately tiny and huge in relation to his surroundings. But mainly he was unaware of anything that made any sense; there were pockets, or moments, of clarity like stills from a forgotten film. The giant white swan of the Erasmus Bridge glowing against the night sky. A heel caught between rails as the first tram of the day screeched around a bend in the track. His hotel room—leaning back against the closed door, astonished to be there at all. Looking at his reflection in the bathroom mirror and not being convinced it was his, until he reminded himself this was how a man might look after drinking as much as he had. Cupping water in his hands from the tap, again and again and again. Finally, lying in bed staring at the door and hallucinating one of Antony Gormley's cast-iron figures standing inside the room with its back to the door.

Waking was a slow process of fear and denial, the inside of his head host to a slideshow of rescued images from the night before. Tattooed flesh, strobe lights, red flashes. Someone grabbing hold of his crotch, taking a handful. A mouth full of teeth. The pulsing LEDs in the kinetic dance floor. The Erasmus Bridge. The Gormley figure in his room.

The open window admitted the sounds of traffic on river and road, the city coming to life.

Knowing he would soon be spending a long period of penance in the bathroom, he looked over toward the door. The figure he had thought he had seen just before falling asleep was not there, but there was something not right about that corner of the room. He closed his eyes, but then opened them again to stop his head spinning. There was something on the wall, something that oughtn't to be there. Feeling his gorge begin to rise, he clambered out of bed, naked. To get to the bathroom he had to pass the end of the bed where there was a bit of space between it and the wall opposite. The door was beyond to the left. There was something there on the floor, some kind of dummy or lifesize doll, or a picture of one painted dark rusty red by a child. There was a lot of red paint splashed on the floor and the walls and the end of the bed, but Joe had to get to the bathroom. He threw up in the toilet, his brain processing the images from the floor of the room, against his will. All he wanted to do was be sick and cleanse his system. As he vomited again, a small knot of pain formed toward the front of his skull, increasing in severity in a matter of seconds. He knew he had to go out of the bathroom and have another look at the floor between the wall and the end of the bed, but he didn't want to do so. He was frightened and he didn't understand. What he had seen was just a picture; hopefully it wasn't even there, it was a hallucination, like the figure as he'd lain in bed.

He turned and looked out of the bathroom door. The bedspread had a busy pattern, but even among the geometric shapes, the purples and the blues, lozenges and diamonds, he could see streaks and splashes of a dirty brown.

He crawled to the doorway, his heart thumping, and peered around the corner. He spent a few seconds looking at the thing that lay on the carpet before retreating into the bathroom and being sick again.

He remembered Mains telling him, at the start of the evening, that he hadn't booked a hotel room. Had they come back together? Or had Mains followed him back and had he—Joe—let him in? Or had he broken in? Had the glimpsed figure been the writer, not one of Gormley's cast-iron facsimiles? Or had Mains already been there passed out on the floor while Joe was drifting into sleep in bed, and had the cast-iron man done this to him?

It was no more bizarre an idea than that Joe had done it. Had slashed at the writer's body until it was almost unrecognizable as that of a human being, never mind as that of Mains. There could be little blood left in the vasculature, most of it having soaked into the carpet and bedspread or adhered to the wall in patterns consistent with arterial spray.

Joe inspected his hands. They were clean. Perhaps too clean. His body was unmarked.

Very deliberately, Joe got dressed. Stepping carefully around the body, he left the room and took the lift down to the ground floor. He glanced at the desk staff as he left the hotel, but they didn't look up.

He walked toward the western end of Nieuwe Binnenweg until he found the mix of shops he needed and returned to the hotel with a rucksack containing a sturdy hacksaw, a serrated knife, some cleaning materials, skin-tight rubber gloves, and a large roll of resealable freezer bags. As he stood facing the mirrored wall in the lift to go back up to the fourth floor, he pictured himself as the boys in the bar would have seen him, shouting at Mains. He recalled the waitress in the restaurant, who had been at their table precisely when Joe had been giving Mains a hard time, and then there was the girl by the bar in WATT. The latter part of the time they had spent in the club was a blank. Anything could have happened and anyone could come forward as a witness.

The lift arrived with a metallic ping and Joe got out and walked the short distance to his room. Once inside, he dumped the rucksack and stripped down to his underpants. He slipped his iPod inside the waistband and inserted the earphones into his ears. "Rotterdam" by Githead, on repeat. If it meant he would never again be able to listen to Githead, so be it. Just as he had never been able to listen to *Astral Weeks* since the traumatic break-up with Marie from Donegal, or to Cranes. He'd been to a Cranes gig in Clapham the night before his father had died and every time he tried to listen to any of their albums, it put him right back where he was the morning he got the phone call from his mother.

He moved a towel and bath mat out of the way, then dragged the body into the bathroom and lifted it into the bath, not worrying too much about the smears of blood this left on the floor and the side of the bath. He stood over the bath with the hacksaw in his hand and suddenly perceived himself as Vos might film him, looking up from the corpse's-eye view. He hesitated, then reached for the towel, which he placed over the head and upper torso.

His first job was to cut away the remaining scraps of clothes, which he dumped in the sink, and then he began working at the left wrist, just below the tattoo. The hacksaw blade skittered when it first met substantial resistance. Blood welled from the cut in the flesh and trickled down toward the hand, causing Joe's hand to slip.

In his earphones, the girl vocalist sang, "It's a nice day," over and over.

It took at least five minutes to get through the radius and another minute or so of sawing to work through the ulna. There was a certain grim satisfaction in having removed one of the hands, but the exertion had brought Joe out in a sweat and his head was throbbing. In his dehydrated state, he could little afford to lose further moisture.

He knew that he had a long job ahead of him and that it would never seem any closer to being completed while he was still thinking forward to—and dreading—the hardest part. He sat down on the bathroom floor for a moment, letting his heart rate slow down. He knew what he was about to attempt. He had decided. It was necessary if he was to survive.

It's a nice day.

Taking a breath, Joe shuffled along the floor. He turned around and leaned over the edge, pulling the hem of the towel up to reveal the neck. He placed the serrated edge of the hacksaw blade against the soft skin just below the Adam's apple. A little bit of pressure and the teeth bit into the skin, causing a string of tiny red beads to appear. He leaned into the saw and extended his arm. Back and forth, back and forth. His hand pressing down on the chest and slithering and sliding.

It took a few minutes. He wasn't timing himself. It felt longer. He bagged the head by touch alone, using a plastic carrier from one of the shops on Nieuwe Binnenweg. He recycled one of Mains's shoelaces to tie it shut, then placed it in the sink.

It would be easier now. It could be anyone.

It's a nice day.

At several points over the next two hours, Joe thought he would have to give up. What he was doing was inhuman. If he carried on, he would lose his humanity. Even if he evaded capture, he would never be at peace. But each time he merely restated to himself his determination to survive. Yes, what he was doing was a crime, but it was the only crime he knew for certain he had committed.

The clean-up operation took longer.

It was some time in the afternoon when Joe presented himself at the front desk to settle his bill. The rucksack was on his back, his own bag, bulkier than on arrival, slung over one shoulder. Outside in the street he stopped and looked back. He counted the floors up and along until he spotted his open window. On an impulse, he walked back toward the hotel. There was a poorly maintained raised flower bed between the pavement and the hotel wall. Joe rested his foot on the lip of the bed as if to tie his shoelace and peered into the gaps between the shrubs. At the back, among the rubbish close to the hotel wall, was a broken brown bottle. Joe reached in and his fingers closed around the neck. He placed the bottle in his shoulder bag and walked away.

On a patch of waste ground at the end of one of the docks behind Keileweg, unobserved, he started a small fire with bits of rubbish, locally sourced. When the fire was going well enough to burn a couple of pieces of wood salvaged from the dockside, Joe took Mains's torn and bloodstained clothing from his bag. He dropped the items into the flames, then added Mains's wallet, from which he had already extracted anything of use. The broken bottle, which could have originally been a beer bottle from WATT but equally might not have been, went over the side of the dock.

Satisfied that the fire had done its most important work, Joe left it burning and started walking back toward the city center, the rucksack still heavy on his back.

At a bus stop across the street from where one of Antony Gormley's ubiquitous cast-iron molds stood guard on the roof of another building, Joe caught a bus to Europort and boarded a ferry bound for Hull, using Mains's ticket. The writer would have approved, he thought. When the ticket control had turned out also to involve a simultaneous passport check, a detail he had somehow not anticipated, Joe's heart rate had shot up and a line of sweat had crept from his hair line, but the check had been cursory at best and Joe had been waved on to the boat. He sat out on the rear deck, glad to relieve his shoulders of the weight of the rucksack. With an hour to go before the ferry was due to sail, he watched the sky darken and the various colors of the port lights take on depth, intensity, richness. Huge wind turbines turning slowly in the light breeze, like fans cooling the desert-warmed air of some alien city of the future. Giant cranes squatting over docksides, mutant insects towering over tiny human figures passing from one suspended cone of orange light to the next. Tall, slender flare-stacks, votive offerings to some unknown god. The lights of the edge of the city in the distance, apartment blocks, life going on.

Soon the ferry would slip her mooring and glide past fantastical wharves and gantries, enormous silos and floating jetties. She would navigate slowly away from this dream of the lowlands and enter the cold dark reality of the North Sea, where no one would hear the odd splash over the side in the lonely hours of the night.

Tempting Providence

JONATHAN THOMAS

Jonathan Thomas is the author of numerous short stories that have appeared in Fantasy and Terror, Studies in the Fantastic, *and other magazines. His first short story collection,* Stories from the Big Black House *(Radio Funk, 1992), is a rare collector's item; a second collection,* Midnight Call and Other Stories, *appeared in 2008 from Hippocampus Press.*

USTIN, TILL A MONTH AGO, HAD NEVER EXPECTED to be here again, but three decades and several dead-end career later, he was back as an "honored alumnus," no less. The room, true to memory, was on the scale of a hospital ward, and the walls were a dull aseptic white, typical of countless other gallery spaces. His photos were of "The Beautiful and the Condemned: Parting Shots," and were on a two-week sojourn in Providence between exhibits in Boston and Philly.

From humble beginnings as snapshots of lopsided red barns, his work had evolved into highly polarized, finely etched silver nitrates of charming landscapes, buildings, or neighborhoods about to be bulldozed for development. Their pathos had touched a mainstream nerve somehow, earning him grants, and articles in the *New York Times*, and NPR interviews, and calendar contracts. Meanwhile, the irony of displaying these images someplace that stood atop a former charming site was evidently lost on the faculty, homecoming alum, and students at the opening, bless their uncritical hearts. If his alma mater wanted to show him off as a successful graduate, he guessed he could live with that much boosterism. No, nothing much had changed about the List Art Building since grad school, except he strongly doubted he'd run into the ghost of H. P. Lovecraft tonight.

Justin, in fact, had never set foot in the building after that incident. He'd been offsetting his tuition as a night watchman for Campus Security, and had refused any further assignments there, and what's more, he'd admitted why. And why not? He saw what he saw, and youthful principles dictated he "tell it like it is," in the parlance of the day. True, he'd been reading up on Lovecraft for his Comparative Literature thesis about local-color fantasists, so he knew that Lovecraft's Early American home had been uprooted and towed over the hill to make way for the List Building. Untrue, however, were rumors he'd been on acid, as fabricated by those intent on a "common sense" rationale for any brush with the supernatural. Luckily, suspicions of drug use rendered nobody a pariah at the time, or the entire university population would have been on the outs with itself. Vexing enough that LSD and "some space cadet" figured in every recap overheard at parties, or worse, thrown back in his face by unknowing raconteurs.

In any case, the unvarnished facts had remained in Justin's drug-free head, and one of the more remarkable was that the ghost had behaved exactly as he'd have anticipated. Justin, in baggy blue uniform, had been on midnight rounds in the building and had entered the room where his work would someday surround him. Track lighting with dimmers set extremely low barely alleviated the darkness; there were no windows.

From out of the murk burst someone pacing rapidly, who nearly collided head-on with Justin before performing a last-second about-face and pacing away. Justin had time only to gasp and stumble to a halt, heart thumping, while the trespasser paced toward him and away once more. At second glance, Justin took note of short hair parted on the left above a high forehead, a thin-lipped mouth that seemed small because of a substantial chin, and a gaunt physique in a 1930s suit replete with white shirt and black tie. The similarity to Lovecraft in off-register photos on yellowing newsprint was unmistakable.

In keeping with his fitful stride, the revenant's expression was of confusion and distress, readily understandable in anyone who found himself in a bleak hall where his snug parlor should be, and in someone so skeptical of the spirit world who was suddenly one of its denizens. Trembling Justin drew flashlight from belt holster and asked meekly, and sympathetically he hoped, "Can I help you?"

The ectoplasm must have been too delicate to withstand spoken vibrations. The agitated Lovecraft failed to re-emerge from the shadows. Darting flashlight beam detected no one anywhere in the gallery. Justin hightailed it out of there, pausing only to lock up behind him with unsteady hands. Thus began and ended his sole occult adventure.

None of his instructors or classmates were at the opening. Good! Chances were minimal of having to endure urban legends about himself. By the grace of free wine, though, numerous alum, whether staid and middle-aged or impossibly young, saw fit to buttonhole him on ever more familiar terms. He extended cordial thanks for generic compliments, even when some cranelike dowager pumped his hand and actually exclaimed, "Nice captures!" And what harm in disclosing that he lived in the Catskills, and that he wasn't going to the "big game" tomorrow against Princeton because he hated football? Or that he was staying on Benefit Street at a Victorian bed-and-breakfast, yes, every bit as quaint and genteel as it sounded, maybe a little rich for his blood in fact. Did he travel with his family? He'd been twice married in haste and divorced at leisure, thanks for asking. "Irreconcilable differences of standards and values," he explained, "but everyone's amicable. The exes are too humane to try squeezing alimony from a stone. Anyway, no children, thank God!" Was Justin coming off as brusque? No matter, if it kept tipsy parents from bragging about their overachiever kids. He'd been hitting the wine himself, after all, and was at the point of wishing Lovecraft's ghost would reappear, if only to light a fire under this whitebread crowd.

Aha, someone with whom Justin needed a word was crossing his line of vision. Dr. Palazzo, head of the Pictorial

Arts division and a darling of *ARTnews* and its slick-paper ilk, was homing in on a few equally overdressed attendees. Sturdy Dr. Palazzo exuded brash corporate airs in powder-blue three-piece suit, yellow tie, and wavy silver hair too majestic to be real. Had he ever in his life so much as handled a crayon? He came across as governor of a military occupation, but Justin steeled himself and essayed an engaging smile. Reimbursement for lodgings had been a condition before Justin agreed to wedge this fortnight into his itinerary at the last minute. The exhibit would otherwise have gone into storage at his Boston or Philadelphia venues, and he'd have been home resting up days ago. Typo-laden e-mails from the gallery director promised that only the formality of Palazzo's signature stood between Justin and repayment, but he had yet to hear a straight answer about that after a full day in town.

Justin flagged Palazzo down and introduced himself. Palazzo congratulated him on the show without acting especially impressed. He was clearly en route to more important conversations. Justin presented his case with all due tact, while ruminating that the sum in question wouldn't have bought one of Palazzo's shoes. Palazzo's curt advice was to discuss petty cash with the gallery director.

"She referred me to you," claimed Justin, a shade archly.

"I can't do anything right now." Oh? That much "petty cash," and then some, was probably wadded up in Palazzo's back pocket.

"Why don't I drop by your office Monday morning? What time is convenient for you?" Justin swallowed a belch an instant before it was too late.

"You'll have to call my secretary." Palazzo rushed off before Justin could say anything else.

The gallery director had been across the room all along, but Justin didn't want to make her evening any worse. She looked like hell. Curly brunette strands were stuck to her clammy brow, her eyes were bulging, and she was dividing frazzled attention between a cell phone and the micromanagement of slowpoke undergrads in catering uniforms. Dr. Palazzo, meanwhile, was hobnobbing with the impeccable few, as if nobody else were around. Justin downed one more plastic goblet of Chablis and slunk out and down the hill to Benefit Street.

He awoke in a sweat under a fleece comforter. Between the cushy down-filled mattress and the hiss of a radiator going full blast before Columbus Day, he felt decadent as much as overheated. He also felt he might have been a bit uncharitable toward last night's attendees, and even Dr. Palazzo. He couldn't, in fairness, object if the lives of others led them to perspectives different from his own.

According to bedside digital clock, it was earlier than he thought. He could still catch the tail-end of breakfast. He rolled out of bed and into the bedraggled, off-balance aftermath of more plastic goblets than he cared to tally. In the dining room downstairs, the other guests had come and gone, and the staff had yet to clear the self-serve table. Justin grabbed three cups of coffee to be sure they'd be there when he wanted them, along with croissants and orange juice. The second cup was lukewarm, but did the trick. His frilly surroundings became sunnier, and he gamely conceded that even if they were overly precious, they attracted the clientele without whom this address might devolve into one of his silver nitrates. Justin had been pleased to find the East Side pretty much as he'd left it, thus far at least, including Geoff's Sandwiches, still in business across the street. Or did it use to be Joe's?

Justin had wisely packed an okay digital camera, to make the best of imposed leisure. The B&B counted homecoming as a "special weekend" and obliged him to book three nights, which was just as well, in view of Monday morning business. At a whim, he headed south on gloriously unchanging Benefit

Street, and at the first major intersection spotted a white cardboard rectangle taped below a "No Left Turn" sign. Big black letters proclaimed "Alumni Tent," with an arrow pointing up the curve of Waterman Street. The phrase put Justin in mind of a circus, and despite the low odds of reality bearing him out, he opted to go see what was what.

The street skirted the drab, postwar School of Design campus and the List Building again and the venerable Main Green of the university, and at the corner of shopping-strip Thayer Street another white placard directed him one block farther, where an arrow sent him north. He winced at vinyl siding on historic walls in a neighborhood that should have known better, and then smiled. A circus tent indeed dominated the little urban meadow of Pembroke Field. Clusters of red, white, and brown balloons bobbed at the tent entrance and along the chain-link fence around the field.

The illusion of a Big Top dissolved as soon as Justin trudged amidst a gaggle of merry old graduates through the gate. Demographically, he was back at the gallery opening, only with a much stronger turnout here, and the addition of many babies in strollers. A guy in a cartoonish bear costume was posing for photos with happy couples. Justin was mildly amused at his inability to look upon the jaunty mascot without thinking "narc." Name tags adhered to the majority of sweaters and jackets, and sociable babel emanated from a dining area where a pregame box brunch was underway. The "Alumni Pub" was doing a lively business, and Justin vetoed the passing thought of a beer to wash down breakfast.

These people were having fun, and more power to them, but black loneliness latched onto him and gnawed deeper, the longer he steeped himself in the festivities. He had a master's degree from this school, and every right to be here, and had come at departmental behest, hadn't he? But he wasn't feeling particularly "honored," and suspected that the Gallery Director's invitation to him had somehow fueled bad politics between her and Palazzo. He also suspected that somebody sooner or later would notice him languishing in solitary discomfort and ask him to leave. He needed no outside confirmation that he didn't belong. Out on the sidewalk, he breathed easier.

He retreated to Thayer Street, and his eyes widened in immediate dismay. Damn his vivid recollections! A dorm complex with red and green brick façade, like a dull-witted kid's Lego project, had replaced a row of classic Victorian mansions, mansard roofs and gingerbread eaves and all. He continued down Thayer and wished he could stop himself. He remembered a second-hand bookshop notorious for buying stolen collections, and a locksmith whose illegal dupes of dorm keys abetted countless student flings, and a hole-in-the-wall deli where a grouchy octogenarian sold expired yogurt and treated the customer like a sissy for not eating it, gray fuzz and all. These and other upwellings of robust personality had no latter-day counterparts. Clothing and restaurant chains were in ascendancy, some chichi, some tacky, but all with deep pockets to absorb the likely sky-high rents. Something he didn't recall was the excessive number of trust fund babies out making fashion statements. He had meager faith in the survival of a record store, a pizza joint, and a few other mom-and-pop operations beyond their next lease renewals. To discover a new generation of panhandlers in front of Store 24 was heartening, though he wasn't about to waste any cash on them. A little scruffiness, a little waywardness remained of the Runyonesque street of his less uptight era. That was the kindest spin he could manage.

Thayer outside the commercial strip was even more appalling. His mental map contained a neighborhood with attractive houses, a popular breakfast place, a clothier who specialized in dated formalwear, and a corner grocer's—Boar's Head Market, wasn't it? Progress, or science, or capitalism, if any distinction applied in this context, had rolled over all of it, and on its dust the university had installed gigantic barracks of lab facilities and gussied-up bunkers of congested dorms. Regrets about hanging his work anywhere on this overreaching campus were weighing more heavily on him. He was glad Lovecraft couldn't see any of this pox of oppressive architecture. Or could he? What was a ghost, and what was the extent of its awareness, its powers of observation? Justin's mind wandered aimlessly in and out of these meditations, while his feet led him back to the solace of Benefit Street. He was sure now only of what he had been sure of all along: he had not been on hallucinogens, that night in List.

He ordered lunch at Geoff's, where sandwiches bore the names of local celebs, none of whom rang a bell. He took his Antoinette Downing a few blocks north, into the secluded old graveyard behind the stately Episcopal cathedral. Poe had courted Sarah Helen Whitman here, and Justin thought he'd read somewhere that Lovecraft had done likewise with his fiancée Sonia. He tried reviving the tradition one night while dating his first wife-to-be, till a humorless geezer cradling a yappy pug appeared at a window overlooking the churchyard and threatened to call the cops on them for "scaring everyone half to death." Today Justin sat on a tabletop sarcophagus off to one remote side and ate in peace. For all he knew, the humorless geezer was buried somewhere in here.

At the B&B again, he slept all afternoon under the fleece comforter, without breaking a sweat. His eyes opened to the waning hour when the outlines of things softened, though he could still navigate by natural light. He retained no contents of any dreams, yet was firmly convinced he'd been dreaming. Or more precisely, he had the sensation of something external impinging on his sleeping self, which, according to received wisdom, had altered the course of those dreams he'd otherwise forgotten. Room service? Intruders? He gave the bedroom a wary once-over and switched on the bedside lamp. Neither his duffel nor the items on top of his bureau showed signs of disturbance. He was picking up none of the eerie vibes he imagined would accompany a haunting. If he couldn't shake the feeling of having been watched, then he'd sensibly ascribe it to pigeons on the windowsill.

What he needed now was to get out and walk, preferably in the direction of supper. He had done nothing to work up an appetite, but hunger pangs and a nervous energy were prodding him toward the door. The East Side had depressed him enough for one day. Grabbing the camera, he headed west, confident of eating well on Federal Hill.

A Holiday Inn on the far side of downtown doubled as a gigantic, informal welcome sign to the Hill, luckily for Justin. Traversing the business district, he felt like a rat in a water-maze. His most substantial old landmarks were proving ephemeral. A puny three decades had obliterated railroad trestles, a Civil War monument, a huge department store, the bus station, and a sprawling annex of the state university. He peevishly navigated around the multiple sore thumbs of upstart high-rises and was never happier to be making steady headway toward a shamelessly box-like hotel. He hadn't planned on going in, but there he was at the desk, asking an aloof clerk about the availability of rooms on Monday. Not a problem, allegedly. All the college types in town for girls' hockey or whatever were checking out tomorrow. Justin said he might be back, and the clerk grunted and re-entrenched himself in a sudoku book.

Like a great X marking the spot, a four-membered arch now spanned the beginning of Atwells Avenue. By way of keystone it featured an outsize bronze pinecone, or maybe a pineapple.

He rejoiced at recognizing the Old Canteen and Blue Grotto, evocative fixtures from yesteryear, and still prosperous. But on his budget, he was more delighted about the warm light from the windows at Angelo's. Inside, the tin ceiling and white enamel tables and the menus nailed like eye charts to big square support posts conceivably looked the same as in 1971 or 1931. And at 5:30, he had his pick of the seats. A chipper waitress called him "sweetie" as she placed his order for sausage, peppers, and French fries, with a glass of the house red. No knots of fat or gristle were hiding in the sausage, the clear outer skin sloughed right off the peppers, and the fries had entered the kitchen as fresh potatoes. The burgundy wasn't bad, either. Justin tapped the bottom of the glass to coax the last drops into his mouth, and pushed away from the table, contented, and thought, This is the good life for me. Should that be so hard? Plus, Justin had beaten the dinner crunch! He left a nice tip and continued up Atwells.

Bewilderment made his steps drag at times. What had happened to the solidly Italian enclave of yesteryear? Chinese and Caribbean takeouts, a nouveau hippie coffee house, an Indian eatery felt incongruous, as if plunked down by some cosmic joker. And where to go from here? The night was in its infancy. If he wasn't mistaken, one of the Lovecraft sites mentioned in his thesis was a few blocks away. Maybe the Historical Society had bolted a commemorative plaque to its door by now.

Justin gradually sped up from minute to minute, till he identified the silhouette of a church across a tiny courtyard. He peered more closely and harrumphed. No, this wasn't it. Too recent, and too wholesome for a horror yarn. And he had gone too far. He was well over the hilltop and halfway down to Olneyville, if memory served. This, unlike the locale in the story, wouldn't be visible from Lovecraft's address on College Hill.

He backtracked. How had he missed an entire church? He

had a bad feeling about an open space at the corner of Sutton Street. The sidewalk widened into a modest plaza, with an ash-gray disk embedded at its center. He glossed its incised text by streetlight, and by the third line was too incensed to follow the rest. Since its founding in 1875, the Catholic church of St. John had been important to "many ethnic groups" and in local working-class history.

Then in 1994 it was demolished. Just like that. Persons unknown to him had designated the resultant vacant lot a park and relinquished it as a "gift to the city."

Disgusted, Justin glared past the plaza and the remnant church steps toward a curb-bound circle of dirt with sparse patches of defeated-looking grass. On the outer perimeter was one park bench, paintless, with a number of broken slats. To its left, springing mushroom-like from the soil, was a pair of cement tables with inlaid checkerboards, flanked by three and four cement chairs, respectively. These furnishings wore a thick coat of rust-orange paint, which reinforced an appearance of being salvaged from a fast-food chain. So even in 1990s Providence, a repository of clear-cut neighborhood and literary value could come to this. What good would it do, though, to burst a blood vessel over other people's disordered priorities?

A wire fence behind the bench denoted one edge of the property. Beyond were three tenements: beige, with flat roof; blue, with pitched roof; and green, with hipped roof. A powerful security light between the uppermost windows in the blue house cast a surprising level of brightness on the park grounds. From stark shadow in back of the checker tables, somebody was careering straight at him. Getting mugged would be the perfect finish for a day like today!

Justin was too stunned to utter a sound and grew faint at a face-to-face glimpse of his assailant, who suddenly U-turned away into the darkness. He stood motionless as the restive ghost of H. P. Lovecraft strode out of the shadows again and beckoned earnestly at arm's-length perigee before withdrawing once more. On Lovecraft's third approach, Justin's professional reflexes nudged him into raising his camera, popping the lens cap, and shooting a rapidfire sequence. His hands were trembling, but at least the automatic flash didn't scare off Lovecraft the way his voice had. In fact, the apparition paused longer and beckoned more demandingly. Maybe verbal communication would work this time. His hands became steadier as he continued to shoot. He gazed through the viewfinder upon Lovecraft's forlorn expression and felt sorry for him, and was at a loss for words. Nonetheless, he wasn't about to follow anyone's ghost into blind obscurity. Lovecraft, a little sadder it seemed, turned on his heel and did not return a fourth time.

Justin lowered the camera and self-consciously checked hither and yon. No other pedestrians were around, and the occasional motorist had tooled by as if nothing unusual was going on. Moreover, the inner-city scene was getting to him now more than when a ghost was flitting through it, because the security light, which must have had some finicky sort of motion sensor, had gone out, to swamp everything beyond the church steps in uneasy mystery.

Justin was shaken, of course, and perplexed, but as he stooped to grope against the paving stones and miraculously find his discarded lens cap, he realized he was also famished as if he'd never had supper, and more antsy than ever, as if some long-awaited desire were near fulfillment. But what did he have in the offing that wouldn't pale beside the sight of a spirit? He had no conscious inkling, and concluded he was too hungry and overwrought for his mind to be doing right by him.

The dinner crunch was just ending as he re-entered Angelo's. His previous table was available, and the chipper waitress remarked that he must really like the food here. He chose the gnocchi because nothing else would be as filling, with sides of rabe and eggplant parm and a half-carafe of the red. The waitress beamed as if gluttony were admirable and called him "sugar." If he looked like he'd seen a ghost, she didn't make anything of it.

And what about the ghost? Justin was in the hapless middle of an emotional pileup, dazed, indignant, intrigued, anxious, excited. Still, his thoughts kept looping back to certain vagaries of what he'd witnessed. He attacked his food and pondered how the ectoplasmic Lovecraft had successfully crossed town but upon arrival was confined, with a single variation in gesture, to performing exactly the same motions as in the List Building. Ghosts might be prone to stereotypy, but that seemed too glib an answer.

Nor was Sutton Street where Justin would have staged a rendezvous if he were in Lovecraft's position. True, the church of St. John had some importance as a story setting, but to Justin's knowledge Lovecraft had only seen it from a few miles' distance. Any number of places closer to home must have been more meaningful to him. Why not materialize at one of those? And why Justin? Twice? Whatever the unquiet spirit wanted, countless others had to be better qualified to help. Yet he'd never heard of Lovecraft haunting anyone else.

He regarded his three clean plates and empty decanter. Everything had been tasty, he'd swear to that, but he couldn't remember consuming any of it. He'd eaten like one possessed. Fortunately, none of the other customers were staring as if he'd been boorish about it.

He got a cannoli to sweeten the return trek through downtown. The ricotta filling burst through cracks in the pastry casing, so his hands were a mess when it finally hit him that he could review all his occult images in-camera this very second, while walking down the street. Going digital was about to pay off already! He stopped himself an inch away from smearing expensive technology with sticky fingerprints. Back in the B&B, he fastidiously washed and dried his hands, but afterward scarcely had the energy to undress before toppling into bed, as if someone somewhere had thrown a lever and cut off his jitters of the last few hours. The pictures would wait.

The heat in his room next morning bordered on stifling, and an unpleasant hint of scorched mold laced the air, a byproduct of antique steam pipes, Justin reckoned. He also awoke with a heightened perception of being an outsider, of not belonging, an echo of what he'd felt at Pembroke Field yesterday, but he connected it now in some dreamtime logic with the excessive heat. Was the management trying to drive him off with too much of a good thing? He opened the window some and discovered that the radiator beneath it was cold. So was the one in the bathroom. Had the warmth wafted up through the floor? These old buildings usually had their anomalies. On the positive side, he was up in plenty of time for breakfast. How fortuitous, seeing as last night's insistent hunger was homing in on him again. And the sooner he was out of the room, the better. Camera in hand, he noted that the corridor was downright chilly. Happily, he'd left the fungal scent behind.

On the last flight of stairs before the foyer, the distinctive rumble of an oil truck reached his ears. A mature woman with bobbed reddish hair and bulky green sweater turned to him from the partly open front door. Justin guessed her to be one of the owners, because she apologized for the furnace running out of fuel in the night. "Not a problem. Please don't give it a thought," he replied without slowing down.

He staked out the table nearest the breakfast bar and pounced at the eggs and sausage and bacon that rewarded early risers. He may have cut off rival guests when going for extra platefuls; he could only vouch for moving faster than whoever else was en route at the same time. To discourage any challenges over his right to multiple helpings, he scowled needlessly at the goateed kid on inattentive duty.

Between every course, he re-examined his new series of shots, as if enough squinting would flush out what he wanted to see. According to his feckless camera, Lovecraft was purely a hallucination, invisible in blurry and sharp exposures alike. The security light upon the blue wall, however, exerted an inordinate presence. It consisted of three bulbs in an upside-down triangle, and though he'd gazed into its glow last night with impunity, in pinpoint reproductions it was burning bright, painfully so within seconds. More inexplicably, it remained in tripartite clarity even when the rest of the frame was smudgy. And toward the end of the sequence, the bulbs were plainly larger, or perhaps in the process of sneaking closer. They weren't playing by the rules of optics in any case, but there his patience for analysis ended. His eyes roved dully over the dwindling contents of chafing dishes. He could always consign more servings to the bottomless pit, but had felt no more satisfied after the last couple. He was becoming too fidgety to stay any longer.

Today's morning walk differed markedly from yesterday's. It proceeded north along Benefit Street and wasn't recreational. Justin wasn't sure yet what it was, but he was averse to letting nostalgia or disappointment enter into it again. Four cups of coffee did not in themselves account for the high-strung nerves that required he range across the landscape, and half a mile of Georgian and Federal elegance was behind him before he understood he was in pursuit of something. Where Benefit merged with North Main, and only dreary new shopping centers and prefab apartments and "professional buildings" lay ahead, he swerved right, up Olney Street. He wasn't out to take stock of his surroundings, but the wrong ones, he sensed, would ill suit his purposes, whatever they were. At the hectic intersection with Hope Street, he marveled that Tortilla Flats, the one Mexican bistro in town way back when, had survived a third of a century. For other than old time's sake, he tried the door. He was now willing to have another go at breakfast, but they weren't open yet.

He forged on, into neighborhoods of Colonial Revival mansions and wedding-cake Victoriana and prim bungalows and rundown triple-deckers that still had more character than anything constructed in Justin's lifetime. Not till he was deep in a terra incognita of broad avenues and manorial pretenses did he grasp that Lovecraft, or his unbodily likeness, had some bearing on this obscure mission. Much keener was his awareness that it must have been lunchtime, and he in a gilded wasteland as far as restaurants were concerned.

Subjective, hungry ages elapsed before he chanced upon a busy artery, with the brackish Seekonk River to the east, and westward, a cluster of businesses. It was dimly familiar, and on its outskirts the words Wayland Square popped into his head after thirty-five years of disuse. Historically it had been an "exclusive" retail hub for the old money, but Justin at present had eyes only for the black and yellow sign that read Minerva's Pizza.

At the cash register, a gray, spindly gent with a gravelly voice told Justin to sit where he liked. A table up front afforded him a view of the sunny street through an expanse of plate glass. Apparently churchgoers didn't come here for Sunday dinner, and none of the homecoming set were in evidence either. Some kids from a prep-school track meet, to judge by the uniforms, were lunching with their families, and that was about it.

He scanned the menu for whatever promised to contain the most meat, and under Subs he gravitated to Steak and Cheese. His cravings and his restlessness were no more subject to free will than were his eyes, drawn irresistibly to the movement on the screen above the mirrored bar. The sound was muted, and the kitchen crew had forgotten the TV was on. How else to explain why nobody changed the channel? Outdoorsmen were fishing in some Deep South cypress swamp, and Justin couldn't imagine a more tedious contest of man against nature. Nonetheless, he had to watch until there was a sandwich to devour. He didn't notice who brought it. But while he bit off and chewed mouthfuls, his mind's eye kept harking back to close-ups of the bait in taunting play, back and forth, back and forth, just below the leaf-strewn surface. He knew he'd seen the like somewhere lately, and it nagged at him and eluded him and made him put down his sandwich and think.

Then the revelation pitched him into momentary vertigo. His putative Lovecraft had shared in the abridged range of motion, the repetition, the agitated beckoning. If ghost he really was, he was under some duress, but of what nature and to what end? Lovecraft, or his puppeteer, had coaxed Justin to follow. That same hidden agency was implicated, coincidentally or not, in firing up Justin's feral appetite and joyless wanderlust. He dared not conjecture further without more to go on. He was in too vulnerable a mood.

His hands had raised the Steak and Cheese halfway to his mouth. He forced himself to put it down again and stared out the window to take his mind off food while he tried to concentrate. Justin's one conceivable source of information to tie together Lovecraft, the two places where he'd seen Lovecraft, and some background on those places was the novelette by Lovecraft himself. But how to get hold of it on short notice, and what was it called, anyway? His eyes were scrutinizing storefronts across the street, as if that would help. Then he laughed out loud and wolfed the rest of his sandwich and a handful of chips with a rush of new determination. In what was once a branch post office, a fanlight-spanned masonry façade. Fanciful lower-case letters in each of its trapezoidal panes spelled out "Myopic Books."

He strode to the cash register without waiting for anyone to bring the check, and was almost out the door before he reversed course and stuck $20 in singles under his water glass. If this manic energy refused to let him alone, maybe he could at least channel it for his own good.

He reined himself in after sprinting up Myopic's front steps. No point in alarming people with a dramatic entrance! The layout was uncommonly airy for a used bookshop. A fetching girl with long black hair and disarming eyes was online at the desk, presumably filling mail orders. She escorted him to the horror section, a free-standing bookcase in a far corner. What jaw-dropping luck! A Lovecraft omnibus stood on top of the case, beside a slipcovered set of Tolkien. "Looks like you found what you wanted," she said.

He had her ring it up and asked if she'd mind him reading it on the premises. She shook her head. "We're open till six." At second glance, she was simply rendering realpolitik its due. A couple of bearded duffers were ensconced in comfy chairs by a coffee table, noses deep between covers. They gave off a vibe of barnacles. Toward the rear wall, he settled into a barber's chair, upholstered in chiffon green. He strove for a semblance of composure, though inwardly he was on a breathless hunt.

His hunch to skim through last stories first proved correct. An allusion to Federal Hill guided him to the title "The Haunter of the Dark," and he resolved to peruse carefully, to stay on track from word to word, despite his jumpiness. In barest outline, a Midwestern visitor to the East Side blunders into mental linkage with a hostile alien while inspecting vestiges of a grisly cult in a deserted Atwells Avenue church. Justin had read the tale before, but so long ago that this amounted to the first time all over again. His reactions, too, were bound to be different now from when his interests were merely academic.

He had to stop sometimes and bathe his eyes in the calming

brightness around him, to divert his racing thoughts from premature conclusions. The protagonist's dread of "something which would ceaselessly follow him with a cognition that was not physical sight" reminded Justin of those hypothetical unseen trespassers during yesterday's nap. And concerning the "unholy rapport he felt to exist between his mind and that lurking horror," why wouldn't that express itself as the insatiable hunger and compulsive restlessness which even now tried to unseat him, and in which he was no willing participant?

He pushed on through the text. More stubborn efforts led only to graver intimations. The victim's despair at "a strengthening of the unholy rapport in his sleep" reminded Justin of how displaced and, yes, alienated he'd felt first thing that morning, and when the hero later stirs from a mesmeric daze in the church and inhales a "stench where a hot, searing blast beat down against him," Justin recalled the heat in his room, and the stink of burnt mold, after a night without oil in the furnace. He felt hemmed in by the pages and looked out the narrow window in front of him, but it was half blocked off by foreign-language dictionaries, and beyond the glass was an antitheft steel latticework, with a claustrophobically nearby brick wall filling the view. Justin dove back into the book on his lap.

The narration laid increasing emphasis on the malign entity's intolerance of light, and Justin had to nod in tentative agreement, since both his Lovecraftian experiences had occurred after dark. Finally he reached the diary excerpts recording the hero's semi-coherent desperation as his nemesis closed in. The climactic image of "the three-lobed burning eye" turned Justin's stricken musings to the camera hanging from his neck, and its documentation of the church site's security light with its three glaring bulbs and disregard for the way objects should take shape in photographs. And in retrospect, how disquieting that the lights had gone out after Justin activated his flash! He twisted his head away from the book, toward a wider window to his left. The shop had a flagstone patio out back, where the blooms on a hydrangea and the leaves of a virginicus were already brown. Must have been nice here in summer! He wondered if he'd live to see it, then grimaced at himself for turning morbid on such a flimsy basis.

The sunshine happened to fade before his eyes. How long had he been in that chair? Had the overhead fluorescent been humming like that all along? He stood too fast and everything spun for several heartbeats. Stiff and creaky legs carried him to the desk, and he started framing an apology for loitering till the last minute. The barnacles had vacated their comfy furniture! A bad sign, but the wall clock above the desk was a tad shy of 5:15. He relaxed a bit and thanked the fetching girl for being very helpful, and hoped his long-term occupancy hadn't been a problem. "As long as nobody heard you snoring," she assured him.

Out on the sidewalk, he slid his purchase into a big inside pocket of his denim jacket. Desires to eat and roam plagued him again. Minerva's was right there, and a large meatball calzone stood out as the shortest wait for the most protein, with the added virtue of portability.

He headed down Angell Street and wondered how far he'd get before tearing the wrapper off dinner. Past the first bend in the road, the green and white sign for a Newport Creamery loomed over him. One more youthful hangout he'd forgotten for decades! Too bad he hadn't scouted ahead; a burger plate and sundae sounded good. Then he saw that nothing was left but the sign. Streetlight penetrated sheet glass sufficiently to indicate an interior gutted of booths, counter, stools, freezer cases and all.

But in the distant recesses, people were moving around, unhindered by gloom, animated, at arm's length from each other.

The more he studied them, the less shadowy they became, as if Justin must have been wrong about the dearth of illumination back there, and they seemed closer than at first. Momentarily in lambent glow he beheld a frail, gaunt oldster presiding over a table of deferential young men. He wore a dark suit of thirties vintage that seemed on the verge of falling apart at the seams, and he retained enough thin white hair to part on the left. His chin projected well ahead of his delicate mouth, into which he was spooning a banana split with laudable gusto when he wasn't offering an opinion. His audience had shoulder-length hair and turtleneck shirts and flared jeans, and were patently not the youth of today.

Back when researching his thesis, he'd woven trivia about Lovecraft and this stretch of Angell into wistful daydreams centering on this restaurant. At seeing them converted into three dimensions, he fought a lump in his throat. Opposite the Creamery hulked a typically boring apartment complex of the fifties, and adding injury to insult, for its sake the beautiful birthplace of H. P. Lovecraft had been destroyed. In the young Justin's reveries of a better Providence, Lovecraft had not been struck down in middle age, overdue royalties had let him regain his ancestral home in the nick of time, and his legendary taste for ice cream frequently enticed him, in his fragile but genial eighties, to cross the street and hold court in the Creamery with Justin's horror-fan contemporaries. Justin still cherished that daydream, and to gaze into its world, not only parallel but long defunct, made him weak with yearning, and his lower lip trembled.

He blinked away tears. The kids at the table were regarding him with anticipation, as if he had agreed to come palaver with them, and the ancient Lovecraft was graciously waving him in. Justin gulped. Who, me? But the door ought to be locked. He stepped over and tugged at the handle. He saw and felt it start to heave open, yet could see through it, at the same time, to a door that wasn't budging, as expected.

Justin let go and shuddered, and his melancholy reddened into anger. What would have happened if he'd set foot across that phantom portal? Lovecraft and the boys were still hopeful of his company. Justin grabbed his camera, stowed the lens cap, and turned on the flash. Not now, not ever had he seen Lovecraft's ghost, but only this soulless effigy. Absurd to suppose a spirit would age posthumously! And what about this coterie of ghost hippies? Whatever was pulling the strings here either thought little of Justin's intellect or had major limitations in its own.

Justin raised the camera. The tableau most likely wouldn't leave a record, but why not see what would? And if something sinister, and photophobic, were trailing him, this was the least he could do. He aimed and shot a sequence. When he lowered the camera, the interior was dim and empty again.

His appetite, however, was unabated. The calzone was reduced to grease on his fingertips, for all the restraint he could summon, blocks away from Benefit Street. Furthermore, knowing that his surplus energy derived from some ominous, furtive source was of no help in suppressing it. He could, at best, shut himself in his room and ride the frazzling current toward a better understanding of whatever was hounding him.

He washed his beefy-smelling hands, flopped into bed, plucked the remote off the nightstand, and turned on the TV. He used whatever began yacking at him as a subliminal anchor to normality, while he examined his series from the Creamery.

Naturally, his was the only human form throughout, camera masking his face, as reflected in the brilliance of the flash upon plate glass. Inside, trackless dust between bare walls showed faintly. All the way back, a rear door opened onto the Deco brick row of Medway Street. That he had to take on faith, because a substantial area within the vague doorway contained three scorching orange discs in triangular arrangement. The security light had followed him to Wayland Square!

After a bout of hot sweat and nausea, Justin noted with perverse satisfaction that a meager five minutes in bed were yielding valuable insights. Lovecraft and anyone with him were figments planted in his mind. The "three-lobed burning eye" was not. And the sentience behind that eye and those figments had even more invasive access to the mind of man, or to Justin's at least, than it had in the story.

As he spooled through the sequence, the "lobes" hovered unwavering, as if in wait. On finer inspection, though, they weren't exactly framed by the door but overlapped it, so that they seemed to shine from vastly farther away than the door, yet were inside the building at the same time.

In the last image, all that changed. The eye, in predictable reaction to the flash, had departed, but in its place was not the formerly hidden portion of doorway. A circular hole was floating there, and not a vacant one. A pattern informed the murky grayness, as of braided strands of dirty smoke or striations in muscle tissue. The printed page had implied a winged and cloudlike entity skulking in the church. Here was a glimpse of detail, intriguing, disturbing, but equally uninformative in practical terms. It was, in fact, petrifying to linger over that fingerprint-sized window onto inexpressibly remote and strange conditions. Justin started feeling dizzy, as if on the brink of physically tumbling into that tiny gateway.

Look away! On television, a silver-whiskered park ranger was calf-deep in reedy wetland, lecturing on the ecology of the Blackstone Valley. A local cable production, Justin surmised. The visuals switched to fishermen flycasting from a grassy riverbank. They jogged his thoughts back to the TV in the pizzeria, and to the bait wiggling on the hook.

Different bait for different fish, he thought, then thought further, depending on the neural circuitry and genetics and much else of which the fish had no clue. And yes, depending also on the mood of the fish. Was his predicament the upshot of being the right person in the right mood, in his case of withdrawal and loneliness, broadcasting a signal from the right place at the right time, perhaps when the stars were right," as Lovecraft put it? Was there a species of angler, a predator whose range was of dimensions rather than miles, receptive to that signal? In that angler's continuum, had that first incident in List happened scant moments ago? If only he could recapture what his mood had been before he'd first sighted Lovecraft. Had he been troubled, depressed, tense? He drew a total blank. In respect to emotions, it may as well have been a stranger in that baggy uniform.

But in common with his younger self, and with Lovecraft too, there was Providence. Justin had never encountered ghosts and aliens elsewhere. And perhaps he could also share with Lovecraft the distinction of being the same kind of fish, in a manner of speaking. Minutiae cluttering his brain for half a lifetime were paying their rent at last! In letter or essay, Lovecraft had reported seeing nymphs and satyrs under the oaks in his backyard during his childhood, and at this time of year. If he'd tried to join them, would he have met the fate Justin had narrowly escaped tonight? Plenty of people disappeared forever, without motive or signs of foul play, from their home streets or front porches. Wasn't there an author, Charles Fort, who based his whole career on compiling hundreds of such cases?

The angler had most definitely made an impression on Lovecraft, subconsciously or not, and a line or two in his mountain of correspondence might testify to that. In one aspect, Lovecraft had been among the lucky ones, insofar as timing and placement and mental state had never combined to block his path with irresistible temptations and a hole in space. How much longer would that luck have held out if Lovecraft hadn't died at forty-six? Had a "Damned Thing" of sorts eventually ambushed the elderly Ambrose Bierce in Mexico? Would even Charles Fort have gone out on that limb to explain Bierce's disappearance?

Justin had to blame the driven presence in his head for the ideas bubbling up so furiously. He'd generally be nodding off by this stage of the evening. His skin, meanwhile, crawled at visions of what had fastened on him. He felt violated, unclean, as at louse or ringworm infestation. Not that he was in immediate danger, for what consolation that offered! As if the barrier between his world and the angler's were a surface of ice on which it impatiently trod, the angler could only lower bait and lure its prey through openings at fixed earthly locations, and at fixed earthly times. As for the sleepwalking toward doom that afflicted the story's character, the entity had needed weeks, and not paltry days, to impose that much influence, if those episodes were ever more than Lovecraft's dramatic invention.

Justin would be leaving town by Tuesday, one way or another. Though his worries had ballooned to a grander order of magnitude over the weekend, he did have business tomorrow with Palazzo. It had seemed so pressing Friday night, without entering into his considerations since. Better late than never, he tried mapping out a plan of attack, how he'd parry attempts by Palazzo or his secretary at the runaround. But the aggressive current was rapidly ebbing from his body, and before he could exploit its sputtering last, he was asleep, fully clothed on top of the blankets, TV nattering through the night.

His eyes opened at the customary 7 a.m. The room temperature was normal for once. However, he needed a minute to remember his age, and what year it was. The public access channel was airing a community bulletin board to the accompaniment of jazz fusion. The remote control still rested on his stomach. He flipped to a so-called morning news program, for the short while he could stand the medley of fluff and atrocities. He gave up during reportage of one more missing pregnant wife and of unfaithful husband under suspicion, when he couldn't tell in which category it belonged. Nagging hunger and raw nerves were in remission, as if they'd been a weekend-long dream. The entity had relented, or the stars had ceased to be right. Either way, Justin could tackle his last B&B breakfast strictly for the sake of returning well nourished and caffeinated to the List Building.

He ate, packed, checked out, and hastened to the parking lot behind the inn. The management probably wasn't sorry to see him go. His dingy '85 Dodge van could only detract from any ambience they intended to cultivate. Yet for all the patches of gray undercoat where cobalt blue paint had flecked off, and rust damage like a row of ragged buttonholes between the front and back wheels, and other cosmetic shortcomings, the old Ram refused to die, and it wasn't in him to junk it. But at his first eyeful of it in days, he winced with the shock of seeing it as others did. Blessedly, that passed as soon as he was in the driver's seat. He was out the gate at a commendable 8:45.

Some forethought before confronting Palazzo would have been preferable, but last night he was too exhausted, and now he was busy navigating. Resigned to winging it, he parked alongside the List Building. So where in all this cement did the division head hole up? The gallery attendant dislodged her designer-punk self from a semiotics primer and answered him audibly the second time. There was an elevator, but climbing the fire stairs to Palazzo's floor possibly delivered more oxygen to Justin's brain.

The door beside the room number was open. Into the breach! This could have been the anteroom of any dentist or accountant, save for the pricier art on ivory-white walls. The trophies included Lichtenstein, Ben Shahn, David Hockney. Justin stopped there. Conspicuous enough consumption for his blood. The receptionist wore tortoiseshell glasses and her brown hair in a bun, and would have looked bookish apart from an ingrained pout. He requested an appointment sometime that day with Palazzo. She didn't know if he'd be in or not and didn't bother asking what his business was, which made him suspect that Palazzo had warned her about him. Through the closed door behind her, he could hear someone tromping around and the scrape of a wastebasket across tiles. Neither of these people seemed to have a very high opinion of him.

He smiled broadly and said he'd wait, that he had all day. He took one of several squeaky leather seats along the wall, and she began typing with unnecessary force at her computer. She sighed a lot. Justin zoned out, to conserve energy. He owed all he had to his refusal to go away, and today was shaping up as no exception.

Half an hour crawled by. He approached the desk, cleared his throat, and asked the frowning secretary for a blank reimbursement form, in case Palazzo had misplaced the one from the gallery director. She claimed not to have any. The door behind her opened silently a hair's breadth, and Justin's eyes chanced to meet the eye that peeked out. The door closed swiftly but silently.

The receptionist's phone chirped several seconds later, while Justin was still watching the door. She swiveled away from him and whispered. She hung up, and the inner door swung wide as if proclaiming Hail fellow, well met. The ever-impeccable Palazzo briskly invited Justin in, but didn't proffer a handshake.

Justin hadn't finished taking the liberty of sitting down when Palazzo launched into preemptive strike. "You've come back at a very exciting time! Great things are underway all over campus. And we're a part of that too, you and I."

Justin greeted this with the polite reflex of a weak nod. Misgivings were already fluttering in his stomach.

"This university is gearing up for the biggest phase of growth in its history, thanks to a hugely successful capital drive. And we're going to be enlarging this department too."

"Enlarge it how? Where is there room? What are you going to do, declare war on the library next door?" The prospect of even more demolition of his beloved old Providence made Justin queasy, and outraged, and remorseful at displaying his work here.

"Oh, we leave that to the professionals." Had Palazzo actually chortled? "So you see, we have tremendous amounts of funding tied up in all this. I don't find any record of contributions from you, though."

That smelled much more like guesswork than the results of research, and not terribly astute guesswork either. Justin's misgivings were fluttering harder.

"If I remember what you're up here for," Palazzo ventured, "I'd consider it a personal favor, and an appropriate gesture, if you'd regard the money in question as a donation to the future of our department." Justin was amazed at how ghastly an ingratiating smile could look.

Easy, now! "Listen, I had an understanding with the gallery director. A deal. There are e-mails to that effect. I put a lot of time and effort into installing the exhibit here on short notice, and I'm getting nothing out of it myself. I really need what you owe me."

"I don't owe you anything." How quickly the worm turned! "She didn't consult with me first. She went over my head, and not for the first time. You made your deal with her, not me. There's plenty I could have done with that wall space for two weeks."

Justin shrugged and spread his hands. "That's not my

problem. I came to town in good faith."

"Well, you invested your faith badly. And yes, it is your problem." With the tiniest adjustment of facial muscles, Palazzo would be gloating.

"You can't be serious. Where is the gallery director, anyway? I'd like to hear her side of this."

"She's called in sick."

Justin wouldn't put it past Palazzo to lie, but he conceded the point. "And I suppose you're going to fire her as soon as she gets well? If you haven't already?"

"Oh no, that would be crude. Her contract is nearly up. We won't renew her, that's all." God forbid that any whiff of discord emanate from Pictorial Arts!

Palazzo had inadvertently helped Justin plot his next move. *Si le geste est beau*, as the French said. But in good conscience, he had to brave the direct route as last resort. "So are you going to pay my hotel bill or not?"

"How simple do I have to make it for you? No!" Justin had pushed the decorous Dr. Palazzo into quaking like an aspen. Maybe that short fuse had propelled Palazzo's rise to the bureaucratic top, Justin speculated.

"Fine, then." Justin stood up unhurriedly. It behooved him to take the high road, though he'd have been more satisfied, and eminently within his rights, to vent a resounding Fuck you. When Justin began to speak, Palazzo lost his cool altogether and shouted at him to get out and stay out, but Justin doggedly followed through on the grounds that he'd always hoped for the occasion to say what he was saying, whether Palazzo was listening or not. "You know, Doc, for some people, the present represents an accumulation of everything past, like it's all there to some degree as a source of inspiration. For others, the present only represents as clean a break from the past as possible, and the less history there is to get in the way of business, the better.

It's just too bad a city like this has you, or anyone like you, in the position you're in."

Palazzo, red, heaving, goggle-eyes hurling malice, was temporarily out of steam.

"Did a word of that sink in?" Justin asked.

Palazzo gathered breath for another tirade, but this time Justin had the drop on him. "Anyway, fuck you," he summed up, ambled out, and closed the door with overweening deliberation till it clicked, amidst new barrage about how vulgar and unimportant he was. The receptionist was gaping at Justin as if he'd blown up the dam. "Boy, he's going to be fun for the rest of the day," Justin forecast. Only when he was on the fire stairs did he realize how much he was shaking.

He paused outside the gallery. A cursory mental survey located reasonably clean blankets and towels in the van, for art-swaddling purposes. He'd removed and stacked three 18" by 24" frames from the wall before the attendant was at his elbow.

"It's all right, I'm the artist," he told her.

"Are you sure it's okay? Isn't this show up for a week or two?" A good do-bee in spite of spiky pink hair!

"If you're worried, call Palazzo. In fact, I wish you would."

She said no more, and was nowhere in sight when Justin set another frame on the pile and debated carrying four at once. He was out to the van and back, and had voted against more loads that size, when Palazzo and the attendant arrived at the doorway. He barked at her to come back in an hour. He stormed in, but halted judiciously out of swinging range while bellowing, "What do you think you're doing? This is unacceptable! What are people going to say when there's nothing on the walls?"

Justin begrudged him a morose glance. "Call it a matter of trust. I don't feel safe leaving my artwork with you. You've already expressed a rather dismissive attitude toward it." He was also, admittedly, loath to stay or return where a grotesque death was in store, were the stars ever "right" again.

"Have you any idea how unprofessional this is?"

Justin shook his head impassively. "Maybe some token on your part would help. Something tangible. Otherwise, I don't know."

"You want money? This is childish! This is blackmail!"

"Well, that's not how I'd describe it." Justin reached for another picture, but stopped as Palazzo charged from the room. Would he enlist campus security? And make a scene strong-arming an exhibiting artist and "honored alum"? Justin doubted it.

Then the gallery lights went out. Brightness from the doorway made negligible impact in the mineshaft blackness. He anticipated Palazzo would let him stew a while and was reconciled to waiting in the dark. If the stalemate dragged on long enough, how would Palazzo respond to inquiries about the gallery blackout and Justin alone inside? Justin was conversant with feeling ridiculous, but he'd wager Palazzo was not. A drawback in these circumstances!

The dark was coming to seem less absolute. Were his eyes adjusting? No, not exactly, because he still couldn't see his pictures on the walls. Just the same, a glow was spreading through the room, as if someone were almost imperceptibly upping a dimmer switch, to reveal surfaces at right and acute angles to each other, which dwindled to a vanishing point miles beyond the rear gallery wall. And as if it had never been absent but only lurking below a subliminal threshold, ravenous appetite welled up in him again. Nor would it scruple to take a bite out of Palazzo at the least provocation.

He also hungered for what had attained depth and sharp outlines in soothing twilight. He was standing on a mossy slate terrace, facing west. No List Building surrounded him, no high-rises rudely interrupted the scarlet horizon of western hills, and even the massive Colonial Revival courthouse on Benefit Street had reverted to rows of antique gables and gambrels. The tallest structure by five stories or so was the bracket-shaped Hospital Trust bank across the canal. A few electric signs lent primary colors to the bricks and masonry of downtown, but only the one for the Old Colony Hotel was within reading distance. Sunset made the gold dome of the Congregational church on Weybosset Street gleam softly. The streetlamps ought to be on in a minute.

Here was the unmodern Providence of his dreams, and of heightened poignancy after a weekend in the brave new Providence. Lovecraft had not emerged beckoning, but that would have been impossible really. This was the Providence of Lovecraft's schooldays, and since Justin couldn't imagine Lovecraft as a child, that version of him couldn't materialize. In any event, it was very beautiful over there, and Justin could have it for the rest of his life, if he simply walked into it.

He was aware at the same time of how short such a life would be, and that the cosmic angler's hidden eye had to be glowering down at him. He also belatedly recognized how cunning the angler had been, to give the fish all the line it wanted, and an illusion of freedom, while that fish spent its strength and the hook stayed embedded in unfeeling lip.

None of this stopped Justin from shuffling his feet eagerly. His hankering for that place was inseparable from the hankering of something that regarded him as food, and he had no means to pull out the psychic hook, any more than a fish could sprout hands to save itself. How covertly active had the entity been after the line had gone slack? What kind of orchestrations had been involved for Justin to end up back at List, in the dark?

A phrase from Lovecraft's story echoed at Justin, even as his left foot rose in defiance of better judgment: "I am it and it is I." Did the "it" in question feel or understand any of Justin's yearning for the mirage it created for him, the way he suffered its hunger pangs, its anxiety, because Justin wasn't in the net yet, and meals were few and far between? Did Justin want to help assuage that cruel hunger? All he had to do was be eaten!

"Now will you please come out and behave reasonably?" Palazzo's outburst confused Justin and threw him off-balance. It sounded so clear and immediate, but how could that be? Justin was virtually a world away. "What are you doing in there?"

Palazzo was too worked up to be observant, or else from outside the gallery was still in darkness. But Justin soon learned that it wasn't necessary to be him to see what he was seeing. Palazzo was beside him, directing eyes wide with horror north and south, east and west. "Where are we? What the hell is going on?"

Justin, despite everything, smiled wryly. "It's Providence."

Palazzo became even more distraught. "Where's our building? Where's everything that's happened in the last hundred years? All that progress gone! Everything we've achieved! This is terrible! Why are you smiling, you little son of a bitch?"

Justin had been about to tell Palazzo it was all in his head, but stopped himself. Not after that abusive tone!

Palazzo wasn't doing especially well at coping with the situation. He began babbling about what they could do to fix all this. Justin could have suggested leaving the room or taking some flash photography, but why put himself out? And would Palazzo listen to someone as unimportant as him? Remarkable, in any case, that Palazzo was so susceptible to psychic influence, taking the reality of their vista at face value. Maybe he had too much else on his mind to think critically about this. Dotted lines of streetlamps were beginning to incandesce hither and yon.

Justin understood what happened next, because it was also happening to him by dint of celestial meeting of minds. Traveling across any surface obviously entailed the risk of slipping on that surface, particularly at stressful moments. Those who fished through a hole in the ice were always one misstep away from an unfriendly medium. And now Justin's idyllic Providence descended instantaneously from mellow dusk to heavy gloom. Big and low in the gray northern sky floated the denser black of what first seemed the moon in eclipse. But pale stars, and not craters, were scattered across its surface, in a range of sizes from pinpoint to grapeshot. Here was the angler's native sky, as glimpsed through the hole in space where the three-lobed eye had glared down and dispensed visions till brief clumsiness dislocated it. If Justin had blinked, he'd have missed it, for there followed a thud that shook the unseen gallery floor and rattled the unseen pictures on the walls, and the hole in space was jammed with frantic, ciliated tissue that bulged like a bubble into the room. On contact with the atmosphere it shone pink, then hot red.

In that span of seconds, a mounting stench of scorching mold and incinerated carcasses made Justin choke, and he reeled at a protracted, inhuman wail that was as much between his ears as in them, and that also spewed from his own mouth. It distorted as if channeled through cheap microphone. The surroundings, meanwhile, kept flickering between darkness and dim simulation of bygone Providence.

Then further sound impinged on him. Palazzo was still babbling in the same rhythm, at the same tempo, but the syllables had devolved into baby talk, and their volume had drastically risen. Callously or not, Justin felt a burden melt from his shoulders, and a release of tension in his chest. Palazzo going mad had saved Justin from doing the same. This chaos wasn't simply an expression of Justin's lone delusion. He needn't doubt, or abandon, his own sanity!

The entity broke free of vacuum seal between dimensions, and in its wake left unmediated the passage between here and there. A sonic boom knocked Justin off his feet, and the walls in the dark room rumbled, and all his artwork plummeted with a crash of shattering glass. The sour air began to whistle by his face. He lay as flat as possible, and his lunging hands bumped and clung to the cold steel siding of the attendant's desk. Praise the Lord, it was bolted down!

A hole in space, left on its own, couldn't be stable. It had to collapse soon. But the leakage between dimensions was still accelerating, lifting Justin off the concrete floor, when Palazzo flopped onto his belly and grabbed Justin's ankles. Justin's sweaty handhold on the sharp edge of slick metal panel began to loosen. He couldn't hang on much longer in this wind tunnel with patrician dead weight doubling his own. He kicked out as if swimming the Australian crawl, once, twice, and screaming Palazzo lost his grip. Had Justin done what was needful to save himself, or had he outright killed a man? The keening airflow was already beginning to tug less fitfully at him, and with a moral issue assailing him on top of everything else, his overtaxed consciousness gave way, though his fingers knew better than to let go.

Justin opened his eyes to bright gallery illumination. The attendant was standing beside him, studying him fretfully. She evidently knew where to find the circuit-breakers, or at least the janitor. Justin was lying on his right side and had unhanded the desk. He and the girl gawked at each other a minute. He didn't feel impelled to say anything yet.

"You okay? You want me to call the infirmary?"

Infirmary? The word dredged up long-lost campus lore of sub-par doctors burning warts off the wrong hand. Last thing he needed now. "Oh no, not those butchers."

She shrugged. "A friend came and got me from upstairs when she heard a noise and saw the lights were out. Was there an earthquake in here or something?"

"Something, yeah." He raised himself on bruised and achy

elbow. By the grace of whatever laws governed pressure or gravitation or aerodynamics between worlds in tangent, little had been scooped up from the edges of the room. Most of his photos lay face-up on the floor, though a lot of busted glass had crossed over. "I'm a lucky bastard," he mumbled.

"What?" The girl wasn't going to freak out, was she? "Where's Dr. Palazzo?"

"I don't know." Not the lie it sounded like! "Pretty sure the earth didn't swallow him up."

She assessed the damage with a few bird-like turns of her head. "There's not much glass." She crinkled her nose. "Do you know what that smell is?"

Pleasantly for her, most of the stink had been funneled into the void. Justin started to get up, but one foot skidded out from under him when he put his weight on it. He sat awkwardly with leg outstretched. The attendant had skipped back several prudent steps, and waved toward his less trustworthy foot. "What's that?"

He shifted the foot aside, drew his leg in, and huddled forward for a closer squint. The item on the floor had the circumference of a pancake, and was related to humanity somehow, but was hard to define because it was so out of context. Aha! Palazzo's majestic head of wavy silver hair really had been a toupee. "It's Palazzo's," he told the girl, who persisted in her puzzled stare. "Looks like he flipped his wig," Justin hinted. Comprehension dawned. Understandably, she made no move to pick it up.

He managed to stand. He might be in shock, but theorized that if he chose not to think about it, he could function indefinitely. "Look, if you're not busy, help me load the rest of my stuff in the van, will you?"

"Are you sure it's all right? I thought Dr. Palazzo wanted everything to stay."

"He left it up to me." Was that less than a half-truth? Did it matter? "Now come on. I want to be in the Catskills by nightfall."

She wavered as if tossing a figurative penny, then with a fraction of a nod capitulated. What the hell, why not? A bigger relief than Justin dared let on! Sooner or later, Palazzo's disappearance would be police business, and they might well talk to the girl and go from there. Justin gave her two frames to carry at a time, and dawdled so that she always went out by herself. The more trips she made, the more chances she had to snoop around the van, fore and aft, and ascertain that it contained no *corpus delicti.*

He thanked her afterward, but she only made a non-committal sound and scurried for the shelter of the List Building. Was he really such an unnerving presence? Just as well she was gone, anyhow. A bothersome soreness and itch below his left ribs called for investigation. He untucked his shirt. Thank God the psychic link was compromised when the careless alien faltered onto the hole! Otherwise, instead of a puffy, flaming red welt, wide and round as a CD, he'd have an empathic third-degree burn to explain at the emergency room. He was a lucky bastard all right. Even if he was stuck with the bed-and-breakfast bill.

He hit the road. Minutes later, according to a sign on the median strip, Massachusetts welcomed him. He'd made a scot-free getaway, or had he? Ten days went by, in which the angry red welt faded; he e-mailed the gallery director an unacknowledged apology for yanking the show, and he reframed his photos, and then the phone rang. The Providence police wanted to have their inevitable talk, and he obliged them on the way home from his Philly opening. They recorded the diffident, submissive Justin for posterity. His account contained no untruths and hoisted no red flags. He did omit any nonsense about nostalgic hallucination, hostile alien, hole in space, and kicking Palazzo into that hole. In the official version, he fell unconscious during a local tremor that interrupted an argument with Palazzo, and when he came to, Palazzo was gone. The police didn't ask about Palazzo's toupee. It must have landed in the trash before anyone realized what it was, before Palazzo was numbered among the missing. And the gallery attendant had forgotten or hadn't troubled to mention it. Justin owed her for that!

The police let him go. He was undeniably the last man on earth to see Palazzo alive, but only he knew that for a fact, and Palazzo must have had longer-standing, uglier imbroglios with others. Hopefully Justin was shut of Providence forever. Foolhardy to second-guess when next the stars above town would be "right" again!

Behind the wheel, it gave him pause to consider how blithely he was sidestepping any remorse about his role in Palazzo's demise. Technically, he'd killed the guy, unavoidably or not, willfully or not. But what about the hundreds of more cold-blooded, premeditated murders on the books that went unsolved? Plainly a crowded field of killers had learned to live with themselves, and go to work every day, and get married, and raise kids, and collect a pension. Justin wasn't even asking as much of life as all that. He too would learn to live with himself, just as he had learned the ropes of so many careers in his checkered adulthood. That malaise seeping up from the bedrock of his conscience would settle down if he ignored it, and stay down for months or years like any of his other wellsprings of guilt. What good would confession do himself or anybody? He was under no illusion that a jail cell or padded cell would "cleanse" him. To be honest, wasn't the world better off minus one arrogant yuppie?

Next afternoon, he was in his sunny, cluttered parlor, with its rugged mountain view that had seemed so breathtaking, prior to his glimpse of interstellar gulf. He was finally unpacking the duffel bag in which dirty clothes had accumulated since homecoming weekend. He should have emptied it before stuffing in more to wear in Philly, but if he'd arrived at a greater appreciation of anything lately, it would be that he wasn't perfect.

From the bottom of upended sack, his digital camera plopped onto a cushion of stale shirts. He couldn't figure out what it was for a second. He started picking it up, then slung it across the table as if it were electrified. In it was documentation, unique in human history, immensely valuable, of alien life, of alien interaction with this unwitting planet. Personally, on the other hand, it was a reminder of near-death experience, a preamble to homicide. If his eyes lingered on the camera for any time, that dizziness from back in the B&B, when he thought he would topple into that viewfinder miniature of a cosmic gateway, overtook him again. Would he always be a fish with an immaterial hook in his lip to draw him into that hole?

He went on with life, as he trusted he would, crisscrossing the world on photo shoots, exhibiting his work, making enough money, and he let the digital camera gather cobwebs where it lay, religiously averting his eyes from it. He never felt or acted particularly crazy, to the best of his knowledge, not even when visitors were apparently looking at his dusty camera on the table, and he startled them by roaring, "There's your murderer, right in there!" Nobody ever dared inquire what he meant, and he always seemed fine after a minute of probing lower lip with upper incisors, as if for a foreign object.

Howling In The Dark

DARRELL SCHWEITZER

Darrell Schweitzer is a prolific fiction writer, critic, and editor. Among his short story collections are We Are All Legends *(Doning, 1982),* Tom O'Bedlam's Night Out *(Ganley, 1985),* Transients and Other Disquieting Stories *(Ganley, 1993),* Refugees from an Imaginary Country *(Owlswick/Ganley, 1999),* Necromancies and Netherworlds *(with Jason Van Hollander; Wildside Press, 1999),* Nightscapes *(Wildside Press, 2000), and* The Great World and the Small *(Wildside Press, 2001). He has written the novels* The Shattered Goddess *(Donning, 1982),* The White Isle *(Weird Tales Library/ Owlswick, 1989), and* The Mask of the Sorcerer *(New English Library, 1995).* Sekenre: The Book of the Sorcerer *(Wildside Press, 2004) is a volume of linked sequels to* The Mask of the Sorcerer, *and* Living with the Dead *(PS Publishing, 2008) is a story-cycle/novella. He has compiled many anthologies of criticism of horror and fantasy fiction and was the editor of* Weird Tales *from 1988 to 2007.*

He sits there in the dark, silent, a hard, lean man of truly indeterminate age, like a creature of living stone. If his eyes seem glowing, that is my imagination. No, they are not.

He wants me to tell this story, so that I may slough it off.

WASN'T AFRAID OF THE DARK AS A CHILD. NO, IN FACT, I enjoyed it. Where my older sister Ann used to huddle at the edge of her bed with her face as close to the nightlight as possible until she got to sleep, I would, whenever I could, listen to her breathing and wait until she was clearly asleep, and then reach over and remove the nightlight from the wall.

The dark contained things that the lighted bedroom did not. I knew that even then. I could feel *presences*. Hard to define more than that. Not ghosts, because they were not remnants of former living people, or human at all. Not guardian angels, because they were not angelic, nor were they in any sense my guardians. But something. There. All around me. Passing to and fro and up and down in the darkness on their own, incomprehensible business, in their own way beckoning me to follow them into spaces far beyond the walls and ceiling of the tiny bedroom.

Then, inevitably, my sister would wake up screaming.

When we were old enough to have separate bedrooms, that solved the immediate problem, but it was not enough. My mother would all too often come in and put her arms around me and ask *Why are you sitting here in the dark? What are you afraid of?* and I could not answer her. Not truthfully, anyway. Because I did not know the answer. But I wasn't afraid.

Sometimes I would drop silently out the window onto the lawn very late at night, into the darkness when the moon was down. I'd stand there in the darkness, under the eaves of the house, as if the roof provided me with a little extra shadow; in my pajamas or just in shorts, barefoot, and if it was cold that was all the better because I wanted the dark to touch me, to embrace me and take me away into the remote reaches of itself, and if I shivered or my toes burned from the cold, that was a good thing. It was an answer. It was the dark acknowledging that I was there.

I'd look up at the stars and imagine myself swimming among them, into some greater darkness, to the rim of some black whirlpool that would carry me down, down and away from even their faint light.

"Are you crazy? You'll catch your death of cold!" was what my mother inevitably said when I got caught. There would be a scolding, followed by hot chocolate, being bundled up in an oversized robe, and eventually being led back to bed.

Yet I could provide no explanation for my behavior. Mom began to talk about doctors and psychiatrists.

There are no words, the man in the dark tells me, the ageless man whose eyes are not glowing. No explanations that can be put into words. Never.

There was a particularly inexplicable incident when I was thirteen and was discovered early one morning by a ranger in Valley Forge Park, twenty miles from where I lived, in the middle of a low-lying area that was half woods and half swamp. It was November and the half-frozen ground crunched underfoot. Here I was wearing only a particularly ragged pair of denim cut-offs, soaked, muddy, exhausted from hypothermia and covered with bruises.

I couldn't remember very much. There were a lot of questions, from the police, from doctors; and yet another round of bundling the poor little darling up nice and warm and giving him hot chocolate. What I *did* know was more about how I had *touched* the presences in the darkness and how they had borne me up into the night sky on vast and flapping wings. But they carried me only for a moment, either because I was afraid, or because I was not ready, or because I was not worthy.

So they let go, and I tumbled into the woods, crashing through the branches, which was how I'd gotten the bruises.

Nobody wants to hear about that. I refused to tell.

It was only after a particularly tearful display on my mother's part that I was allowed to go home at all.

Oh, I knew what my interrogators wanted me to say. Things were not going well at home, it was true. My father and mother screamed at one another. There were fights, violent ones. Things got smashed up. My sister Ann had bloated up into a 300-pound, terminally depressed monstrosity, who was ceaselessly excoriated by the kids at school as a retard, a whore, and a smelly bag of shit. I got a lot of that too, as the kid brother of same. Ann used to sit up long nights in the bright glare of lights cutting herself all over with a razor, carving intricate hieroglyphs into her too, too voluminous flesh, so that the pain would reassure her that she was somehow still alive.

She had her little ways. I had mine.

I was beaten regularly too, usually by my father, with fists or a belt or whatever happened to be handy, but no, it wasn't like what the police or the doctors or my teachers were trying to get me to blurt out. No one had the slightest lustful interest in my nubile young body. I was just the weird and silent kid at the back of the class who had a secret he didn't want to share, who would never make it as a poster boy for child abuse.

Such preconceptions must be cast aside. Humanity must be cast aside. Sloughed off.

I met the living stone man whose eyes do not really glow on the night my mother and sister both committed suicide. We will not go into details. Those things must be cast aside. Lives end. My mother, who had been a teacher, and my sister, who wanted to be a singer, terminated themselves. My father, who worked as an electrician when he managed to work, would drink himself to death within the year.

It is the way of things, which are to be sloughed off, discarded and forgotten.

That night, relishing both the cold and the danger—it was winter; there was snow on the ground—I went out into the back yard, completely naked. I understood by then that if you are to surrender yourself utterly to the darkness, you must achieve total vulnerability, which is why virgin sacrifices are always naked.

The stone man, whom I had known only in dreams before that night, was waiting for me. He took me by the hand. His touch was indeed as hard and fleshless as living stone, and yet somehow lighter in a way my senses could not define, as if he were only partially made of material substance at all.

He led me into the further dark, heedless of my nakedness, because the human body is just one more thing to be sloughed off in the darkness, and of no interest to him. If we are to achieve our place in the whirling darkness beyond the stars, he explained to me, inside my head without words, we must become *nihil*, nothing.

He didn't have a name. Childishly, I made up a whole series

of names for him, Mr. Graveshadow, Mr. Midnightman, Mr. Deathwalker, but names, too, are to be sloughed off.

I remember opening the back gate, but beyond that I do not think we walked through familiar places at all, certainly not across suburban back yards and streets, beneath the widely spaced streetlights, the strange, dark man and the naked, pale boy, who surely would have caused some consternation when caught in the headlights of the occasional passing car.

I wonder if we even left footprints in the snow. I am certain only that we came to a high, dark place beneath brilliant stars and perched at the edge of a precarious precipice, so that with the slightest tumble, not to mention an intentional leap, we could have hurled ourselves off into the black sea of infinity forever.

The presences gathered all around us. I could feel their wings brushing against my bare back and shoulders like the wind.

That was when the man who had waited for me all this time, who had brought me here to this place, first taught me how to speak the speech of the dark spaces. Maybe he began with a series of syllables that went something like *whao-ao-ao*—but it was a howl, high and shrill like nothing I had ever imagined a human throat could produce, a screaming beacon that could reach across interstellar spaces, beyond the universe itself, into the great, black whirlpool at the core of Being. It was so *loud*. It filled everything, obliterated everything. Did my eardrums burst? Was there blood oozing out of my ears? The body is to be discarded, and for a moment it seemed it was, as in a kind of vision my companion bore me up, surrounded by howling, dark angels, and we hurled through infinities without number until we came at last to a flat and frozen plain, beneath two black suns, and we knelt down and abased ourselves, and shrieked that impossible shriek before a miles-high eidolon that might have had the form of a man, but *never was* a man. And this thing opened its stone jaws to join us in our song. It spoke, without words, the secret name of the primal chaos that turns in the heart of the black whirlpool, that unnameable name which no human tongue can ever form, nor can any human ear—with or without broken eardrums—ever hear.

That was almost thirty years ago, I say, uselessly. A lot of water under the bridge since then.

There no time, the stone man says.

Indeed, he has not changed at all. If he is truly alive, he does not age.

You are ready, then?

Yes. I have done a terrible thing.

Somehow I found my way back home. I must have arrived a while after my father came home from work, because I discovered him sitting amid the ruins of our trashed living room, staring at the heavy-caliber pistol on the floor and at the brains and blood splattered all over the furniture and walls. My sister was sprawled head-first down the front stairs. My mother lay right in front of Dad, curled up as if she were asleep.

He was weeping uncontrollably.

He never noticed that I was naked and wet and half frozen, or that I was burned where either the stone man or any of the winged ones had touched me. I stank of sweat the way you do when you've shivered really hard. When I tried to say something it came out as a weird, trailing howl. Lights glared and whirled all around the house, blinding me, and the sounds were all strange and distorted, people talking to me at the wrong speed, all growling and distorted, like the voices of broken machinery. Maybe there was blood running down my cheeks. One of my eardrums had burst. I've been partially deaf in that ear ever since. The house was spinning, shifting, and nothing made a great deal of sense. My feet hurt intensely from where they had touched the stars, as if I had been wading ankle-deep in the burning sky.

In the end, guess what? Somebody really did wrap me up in a blanket like a little baby and hand me a cup of hot chocolate.

Yes, I did time in institutions after that, in high, red-brick prisons where you have to wear pajamas all day and night in the company of crazy people who think you are one of them, where the bright lights are always on and there is no darkness, except what you can carefully, secretly nurse within yourself, despite the best efforts of so many cooing and clucking Professionals to gently probe you with words and drugs and Get To The Root Of Your Problem. They want you to confess, confess, *confess*, as relentless as any Inquisition, their pretend-gentleness as insidious as the rack and the thumbscrew.

Confess.

Yet I held out. I hoarded my secrets. Eventually, for lack of evidence or lack of guilt or lack of interest, or maybe something as mundane as lack of continuing funds, after many stern lectures about how I was apparently devoid of all normal human emotions, I was cast up at eighteen, an orphan, shipwrecked and alone, onto the shore of the Real World to make my way in it.

The rest is fraud. Imposture. With darkness in my heart, with my secret cunningly concealed, I gained, at first, marginal jobs and marginal acquaintances, and learned to impersonate a human being, going through all the motions of "normal" life, becoming so convincing in my falsehood that I even managed to marry Marguerite, a much more accomplished person than myself, and to father a daughter by her, whom we called Anastasia, whose name means "resurrection," as in the resurrection of hope.

But it was all just one more part of my plan. Another part was that we had to leave our native Pennsylvania, and by cunning degrees I eased us into the necessity of moving the entire family to Arizona.

It spooked them. No doubt about it. A place of vast *emptiness*, where there are immensities that no one from the East can really comprehend, and you can easily go hundred miles at night between the last gas station and a truck stop, seeing absolutely nothing in between. A little town like Page perched on a hilltop with its stores and green lawns seems like a whimsical speck of paint on an otherwise completely empty canvas. Ten miles down the road can be as barren as the moon. I took Marguerite to see the Grand Canyon by starlight, and she was terrified of its vastness even as I wanted to leap out and swim into its abyss, in which there was no up or down and no distance, where infinity is very close, and at its heart swirls the black chaos whose name may never be spoken.

You came to me.

I knew the way.

An awakening, into darkness.

Yes. Because I have done a terrible thing.

Then listen.

And we both listen. It makes no difference that I am partially deaf in the real world, because this is a sound from out of the immensity of the darkness. We gaze down from atop a remote mesa over a desert landscape that stretches off into black nothingness, without the light of a house or a highway or any glow on the horizon to suggest that mankind has ever set foot on this planet—from out of that distance and that darkness, from beyond the squat, round hills that are visible only because they block out the starlight, comes a howling which I have indeed heard before and have never stopped hearing all the days of my life, a sound no human throat ought ever to be able to utter.

You hear it? my companion asks.

Yes, of course.

In such places, in the darkness, we are closer to the outer spheres. Dimensions, gateways, whatever you want to call them, touch.

Do other people hear this?

The Christians say it is the howling of a damned soul. The Native peoples, who have been here longer, have other, older ideas.

We stand in the darkness, gazing into the farthest distance, and for an instant the stars seem to be rippling, as if they're a reflection in a mirror-smooth pond and something has just gone skittering over the surface.

My companion takes my hand, as he did that first time, in the dark. It is a surprisingly human, tender gesture.

The howling sound is all. It fills the universe. I cannot hear anything else. I cannot speak or hear, and we two reply, joining an impossible chorus even as the presences close in around us, and I feel their wings beating against me like the wind. Their claws or hands or whatever it is they have tear at my to-be-sloughed-off flesh as they seize hold of us and lift us into the air, off the top of the mesa, sweeping over the landscape, into the stars and the darkness beyond.

I am still able to touch the thoughts of my companion and converse with him after a fashion that is not speech, except perhaps the speech of dreams. His words form inside my mind, as if they are my own.

This is my tragedy, I come to understand.

I have done a terrible thing, but not terrible enough.

For a while, during the years of my imposture, I didn't feel like a damned soul at all. It was very beguiling. Marguerite awakened within me emotions I did not know I even had. We were *happy*. When our daughter was born, it was a *joy*. She taught me how to *laugh*, something I had not done in a very long time.

That must be sloughed off.

I had a life.
And I lost it.
Again.
I have done a terrible thing.

It is of no matter. Such things do not exist in the dark.

But what if I can't slough it all off? What if the condition of *nihil* is only incompletely achieved? What if, in the end, my sin is a very petty and human one, a routine mixture of cowardice and prideful despair?

Now the stars swirl around us in a vast whirlpool, and then there are more dark dust clouds whirling, obscuring the light, and we pass through, borne by our captors, for I believe that is what they are, the ones to whom we have surrendered ourselves. Once again the ice-plain stretches below us, beneath the black suns, and the enormous stone visage looms before us, and the stone jaws grind and the stone throat howls, speaking the names of the lords of primal chaos, and of the chaos itself which cannot be named at all.

I have done a terrible thing.

History, family history, has a way of repeating itself, and the sins of the fathers are visited, etc., etc., but not precisely and not the way you think, because the terrible thing was simply this, that at the end of many long and happy years together with Marguerite, she began to leave me, not because she was unfaithful or wanted a divorce, much less because I blew her brains out with a heavy-caliber pistol or induced her to do the same to herself. More simply, she developed brain cancer, and after the seizures and delirium and withdrawals into hospital wards, where I last saw her hooked up to monitors and tubes like a thing, not the person I loved, who had taught me, quite unexpectedly, how to be human—after I no longer had the courage to visit her or whisper her name, I looked into the darkness once more and remembered all those strange things from my youth, and my companion, my mentor, my friend with the many funny names I'd made up for him and no name at all, was waiting for me as if no time had passed.

OWARDICE AND DESPAIR. HOW TERRIBLY, disappointingly human at the last.

Falling down from out of the black sky toward the immense thing that is more of a god than anything imagined in human mythologies, I realize that my only crime is that I am a liar, that I claimed to be ready for this journey when I am not, that I have not managed to slough off my humanity at all; that if anything I have suddenly regained it.

I call out to my companion. I speak strange words, like an apostle babbling in tongues. I ask him if he is my friend, if he has been my friend all my life. I tell him that I have a name, which is Joseph. I ask him his own name, and somehow I am able to press into his mind. I catch glimpses of his life and learn that he was an astronomer who worked in Arizona about 1910, named Ezra Watkins, and he too has some deeply buried core of sorrow, a secret pain that he is terrified I might uncover and force him to confront before the darkness can swallow him up utterly and forever.

He draws away from me in something very much like panic, shouting that these things must be gotten rid of, discarded, sloughed off—the phrase he uses over and over again, chanting it like a mantra—and I can feel his immeasurable, helpless, despair as memories of his discarded humanity begin to awaken within him.

He begins to scream, to make that unbelievable, indescribable howling noise, and for once I cannot join him in his song. From out of my mouth issue only words, like a little boy's voice, not loud enough to be heard, breaking, shrill.

Consternation among our winged bearers.

This one is too heavy. He is not pure.

They let go of me. I am falling from them, through space, burning among the stars, blinded by light, away from the stone god, away from the black suns and the swirling dark.

I call out to Ezra Watkins. I reach for his hand.

But he is not there, and I can feel my ears bleeding.

Maybe my daughter Anastasia inherited my alleged total lack of human emotions, because she disappeared about the time her mother became ill, and I never heard from her again; but I am, alas, a very poor liar, which is my single crime, of which prideful despair, cowardice, and self-delusion are mere subsets, what I have failed to slough off.

I alone have escaped to tell thee.

My eyes do not glow. That is an illusion. In the dark, there is no light.

I wait. I have walked too far in the dark spaces. I have waded barefoot among the fiery stars and the black stars and burned myself. I cannot walk upon the Earth again, but only wander in the darkness, howling.

The Christians say it is the howling of a damned soul. The Native peoples, who have been here longer, have other, older ideas.

They're both right.

Nobody is going to make this better with a blanket and a cup of hot chocolate.

Now that you have come to me, you must tell the story.

The Truth About Pickman

BRIAN STABLEFORD

Brian Stableford is an acclaimed British author of science fiction and horror novels, including The Empire of Fear *(Simon & Schuster UK, 1988),* Young Blood *(Simon & Schuster UK, 1992),* The Hunger and Ecstasy of Vampires *(Mark V. Ziesing, 1996),* The Werewolves of London *(Simon & Schuster UK, 1990),* The Angel of Pain *(Simon & Schuster UK, 1991), and* The Carnival of Destruction *(Simon & Schuster UK, 1994). He has also edited* The Dedalus Book of Decadence *(Dedalus, 1990–92; 2 vols.) and is the author of such critical studies as* Scientific Romance in Britain 1890–1950 *(Fourth Estate, 1985) and* The Sociology of Science Fiction *(Borgo Press, 1987).*

THE DOORBELL DIDN'T RING UNTIL FIFTEEN MINUTES after the time we'd agreed on the telephone, but I hadn't even begun to get impatient. Visitors to the island—even those who've only come over the Solent from Hampshire, let alone across the Atlantic from Boston—are always taken by surprise by the slower pace of life here. It's not so much that the buses never run on time as the fact that you can't judge the time of a walk by looking at the map. The map is flat, but the terrain is anything but, especially here on the south coast, where all the chines are.

"Do come in, Professor Thurber," I said, when I opened the door. "This is quite a privilege. I don't get many visitors."

His face was a trifle blanched, and he had to make an effort to unclench his jaw. "I'm not surprised," he muttered, in an accent that was distinctly American but by no means a drawl. "Who ever thought of building a house here, and how on earth did they get the materials down that narrow track?"

I took his coat. There were scuff-marks on the right sleeve because of the way he'd hugged the wall on the way down rather than trust the hand-rail on the left. The cast-iron struts supporting it were rusted, of course, and the wood had grown a fine crop of fungus because we'd had such a wet August, but the rail was actually quite sound, so he could have used it if he'd had the nerve.

"It is a trifle inconvenient nowadays," I admitted. "The path was wider when the house was built, and I shudder to think what the next significant landslip might do to it, but the rock face behind the house is vertical, and it's not too difficult to rig a block-and-tackle up on top. The biggest thing I've had to bring down recently is a fridge, though, and I managed that on the path with the aid of one of those two-wheeled trolleys. It's not so bad when you get used to it."

He'd pulled himself together by then and stuck out his hand. "Alastair Thurber," he said. "I'm truly glad to meet you, Mr. Eliot. My grandfather knew your…grandfather." The hesitation was perceptible, as he tried to guess my age and estimate whether I might conceivably be Silas Eliot's son rather than his grandson, but it wasn't so blatant as to seem impolite. Even so, to cover up his confusion, he added: "And they were both friends of the man I wrote to you about: Richard Upton Pickman."

"I don't have a proper sitting-room, I'm afraid," I told him. "The TV room's rather cluttered, but I expect you'd rather take tea in the library in any case."

He assured me, quite sincerely, that he didn't mind. As an academic, he was presumably a bibliophile as well as an art-lover and a molecular biologist: a man of many parts, who was probably still trying to fit them together neatly. He was, of course, younger than me—no more than forty-five, to judge by appearances.

I sat him down and immediately went into the kitchen to make the tea. I used the filtered water and put two bags of Sainsbury's Brown Label and one of Earl Grey in the pot. I put the milk in a jug and the sugar in a bowl; it was a long time since I'd had to do *that*. On the way back to the library I had a private bet with myself as to which of the two salient objects he would comment on first, and won.

"You have one of my books," he said, before I'd even closed the door behind me. He'd taken the copy of *The Syphilis Transfer* off the shelf and opened it, as if to check that the words on the page really were his and that the book's spine hadn't been lying.

"I bought it after you sent the first letter," I admitted.

"I'm surprised you could find a copy in England, let alone the Isle of Wight," he said.

"I didn't," I told him. "The public library at Ventnor has Internet connections. I go in twice a week to do the shopping and often pop in there. I ordered it from the U.S. via Amazon. I may be tucked away in a chine, but I'm not entirely cut off from civilization." He seemed skeptical—but he had just walked the half a mile that separated the house from the bus stop on the so-called coast road, and knew that it wasn't exactly a stroll along Shanklin sea-front. His eyes flickered to the electric light bulb hanging from the roof, presumably wondering at the fact that it was there at all rather than the fact that it was one of the new curly energy-saving bulbs. "Yes, I said, "I even have mains electricity. No gas, though, and no mains water. I don't need it—I actually have a spring in my cellar. How many people can say that?"

"Not many, I suppose," he said, putting the book down on the small table beside the tea-tray. "You call this place a chine, then? In the U.S., we'd call it a gully, or maybe a ravine."

"The island is famous for its chines," I told him. "Blackgang Chine and Shanklin Chine are tourist traps nowadays—a trifle gaudy for my taste. It's said that there are half a dozen still unspoiled, but it's difficult to be sure. Private land, you see. The path isn't as dangerous as it seems at first glance. Chines are, by definition, wooded. If you were to slip, it would be more a slide than a fall, and you'd probably be able to catch hold of the bushes. Even if you couldn't climb up again you could easily let yourself down. Don't try it at high tide, though."

He was already halfway through his first cup of tea, even though it was still a little hot. He was probably trying to calm his nerves, although he had no idea what *real* acrophobia was. Finally, though, he pointed at the painting on the wall between the two freestanding bookcases, directly opposite the latticed window.

"Do you know who painted that, Mr. Eliot?" he asked.

"Yes," I said.

"I knew the moment I looked at it," he told me. "It's not on the list I compiled, but that's not surprising. I knew it as soon as I looked at it—Pickman's work is absolutely unmistakable." His eyes narrowed slightly. "If you knew who painted it," he said, "You might have mentioned that you had it when you replied to my first letter."

Not wanting to comment on that remark, I picked up *The Syphilis Transfer.* "It's an interesting thesis, Professor," I said. "I was quite intrigued."

"It was quite a puzzle for a long time," he said. "First the Europeans argued that syphilis had started running riot in the sixteenth century because sailors imported it from the Americas, then American scholars motivated by national pride started arguing that, in fact, European sailors had imported it to the Americas. The hypothesis that different strains of the spirochaete had evolved in each continent during the period of separation, and that each native population had built up a measure of immunity to its own strain—but not to the other—was put forward way back in the seventies, but it wasn't until the people racing to complete the Human Genome Project developed advanced sequencers that we had the equipment to prove it."

"And now you're working on other bacterial strains that might have been mutually transferred?" I said. "When you're not on vacation, investigating your grandfather's phobic obsessions, that is?"

"Not just bacteria," he said ominously—but he was still on vacation, and his mind was on Richard Upton Pickman. "Does it have a title?" he asked, nodding his head toward the painting again.

"I'm afraid not. I can't offer you anything as melodramatic

as *Ghoul Feeding*, or even *Subway Accident*."

He glanced at me again with slightly narrowed eyes, registering the fact that I was familiar with the titles mentioned in the account that Lovecraft had reworked from the memoir that Edwin Baird had passed on to him. He drained his cup. While I poured him another, he stood up and went to the picture to take a closer look.

"This must be one of his earlier works," he said, eventually. "It's a straightforward portrait—not much more than a practice study. The face has all the usual characteristics, of course—no one but Pickman could paint a face to make you shudder like that. Even in the days of freak-show TV, when the victims of genetic disasters that families used to hide away get tracked through courses of plastic surgery by documentary makers' camera crews, there's still something uniquely strange and hideous about Pickman's models…or at least his technique. The background in this one is odd, though. In his later works, he used subway tunnels, graveyards, and cellars, picking out the details quite carefully, but this background's very vague and almost bare. It's well-preserved, though, and the actual face…"

"'Only a real artist knows the actual anatomy of the terrible or the physiology of fear,'" I quoted.

He wasn't about to surrender the intellectual high ground. "'The exact sort of lines and proportions that connect up with latent instincts or hereditary memories of fright,'" he went on, completing the quote from the Lovecraft text, "'and the proper color contrasts and lighting effects to stir the dormant sense of strangeness.'"

"But you're a molecular biologist," I said, as smoothly as if it really were an offhand remark. "You don't believe in latent instincts, hereditary memories of fright, or a dormant sense of strangeness."

It was a mistake. He turned round and looked me straight in the eye, with a gaze whose sharpness was worth more than vague suspicion. "Actually," he said, "I do. In fact, I've become very interested of late in the molecular basis of memory and the biochemistry of phobia. I suppose my interest in my grandfather's experiences has begun to influence my professional interests, and vice versa."

"That's only natural, Professor Thurber," I told him. "We all begin life as men of many parts, but we all have a tendency to consider ourselves as jigsaw puzzles, trying to fit the parts together in a way that makes sense."

His eyes went back to the painting—to that strange distorted face, which seemed to distill the very essence of some primitive horror, more elementary than a pathological fear of spiders, or of heights.

"Since you have the painting," he said, "you obviously do have some of the things that Silas Eliot brought back to England when he left Boston in the thirties. May I see them?"

"They're not conveniently packed away in one old trunk and stowed neatly in the attic or the cellar," I said. "Any items that remain have been absorbed into the general clutter about the house. Anyway, you're really only interested in one thing, and that's something I don't have. There are no photographs, Professor Thurber. If Pickman really did paint the faces in his portraits from photographs, Silas Eliot never found them—at least, he didn't bring any back with him from Boston. Believe me, Mr. Thurber, I'd know if he had."

I couldn't tell whether he believed me or not. "Would you be prepared to sell me this painting, Mr. Eliot?" he asked.

"No," I said. "I'm sorry if that ruins your plan to corner the market—but who can tell what a Pickman might fetch nowadays if one ever came into the saleroom? It's not as if he's fashionable."

The red herring didn't distract him. He wasn't interested in saleroom prices, and he knew that I wasn't angling for an offer. He sat down and picked up the second cup of tea I'd poured for him. "Look, Mr. Eliot," he said. "You obviously know more about this than you let on in your letters, and you seem well enough aware that I didn't tell you everything in mine. I'll level with you, and I hope that you might then be more inclined to level with me. Did your grandfather ever mention a man named Jonas Reid?"

"Another of Pickman's acquaintances," I said. "The supposed expert in comparative pathology. The one who thought that Pickman wasn't quite human—that he was somehow akin to the creatures he painted."

"Exactly. Back in the twenties, of course, knowledge of genetics was primitive, so it wasn't possible for Reid to entertain anything more than vague suspicions, but there was a time when colonial America was home to numerous isolated communities, who'd often imported sectarian beliefs that encouraged inbreeding. You don't expect to find that sort of thing in a big city, of course, but Pickman's people came from Salem, and had been living there at the time of the witch-panic. The people who moved into cities as the nation industrialized—especially to the poorer areas like Boston's North End and Back Bay—often retained their old habits for a generation or two. The recessive genes are all scattered now, mind, so they don't show up in combination nearly as often, but back in the twenties..."

I felt an oddly tangible, if slightly premature, wave of relief. He seemed to be on the wrong track or, at least, not far enough along the right one. I tried hard not to smile as I said: "Are you trying to say that what you're actually looking for is a sample of Pickman's DNA?" I asked. "You want to buy that painting because you think it might have a hair or some old saliva stain somewhere about it—or even a blood drop, if he happened to prick himself white fixing the canvas to the frame?"

"I already have samples of Pickman's DNA," he told me, in a fashion that would have wiped the smile off my face if I hadn't managed to suppress it. "I've already sequenced it and found the recessive gene. What I'm looking for now is the mutational trigger."

I'd cut him off too soon. He was a scientist, after all—not a man to cut to the bottom line without negotiating the intermediary steps. He must have mistaken my dismay for incomprehension, because he continued without waiting for me to speak.

"We all have numerous recessive genes of various sorts, Mr. Eliot," he said, "which are harmless as long as the corresponding gene on the paired chromosome is functioning normally. The ones that give us the most trouble nowadays are those that can cause cancer, if and when their healthy counterpart is disabled in a particular somatic cell, causing that cell to start dividing repeatedly, forming a tumor. Normally, such tumors are just inchoate masses of cells, but if the recessive is paired with one of the genes that's implicated in embryonic development, the disabling of the healthy counterpart can activate bizarre metamorphoses. When such accidents happen in embryo, they result in monstrous births—the sort DeVries was referring to when he first coined the word *mutation*. It's much rarer for it to occur in the mature soma, but it does happen.

"Most disabling incidents are random, caused by radiation or general toxins, but some are more specific, responding to particular chemical carcinogens: mutational triggers. That's why some specific drugs have links with specific cancers, or other mutational distortions—you probably remember the thalidomide scandal. Jonas Reid didn't know any of this, of course, but he did know enough to realize that something odd was going on with Pickman, and he made some notes about the changes he observed in Pickman's physiognomy. More importantly, he also went looking for other cases—some of the individuals that Pickman painted—and found some, before he gave up the inquiry when disgust overwhelmed his scientific curiosity.

"People were so anxious to hide the monsters away, of course, that Reid couldn't find very many, but he was able to observe a couple. His examinations were limited by available technology, of course, and he wasn't able to study the paintings *in sequence*, but I've got the DNA, and I've also pieced together as complete a list of Pickman's paintings as is still possible, along with the dates of composition of the later items. I've studied the progression from *Ghoul Feeding* to *The Lesson*, and I think I've figured out what was happening. It's not traces of Pickman's DNA for which I want to search your canvas—and any other Pickman-connected artifacts your grandfather might have left you—but traces of some other organic compound, probably a protein: the mutational trigger that activated Pickman's gradual metamorphosis, and the not-so-gradual metamorphoses of his subjects. If you won't sell me the painting, will you let me borrow it, so that I can run it through a lab? The University of Southampton might let me use their facilities, if you don't want me to take the painting all the way to America."

I was glad of his verbosity, because I needed to think, and decide what to do. First of all, I decided, I had to be obliging. I had to encourage him to think that he might get what he wanted, at least in a superficial sense.

"All right," I said. "You can take the painting to Southampton for further examination, provided that it doesn't go any further and that you don't do any perceptible injury to it. You're welcome to look around for any other objects that take your fancy, but I doubt that you'll find anything useful."

I cursed, mentally, as I saw his gaze move automatically to the bookcases on either side of the painting. He was clever enough to identify the relevant books, even though none of them had anything as ludicrously revealing as a bookplate or a name scribbled in ink on the flyleaf. The painting was almost certainly clean, but I wasn't entirely sure about the books—and if he really did decide to scour the rest of the house with minute care, including the cellars, he'd have a reasonable chance of finding what he was looking for, even if he didn't know it when he found it.

"It's odd, though," I observed, as he opened one of the glass-fronted cases that contained older books, "that you've come all the way from America to the Isle of Wight in search of this trigger molecule. I'd have thought you'd stand a much better chance of finding it in the Boston subway, or the old Copp's Hill Burying Ground—and if it's not there, your chances of finding it anywhere must be very slim."

"You might think so," he said, "but if my theory is correct, I'm far more likely to find the trigger here than there."

My sinking heart touched bottom. He really had figured it out—all but the last piece of the jigsaw, which would reveal the whole picture in all its consummate horror. He began taking the books off the shelves one by one, very methodically, opening each one to look at the title page, checking dates and places of publication as well as subject-matter.

"What theory is that?" I asked, politely, trying to sound as if I probably wouldn't understand a word of it.

"It wasn't just the syphilis spirochaete that was subject to divergent evolution while the Old World and the New were separated," he told me. "The same thing happened to all kinds of other human parasites and commensals: bacteria, viruses, protozoans, fungi. Mostly, the divergence made no difference; where it did—with respect to such pathogens as smallpox, for instance—the effect was a simple loss of immunity. Some of the retransferred diseases ran riot briefly, but the effect was temporary, not just because immunities developed in the space of four or five human generations but because the different strains of the organisms interbred. Their subsequent generations, being much faster than ours, soon lost their differentiation. The outbreak of monstrosity that occurred in Boston in the twenties, as variously chronicled by Pickman and Reid, was a strictly temporary affair; it hardly spanned a couple of human generations. My theory is that the trigger lost its potency, because the imported organism carrying it either interbred with its local counterpart or ran into some local pathogen or predator that wiped it out. The reverse process might easily have occurred, of course—at least in big cities—but I believe that there's a better chance of finding the trigger molecule over here, where families like the Pickmans and the Eliots probably originated, than there is in Boston or Salem."

"I see," I said. While he was leafing through the books, I went to the window to look out over the chine.

To the right was the English Channel, calm at present, meekly reflecting the clear blue September sky. To the left was the narrow cleft of the chine, thickly wooded on both sheer slopes because the layers of sedimentary rock were so loosely aggregated and wont to crumble that they offered reasonable purchase to bushes, whose questing roots could burrow deep enough not only to support their crowns but to feed them gluttonously on the many tiny streams of water filtering through the porous rock. Because the chine faced due south, both walls got plenty of sunlight in summer in spite of the acute angle of the cleft.

Directly below the window, there was only a narrow ledge—almost as narrow now as the pathway leading down from the cliff-top—separating the front doorstep from the edge. When the house had been built, way back in the seventeenth century—some fifty or sixty years before Richard Upton

Pickman's ancestor had been hanged as a witch in Salem—the chine had been even narrower and the ledge much broader, but it had been no fit home for acrophobes even then. If it hadn't been for the vital importance of the smuggling trade to the island's economy, the house would probably never have been built, and certainly wouldn't have been kept in such good repair for centuries on end by those Eliots who hadn't emigrated to the New World in search of a slightly more honest way of life. The bottom had dropped out of the smuggling business now, of course, thanks to the accursed European Union, but I didn't intend to let the place go—not, at least, until one landslip too many left me no choice.

By the time I turned round again, Alastair Thurber had sorted out no less than six of Pickman's old books, along with a mere four that just happened to be of similar antiquity.

"That's about it, I think," he said. "Would you care to show me around the rest of the house, pointing out anything that your grandfather might have brought back from Boston?"

"Certainly," I said. "Would you prefer to start at the top or the bottom?"

"Which is more interesting?" he asked.

"Oh, most definitely the bottom," I said. "That's where all the most interesting features are. I'll take you all the way down to the smugglers' cave, via the spring. We'll have to take an oil-lamp, though—I never have got around to running an electric cable down there."

As we went down the cellar steps, which he handled with rigid aplomb, I filled in a few details about the history of smuggling along the south coast—the usual tourist stuff—and added a few fanciful details about wreckers. He didn't pay much attention, especially when we went down through the trapdoor in the cellar into the caves. He was a little disappointed by the spring, even though he was obviously relieved to reach the bottom of the parrot-ladder. He had obviously expected something more like a gushing fountain, and probably thought that the Heath-Robinson-esque network of copper and plastic tubing attached to the pumps wasn't in keeping with the original fitments. I was careful to point out the finer features of the filtration system.

"The water's as pure as any mains water by the time it gets up to the tank in the loft," I told him. "Probably purer than much mainland water, although it's pretty hard. The real problem with not being connected to the mains is sewerage; the tanker that comes once a fortnight to drain the cesspool has to carry a specially extended vacuum tube just for this house. They have to do it, though—regulations."

He wasn't interested in sewerage, either. In fact, he lost interest in the whole underground complex as soon as he realized how empty it was of artifacts that might have been brought back to the old country from the home of the bean and the cod. The smugglers' cave left him completely cold; there obviously wasn't a lot of romance in his soul.

He didn't notice anything odd about the kitchen, but he scanned the TV room carefully, in search of anything un-modern. Then I took him upstairs. He didn't waste much time in the bedroom, but when he got to the lumber room, his eyes lit up.

"If there's anything else," I said, unnecessarily, "this is where you'll find it. It'll take time, though. Help yourself, while I fix us some lunch."

"You don't have to do that," he said, for politeness' sake.

"It's no trouble," I assured him. "You'll probably be busy here all afternoon—there's a lot of stuff, I'm afraid. Things do build up, don't they? It was a lot tidier when I last moved back in, but when you live alone..."

"You haven't always lived here, then?" he said, probably

fearing that there might be some other premises he might need to search.

"Dear me, no," I said. "I was married for ten years, when we lived in East Cowes, on the other side of the island. This is no place for small children. I moved back here after the divorce—but anything that came back from the U.S.A. in the thirties will have stayed here all along. Couldn't rent the place, you see, even as a holiday cottage. It was locked up tight and nobody ever broke in. Not a lot of crime on the island."

I left him alone then in order to make the lunch: cold meat from the farmers' market and fresh salad, with buttered bread and Bakewell tarts, both locally baked, and a fresh pot of tea. This time I used two bags of Earl Grey to one of Brown Label, and I ran the water from the other tap.

"What I don't understand," I said, as he tucked in, "is where the anatomy of the terrible and the physiology of fear fit in. What do cancers and trigger molecules have to do with latent instincts and hereditary memories?"

"Nobody understands it yet," he told me. "That's why my research is important. We understand how genes function as a protein factory, and the associated pathology of most cancers, but we don't understand the heredity of structure and behavior nearly as well. The process controlling the manner in which the fertilized ovum of a whale turns into a whale, and that of a hummingbird into a hummingbird, even though they have fairly similar repertoires of proteins, is still rather arcane, as is the process by which the whale inherits a whale's instincts and the hummingbird a hummingbird's. Most of human behavior is learned, of course—including many aspects of fear and horror—but there has to be an inherited foundation on which the learning process can build. The fact that Pickman's recessive gene, once somatically activated, caused a distinctive somatic metamorphosis rather than simple undifferentiated tumors indicates that it's linked in some way to the inheritance of structure. It's a common fallacy to imagine that individual genes only do one thing—usually, they have multiple functions—and the genes linked to structural development routinely have behavioral effects too. I suspect that the effects Pickman and his relatives suffered weren't just manifest in physical deformation; I suspect that they also affected the way he perceived and reacted to things."

"You think that's why he became an artist?"

"I think it might have affected the way he painted, and his choice of subject-matter—his understanding of the anatomy of the terrible and the physiology of fear."

"That's interesting," I said. "It took your grandfather differently, of course."

Mercifully, he wasn't holding his tea-cup. It was only his fork that he dropped. "What do you mean?" he asked.

"Art isn't a one-way process," I said, mildly. "Audience responses aren't created out of nothing. Mostly, they're learned—but there has to be an inherited foundation on which the learning process can build. It's right there in the story, if you look. Other people just thought that Pickman's work was disgustingly morbid, but your grandfather saw something more. It affected him much more profoundly, on a phobic level. He knew Pickman even better than Silas Eliot—they, your grandfather, and Reid were all members of the same close-knit community. It must have been much easier for you to obtain a sample of his DNA than Pickman's, and you already had your own for comparison. Are you carrying the recessive gene, Professor Thurber?"

A typical academic, he answered the question with a question: "Would you mind providing me with a sample of your DNA, Mr. Eliot?" he asked, reaching the bottom line at last.

"You've been trampling all over my house for the last two

hours," I riposted. "I expect you probably have one by now."

He'd picked up his fork automatically, but now he laid it down again. "Exactly how much do you know, Mr. Eliot?" he asked.

"About the science," I said, "not much more than I read in your excellent book and a couple of supplementary textbooks. About the witchcraft…well, how much of that can really be described as *knowledge*? If what Jonas Reid understood was vague, what I know is…so indistinct as to be almost invisible." I emphasized the word *almost* very slightly.

"Witchcraft?" he queried, doubtless remembering the allegation in Lovecraft's story that one of Pickman's ancestors had been hanged in Salem—although I doubt that Cotton Mather was really "looking sanctimoniously on" at the time.

"In England," I said, "they used to prefer the term *cunning men*. The people themselves, that is. Witches was what other people called them when they wanted to abuse them—not that they always wanted to abuse them. More often, they turned to them for help—cures and the like. The cunning men were social outsiders, but valued after their fashion—much like smugglers, in fact."

He looked at me hard for a moment or two, then went back to his lunch. You can always trust an American's appetite to get the better of his vaguer anxieties. I watched him drain his teacup and filled it up again immediately.

"Is the ultimate goal of your research to find a cure for…shall we call it *Pickman's syndrome*?" I asked, mildly.

"The disease itself seems to be virtually extinct," he said, "at least in the form that it was manifest in Pickman and his models. To the extent that it's still endemic anywhere, the symptoms generally seem to be much milder. It's not the specifics I'm interested in so much as the generalities. I'm hoping to learn something useful about the fundamental psychotropics of phobia."

"And the fundamental psychotropics of art," I added, helpfully. "With luck, you might be able to find out what makes a Pickman…or a Lovecraft."

"That might be a bit ambitious," he said. "Exactly what did you mean just now about *witchcraft*? Are you suggesting that your cunning men actually knew something about phobic triggers—that the Salem panic and the Boston scare might actually have been *induced*?"

"Who can tell?" I said. "The Royal College of Physicians, jealous of their supposed monopoly, used the law to harass the cunning men for centuries. They may not have succeeded in wiping out their methods or their pharmacopeia, but they certainly didn't help in the maintenance of their traditions. A good many must have emigrated, don't you think, in search of a new start?"

He considered that for a few moments, and then demonstrated his academic intelligence by experiencing a flash of inspiration. "The transfer effect doesn't just affect diseases," he said. "Crop transplantation often produces new vigor—and the effect of medicines can be enhanced too. If the Salem panic was induced, it might not have been the result of malevolence—it might have been a medical side-effect that was unexpectedly magnified. In which case…the same might conceivably be true of the Boston incident."

"Conceivably," I agreed.

"Jonas Reid wouldn't have figured that out—he wouldn't even have thought of looking. Neither would my grandfather, let alone poor Pickman. But *your* grandfather…if he knew something about the traditions of cunning men…"

"Silas Eliot wasn't my grandfather," I told him, unable this time to repress a slight smile.

His eyes dilated slightly in vague alarm, but it wasn't the effect of the unfiltered water in his tea. That wouldn't make itself manifest for days, or even weeks—but it *would* make itself manifest. The contagion wasn't the sort of thing that could be picked up by handling a book, a damp wall, or even a fungus-ridden guardrail, and it wouldn't have the slightest effect on a local man even if he drank it…but Professor Thurber was an American, who'd probably already caught a couple of local viruses to which he had no immunity. The world is a busy place nowadays, but not that many Americans get to the Isle of Wight, let alone its out-of-the-way little crevices.

I really didn't mean him any harm, but he had got too close to the truth about Pickman, and I had to stop him getting any closer—because the truth about Pickman had, unfortunately, become tangled up with the truth about me. It wasn't that I had to stop him *knowing* the truth—I just had to affect the way he looked at it. It wouldn't matter how much he actually knew, always provided that the knowledge had the right effect on him. Pickman would have understood that, and Lovecraft would have understood it better than anyone. Lovecraft understood the true tenacity and scope of the roots of horror, and knew how to savor its aesthetics.

"You're not claiming that you *are* Silas Eliot?" said Professor Thurber, refusing to believe it—for now. His common sense and scientific reason were still dominant.

"That would be absurd, Professor Thurber," I said. "After all, I haven't got the fountain of youth in my cellar, have I? It's just water—it isn't even polluted most of the time, but we have had a very wet August, and the woods hereabouts are famous for their fungi. Some poor woman in Newport died from eating a deathcap only last week. You really have to know what you're doing when you're dealing with specimens of that sort. The cunning men could probably have taught us a lot, but they're all gone now—fled to America, or simply dead. The Royal College of Physicians won; we—I mean *they*—lost."

The trigger hadn't had the slightest effect on him yet, but my hints had. He looked down at his empty tea-pot, and he was already trying to remember how many taps there had been in the kitchen.

"Please don't worry, Professor Thurber," I said. "As you said yourself, the disease is very nearly extinct, at least in the virulent form that Pickman had. The attenuated form that your grandfather had, on the other hand...it's possible that you might still catch that—but what would it amount to, after all? You might become phobic about subways and cellars, and your acrophobia might get worse, but people mostly cope quite well with these things. The only that might be seriously inconvenient, given your particular circumstances, is that it might affect your attitude to your hobby...and to your work. Jonas Reid had to give it up, didn't he?"

His eyes were no longer fixed on me. They were fixed on something behind me: the painting that he had mistaken, understandably enough, for a Pickman. He still thought that it *was* a Pickman, and he was wondering how the mild fear and disgust it engendered in him might increase, given the right stimulus. But biochemistry only supplies a foundation; in order to grow and mature, fears have to be nurtured and fed with doubts and provocations. Pickman had understood that, and so had Lovecraft. It doesn't actually matter much, if you have the right foundation to build on, whether you feed the fears with lies or the truth, but the truth is so much more *artistic*.

"Actually," I told him, "when I said that I knew who'd painted it, I didn't mean Pickman. I meant me."

His eyes shifted to my face, probing for tell-tale stigmata. "You painted it," he echoed, colorlessly. "In Boston? In the 1920s?"

"Oh no," I said. "I painted it right here in the chine, about twenty years ago."

"From memory?" he asked. "From a photograph? Or from life?"

"I told you that there aren't any photographs," I reminded him. I didn't bother shooting down the memory hypothesis—he hadn't meant that one seriously.

"You do carry the recessive gene, don't you?" he said, still the rational scientist, for a little while longer.

"Yes," I said. "So did my wife, unlikely as it might seem. She was Australian. If I'd known...but all I knew about then was the witchcraft, you see, and you can't really call that *knowledge*."

His jaw dropped slightly, then tightened again. He was a scientist, and he could follow the logic all the way—but he was a scientist, and he needed confirmation. Our deepest fears always need confirmation, one way or another, but once they have it, there's never any going back...or even, in any meaningful sense, going forward. Once we have the confirmation, the jigsaw puzzle is complete, and so are we.

"The chance was only one in four," I said. "My other son's body is a veritable temple to human perfection...and he can drink the water with absolute impunity."

Now, the horror had begun to dig in, commencing the long and leisurely work of burrowing into the utmost depths of his soul.

"But I have a family of my own at home in Boston," he murmured.

"I know," I said. "They have the Internet in Ventnor public library; I looked you up. It's not really that contagious, though—and even if you do pass it on, it won't be the end of the world: it'll just engender a more personal and more intimate understanding of the anatomy of the terrible, and the physiology of fear."

Tunnels

PHILIP HALDEMAN

Philip Haldeman has written for a wide variety of publications. His fiction has appeared in Alfred Hitchcock's Mystery Magazine, The Silver Web, Weirdbook, *and others. His novel* Shadow Coast *was published in 2007. For ten years he was a classical music critic for* American Record Guide. *He has been a spokesperson on science vs. superstition for local and national media and has retained a lifelong love of the supernatural in fiction.*

HE INSIDE OF OUR 1920S BRICK APARTMENT BUILDING was intersected with Oriental-carpeted hallways that might have been those of a luxurious mausoleum; except that these particular passages were haunted not by dead souls, but by living ones. I lived there, at the age of six, with my two grandparents and an aunt, but it wasn't the building's faded elegance or its aging tenants that was the focus of my childhood imagination. For some reason, in that peculiar four-story structure, I began to have disturbing, surrealistic dreams. The images were vague at first, then became more distinct, vivid, and aggressive. Over several nights of quiet terror, I came to believe, without any previous associations, that huge white worms were tunneling up from far under the ground beneath the apartment building.

My grandparents, who had recently moved from Billings, Montana, explained how common such nightmares were in the mind of an imaginative six-year-old. My aunt Evelyn was some what more blunt and disapproving: "Well, you mustn't worry. They can't tunnel up into your room if we're on the fourth floor." My grandmother merely said, "Now go back to bed and don't let such nonsense bother you."

Grandfather sat in his velvet-flocked overstuffed chair, his head resting against the embroidered antimacassar, listening to Amos 'n' Andy. It was 1950. He had recently been a lumberman in Montana and Minnesota, and it was reputed that he could tell on sight how many board feet of lumber were on a given railroad flat car. But in the late forties, he decided to come to

Seattle, partly to work at another lumber mill, and because he was in the habit of moving from one place to another. His greatest desire was to visit Sogndal, Norway, his birthplace. Grandfather was the sort of person you could depend on for advice.

"They're real," I said, shifting toward a whine. "If I let my hand out over the edge of the bed they'll bite onto it and pull me under the ground."

"Don't let your hand dangle over the edge of the bed," said Grandfather.

In the winter, Grandmother and I had built a snowman in the open courtyard at the front of the gabled apartment building. Mrs. Murphy peered down disapprovingly from her window because we were destroying the coat of virgin snow with our galoshes, rolling snowballs, and acting as if the courtyard were our own private domain. Perhaps because the building was in an old section of the city, it contained no children other than myself, at least none I can recall.

I remember that the hallway on the fourth floor was carpeted with an intricately patterned, wine-red runner, and it led down the hall to the corner I did not travel beyond. Near the end of the hall was Mr. Worklan's apartment. Mr. Worklan was a journeyman fur worker who spent much of his time in the cool storage vault of Weisman's Clothing on Third Avenue. One day he stared at me for a long time as I went up the main staircase (a dark forest of polished mahogany posts and railings). On the landing between floors, I saw him finally walk down toward his door like a drunken man lost in the depths of a sinking ocean liner, certain that only women and children would be saved.

GRANDMOTHER PUT HER HAND GENTLY ON MY FOREHEAD. "Goodnight, David."

"When will Mother be back?" I asked, as I had asked every night. And Grandmother answered, as she had answered every night, that she didn't know.

"Where is she?"

"We're not really sure, dear, but we love you and you'll stay with us. Go to sleep now and I'll leave your door open a crack."

With the narrow column of light coming from the short hall outside my room, I put my cheek on the cool pillow and began to sleep, and to dream about Mother.

When Mother and I had moved in, Mother shared a bedroom with my aunt. Father had moved "across town," I was told. We had left him, actually. Since I'd only a nursery-schooler's experience with Father, no one felt obligated to explain our flight and the subsequent divorce. As for my mother, one day she'd been in the apartment helping Grandmother with the ironing; the next day she was gone. Her disappearance was a shock, but after several days of confusion I decided to just wait for her to come back. Each night I would ask about her, and each night I perceived in my grandmother's answer a lingering doubt.

Mr. Worklan knocked on our door one night that summer. Grandfather let him in, and from my room I could hear their agitated voices. Worklan spoke in low, worried tones, his voice rising in fearful expressions, then subsiding into barely audible whispers. Grandfather spoke calmly; then I heard something like "…happened so fast" when the door of my room was closed, blacking out the secure crack of light from the hall. For several minutes I lay awake in the dark. I fell asleep listening to muffled voices.

Again, I dreamed of the big white worms tunneling up from under the ground. Their thick, blind, segmented bodies, unused to light, smelled like water in a limestone cave. Nothing in my humble experience prepared me for their existence, and my repeated nightmare became more terrifying and vivid with each occurrence. To ease my mind, Grandfather described the Orson Welles radio broadcast of *The War of the Worlds* in 1938, and how everyone thought Martians had landed in New Jersey. "We may be frightened by strange ideas, but sometimes we have to ignore them."

The creatures in my dreams were only as real as those Martians, I told myself, and they couldn't find their way into my room.

The next week, Grandmother, in her brown plaid overcoat, walked with me to Caroline's Bakery on 15th Avenue, where I stared into the long glass cases that contained fresh-baked birthday cakes. The baker often decorated these cakes with small plastic cowboys and Indians. We came for the homemade cinnamon rolls, however, and left quickly, passing Fire Station No. 7 on the way home. The back of our apartment house bordered an alley directly behind the fire station, and the gridded metal fire escape, whose uppermost platform was outside our kitchen window, could be seen winding downward to the alley where the garbage cans were grouped like big aluminum mushrooms near a brick wall. A fireman named John often threw a tennis ball back and forth to me in the alley. He had become a father figure, encouraging me to catch the ball and throw straight.

"He's learning to be a real ball player," John had told my grandmother.

At the front of the apartment building, I opened the tall, wood-framed glass door to the entry hall. Grandmother took a key out of her purse to check the mailbox.

That day, as we reached the second floor, Mrs. Schulte came running down the hall. She held my grandmother not so gently by the arm.

"Mr. Worklan in 8 is moving out!" Her face, not as aged as my grandmother's, nevertheless looked older right then. She might well have been announcing the Japanese attack on Pearl Harbor.

"*Oh?*" said Grandmother, looking significantly down at me for a brief moment.

"Yes…he…told us this morning. I thought you'd like to know." She backed away. "It's too bad when people want to leave," she said emphatically, and walked back down the hallway.

The next day, movers began to take furniture out of Mr. Worklan's apartment. Some of the tenants, including my grandfather, gathered on the hot summer sidewalk near the moving van to talk to him. I sneaked into the alley to listen to them from around the corner of the building.

"No, I won't stay. I won't stay now," said Mr. Worklan angrily.

"They couldn't have found us so soon," said Mr. Sorensen, an older tenant on the second floor.

"We've got to *do* something this time," said Mrs. Schulte in a violent whisper, and I could hear an edge of hysteria in her voice.

"Look, I know we've kept from meeting each other—since *we* aren't the only people in this building—but we sure as hell can't meet on the sidewalk," said Sorensen. He stared at Worklan. "The movers are coming out again. Why not go inside and talk? Why couldn't you wait, Worklan?"

Worklan stood there, stiff and straight, eyeing the apartments, his lips quivering slightly, his gaze scanning the courtyard and the windows as if trying to recall some lost or forgotten memory. He shook his head.

"Come on, Worklan," said Sorensen. "We should stay together."

"You're making a mistake," said Worklan. "We've been safe. But *all* of us should move now."

The movers came out carrying a mirrored bureau that

brilliantly reflected the windows and brick of the apartment house. They brought it down the steps and across the courtyard toward the sidewalk while the small group of tenants made room. A determined Worklan shook hands with Grandfather, then nodded to the others. "Goodbye."

By sundown, the movers had gone, and Mr. Worklan's apartment at the end of the second-floor hall was empty.

"He's left, and we might not hear from him again," said Grandfather that night.

"We won't really know..." said Aunt Evelyn.

"Keep your voices down," said Grandmother. "David might hear."

"He's asleep," said Aunt Evelyn.

But instead, I lay awake listening, thinking, wondering anxiously. Was there an essential fact about our lives I didn't know, that no one talked about? Would everyone leave? Where would I go?

"If we just stick together..." said Aunt Evelyn. "We should never have left Billings."

"You don't *mean* it, Evelyn," said Grandmother. "We got away."

"What about Worklan?" said Aunt Evelyn. "There aren't as many of us now. It's not fair."

"Is it supposed to be *fair*?" said Grandfather. "For Chrissake!"

"*Please* keep it down," said Grandmother. For a moment there was silence, and I thought someone would come to check on whether I was still asleep, but no one did.

"Worklan could turn up missing like Lars Johnson," said my aunt. "Remember Johnson, the boss on the East River side?"

"I remember them all," said Grandfather.

"They run away," said Aunt Evelyn nervously. "Why don't they stay? They run away and eventually they disappear. What happens if..."

"I don't blame them," said Grandfather.

"Oh, why can't we just get someone to help us?" said Aunt Evelyn. She was crying. Her fretful, harsh sobs drifted through the hall into my room, where this time the door had been accidentally left ajar.

"We've been through that, too," said Grandmother resignedly.

"We should find David's father," said my Aunt. "We should get David to his father."

"He thought we were insane."

"*Please* keep it down," said Grandmother.

"Sorry," said Grandfather in a barely audible voice. "But Evelyn's right. It was fine as long as David was living with his mother and father, but now he's not safe with us, and we're getting too old to move again. We have to make a stand."

"God," said Aunt Evelyn, "I don't know."

"This time we'll have to wait," said Grandfather.

"What will we tell David?" said Aunt Evelyn. There was a long silence, and during the silence I struggled to keep from yelling in terror, rushing into the living room and pleading with them to tell me what was happening to us. Eventually, I fell asleep exhausted. And in my dreams *they* came again from below in their tunnels—slick, pasty horrors without eyes…

In the morning I watched Grandfather sitting in his chair, smoking his pipe, occasionally looking toward me where I played grimly with toy horses. His gray features were a cruel poker face. I fought with the determination of a chess player to stay calm. I was afraid to speak.

When the sun was low one day and the light glared through the front-door glass into the building's entry hall, I sat on the lower step of the staircase. Mrs. Turnbull was cleaning her apartment and had made one or two trips out the back door behind the main staircase, now carrying a grocery bag of garbage that smelled of used coffee grounds. I heard the garbage can lid rattle onto the can in the alley, and from Mrs. Turnbull's open apartment door I could hear the soap-opera voices of *Stella Dallas* coming from her radio. I heard the back door close, watched Mrs. Turnbull start back down the long hallway, then turn.

She suddenly walked back toward me, a hurricane of thick makeup and bright red lipstick. Her face was like a shrunken plaster cast, her pale eyes like marbles of blue and white fire. "Your grandmother hasn't *told* you anything," she said hastily. "They spoil you." Her left eye twitched slightly in its cavity of dry flesh. "You shouldn't be here. Do you think we're all going to pack up and move *again?* Tell your grandpa and grandma what I said." She bent down, a frightened caricature. "It doesn't matter because I'm not going to live much longer, you know what I mean? What dying is? Or," she smiled, "haven't they mentioned that little item to you either?" She started to say more, but saw tears in my eyes. She quickly turned, as if from the scene of a crime, and retreated toward her apartment with the soap-opera voices.

Late that evening, I believe some kind of a meeting was held. After I heard my grandmother, grandfather, and aunt go out and shut the front door, I put on my robe, came out of my room, and went into the outside hall. There was the sound of people treading through the lower hallways and down the stairs to the first floor. There was that feeling, barely comprehensible to me then: I am inside a tomb, here are the dead people moving around. I went back into the living room and sat in Grandfather's overstuffed chair.

I didn't know how long I slept, but when I awoke, I pictured the downstairs hall in my mind, thought about the first-floor tenants and the front-door glass, which must have been a tall dark rectangle at that time of night.

Aunt Evelyn had said, "How could they come from

under the ground if we're on the fourth floor?" I realized how misleading that comment had been, and I remembered Mrs. Turnbull taking out her garbage along the short passage that went past a door that led to the basement. Down there, our storeroom locker was packed with old furniture, boxes of bedding, tools, and other things. The basement room with its rows of wooden foundation posts extended under the entire length of the building and included a big boiler. I had been down there once or twice with Grandfather, but never alone.

I went out into the hall. It was dark because of a burned-out light bulb, but a flood of light came up the stairwell. I went downstairs to the short hall that led to the alley. Midway along it was the cellar door. Ten feet away was the alley exit door, and through its window I could see a dim illumination of streetlight on the bricks of the old fire station.

I turned the cold brass of the cellar doorknob. A light was on in the basement; the old stairs descended into dimly lit space. Frightened but curious, I stepped down one at a time.

The underground room extended into the dark shadows among the row of foundation posts.

In this bizarre place, under a dim light bulb near the center of the bare floor, sat my grandmother. She was rocking slowly back and forth in a high-backed rocking chair. Her hands worked a pair of knitting needles, nervously starting and stopping while the chair creaked. I recognized the chair as one that had recently been put in our storage locker next to a pair of old snow tires. She had rocked me in that chair many times.

I stepped quietly down to the bottom of the stairs. Grandmother wore the brown plaid overcoat she'd used while walking with me. It was cold down here.

"Grandmother?" I whispered.

Her hands stopped knitting.

"Grandmother?"

The chair stopped, she looked up in surprise and stared in my direction.

"David?"

"It's me."

"Why are you down here?" she said in a dry voice. She started to get up. The knitting fell from her lap onto the concrete floor. She stood up. "Oh…you have to go back upstairs. How did you find your way down here?"

"I didn't know where anyone was."

"Well, you're supposed to be in bed." Her voice fluttered in an unnatural way. "You'd better go now, right away."

I turned.

"Wait," she said. She motioned me to come to her. I walked across the cold floor, and when she sat back down I eased myself onto her lap.

"It *is* a long night," she said. "You know, David, I love you. Sit with me for a while, like we used to do."

We sat there rocking for some time, until I could hear the floorboards creaking slightly overhead with the movement of footsteps while Grandmother looked up in silence.

"Why are you down here, Grandma?"

"Well, because it's cool down here after such a hot day. You know how hot it was today, don't you? Well, down here it's cool."

"Are you coming upstairs now, Grandma?"

"Not yet, dear. I can't come back upstairs right away. I'm really supposed to be down here for a while. Will you do me a favor, David?"

"Yes," I said with tearful eyes, knowing that something was wrong.

"Will you tell your grandfather that I'm all right, and that you were here?"

"Yes."

"And remember that we love you."

I kissed her on the cheek, and she let me off of her lap.

I went back to our apartment on the fourth floor. A pale yellow light came from the kitchen. Grandfather sat alone at the kitchen table, his elbow on the table, eyes downcast. He looked up at me when I came in and brought a handkerchief out of his deep pants pocket.

"Grandma says to tell you she's all right," I said.

Grandfather looked at me with wide eyes. He hadn't expected me to come in by the front door and didn't know I'd been gone.

He lifted me up and held me tightly on his lap. He spoke calmly and treated me as if by some remote chance, after his words changed the world forever, I would be able to cope. He proceeded slowly at first.

"You are becoming aware of certain things, David, so it's time you knew that the world isn't exactly what it appears." He shifted me on his lap, trying to get more comfortable.

"You remember I came on the boat to New York in 1906? Well, about a year later I got a job working on the New York subway system, which was being built then. I had a friend who'd come with me from Norway—Nels Hanson. We worked in the tunnels because, well, we needed the money to pay rent and buy food; so we stayed. We had to work, Hanson and I and the rodmen—Worklan, Turnbull, and Murphy. A fellow named Benson was an engineer—and there was some odd slumping of the ground he didn't expect. A few of the men were afraid because they didn't know how safe we were down there. I was afraid, too, but we were there to do a job—the sand hoggers, drillers, and the bosses, bless their black hearts."

"Sand hoggers?"

"That's what they were called." He paused. "Building a tunnel is a big job, David. Things happen, people die, people leave, people go through a lot of trouble. Working underground is like working in a city with no sky—a big, dark, dreary place. It was down near the Hudson Terminal, in one of the two lower tubes, that the bad thing happened.

"Benson, the engineer, was ahead down the line, checking out the ground problem. This was before the concrete had been poured. There was a lot of water down there, freezing cold, so we all had our heavy clothes and rubber boots on... We heard this terrible scream coming from down the line, but we couldn't get there very fast. Something had happened to Benson... You know, when some people are frightened really bad, they just aren't themselves anymore. That's what happened to Benson. He kind of fell asleep in his mind."

"Why?" I asked.

"We didn't know. But later, when he recovered from shock, he said there were strange things in the deepest parts of the tunnel. He said they had been crawling down there and affecting his mind.

"A month later we were down there again, in the lower tunnel, just a few of us: Lars Johnson, our boss—Murphy, McShay, and Sorensen, the man who'd taken over for Benson—and some others, some of the people who live right here in our apartments, David, and who've stuck together for over forty years. I guess there were a half-dozen of us down there on that day.

"It was like a bad dream, David, like the dream you've been having. McShay and Bailey came running back from below. They said that huge white things were in the ground—worms, they said—and Farley, he was a non-union man but tough-minded; he had a pick ax, McShay said, and he tried to kill one of them but couldn't, and they took hold of Farley with big sucking jaws and dragged him down under the ground. It was horrible. No one could help Farley, and we ran back through the tunnel—and in the days following we had horrible thoughts—thoughts we were told by Benson came from underground, thoughts we couldn't understand because the underground things were blind, yet they lived in a world of sound and vibration, and they could hear us.

"For days, no one would go back down there, and construction was held up until a new crew could be found. There were some transfers to other parts of the project. There were rumors that a large hole had been filled in, but there were no more strange stories. The men I worked with scattered from job to job until the subway was finished. But none of them who were in the tunnel *that* day have ever been able to live in one place for long—because of the dreams. Dreams that may not be dreams at all. Or memories either. Some said McShay and Bailey killed Farley themselves because he was a non-union man. But Mr. Worklan, he thinks maybe those blind creatures under the ground permanently locked into our minds because they can't see or talk, and they got to know where we are. We've come up with all kinds of ideas, but the one that sticks is that those things under the ground are trying to find us again. We don't know why.

"But that's sometimes the way the world is, David. Our idea is that they share our planet but don't know what *we* are, and maybe no one but us knows about them. So we've been moving around the country, because after each move the dreams stop. We think the dreams mean they are getting close to finding us again, and we don't know what will happen if they do. Most of us decided to band together. We began to study books about a hollow earth, UFOs, and things like that, and we formed a kind of club to delve into these matters. None of it was the truth. I set up the lumber business, first in Minnesota, so we could work and stay together."

"How can the underground things stay secret?"

"We don't know—but sometimes you can be near something for a long time and not know it's there. We've been trying to find other people who know about them. Once, we thought we'd found someone. He wrote in a magazine that he'd been exploring a deep cave and had seen moving white things in a grotto, but he wouldn't respond to our letters asking if he'd had strange dreams. We tried to tell him about how the underground world is inhabited by these creatures and how they may threaten us. The world is a confusing place, David, and we alone had discovered the strangest thing about it. The man who wrote the article teaches at a university, and in the article he said he believes that there may be many discoveries yet to come about life underground. But we gave up writing to him."

Grandfather's voice wavered slightly. "Most of us are tired now, David, like Turnbull's wife, but still afraid. Now and then one of us tried to tell someone else about the creatures, but no one believed—because none of their experiences included what was seen in the tunnel that day. They are right not to believe, David, because what was seen doesn't jibe with what's known. When we began to dream about them again, there was usually time to move, pack up, and run. But we're getting old, and we can't run anymore."

His voice weakened. "We kept the secret from our children for a long time. Your Aunt Evelyn found out because she came back to live with us. Your mother was lucky because she'd grown up during a time when there weren't any bad dreams. We think the dreams come when the things are near, and they affect those close to us. When the children were growing up, we had to move only once, from Minnesota to Montana. When all our children were old enough, we told them the story, but they didn't know what to think about it. We told your father, too, but he thought we were crazy. He said maybe we had been given drugs in our water supply down in the tunnel."

"Where's Mother?" I asked. "Why didn't she take me with her?"

His hands shook slightly. "We haven't heard from her. She was very upset after her divorce from your father. She talked about getting an apartment and finding a job before sending for you. She knew you'd be safe for a while. We couldn't understand why she didn't tell anyone before she left. It was very cruel, David, and we didn't know what to say or do. We're sure she'll come back for you, David. Perhaps she started to have dreams, too."

Aunt Evelyn came into the kitchen.

"Most of us decided to stay," Grandfather continued, "to keep watch, and see what happens, though the dreams are strong now." He smiled grimly. "It's early, but I'm going to take your grandmother's watch now. Mr. Sorensen will take my place in two hours. We are going to take turns listening in the basement. Our only chance now is to wait for them."

"Maybe it's just *dreams*, Grandfather!"

Grandfather eased me off his lap. He bent forward and hugged me with his lumberman's strength.

Then he brushed by Aunt Evelyn and went out through the living room. I started to run after him, but my aunt grabbed me and held onto me.

Grandfather left to go downstairs.

My mind, half numb, groped for whatever reality I could cling to in my now disassembled universe: the horrible creatures, Grandfather's story. Might there not have been some other explanation for the dreams?

I went into the living room and sat on the sofa. Finally I said, "We have to get help!"

"Yes," said my aunt, "when the time comes." She reached out and gripped me gently by the shoulder.

I got up, broke angrily free of her grip, and ran out of the apartment into the hall. I hurried down the main stairs and to the cellar door.

I went down into the basement. Grandfather rocked

peacefully in the chair. He was holding a book, and looked up at me slowly. Grandmother turned to leave, then also saw me.

"David. My God, what are you…down here again! Listen to me! Get upstairs right now!" Her voice echoed among the foundation posts.

"I…can't," I said. "Not until you come."

Grandfather got up from the chair, took me firmly by the hand, and they both led me up the basement stairs.

"Come on, David!" said Grandmother.

"I'd better stay," said Grandfather.

"No!" I yelled.

"Better help me get him upstairs," said Grandmother. "It won't take but a few seconds."

We three came out of the basement and rounded the landing halfway to the second floor while I slid my hand miserably along the railing.

I was put to bed. The room was black except for a bit of light that shafted under the door, illuminating a few floorboards. I listened intently for my grandparents, wishing the time forward. I fought to keep from calling out, and the window shade next to my bureau seemed to symbolize what had been kept from me. After a time, I fell asleep.

Our ability to confirm the memories of childhood is often based upon cruel or doubtful reconstructions, but it was in the confusion that followed that I learned how tenuous our grip on reality can be.

I was awakened by a frightening noise.

A thunder sound, coming up from far below, tore at my senses. I'd never heard a sound like it—or was I dreaming?—the sound of thick concrete cracking deep down in the basement. The building shook slightly, as if in an earthquake.

I jumped out of bed and rushed into the living room, where my aunt grabbed onto me. Ripping my pajama top, I wrenched free of her and ran out into the upper hall. I had to find Grandfather. I heard his familiar voice coming up from the stairwell.

"Timing!" he yelled angrily, his voice distinguishable amid the noises of people shouting and running in the hallways.

I ran barefoot down the stairs, my aunt yelling after me. I got to the first floor. My grandfather was standing at the entrance to the cellar door. Huge cracking sounds, as of thick concrete snapping, wooden supports breaking, came from below. Mr. Sorensen was handing Grandfather cans of gasoline that he then poured down the cellar stairs. The other people in the entry hall, including my grandmother, began to run back up the stairs or out through the front door. People were yelling "*Fire!*" They ran through near or far exits of the building. Mrs. Schulte stayed behind. She was holding two unlit torches. One of these she passed to Grandfather, who tensely lit it with a cigarette lighter and then threw it down into the cellar. Flames quickly roared up through the cellar door as Grandfather and Mrs. Schulte backed away. Grandfather turned, saw me standing there, ran toward me, picked me up in his huge hands, and, without seeming to think, bounded back up the stairs with me in his arms.

He set me down on the second-floor landing.

"Stay here!" he yelled at me. "I was supposed to be on the first floor!"

I grabbed onto him. "No!"

He got loose from me and stumbled back down the stairs to the entry hall. The hot flames burst across the downstairs ceiling and licked up into the stairwell. I heard a commotion. I looked up, and there were other tenants, the familiar faces I knew, peering down from the various landings toward Grandfather, who yelled up at them from below. "Get to the fire escapes!" Then he turned his attention to a red-framed glass box on the wall. I'd seen it many times before. He grabbed the little hammer and smashed the glass. The alarm, which was attached to our apartment house, rang fiendishly in the alley out by the garbage cans. Now Mr. Sorensen, holding two more cans of gasoline, rushed by me on the landing. Grandfather came up the stairs to meet him, and together they poured the gasoline, which sloshed down the stairs, splashing onto the walls and railing.

The cans were almost empty when we heard what sounded like the floor below breaking all along the length of the building. We heard people yelling "Fire!" and banging on doors in the distance. Mrs. Schulte, from a few steps up, handed Mr. Sorensen the second handmade torch, this time already lit. Grandfather tossed it down onto the stairs where the gasoline pooled and dripped into the soaking carpet. The stairwell exploded in a tempest of heat and flames. The walls, carpet, and woodwork caught fire all at once. While I was dragged up to the fourth floor, I looked down into the roaring conflagration. People die in fires, I thought. Die!

An acrid smell filled the air. *In the flames and smoke I saw something alive*. Something monstrously white was writhing in or behind the waves of heat, fire, and smoke roaring up the stairwell. A second one appeared. Then up into the mid-air blackness, screaming, I was lifted and carried into our apartment. Grandmother, Grandfather, Aunt Evelyn, and I made our exit through the big double-hung kitchen window and out onto the fire escape. We descended amid the sounds of the fire station alarm and the apartment alarm. Other tenants did the same. A fire engine roared around to the front of the apartment building while we huddled on the lower escape landing. Grandfather lowered a metal ladder—an object I'd always failed to see because it had been part of the metal grid. We climbed down to the pavement.

The old people gathered near the fire station wall. They whispered to each other in the darkness; then, in a group, they moved down the alley and out to the street in front of the old apartment building.

I watched the firemen point their brass-nozzle hoses toward the orange flames that beat out of the second-story windows like tattered rags in a harsh wind. People were talking, shouting, while the alarms continued to sound. I stood on the cool pavement while the fire spread upward.

That building, which on the outside looked like one of Poe's haunted mansions and on the inside like a tomb, was now engulfed in flames. The firefighters had been right next door, but the fire had started so quickly and spread so fast that even the advantage of location was minimized, and in the glow of the fire people were expressing astonishment all around me, now pointing toward the burning roof. The alley was soon blocked by policemen, and I could only stand with my bare feet on the pavement and gaze at the tall brick walls. High up, at the fire escape landing, smoke poured through our broken kitchen window. I heard the sounds of breaking glass and hissing steam; and finally, as the fire was at last extinguished in that huge sooty building, the survivors remained huddled together, the crowd thinned out, and within the hour I could hear the lonely sound of dripping water.

There was the familiar face of John, the fireman, from Station No. 7, standing next to us, looking upward at the black windows, annoyed and bewildered. He looked at the dozen anxious wrinkled faces in the darkness.

When he spoke, some unaccountable fragment of confusion clung to his words. "How'd it start?" he asked quietly.

Grandfather looked at John for a few seconds, watching his youthful face, seeming to ponder an act of trust that I later realized might have been planned, but in the end he said nothing.

John removed his helmet and ran his hand through a tangle of thick brown hair. He was uneasy, frightened, looking back at my grandfather's silent expression, visions perhaps of something incredible retreating in the flames. He looked at the old faces.

"What in God's name were they?" he asked.

T WAS SWEPT INTO THE PAST, ALL THE UNACCEPTABLE facts or fantasies, but I stayed the rest of that night and all the next day in the fire station. Our dark blue 1940 Ford miraculously contained family treasures—photo albums, jewelry, clothing, a few books, some phonograph records, and even some of my toys—all the important things that had been placed in it by Grandmother and Aunt.

My mother found out about the fire. She returned and took me away to the suburbs, where I went to grade school. No one ever admitted starting the fire, so it was attributed to persons unknown. Aunt Evelyn eventually moved to Boise, Idaho, while my grandparents went south to California.

My mother tried to make me forget what she called a cult of delusion and the fantasies told by my grandfather of his days in the Hudson tubes. It was a story concocted to scare off non-union workers, she said—and in time I might have begun to question the reality of my dreams and the accuracy of my memories.

Yet, even as she spoke, the Seattle papers printed the story of unexplained tunnels under the old apartment building, nearly vertical tunnels that had collapsed into unaccountable depths.

City officials chose not to speculate as to the origin of the passages, the men of Fire Station No. 7 declined comment, and the mysterious holes were eventually filled by many tons of earth and rock.

My grandparents passed away, and Aunt Evelyn, now

eighty-six, has not reported any bad dreams. Yet I wonder if workers in some underground project will make a new report. Has some shift in habitat or consciousness started to bring the worms to the surface? Given what I have seen, and what we know of their tiny brethren on our planet, their number may be too horrifying to contemplate.

The Correspondence of Cameron Thaddeus Nash

ANNOTATED BY RAMSEY CAMPBELL

Ramsey Campbell is one of the most distinguished authors of supernatural fiction of his generation. He published a collection of Cthulhu Mythos tales, The Inhabitant of the Lake and Other Unwelcome Tenants *(Arkham House, 1964), at the age of eighteen. His second collection,* Demons by Daylight *(1973), was a landmark in the history of weird fiction. Among his later collections are* Dark Companions *(Macmillan, 1982),* Waking Nightmares *(Tor, 1991),* Alone with the Horrors *(Arkham House, 1993), and* Told by the Dead *(PS Publishing, 2003). Among his many novels are* Incarnate *(Macmillan, 1983),* Midnight Sun *(Macdonald, 1990),* The Long Lost *(Headline, 1993),* The House on Nazareth Hill *(Headline Feature, 1996), and* The Darkest Part of the Woods *(PS Publishing, 2002). Most of his Lovecraftian tales were gathered in* Cold Print *(Tor, 1985; rev. ed. Headline, 1993). PS Publishing is to publish the definitive set of his Lovecraftian short fiction.*

N 1968 AUGUST DERLETH WAS SENT A NUMBER OF letters that had apparently been received by H. P. Lovecraft. The anonymous parcel bore no return address. Although the letters had been typed on a vintage machine and on paper that appeared to be decades old, Derleth was undecided whether they were authentic. For instance, he was unsure that someone living in a small English village in the 1920s would have had access to issues of *Weird Tales*, and he could find no obvious references to Nash in any of Lovecraft's surviving correspondence. Derleth considered printing some or all of Nash's letters in the *Arkham Collector* but decided against using them in the Winter 1969 issue devoted to Lovecraft. Later he asked me to think about writing an essay on Lovecraft for a new Lovecraftian volume that might offer the letters a home, but the project was shelved. Intrigued by his references to the Nash letters, I persuaded him to send me copies, including the other documents. It isn't clear what happened to the originals. When I visited Arkham House in 1975, James Turner knew nothing about them, and he was subsequently unable to trace them. He did mention that in *Howard Phillips Lovecraft: Dreamer on the Nightside*, Frank Belknap Long referred to an English writer who "thought it was amusing to call people names," by whom Lovecraft had supposedly been troubled for several years. Since Long was unable to be more specific, Turner deleted the reference. I reproduce all the letters here, followed by the final documents. Nash's signature is florid and extends across the page. It grows larger but less legible as the correspondence progresses.

7, Grey Mare Lane,
Long Bredy,
West Dorset,
Great Britain.
April 29th, 1925

My dear Mr. Lovecraft,

FORGIVE A SIMPLE ENGLISH VILLAGER FOR TROUBLING such a celebrated figure as yourself. I trust that the proprietors of your chosen publication will not think it too *weird* that a mere reader should seek to communicate with his idol. As I pen these words I wonder if they might not more properly have been addressed to the *eerie* letter-column of that magazine. My fear is that the editor would find them unworthy of ink, however, and so I take the greater risk of directing them to you. I pray that he will not find me so presumptuous that he forwards them no farther than the bin beside his desk.

May I come swiftly to my poor excuse for this intrusion into your inestimably precious time? I have sampled six issues of the Unique Magazine, and I am sure you must be aware that it has but a single claim to uniqueness—the contributions of your good self. I scarcely know whether to marvel or to be moved that you should allow them to appear amongst the motley fancies which infest the pages of the journal. Do you intend to educate the other contributors by your example? Are you not concerned that the ignorant reader may be repelled by this commonplace herd, thereby failing to discover the visions which you offer? The company in which you find yourself reads like the scribbling of hacks who have never dared to dream. I wish that the magazine would at least emblazon your name on the cover of every number which contains your prose. I promise you that on the occasion when I mistakenly bought an issue which had neglected to feature your work, I rent it into shreds so small that not a single vapid sentence could survive.

I am conscious how far any words of mine will fall short of conveying my admiration of your work. May I simply isolate those elements which remain liveliest in my mind? Your parable of Dagon seems to tell a truth at which the compilers of the Bible scarcely dared to hint, but I am most intrigued by the dreams which the narrator is afraid to remember in daylight. The quarry of your hideous hound declares that his fate is no dream, yet to this English reader it suggests one, brought on by the banal Baskerville investigations of Sherlock Holmes. Your narrator de la Poer dreams whilst awake, but are these reveries shaped by awful reality or the reverse? As for the descendant of the African union, perhaps he never dreams of his own nature because he has a *germ in* him—the same germ which infects the minds of all those who believe we are as soulless as the ape. But it is your *hypnotic* tale of Hypnos which exerts the firmest hold on my imagination. May I press you to reveal its source? Does it perhaps hint at your own experience?[1]

As to myself, I am sure you will not want to be fatigued by information about me. I am but a player at the human game. However long I sojourn in this village, none of its natives will tempt me to grow *breedy*. While my body works behind a counter, my spirit is abroad in the infinity of imagination. At least the nearby countryside offers solitude, and it harbours relics of the past, which are keys to dreams. Please accept my undying gratitude, Mr. Lovecraft, for helping to enliven mine. If you should find a few moments to acknowledge this halting missive, you will confer existence on a dream of your most loyal admirer.

---

[1] Nash refers here to Lovecraft's tales "Dagon", "The Hound", "The Rats in the Walls", "Arthur Jermyn" and "Hypnos", all recently published in *Weird Tales*.

I have the honour to remain, Mr. Lovecraft,

Your respectful and obedient servant,
Cameron Thaddeus Nash

7, Grey Mare Lane,
Long Bredy,
West Dorset,
Great Britain.
August 12th, 1925

My esteemed Mr. Lovecraft,

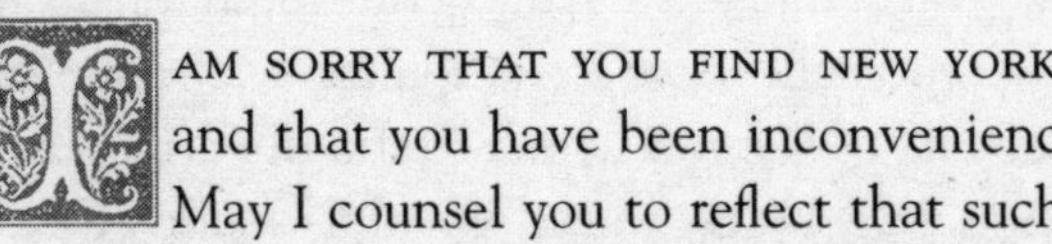
AM SORRY THAT YOU FIND NEW YORK INHOSPITABLE and that you have been inconvenienced by burglary. May I counsel you to reflect that such disadvantages are negligible so long as one's fancies remain unfettered? Your corporeal experiences count for naught unless they prevent you from dreaming and from communicating your dreams. Let me assure you that they have reached across the ocean to inspire a fellow voyager.

I was sure that your stories which I have read gave voice to your dreams, and I rejoice to understand that other tales of yours do so. But why must these pieces languish in amateur publications? While the mob would doubtless greet them with brutish incomprehension, surely you should disseminate your visions as widely as possible, to give other dreamers the opportunity to chance upon them. I hope some of our kind made themselves a Yuletide present of your tale about the festival in the town which you had never visited except in dreams. I fear that any reader with a brain must have been seasonably inebriated to enjoy the other contents of that number of the magazine. How can it still neglect to advertize your presence on the cover? I remain appalled that the issue which contained your tale of Hypnos chose to publicize Houdini's contribution instead. How misguided was the editor to provide a home for those ridiculous Egyptian ramblings? Houdini even dares to claim that the tale is the report of a dream, but we genuine dreamers see through his charlatanry. I believe he has never dreamed in his life, having been too bent on performing tricks with his mere flesh.[2]

May I presume to pose a question? I wonder if Hypnos represents only as terrible an aspect of dream as you believe the reader could bear to confront, unless this evasion is born of your own wariness. For myself, I am convinced that at the farthest reach of dream we may encounter the source, whose nature no deity ever imagined by man could begin to encompass. Perhaps some Greek sage glimpsed this truth and invented Hypnos as a mask to spare the minds of the multitude. But, Mr. Lovecraft, our minds stand above the mass, and it is our duty to ourselves never to be daunted from dreaming.

I wish you could have shared my midsummer night's experience, when I spent a midnight hour with the Grey Mare and her colts. They are fragments of an ancient settlement, and I seemed to dream that I found the buried entrance to a grave. It led into a labyrinth illuminated only by my consciousness. As I ventured deeper I became aware that I was descending into an unrecorded past. I understood that the labyrinth was the very brain of an ancient mage, the substance of which had fertilized the earth, where his memories emerged in the form of aberrant subterranean

[2] In this paragraph Nash refers to "The Festival" and "Imprisioned with the Pharaohs".

growths. One day I may fashion this vision into a tale.

I have done so, and I take the great liberty of enclosing it. Should you ever be able to spare the time to glance over it, I would find any comments that you cared to offer beyond price. Perhaps you might suggest a title more fitting than *The Brain Beneath the Earth*?

I bid you adieu from a land which you have dreamed of visiting.

Yours in inexpressible admiration,
Cameron Thaddeus Nash

18, Old Sarum Road,
Salisbury,
Wiltshire,
Great Britain.
October 30th, 1925

Dear H. P. Lovecraft,

THANK YOU FOR YOUR KIND PRAISE OF MY LITTLE TALE, and thank you for taking the trouble to think of a title. Now it sounds more like a story of your own. Please also be assured of my gratitude for the time you spent in offering suggestions for changes to the piece. I am sure you will understand if I prefer it to remain as I dreamed it. I am happy that in any case you feel it might be worthy of submission to the "unique magazine," and I hereby authorize you to do so. I am certain that *Beneath the Stones* can only benefit from your patronage.

I must apologize for my mistake over the "Houdini" tale.

Had it appeared as *Under the Pyramids* by none other than the great Howard Phillips Lovecraft, I promise you that it would have excited a different response from this reader. I should have guessed its authorship, since it proves to be the narration of a dream. May I assume that Houdini supplied some of the material? I believe this robs the tale of the authenticity of your other work. Only genuine dreamers can collaborate on a dream.

I was amused to learn that you had to devote your wedding night to typing the story afresh. Perhaps your loss of the original transcription was a lucky chance which you should continue to embrace. I trust you will permit a fellow dreamer to observe that your courtship and marriage appear to have distracted you from your true purpose in the world. I fervently hope that you have not grown unable to dream freely now that you are no longer alone. May your wife be preventing you from visiting sites which are fertile with dreams, or from employing relics to bring dreams to your bed? You will have noticed that I have moved onwards from my previous abode, having exhausted the site of which I wrote to you. I believe my new situation will provide me with a portal to dreams no living man has begun to experience.

In the meantime I have read your brace of tales which recently saw publication. The musician Zann and his street are dreams, are they not? Only in dreams may streets remain unmapped. Is the abyss which the music summons not a glimpse or a hint of the source of the ultimate dream? And Carter's graveyard reverie conjures up the stuff of dream.[3] It rightly stays unnameable, for the essence of dreams neither can nor should be named. You mentioned that these tales were composed before your courtship. May I take the liberty of suggesting that they remind you what you are in peril of abandoning? The dreamer ought to be a solitary man, free to follow all the promptings of his mind.

---

[3] Nash is referring to "The Music of Erich Zann" and "The Unnamable".

At least while you are unable to write, you are still communicating visions—my own. Now that you have become my American representative I shall be pleased if you will call me Thad. It is the name I would ask a friend to use, and it sounds quite American, does it not? Let me take this opportunity to send you three more tales for your promotion. I am satisfied with them and with their titles. May I ask you not to show them to any of your circle or to mention me? I prefer not to be heard of until I am published. I hope that the magazine will deign to exhibit both of our names on the cover. Let the spiritless scribblers be confined within, if they must continue to infest its sheets.

Yours in anticipation of print,
Thad Nash

18, Old Sarum Road,
Salisbury,
Wiltshire,
Great Britain.
February 14th, 1926

Dear Howard Phillips Lovecraft,

I AM GRATEFUL TO YOU FOR YOUR ATTEMPT TO PLACE my work. You had previously mentioned that Farthingsworth Wrong[4] tends to be unreceptive to the truly *unique*. I am certain that you must have done

[4] Farnsworth Wright, editor of *Weird Tales*.

everything in your power to persuade him to your opinion of my tales. Are there other markets where you will do your best to sell them, or is it more advisable to wait for his tastes to mature? You will appreciate that I am relying on your experience in these matters.

I do not recall your mentioning that you had written new fiction last summer. I am relieved to learn that your marital subjugation has not permanently crippled your ability to dream. May I assume that these stories did not hinder your marketing of my work? I believe that our writing has little in common other than the title you provided, but I wonder if the editor's judgement may have been adversely affected by your sending him too many pieces all at once. Perhaps in future it would be wise to submit my work separately from your own, and with a reasonable interval between them.

I am heartened by the information that you plan to write a history of supernatural literature. I am sure that your appreciation of the form will produce a guide which should be on the shelves of every dreamer. I look forward eagerly to reading it. If I can advise or in any way aid you, please do not hesitate to ask.

You will be anxious to hear about the progress of my own work. Please reassure yourself that your failure to place my stories has not cast me down. Rather has it goaded me to venture deeper into dream, whence I shall return bearing prizes no less wonderful than dreadful. I shall tell ancient truths which no reader will be able to deny and no editor dare to suppress. I am certain that the nearby sites contain unsuspected relics, although soon I may have no more need of them. However it is used, a relic is but the germ of a dream, just as your dreams are the germs of your fiction. I wonder to what extent your dreams have become fixed on your native Providence? Perhaps your desire to return there is draining your imagination of the energy to rise higher and voyage farther. I hope you will ultimately find as congenial an environment as I have myself.

I await news of your efforts.

Yours for the supremacy of dream,
Cameron Thad Nash

1, Toad Place,
Berkeley
Gloucestershire,
Great Britain.
May 23rd, 1926

Dear HPL,

WRITE TO ALERT YOU THAT, LIKE YOURS, MY BODY HAS found a new lodging. It became necessary for me to decamp to an unfamiliar town. I had been surprised one night in the process of obtaining a relic. The donor of the item could have made no further use of it, but I fear that the mob and its *uninformed*, *uniformed* representatives of *unformed uniformity* have little understanding of the dreamer's needs. The resultant pursuit was unwelcome, and a source of distraction to me. For several nights I was annoyed by dreams of this mere chase, and they led to my seeking a home elsewhere.

Well, I am done with graves and brains and the infusion of them. I am safe inside my skull, where the mob cannot spy, nor even dreamers like yourself. I have learned to rise above the use of material aids to dream. I require but a single talisman—the night and the infinite darkness of which it is the brink. Let the puny scientists strive to design machines to fly to other worlds! This dreamer has preceded them, employing no device save his own mind. The darkness swarms with dreams, which have been formed by the consciousnesses of creatures alien beyond the wildest fancies of man. Each dream which I add to my essence leads me deeper into uncharted space. A lesser spirit would shrivel with dread of the ultimate destination. In my tales I can only hint at the stages of my quest, for fear that even such a reader as yourself may quail before the face of revelation.

I see you are content to have reverted to your native Providence. I hope that your contentment will provide a base from which you may venture into the infinite. I have read your recent contributions to Farthingsworth's rag. Will you forgive my opining that your story of the dreamer by the ancestral tomb seems a trifle earthbound? I had higher expectations of the other tale, but was disappointed when the narrator's dreams urged him to climb the tower not to vistas of infinity but to a view of the dull earth. No wonder he found nothing worthy of description in the mirror.[5] I wonder if, while immolated in your marriage, you became so desperate to dream that you were unable to direct the process. I counsel you to follow my example. The dreamer must tolerate no distractions, neither family nor those that call themselves friends. None of these is worth the loss of a solitary dream.

At your urging I recently viewed the moving picture of *The Phantom of the Opera*. You mentioned that you fell asleep several times during the picture, and I have to inform you that you must have been describing your own dream of the conclusion rather than the finale which appears on the screen. I assure you that no "nameless legion of *things*" welcomes the Phantom to his watery grave. I am glad that they at least remained nameless in your mind.

---

[5] "The Tomb" and "The Outsider".

No dream ought to be named, for words are less than dreams.

I look forward to reading your short novel about the island raised by the marine earthquake, although would an unknown island bear such a name as "L'yeh" or indeed any name?[6] And I am anxious to read your survey of supernatural literature when it, too, is completed. In the meantime, here are three new tales of mine for your perusal and advancement. Please do make all speed to advise me as soon as there is news.

Yours in the fellowship of dreams and letters,
CTN

P.S. Could you make sure to address all correspondence to me under these initials?

1, Toad Place,
Berkeley
Gloucestershire,
Great Britain.
April 17th, 1927

Dear HPL,

I TRUST THAT YOU HAVE NOT BEEN ALARMED BY MY prolonged silence. I thought it wise not to attract the attention of the mob for a judicious period. I also felt obliged to give you the opportunity to place some of your fiction and to compose new tales before I favoured you with the first sight of my latest work. I think now you have been amply represented in Farthingsworth's magazine, and I am encouraged to learn that you have recently been productive. I believe it is time that you should have reports of my nocturnal voyaging, and I shall include all those which I judge to be acceptable to my audience. Some, I fear, might overwhelm the mind of any other dreamer.

I hope those which I send you will go some way towards reviving your own capacity to dream. May I assume that the anecdote about the old sea captain and his bottles was a sketch for a longer story and saw publication by mistake? I suppose it was trivial enough for Farthingsworth's mind to encompass. I note that the narrator of your tale about the Irish bog is uncertain whether he is dreaming or awake, but his dream scarcely seems worth recording. Your tale of the nameless New Yorker is no dream at all, since the narrator's night is sleepless, and the only fancy you allow him is your own, which you have already achieved—to return to New England. As for the detective in Red Hook, he needs specialists to convince him that he dreamed those subterranean horrors, but I am afraid the medical view failed to persuade this reader.[7]

I am glad to hear that you wrote your story of the upraised island. May I trust that it has greater scope than the tales I have discussed above? Perhaps this may also be the case with your most recent piece, though I confess that the notion of a mere colour falls short of rousing my imagination. No colour can be sufficiently alien to paint the far reaches of dream, which lie beyond and simultaneously at the core of the awful gulf which is creation. Of the two novels you have recently completed, does the celebration of your return to Providence risk being too provincial? I hope that the account of your dreamquest is the opposite, and I am touched that you should have hidden my

---

[6] Lovecraft's original name for the island in "The Call of Cthulhu".

[7] "The Terrible Old Man", "The Moon-Bog", "He" and "The Horror at Red Hook".

name within the text for the informed reader to discover. But I am most pleased by the news that you have delivered your essay on supernatural literature to the publisher. Could you tell me which living writers you have discussed?[8]

Let me leave you to do justice to the enclosed pieces. Perhaps in due time I may risk sending those I have withheld, when you have sufficiently progressed as a dreamer. Have you yet to loose your mind in the outer darkness? Every dream which I encounter there is a step towards another, more ancient or more alien. I have shared the dreams of creatures whose bodies the mob would never recognize as flesh. Some have many bodies, and some have none at all. Some are shaped in ways at which their dreams can only hint, and which make me grateful for my blindness in the utter dark. I believe these dreams are stages in my advance towards the ultimate dream, which I sense awaiting me at the limit of unimaginable space.

Yours in the embrace of the dark,
CTN

---

[8] "The Call of Cthulhu", "The Colour out of Space", *The Case of Charles Dexter Ward*, *The Dream-Quest of Unknown Kadath* and *Supernatural Horror in Literature*.

1, Toad Place,
Berkeley
Gloucestershire,
Great Britain.
June 23rd, 1927

Dear HPL,

F COURSE YOU ARE CORRECT IN SAYING THAT MY NEW pieces have progressed. I hope that you will be able to communicate your enthusiasm to Farthingsworth and to any other editors whom you approach on my behalf.

Thank you for the list of living writers whose work you have praised in your essay. May I take it that you have withheld one name from me? Perhaps you intended me to be surprised upon reading it in the essay, unless you wished to spare my modesty. Let me reassure you that its presence would be no surprise and would cause me no embarrassment. If by any chance you decided that my work should not be discussed in the essay because of its basis in actual experience, pray do remind yourself that the material is cast in fictional form. In the case of such an omission, I trust that the error will be rectified before the essay sees publication.

Yours in urgency,
CTN

1, Toad Place,
Berkeley
Gloucestershire,
Great Britain.
August 25th, 1927

Dear HPL,

WAS GLAD TO RECEIVE YOUR APOLOGY FOR NEGLECTING to include me in your essay. On reflection, I have concluded that your failure to do so was advantageous. As you say, my work is of a different order. It would not benefit from being discussed alongside the fanciful yarns of the likes of Machen and Blackwood. It is truth masquerading as fiction, and I believe you will agree that it deserves at least an essay to itself. I hope its qualities will aid you in placing your appreciation in a more prestigious journal, and one which is more widely read. To these ends I sent you yesterday the work which I had previously kept back. I trust that your mind will prove equal to the truths conveyed therein. While you assimilate their implications, I shall consider how far they are suitable for revelation to the world.

Yours in the darkest verities,
CTN

1, Toad Place,
Berkeley
Gloucestershire,
Great Britain.
November 1st, 1927

Dear HPL,

I AM ASSURED BY THE POSTMISTRESS THAT THE PARCEL of my work has had ample time to reach you. I hope that the contents have not rendered you so speechless that you are unable to pen a response. Pray do not attempt to comment on the pieces until you feel capable of encompassing their essence. However, I should be grateful if you would confirm that they have safely arrived.

Yours,
CTN

1, Toad Place,
Berkeley
Gloucestershire,
Great Britain.
January 1st, 1928

Lovecraft,

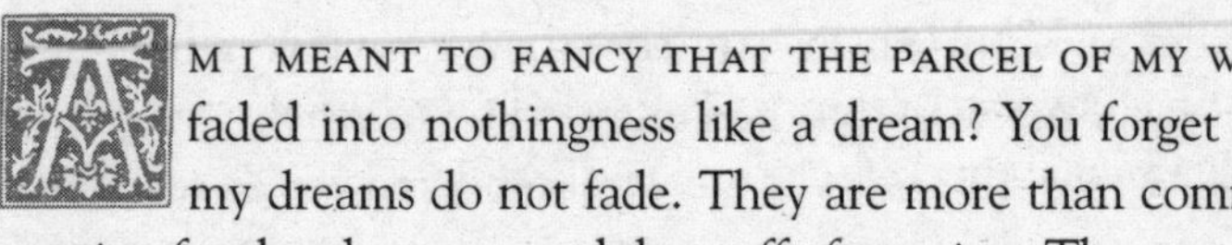

AM I MEANT TO FANCY THAT THE PARCEL OF MY WORK faded into nothingness like a dream? You forget that my dreams do not fade. They are more than common reveries, for they have grasped the stuff of creation. The accounts which I set down may be lost to me, but their truths are buried in my brain. I shall follow wherever they may lead, even unto the unspeakable truth which is the core of all existence.

I was amused by your lengthy description of your Halloween dream of ancient Romans. I fear that, like so many of your narrators, you are shackled to the past, and unable to release your spirit into the universe. I read your *amazing* story of the alien colour, but I failed to be *amazed* except by its unlikeness.[9] How can there be a colour besides those I have seen? The idea is nothing but a feeble dream, and your use of my name in the tale is no compliment to me. When I read the sentence "The Dutchman's breeches became a thing of sinister menace," I wonder if the story is a joke which you sought to play on your ignorant audience.

Nevertheless, it has some worth, for it convinces me that you are by no means the ideal agent for my work. I ignored your presumption in suggesting changes to my reports as if they

---

[9] "The Colour out of Space" was published in *Amazing Stories*.

were mere fiction, but I am troubled by the possibility that you may regard your work as in any way superior to mine. Is it conceivable that you altered the pieces which you submitted on my behalf? I suspect you of hindering them for fear that your fiction might be unfavourably compared to them, and in order that it might reach the editors ahead of them. I am sure that you excluded my work from your essay out of jealousy. I wonder if you may have resented my achievement ever since I gave you my honest appraisal of your Houdini hotchpotch. For these reasons and others which need not concern you, I hereby withdraw my work from your representation. Please return all of it immediately on receipt of this letter.

Sincerely,
Cameron Thaddeus Nash

1, Toad Place,
Berkeley
Gloucestershire,
Great Britain.
March 3rd, 1928

Loathecraft,

WHERE IS MY WORK? I HAVE STILL NOT HAD IT BACK.

C. T. Nash

1, Toad Place,
Berkeley
Gloucestershire,
Great Britain.
May 1st, 1928

Lovecramped,

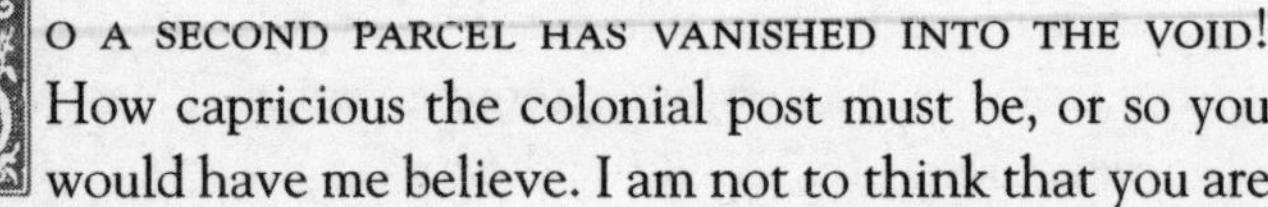

SO A SECOND PARCEL HAS VANISHED INTO THE VOID! How capricious the colonial post must be, or so you would have me believe. I am not to think that you are fearful of my seeing any alterations that you made to my work. Nor should I suspect you of destroying evidence that you have stolen elements of my work in a vain attempt to improve your own. You say that I should have kept copies, but you may rest assured that the essence is not lost. It remains embedded in my brain, where I feel it stirring like an eager foetus as it reaches for the farthest dream.

I wonder if its undeveloped relative may have made its lair in your brain as you read my work. Perhaps it is consuming your dreams instead of helping send them forth, since your mind falls so short of the cosmos. Your limits are painfully clear from your tale of the regurgitated island. Could you imagine nothing more alien than a giant with the head of an octopus? You might at least have painted it your non-existent colour. Giants were old when the Greeks were young, and your dreams are just as stale. No doubt your acolytes—Augur Dulldeath and Clerk Ashen Sniff and Dullard Wantdie and Stank Kidnap Pong and the rest of your motley entourage[10]—will counterfeit some admiration of the tale.

I assume they have been deluded into valuing your patronage, and are so afraid of losing it that they dare offer you no criticism. I would demonstrate to you how your tale should have been written if it included any matter worthy of my attention. In any case, all my energy is necessary to dealing with my dreams. I doubt that I shall write them down in future. I am unaware of anyone who deserves to learn of them. Let mankind experience them for itself when it has sufficiently evolved to do so.

C. T. Nash

1, Toad Place,
Berkeley
Gloucestershire,
Great Britain.
December 25th, 1929

Lugcraft,

DID YOU DREAM THAT YOU WOULD NEVER HEAR FROM ME again? Had you, perhaps, even forgotten my existence, since reading my work has evidently taught you nothing as a writer? You are but a shell in which a few dreams writhed and then withered when exposed to daylight. I had the misfortune to leaf through your claptrap about Dunwich.[11] I suppose you must have chosen to write about the submarine village before you remembered that you had already written about a submarine

---

[10] August Derleth, Clark Ashton Smith, Donald Wandrei and Frank Belknap Long.
[11] "The Dunwich Horror".

island.[12] You would have done better to leave both of them sunken. Can you dream of nothing except tentacles? It seems to me that your writing is a decidedly *fishy* business. Has my mislaid work yet to put in a mysterious reappearance?

I was reminded of you upon recently encountering Mr. Visiak's novel *Medusa*.[13] He, too, writes of a tentacled colossus which inhabits an uncharted rock. His prose is infinitely subtler and more skilled than your own, and evokes the dream which must have been its seed. Have you read the book? Perhaps it is one reason why you appear to have written so little of late. He has achieved all that you strain to achieve and more, with none of your symptoms of labour. He is rightly published by a reputable London house, whereas your efforts are removed from view within a month. Pulp thou art, and pulp thou shalt remain.

Are you struggling to shape some kind of myth out of the mumbo-jumbo in your recent effusions? It does not begin to hint at any kind of truth. You can never hope to touch upon that until you approach the ultimate, the source, the solitary presence, the very secret of all being. What is the universe but the greatest dream, which dreamed itself into existence? At its core, which is also its farthest boundary, is the lair of its creator. That awful entity is the essence of all dreams, and so it can be glimpsed only through them. The visionary dreams of the inhabitants of the universe are fragments of its nature, and it is jealous of bestowing them. Could you convey any of this in your spiritless fiction? I am certain you could not. Even I flinched from the merest distant glance upon the presence which hovers in the deepest dark, mouthing vast secrets while it plucks many-legged at the fabric of the universe. Perhaps I shall capture its essence in a final literary offering, *The Eater of Dreams*. Should it see print, your attempts and those of all your acolytes will fade into deserved oblivion.

C. T. Nash

1, Toad Place,
Berkeley
Gloucestershire,
Great Britain.
November 1st, 1931

Lumpcraft,

HAVE YOU STILL FAILED TO LAY YOUR HANDS ON MY misplaced work? It is evident that you have learned nothing from its example. When I saw the title of your latest washout I wondered if the whisperer might have been your feeble version of the truth to which I previously alluded, but it is even weaker than I would have expected of you.[14] The conclusion of the tale was obvious to me before I read the first page. You have always donned the mask of fiction to aid you in your pitiful attempts to scare your few admirers, but now it should be plain to the dullest of them that there is nothing behind the mask.

Your day is done, Lumpcraft, such as it ever was. I was amused to see that you have rendered Farthingsworth's rag even less *unique* by reprinting your tired tales of the hound and the rats. Are you now so bereft of imagination that you must resort to reanimating these soulless cadavers? Perhaps you have realized that, enervated though they are, they have more life than your latest efforts.

Which of those has lured in your new lickspittle, Rabbity Cowherd?[15] I presume he is avid for the world to notice that

---

[12] Dunwich is a submerged town off the Suffolk coast.

[13] *Medusa: A Story of Mystery, and Ecstasy, & Strange Horror* (Gollancz, 1929).

[14] "The Whisperer in Darkness".

[15] Robert E. Howard.

he refers in his own scribblings to your mumbo-jumbo. Is this intended to delude the reader into mistaking your puerile fancies for truth, or is it simply a game which you and your courtiers play? If you had been granted even the briefest glimpse of the denizen of the ultimate darkness, you would not dare to misuse your dreams in this fashion. You would recognize that you are but the least of its countless dreams. If you had discerned the merest hint of its nature, you would know that by attempting to perceive it, you had attracted its attention. How shall I describe the experience in words that the likes of you may understand? It feels as though some embryonic organ has become embedded in my brain. Sometimes I feel it stir, and then I know that I am observed by a consciousness so vast and so indifferent to me that it shrivels my being to less than an atom. Perhaps these moments are immeasurably brief, and yet they last for an eternity, both of which are constant states of the denizen of the infinite. In such a moment I become aware that time is as much of an illusion as space and all the materials which compose the universe. Nothing is real except the dreams of the source that clutches with its countless limbs at its creation. What would you write if you grasped even a fraction of its nature, Lumpcraft? I believe that you would never write again. What a boon that would be! For myself, I have done writing to you. You are no more to me than I am to the boundless dreamer.

C. T. Nash

1, Toad Place,
Berkeley
Gloucestershire,
Great Britain.
September 3rd, 1933

Pulpcraft,

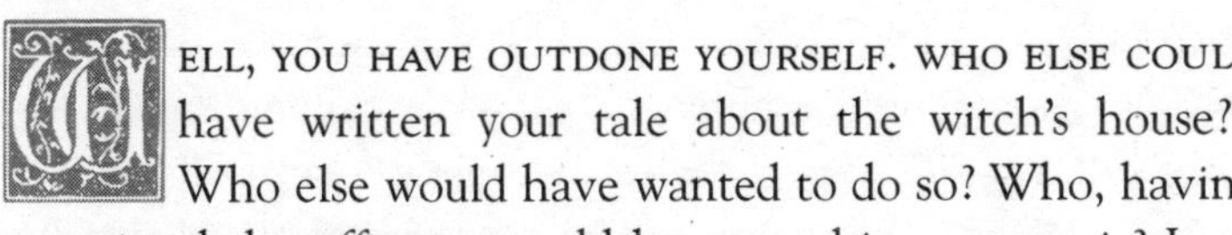

WELL, YOU HAVE OUTDONE YOURSELF. WHO ELSE COULD have written your tale about the witch's house?[16] Who else would have wanted to do so? Who, having committed the offence, would have put his name to it? I am beginning to think that you may indeed not have received my later work. Certainly its example is nowhere to be seen, although the same may equally be said of my work which you admitted to receiving. This latest farrago is an insult to the very name of dream, and I suspect that even your fawning friends will search in vain for elements to praise. Since they all write fiction, no doubt they will produce some to comfort you. Are you so timid or so dishonest that you cannot admit your failings as a writer even to yourself? Were I you, Pulpcraft, I should give up the struggle before I perpetrated worse embarrassments. I writhe in disgust at your humdrum pulpy prose, and so does the mouth in my brain.

It is indeed the semblance of a mouth. Just as the glimpses of the presence with which I tantalized you were no more than similes, so this may be the merest hint of the reality. All the same, I often feel its moist lips shift within my cranium, and sometimes I have felt a tongue explore the folds of my brain, probing among them. Increasingly I seem to sense its whispered

[16] "The Dreams in the Witch House".

secrets seeping into the substance of my cerebrum. At times I have to overcome a compulsion to voice them as I deal with the mob beyond the counter. Does this raise your hope that I may reveal some of them to you? You will have no further opportunity to steal the fruits of my dreaming. You lack the courage to venture where my spirit travels, and so you are unworthy of the reward. Let your prudent *providence* provide you with the prize you earn.

C. T. Nash

1, Toad Place,
Berkeley
Gloucestershire,
Great Britain.
October 24th, 1935

Cravecraft,

BEHOLD, YOU HAVE ENTICED A NEW FOLLOWER TO yourself! Bobby Blob writes like a very young man.[17] Was Dulldeath not one, too? Doubtless you find their kind easiest to influence. Do you now require your lackeys to imitate your awkward prose besides including your mumbo-jumbo in their fiction? Perhaps you should be wary of accepting young Blob's tale of the shambler as a tribute.[18] The narrator appears to need very little excuse to do away with the writer from Providence. I am reminded that Stank Pong also exterminated such a writer.[19] He had an even better reason, since his image of the hand which plays with brains comes closer to the cosmic truth than all your slime and tentacles and gibberish.

You should heed the message of your minions. You are redundant, Cravecraft, and a burden on your scanty audience. Do you not see that your friends feel obliged to praise you? I believe your lack of inspiration has finally overwhelmed you, since your pen appears to have dribbled its last. You are reduced to disinterring the decayed carcasses of tales which should have been left in their unmarked graves. The fiddler Zann begs for pennies once more, and the white ape joins in with a jig. Why, you have given the tale of the ape a new name in the hope of misleading the reader that its publication is *unique*![20] I doubt that even Farthingsworth's dull audience will be deluded. No mask can disguise material which is so uninspiringly familiar, and all the perfumes in the world cannot swamp the stench of rot.

You will be interested to learn that one of the conduits through which I was dreamed into the world has ceased to function. He leaves a sizeable amount of money and his fellow channel, my mother. Both are useful in relieving me of the need to remain in prosaic employment. As well as dealing with domestic matters, my mother will act as my envoy to the mundane world. I am glad to be free of the distractions of customers and fellow butchers, for their incomprehension was becoming an annoyance. The secrets that are mouthed within my brain must be pronounced aloud, but only the enlightened should hear them. Do not dream for an instant that you are numbered among that fellowship.

C. T. Nash

---

[17] Robert Bloch.

[18] "The Shambler from the Stars".

[19] "The Space-Eaters" by Frank Belknap Long.

[20] The tale originally published as "The White Ape" was reprinted as "Arthur Jermyn".

1, Toad Place,
Berkele,
Gloucestershire,
Great Britain
June 19th, 1936

Strivecraft,

NEVER IMAGINE THAT YOU CAN PASS OFF MY DISCOVERIES as your own. Wherever you are published, I shall find you. Do you now seek to *astound*? You appear to have *astounded* your new readers solely by your unwelcomeness.[21] They are as unimpressed by all your slime and tentacles as any audience should be. What possessed you to inflict your outmoded fancies on a readership versed in science? Since you claimed Farthingsworth as your most sympathetic editor, have you perhaps thrown yourself upon an agent? He must be poor, both financially and intellectually, to accept your work. At least, if I am not mistaken, he has revised it to improve your prose. No doubt your craven sycophants will chorus that your enfeebled work goes from strength to strength.

The true visionary neither requires supporters nor expects them. My mother's only functions are to keep the house in order and to deal with the mob on my behalf. Her interpretations of my pronouncements are none of my concern, and I shall not allow them to annoy me. It is only to retain her usefulness that I exert myself to keep my secrets from her, instead sharing them with the lonely hills when the night permits. There I can release the truths which the lips constantly shape in my brain. Sometimes things consumed by ancientness gather about me to listen to my utterances, and sometimes I am witnessed by creatures that will inhabit the earth when the mob is no more.

As to you, Strivecraft, will you persist in scribbling when you have less than nothing to communicate? Perhaps you should be shown what a true seer looks like. The next time I dispatch my mother to the shops I may have her bring me a camera. While your mind would shrivel at the merest glimpse of the source of all dreams, perhaps you can bear to look upon its human face, although I do not think you will survive the comparison. I think you will never again want to face yourself in a mirror.

C. T. Nash

1, Toad Place,
Berkeley,
Gloucestershire,
Great Britain
October 12th, 1936

Limpcraft,

SEE THAT RABBITY COWARD HAS CEASED TO PLAY THE brave barbarian. His dreams must have been as frail as your own. Or might he have intended to set you an example by ridding the world of himself? How long will you persist in loitering where you are unwanted? The readers of the scientific fiction magazine have made your unwelcomeness

[21] On its appearance in *Astounding Stories*, "At the Mountains of Madness" attracted hostile comment in the letter-column.

plainer still.[22] What delusion drives you to seek publication where you must know you will be loathed? Even Farthingsworth is not so desperate that he feels compelled to disseminate your latest flops. Limpcraft, you are but a dismal caricature of the man I once sought to be. As well as burdening literature, your inert presence weighs me down and binds me to the earth. My brain aches at the thought that you continue to infest the world, just as my jaws ache with declaration.

I have the camera, but I do not think any technician could look upon the photograph which would be developed. Whenever my mother is at home I keep to my room. I have trained her to leave my meals outside the door, since it would be inconvenient to have her flee. The curtains shut out the attentions of the mob. I have no need of mirrors, because I know that I am transformed by dreaming. Perhaps I am growing to resemble the source, or perhaps its awareness has begun to consume me. Perhaps I am how it mouths its way intro the world. By now the lips that gape within me feel as vast as space. Your puny skull could never contain even the notion of them.

C. T. Nash

1, Toad Place,
Berkeley
Gloucestershire,
Great Britain.
January 18th, 1937

Lovecrass,

O YOU ARE DREAMING OF ME, ARE YOU? OR YOU ARE so bereft of dreams that you have to write tales about me. I am a *haunter* of the *dark*, am I, and a shell which owes its vitality to the presence of a woman.[23] It is time that you were confronted with the truth. I shall convey a revelation from which even your mind will be unable to hide. I vow that you will no longer be able to ignore your ignorance.

I shall enclose my photograph. There is, of course, no need for my to delegate my mother to obtain a print, since you can have the film developed yourself. Have you the courage to gaze upon the face of dream, or has all your dreaming been a sham? Perhaps you will never sleep again while you remain in the world, but whenever you dream, there shall I be. Do not imagine that your death will allow you to escape me. Death is the dream from which you can never awaken, because it returns you to the source. No less than life, death will be the mirror of your insignificance.

C. T. Nash

---

[22] After the publication of "The Shadow out of Time", *Astounding Stories* ran further hostile correspondence.

[23] Nash is referring to "The Haunter of the Dark" and "The Thing on the Doorstep", published in the most recent issues of *Weird Tales*.

HIS WAS APPARENTLY NASH'S FINAL LETTER. TWO ITEMS are appended to the correspondence. One is a page torn from a book. It bears no running title, and I have been unable to locate the book, which seems to have been either a collection of supposedly true stories about Gloucestershire or a more general anthology of strange tales, including several about that area. Presumably whoever tore out the sheet found the following paragraph on page 232 relevant:

> *Residents of Berkeley still recall the night of the great scream. Sometime before dawn on the 15th of March 1937, many people were awakened by a sound which at first they were unable to identify. Some thought it was an injured animal, while others took it for a new kind of siren. Those who recognised it as a human voice did so only because it was pronouncing words or attempting to pronounce them. Although there seems to have been general agreement that it was near the river, at some distance from the town, those who remember hearing it describe it as having been almost unbearably loud and shrill. The local police appear to have been busy elsewhere, and the townsfolk were loath to investigate. Over the course of the morning the sound is said to have increased in pitch and volume. A relative of one of the listeners recalled being told by her mother that the noise sounded "as if someone was screaming a hole in himself". By late morning the sound is supposed to have grown somehow more diffuse, as though the source had become enlarged beyond control, and shortly before noon it ceased altogether. Subsequently the river and the area beside it were searched, but no trace of a victim was found.*

HE SECOND ITEM IS A PHOTOGRAPH. IT LOOKS FADED with age, a process exacerbated by copying. The original image is so dim as to be blurred, and is identifiable only as the head and shoulders of a man in an inadequately illuminated room. His eyes are excessively wide and fixed. I am unable to determine what kind of flaw in the image obscures the lower part of his face. Because of the lack of definition of the photograph, the fault makes him look as if his jaw has been wrenched far too wide. It is even possible to imagine that the gaping hole, which is at least as large as half his face, leads into altogether too much darkness. Sometimes I see that face in my dreams.

Violence, Child Of Trust

MICHAEL CISCO

Michael Cisco is the author of the short story collection Secret Hours *(Mythos Books, 2007) and the novels* The Divinity Student *(Buzzcity Press, 1999; winner of the International Horror Guild Award for best first novel),* The Tyrant *(Prime, 2004),* The San Veneficio Canon *(Prime, 2005), and* The Traitor *(Prime, 2007).*

GROVER

I WATCH.

The fly rubs its things. It came out of the well. That well is full of flies. There are always more after for a while. Julius didn't need to take the bucket off the rope and put it away in the cellar to stop me drinking any more well water because I kept forgetting not to drink it because I stopped liking the taste since the pit was filled in and there are too many flies. Now there's just the loop.

I used to come out to the well all the time because Father didn't give me water in the house. They didn't remember me because I was always quiet even before I stopped talking. Julius had the pump put in so we don't have to use the well water anymore. After Father left.

Grass. The up and down where the wood starts. Sun in my eye. The rough grey wood of the well. The hum the flies make in the well. One of them lands on my hand. I shake it off. Todd said it has to be soon. But we just did the it. We just did one. Julius is angry about it. I wish Todd would just tend the women and quit fussing with Julius, because Julius shouts when he gets mad. And he hits me for *no reason*.

The day sure is fine. It might be today.

JULIUS

"YOU TOOK YOUR TIME," I SAID WHEN TODD CAME IN.

I was certainly ready for him. I was braced and ready. I took a good hard look at him. He didn't answer me. He was always backtalking me but this time he kept his peace. That irregularity put me up.

"What kept you, Todd?"

He rubbed his brow. I hadn't expected that. I thought he might be shamming.

"Are you ailing, Todd?" I asked.

He wouldn't meet my gaze.

"You look at me when I address you, *Todd,*" I said, without raising my voice.

He shook his head once, almost as if he wanted to shush me. The day he shushes me—but then I thought again.

"Is it—?"

After some dither he managed to get it out. He said he thought.

"You think?" I demanded. He could sham that too.

But he told me it was still going on, that he was coming out of it. His Lordship. The Prophet.

Right then he looked at me. I knew that was the look. Todd couldn't have shammed that look if he'd practiced day and night.

"Again?"

TODD

THE WORD JUST DROPPED OUT OF HIS MOUTH, AND HE leaned against the lintel like he'd been biffed on the head. His eyes blundered from nothing to nothing.

Stupidity washed down his seamy white face and made it even longer. I had to keep my eye on him now that I'd looked at him; it was helping me to come back out of it.

It came over me with more force than ever, as I was coming back from tending the women. The one Julius dubbed Elaine, her name was Katey or something like that actually, had given me a bit of smart mouth and I'd had to crack her in the chops. Then I reminded her why she was there. In that frame of mind it is not for me a protracted matter and Julius never suspects. I don't think he hardly goes out there any more. Perhaps he can't manage it, in his senescence.

It doesn't really start until you notice. I had been feeling good, although my hand was a little sore, then I realized that, now that I was out of the dark, that close little cell with the women, the sun dazzle isn't diminishing. Every time I move my eyes I see streaks. Then my breath whistles in my teeth and I know this is really it. I don't like to fall down. I keep myself clean, I hate to get even the slightest bit dirty. So I hold myself up.

My mouth watered and my stomach turned over. My arms and legs got weak, hateful. Next I notice some dark spot; in this case, it was the shadow that fell between the house and the tupelo tree. I saw the sign in there. The dark opened and spread itself around me, and then the palaces.

We'd had to know it would come to this sooner or later. The last time hadn't been but a month ago, less than a month. Julius had relaxed. I have to admit I'd let myself relax too. I shouldn't have.

We're not ready. We haven't got a girl and we haven't got time to grab one. The last time was a close call—she was a tussler and Julius came back white as a sheet and swearing, pacing and swearing up and down he'd been seen. Nothing came of it. Nothing has as yet come of it.

He asked me how long, still gawking at me as if there were

ever any variation how long between the sign and the time, as if I set the time.

"Tomorrow dusk like always," I said, throwing it at him.

His mouth was hanging open, and I could see he hadn't a thought in his head. Not an uncommon condition.

No.

He did have a thought in his head—I had it, too. We *were* ready, that was the thing. There *were* girls. He was thinking of Claire. I was thinking of Ruth.

He was thinking of Ruth.

We had always known something like this might happen, and Father had seen to it we knew what to do if it did. He'd said the elders had given us the measure.

JULIUS

"We can't use any of the women?"

I knew we couldn't of course. But it was Todd's job to tend them, and there was a slim chance he might know something I didn't. He'd brought them. They were always to his taste.

Todd looked at me with his eyes slitted up and asked me if I meant were any of the women young enough. I could have busted the lamp over his head then. I nearly started to shake, but I can keep my composure.

I take the risks. I do all the planning. I'm the oldest, and I do it. I'm the only one who can. And he knows what'll happen if I don't do it.

You never ignore the sign. Father took us as boys to see where the old place had been, and even in the broad light of day it was a screaming piece of land, just screaming. It turned Grover inside out. I was the only one who could come back from there on his own two feet and that was why it was entrusted to me. Todd had to go get in bed and stay there.

But when it's time, the sign comes to Todd. I have to hop to like a slave and start it all over again every time he gets the sign.

I squeezed the bridge of my nose, rubbed my face.

Father said it was bound to happen.

"I'll get the lots," I said.

Claire looked up when I came in. I crossed the room and got the case. She didn't take her eyes off me. I told her to get back to her reading.

TODD

ULIUS BROUGHT DOWN THE CIGAR BOX OPEN AND SET it on the table beside me. I had sat myself by the bay window, looking out at Grover who was sitting in the grass like a sack of potatoes. The checkers, red and black, were all jumbled together, and Julius was letting me see them all first. I nodded, numbly, and thinking about what we had to do was setting in and my mouth went dry and my hands turned cold.

Julius shut the box and shook it, still standing over me. It's hot and stuffy upstairs and I could see sweat swarm down the gnarls in his brow. He stank. He made us keep the house neat as a pin but he couldn't be bothered to wash. The whole place smelled like him.

He rattled the opposite chair back and dropped into it, putting the shaken box on the shelf under the table, where we both could reach it and neither of us see it.

We stared at each other. He said we would pick to see who went first. I got red. That color seemed to burn against my hand. It was just that particular color red. We put the checkers back and shook the box again, both of us, out of sight. Then we put our hands on the table. I thought of Ruth out in the woods and stubbed out that thought.

I pulled black.

You lie down in the dark, and wait.

At first you would see something like a forearm crossing the room. Just the forearm. It isn't a forearm, it only so happens to look like one just then, and it's what occurs to you. It just flashes by. Then, after a while, the dark and the quiet open up, right where you saw it. I can't say what the others see, I see only dim colors. For a long time, there are only dim colors there, and something will flit through the field now and then, quick as a wink. You have to make the effort not to ask it anything; it isn't hard. Eventually, you'll be shown the palaces, five figures of light or maybe more, and then they're all over the room like fog. The fog is blue, like cigarette smoke, but the light is white and gold. The palaces are like chandeliers. Hanging from nothing. We all lie in our separate rooms and go into the walls, I believe the girls too, slipping out into our palaces at night, in perfect silence. That's our beauty; we inherited it from Father, and he from long before.

JULIUS

ODD SAT ACROSS FROM ME, BLANCHED TO THE BONE. He'd scrunched up that cat face of his. I told myself that if I heard anything like fumbling around down there, anything but a straight pick, I'd shoot out my arm across that table and shove his adam's apple in.

Black.

Dirty cheater—

I just reached out and grabbed one. It felt like it wanted to slip out of my hand. I slapped it down hard on the table. Black.

Todd rocked a little. My nerves were steady.

I was going to win.

He pulled black.

Must have been the shuffle put them all back in order I thought. Could I count them—how many were there?

I pulled black.

Todd hesitated. He rubbed his fingers together. Nails all clean and buffed.

You're going to lose, I thought at him.

He pulled.

I got up and swept the checkers back into the box.

"Red for Ruthie," I said.

I left him sitting there.

GROVER

ULIUS ASKED ME WHERE TODD IS AND I POINTED TO where Todd was waiting for Ruth on the veranda because he wanted to see her. Julius made a noise and went back into his office to get ready.

It's supposed to work like, Julius gets the girl and brings her here. Todd puts casts on her legs so she can't run. Then he puts her in with the women but separate so they don't mix. Todd holds, normally, because Julius has to do it himself. No one hears because nobody lives around here. When Todd gets the sign, she's there. All ready. You always keep a girl, because you never know when Todd will get the sign. But there's no girl now, because we just did the it. Julius can't go back so soon because they'll be on the look out. But Todd says it has to be tonight.

The last girl was black. Julius said it didn't matter. He also said no one would care because she was colored. She was here three months, nearly. I only got to see her twice. Todd saw the sign and the next night he took her into the thing. She was so scared she didn't even move. Julius did the it. He called when we have to bring her in because he has to start by himself, because he doesn't like us to see how it's done. He wants to be the only one who knows.

Todd knows the time, and Julius does the it, but I'm the only one who can put the right mark on the girl. That's been since Father took us out to the first farm. Julius says it made me slow. He opens the girls up and gets the sack away, and then tells me put on the mark. It's hard because the heart jumps all over. You can't smudge. I always get it right because I practice. Then Julius grabs it and cuts all around and pulls it out. He always gets soaked because they take a while to stop going. Todd has to come up with the bowl and Julius puts it in it, because they have to burn it, and then it gets burnt and the sparerib smell, smoke all over and then they come, they get into the girl, then we can go in the palaces.

The mark always looks different. I just paint it because I don't know it. I see it and then I paint it on. I tried painting it on me once but the brush tickles and I don't see anything. I think the it has to be happening. I try not to tickle the girl's heart too much.

TODD

CLAIRE CAME DOWN AND SET OUT THE DISHES FOR SUPPER. Julius kept her locked up in the attic room during the day and didn't want her to "mix" with Ruth. He never let her out and made her read the books all day long, over and over. He allows her to put on a frock before coming down to eat. When he feels like showing off, he makes her conjugate, standing by the table, in her miserable, reedy little voice.

I left Ruth to herself and out of the way. I didn't watch her, but I watched him. He never forgave me getting ahead of him.

She looked nothing like Lorraine. She was less than a year old when Lorraine last saw her, and time has disguised her. I took great pains to get her away, recruited Amelia to carry her back home on the train while I hitched. Julius must have made up his mind about Amelia the moment he saw her coming in with the baby. I'll bet she was pregnant by the time I made it back.

I went out to wait for Ruth on the veranda, and she came along through the tall grass, just at the reddening of the setting sun. She was quiet, from being alone all day. I took her by the hand and led her to the table.

JULIUS

HEY'RE OUTSIDE NOW. ONE GLANCE IS ALL I HAVE TIME for. Grover is standing in front this time, and between him and Todd there's Ruthie with her shoulders in their hands.

I move into the second part. I have to go on and on and on, remembering how Father did it. The way he did what the elders did. They showed it me through him. I have to time each breath right. I can't stop in the wrong spot. Not even to draw breath. Every word has to get out exactly right. It's like a long elastic that draws me in closer. They're far away, but I feel them stirring. They hear me. It's stepping out into the light.

I finish that part and wait. My breath comes tight and I can feel the sweat run down my sides. The fane is stifling, like a grave. They will call in Todd and Grover.

Now the smell—I never could get used to that.

I begin to recite. They're taking their time coming in but I have to keep my mind on the words and not stumble. I close my eyes and I can hear them shuffling. I'm in the dark, and the palaces shine out there and I pull up to them like rowing up to still islands in a black lake. That gold light spills over my face I open my eyes and turn as Todd is throwing her up on the stone and as her hair falls back from her face I lock eyes with Claire.

TODD

E HAS TO KEEP GOING AND HE CAN'T SO MUCH AS FALTER. He knows what will happen.

You're the one who does it, Julius.

Well.

Just go ahead on and do it.

I'm not afraid of Julius. Without me he'd miss the sign and we all know what'll happen if the sign comes and we don't act on it.

That gold light is all around—I can feel their greed blending in with his hatred in a cold, steady gush.

I pick the time.

He looks down at her. His eyes are in the shade.

I tear her frock open, baring her skinny chest. She doesn't even cry out, just stares into her father's face.

Any idiot can break a lock, *Julius*.

Lesser Demons

NORMAN PARTRIDGE

Norman Partridge is the author of the short story collections Mr. Fox and Other Feral Tales *(Roadkill Press, 1992),* Bad Intentions *(Subterranean Press, 1996),* The Man with the Barbed Wire Fists *(Night Shade Books, 2001), and the horror novels* Slippin' into Darkness *(Cemetery Dance, 1994),* Wildest Dreams *(Subterranean Press, 1998),* Wicked Prayer *(HarperPrism, 2000), and* Dark Harvest *(Tor, 2007). He has also written the hardboiled detective novels* Saguaro Riptide *(Berkley, 1997) and* The Ten-Ounce Siesta *(Berkley, 1998) and has edited the horror anthology* It Came from the Drive-In! *(I Books, 2004).*

OWN IN THE CEMETERY, THE CHILDREN WERE LAUGHING.

They had another box open.

They had their axes out. Their knives, too.

I sat in the sheriff's department pickup, parked beneath a willow tree. Ropes of leaves hung before me like green curtains, but those curtains didn't stop the laughter. It climbed the ridge from the hollow below, carrying other noises—shovels biting hard-packed earth, axe blades splitting coffinwood, knives scraping flesh from bone. But the laughter was the worst of it. It spilled over teeth sharpened with files, chewed its way up the ridge, and did its best to strip the hard bark off my spine.

I didn't sit still. I grabbed a gas can from the back of the pickup. I jacked a full clip into my dead deputy's .45, slipped a couple spares into one of the leather pockets on my gun belt, and buttoned it down. Then I fed shells into my shotgun and pumped one into the chamber.

I went for a little walk.

IVE MONTHS BEFORE, I STOOD WITH MY DEPUTY, ROY Barnes, out on County Road 14. We weren't alone. There were others present. Most of them were dead, or something close to it.

I held that same shotgun in my hand. The barrel was hot. The deputy clutched his .45, a ribbon of bitter smoke coiling from the business end. It wasn't a stink you'd breathe if you had a choice, but we didn't have one.

Barnes reloaded, and so did I. The June sun was dropping behind the trees, but the shafts of late-afternoon light slanting through the gaps were as bright as high noon. The light played through black smoke rising from a Chrysler sedan's smoldering engine, and white smoke simmering from the hot asphalt piled in the road gang's dump truck.

My gaze settled on the wrecked Chrysler. The deal must have started there. Fifteen or twenty minutes before, the big black car had piled into an old oak at a fork in the county road. Maybe the driver had nodded off, waking just in time to miss a flagman from the work gang. Over-corrected and hit the brakes too late. Said: *Hello tree, goodbye heartbeat.*

Maybe that was the way it happened. Maybe not. Barnes tried to piece it together later on, but in the end it really didn't matter much. What mattered was that the sedan was driven by a man who looked like something dredged up from the bottom of a stagnant pond. What mattered was that something exploded from the Chrysler's trunk after the accident. That thing was the size of a grizzly, but it wasn't a bear. It didn't look like a bear at all. Not unless you'd ever seen one turned inside out, it didn't.

Whatever it was, that skinned monster could move. It unhinged its sizable jaws and swallowed a man who weighed two-hundred-and-change in one long ratcheting gulp, choking arms and legs and torso down a gullet lined with razor teeth. Sucked the guy into a blue-veined belly that hung from its ribs like a grave-robber's sack and then dragged that belly along fresh asphalt as it chased down the other men, slapping them onto the scorching roadbed and spitting bloody hunks of dead flesh in their faces. Some it let go, slaughtering others like so many chickens tossed live and squawking onto a hot skillet.

It killed four men before we showed up, fresh from handling a fender-bender on the detour route a couple miles up the road. Thanks to my shotgun and Roy Barnes's .45, all that remained of the thing was a red mess with a corpse spilling out of its gutshot belly. As for the men from the work crew, there wasn't much you could say. They were either as dead as that poor bastard who'd ended his life in a monster's stomach, or they were whimpering with blood on their faces, or they were running like hell and halfway back to town. But whatever they were doing didn't make too much difference to me just then.

"What was it, Sheriff?" Barnes asked.

"I don't know."

"You sure it's dead?"

"I don't know that, either. All I know is we'd better stay away from it."

We backed off. The only things that lingered were the afternoon light slanting through the trees, and the smoke from that hot asphalt, and the smoke from the wrecked Chrysler. The light cut swirls through that smoke as it pooled around the dead thing, settling low and misty, as if the something beneath it were trying to swallow a chunk of the world, roadbed and all.

"I feel kind of dizzy," Barnes said.

"Hold on, Roy. You have to."

I grabbed my deputy by the shoulder and spun him around. He was just a kid, really—before this deal, he'd never even had his gun out of its holster while on duty. I'd been doing the job for fifteen years, but I could have clocked a hundred and never seen anything like this. Still, we both knew it wasn't over. We'd seen what we'd seen, we'd done what we'd done, and the only thing left to do was deal with whatever was coming next.

That meant checking out the Chrysler. I brought the shotgun barrel even with it, aiming at the driver's side door as we advanced. The driver's skull had slammed the steering wheel at the point of impact. Black blood smeared across his face, and filed teeth had slashed through his pale lips so that they hung from his gums like leavings you'd bury after gutting a fish. On top of that, words were carved on his face. Some were purpled over with scar tissue and others were still fresh scabs. None of them were words I'd seen before. I didn't know what to make of them.

"Jesus," Barnes said. "Will you look at that."

"Check the back seat, Roy."

Barnes did. There was other stuff there. Torn clothes. Several pairs of handcuffs. Ropes woven with fishhooks. A wrought-iron trident. And in the middle of all that was a cardboard box filled with books.

The deputy pulled one out. It was old. Leathery. As he opened it, the book started to come apart in his hands. Brittle pages fluttered across the road—

Something rustled in the open trunk. I pushed past Roy and fired point-blank before I even looked. The spare tire exploded. On the other side of the trunk, a clawed hand scrabbled up through a pile of shotgunned clothes. I fired again. Those claws clacked together, and the thing beneath them didn't move again.

Using the shotgun barrel, I shifted the clothes to one side, uncovering a couple of dead kids in a nest of rags and blood. Both of them were handcuffed. The thing I'd killed had chewed its way out of one of their bellies. It had a grinning, wolfish muzzle and a tail like a dozen braided snakes. I slammed the trunk and chambered another shell. I stared down at the trunk, waiting for something else to happen, but nothing did.

Behind me…well, that was another story.

The men from the road gang were on the move.

Their boots scuffed over hot asphalt.

They gripped crow bars, and sledge hammers, and one of them even had a machete.

They came toward us with blood on their faces, laughing like children.

THE CHILDREN IN THE CEMETERY WEREN'T LAUGHING anymore.

They were gathered around an open grave, eating.

As always, a couple seconds passed before they noticed me. Then their brains sparked their bodies into motion, and the first one started for me with an axe. I pulled the trigger, and the shotgun turned his spine to jelly, and he went down in sections. The next one I took at longer range, so the blast chewed her over some. Dark blood from a hundred small wounds peppered her dress. Shrieking, she turned tail and ran.

Which gave the third bloodface a chance to charge me. He was faster than I expected, dodging the first blast, quickly closing the distance. There was barely enough room between the two of us for me to get off another shot, but I managed the job. The blast took off his head. That was that.

Or at least I thought it was. Behind me, something whispered through long grass that hadn't been cut in five months. I whirled, but the barefoot girl's knife was already coming at me. The blade ripped through my coat in a silver blur, slashing my right forearm. A twist of her wrist and she tried to come back for another piece, but I was faster and bashed her forehead with the shotgun butt. Her skull split like a popped blister and she went down hard, cracking the back of her head on a tombstone.

That double-punched her ticket. I sucked a deep breath and held it. Blood reddened the sleeve of my coat as the knife-wound began to pump. A couple seconds later I began to think straight, and I got the idea going in my head that I should put down the shotgun and get my belt around my arm. I did that and tightened it good. Wounded, I'd have a walk to get back to the pickup. Then I'd have to find somewhere safe where I could take care of my arm. The pickup wasn't far distance-wise, but it was a steep climb up to the ridgeline. My heart would be pounding double-time the whole way. If I didn't watch it, I'd lose a lot of blood.

But first I had a job to finish. I grabbed the shotgun and moved toward the rifled grave. Even in the bright afternoon sun, the long grass was still damp with morning dew. I noticed that my boots were wet as I stepped over the dead girl. That bothered me, but the girl's corpse didn't. She couldn't bother me now that she was dead.

I left her behind me in the long grass, her body a home for the scarred words she'd carved on her face with the same knife she'd used to butcher the dead and butcher me. All that remained of her was a barbed rictus grin and a pair of dead eyes staring up into the afternoon sun, as if staring at nothing at all. And that's what she was to me—that's what they all were now that they were dead. They were nothing, no matter what they'd done to themselves with knives and files, no matter what they'd done to the living they'd murdered or the dead they'd pried out of burying boxes. They were nothing at all, and I didn't spare them another thought.

Because there were other things to worry about—things like the one that had infected the children with a mouthful of spit-up blood. Sometimes those things came out of graves. Other times they came out of car trunks or meat lockers or off slabs in a morgue. But wherever they came from they were always born of a corpse, and there were corpses here aplenty.

I didn't see anything worrisome down in the open grave. Just stripped bones and tatters of red meat, but it was meat that wasn't moving. That was good. So I took care of things. I rolled the dead bloodfaces into the grave. I walked back to the cottonwood thicket at the ridge side of the cemetery and grabbed the gas can I'd brought from the pickup. I emptied it into the hole, then tossed the can in, too. I wasn't carrying it back to the truck with a sliced-up arm.

I lit a match and let it fall.

The gas *thupped* alive and the hole growled fire.

Fat sizzled as I turned my back on the grave. Already, other sounds were rising in the hollow. Thick, rasping roars. Branches breaking somewhere in the treeline behind the old funeral home. The sound of something big moving through the timber—something that heard my shotgun bark three times and wasn't afraid of the sound.

Whatever that thing was, I didn't want to see it just now.

I disappeared into the cottonwood thicket before it saw me.

BARNES HAD LIVED IN A CONVERTED HUNTING LODGE on the far side of the lake. There weren't any other houses around it, and I hadn't been near the place in months. I'd left some stuff there, including medical supplies we'd scavenged from the local emergency room. If I was lucky, they would still be there.

Thick weeds bristled over the dirt road that led down to Roy's place. That meant no one had been around for a while. Of course, driving down the road would leave a trail, but I didn't have much choice. I'd been cut and needed to do something about it fast. You take chances. Some are large and some are small. Usually, the worries attached to the small ones amount to nothing.

I turned off the pavement. The dirt road was rutted, and I took it easy. My arm ached every time the truck hit a pothole. Finally, I parked under the carport on the east side of the old lodge. Porch steps groaned as I made my way to the door, and I entered behind the squared-off barrel of Barnes's .45.

Inside, nothing was much different than it had been a couple of months before. Barnes's blood-spattered coat hung on a hook by the door. His reading glasses rested on the coffee table. Next to it, a layer of mold floated on top of a cup of coffee he'd never finished. But I didn't care about any of that. I cared about the cabinet we'd stowed in the bathroom down the hall.

Good news. Nothing in the cabinet had been touched. I stripped to the waist, cleaned the knife wound with saline solution from an IV bag, then stopped the bleeding as best I could. The gash wasn't as deep as it might have been. I sewed it up with a hooked surgical needle, bandaged it, and gobbled down twice as many antibiotics as any doctor would have prescribed. That done, I remembered my wet boots. Sitting there on the toilet, I laughed at myself a little bit, because given the circumstances it seemed like a silly thing to worry about. Still, I went to the first-floor bedroom I'd used during the summer and changed into a dry pair of Wolverines I'd left behind.

Next I went to the kitchen. I popped the top on a can of chili, found a spoon, and started toward the old dock down by the lake. There was a rusty swing set behind the lodge that had been put up by a previous owner; it shadowed a kid's sandbox. Barnes hadn't had use for either—he wasn't even married—but he'd never bothered to change things around. Why would he? It would have been a lot of work for no good reason.

I stopped and stared at the shadows beneath the swing set, but I didn't stare long. The dock was narrow and more than a little rickety, with a small boathouse bordering one side. I walked past the boathouse and sat on the end of the dock for a while. I ate cold chili. Cattails whispered beneath a rising breeze. A flock of geese passed overhead, heading south. The sun set, and twilight settled in.

It was quiet. I liked it that way. With Barnes, it was seldom quiet. I guess you'd say he had a curious mind. The deputy liked to talk about things, especially things he didn't understand, like those monsters that crawled out of corpses. Barnes called them lesser demons. He'd read about them in one of those books we found in the wreck. He had ideas about them, too. Barnes talked about those ideas a lot over the summer, but I didn't want to talk about any of it. Talking just made me edgy. So did Barnes's ideas and explanations…all those *maybes* and *what ifs*. Barnes was big on those; he'd go on and on about them.

Me, I cared about simpler things. Things anyone could understand. Things you didn't need to discuss, or debate. Like waking up before a razor-throated monster had a chance to swallow me whole. Or not running out of shotgun shells. Or making sure one of those things never spit a dead man's blood in my face, so I wouldn't take a file to my teeth or go digging in a graveyard for food. That's what I'd cared about that summer, and I cared about the same things in the hours after a bloodfaced lunatic carved me up with a dirty knife.

I finished the chili. It was getting dark. Getting cold, too, because winter was coming on. I tossed the empty can in the lake and turned back toward the house. The last purple smear of twilight silhouetted the place, and a pair of birds darted into the chimney as I walked up the dock. I wouldn't have seen them if I hadn't looked at that exact moment, and I shook my head. Birds building nests in October? It was just another sign of a world gone nuts.

Inside, I settled on the couch and thought about lighting a fire. I didn't care about the birds—nesting in that chimney was their own bad luck. I'd got myself a chill out at the dock, and there was a cord of oak stacked under the carport. Twenty minutes and I could have a good blaze going. But I was tired, and my arm throbbed like it had grown its own heartbeat. I didn't want to tear the stitches toting a bunch of wood. I just wanted to sleep.

I took some painkillers—more than I should have—and washed them down with Jack Daniel's. After a while, the darkness pulled in close. The bedroom I'd used the summer before was on the ground floor. But I didn't want to be downstairs in case anything came around during the night, especially with a cool liquid fog pumping through my veins. I knew I'd be safer upstairs.

There was only one room upstairs—a big room, kind of like a loft.

It was Barnes's bedroom, and his blood was still on the wall.

I didn't care. I grabbed my shotgun. I climbed the stairs.

Like I said: I was tired.

Besides, I couldn't see Barnes's blood in the dark.

AT FIRST, ROY AND I STUCK TO THE SHERIFF'S OFFICE, which was new enough to have pretty good security. When communication stopped and the whole world took a header, we decided that wasn't a good idea anymore. We started moving around.

My place wasn't an option. It was smack dab in the middle of town. You didn't want to be in town. There were too many blind corners, and too many fences you couldn't see over. Dig in there, and you'd never feel safe no how many bullets you had in your clip. So I burned down the house. It never meant much to me, anyway. It was just a house, and I burned it down mostly because it was mine and I didn't want anyone else rooting around in the stuff I kept there. I never went back after that.

Barnes's place was off the beaten path. Like I said, that made it a good choice. I knew I could get some sleep there. Not too much, if you know what I mean. Every board in the old lodge seemed to creak, and the brush was heavy around the property. If you were a light sleeper—like me—you'd most likely hear anything that was coming your way long before it had a chance to get you.

And I heard every noise that night in Barnes's bedroom. I didn't sleep well at all. Maybe it was my sliced-up arm or those painkillers mixing with the whiskey and antibiotics—but I tossed and turned for hours. The window was open a crack, and cold air cut through the gap like that barefooted girl's knife. And it seemed I heard another knife scraping somewhere deep in the house, but it must have been those birds in the chimney, scrabbling around in their nest.

Outside, the chained seats on the swing set squealed and squeaked in the wind. Empty, they swung back and forth, back and forth, over cool white sand.

FTER A COUPLE MONTHS, BARNES WASN'T DOING SO well. We'd scavenged a few of the larger summer houses on the other side of the lake—places that belonged to rich couples from down south. We'd even made a few trips into town when things seemed especially quiet. We'd gotten things to the point where we had everything we needed at the lodge. If something came around that needed killing, we killed it. Otherwise, we steered clear of the world.

But Barnes couldn't stop talking about those books he'd snatched from the wrecked Chrysler. He read the damned things every day. Somehow, he thought they had all the answers. I didn't know about that. If there were answers in those books, you'd have one hell of a time pronouncing them. I knew that much.

That wasn't a problem for Barnes. He read those books cover to cover, making notes about those lesser demons, consulting dictionaries and reference books he'd swiped from the library. When he finished, he read them again. After a while, I couldn't stand to look at him sitting there with those reading glasses on his face. I even got sick of the smell of his coffee. So I tried to keep busy. I'd do little things around the lodge, but none of them amounted to much. I chainsawed several oak trees and split the wood. Stacking it near the edge of the property to season would also give us some cover if we ever needed to defend the perimeter, so I did that, too. I even set some traps on the other side of the lodge, but after a while I got sloppy and began to forget where they were. Usually, that happened when I was thinking about something else while I was trying to work. Like Barnes's *maybes* and *what ifs*.

Sometimes I'd get jumpy. I'd hear noises while I was working. Or I'd think I did. I'd start looking for things that weren't there. Sometimes I'd even imagine something so clearly I could almost see it. I knew that was dangerous…and maybe a little crazy. So I found something else to do—something that would keep my mind from wandering.

I started going out alone during the day. Sometimes I'd run across a pack of bloodfaces. Sometimes one of those demons… or maybe two. You never saw more than two at a time. They never traveled in packs, and that was lucky for me. I doubted I could have handled more than a couple, and even handling two…well, that could be dicey.

But I did it on my own. And I didn't learn about the damn things by reading a book. I learned by reading them. Watching them operate when they didn't know I was there, hunting them down with the shotgun, blowing them apart. That's how I learned—reading tales written in muscle and blood, or told by a wind that carried bitter scent and shadows that fell where they shouldn't.

And you know what? I found out that those demons weren't so different. Not really. I didn't have to think it through much, because when you scratched off the paint and primer and got down to it those things had a spot in the food chain just like you and me. They took what they needed when they needed it, and they did their best to make sure anything below them didn't buck the line.

If there was anything above them—well, I hadn't seen it.

I hoped I never would.

I wouldn't waste time worrying about it until I did.

OME AUGUST, THERE WERE FEWER OF THOSE THINGS around. Maybe that meant the world was sorting itself out. Or maybe it just meant that in my little corner I was bucking that food chain hard enough to hacksaw a couple of links.

By that time I'd probably killed fifteen of them. Maybe twenty. During a late summer thunderstorm, I tracked a hooved minotaur with centipede dreadlocks to an abandoned barn deep in the hollow. The damn thing surprised me, nearly ripping open my belly with its black horns before I managed to jam a pitchfork through its throat. There was a gigantic worm with a dozen sucking maws; I burned it down to cinders in the water-treatment plant. Beneath the high-school football stadium, a couple rat-faced spiders with a web strung across a cement tunnel nearly caught me in their trap, but I left them dying there, gore oozing from their fat bellies drop by thick drop. The bugs had a half-dozen cocooned bloodfaces for company, all of them nearly sucked dry but still squirming in that web. They screamed like tortured prisoners when I turned my back and left them alive in the darkness.

Yeah. I did my part, all right.

I did my part, and then some.

Certain situations were harder to handle. Like when you ran into other survivors. They'd see you with a gun, and a pickup truck, and a full belly, and they'd want to know how you were pulling it off. They'd push you. Sometimes with questions, sometimes with pleas that were on the far side of desperate. I didn't like that. To tell you thc truth, it made me feel kind of sick. As soon as they spit their words my way, I'd want to snatch them out of the air and jam them back in their mouths.

Sometimes they'd get the idea, and shut up, and move on. Sometimes they wouldn't. When that happened I had to do something about it. Choice didn't enter in to it. When someone pushed you, you had to push back. That was just the way the world worked—before demons and after.

ONE DAY IN LATE SEPTEMBER, BARNES CLIMBED OUT OF his easy chair and made a field trip to the wrecked Chrysler. He took those books with him. I was so shocked when he walked out the door that I didn't say a word.

I was kind of surprised when he made it back to the lodge at nightfall. He brought those damn books back with him, too. Then he worked on me for a whole week, trying to get me to go out there. He said he wanted to try something and he needed some backup. I felt like telling him I could have used some backup myself on the days I'd been out dealing with those things while he'd been sitting on his ass reading, but I didn't say it. Finally I gave in. I don't know why—maybe I figured going back to the beginning would help Barnes get straight with the way things really were.

There was no sun the day we made the trip, if you judged by what you could see. No sky either. Fog hung low over the lake, following the roads running through the hollow like they were dry rivers that needed filling. The pickup burrowed through the fog, tires whispering over wet asphalt, halogen beams cutting through all that dull white and filling pockets of darkness that waited in the trees.

I didn't see anything worrisome in those pockets, but the quiet that hung in the cab was another story. Barnes and I didn't talk. Usually that would have suited me just fine, but not that day. The silence threw me off, and my hands were sweaty on the steering wheel. I can't say why. I only know they stayed that way when we climbed out of the truck on County Road 14.

Nothing much had changed on that patch of road.

Corpses still lay on the asphalt—the road gang, and the bear-thing that had swallowed one of them whole before we blew it apart. They'd been chewed over by buzzards and rats and other miserable creatures, and they'd baked guts-and-all onto the road during the summer heat. You would have had a hell of a time scraping them off the asphalt, because nothing that mattered had bothered with them once they were dead.

Barnes didn't care about them, either. He went straight to the old Chrysler and hauled the dead driver from behind the steering wheel. The corpse hit the road like a sack of kindling ready for the flame. It was a sight. Crows must have been at the driver's face, because his fishgut lips were gone. Those scarred words carved on his skin still rode his jerky flesh like wormy bits of gristle, but now they were chiseled with little holes, as if those crows had pecked punctuation.

Barnes grabbed Mr. Fishguts by his necktie and dragged him to the spot in the road where the white line should have been but wasn't.

"You ready?" he asked.

"For what?"

"If I've got it figured right, in a few minutes the universe is going to squat down and have itself a bite. It'll be one big chunk of the apple—starting with this thing, finishing with all those others."

"Those books say so?"

"Oh, yeah," Barnes said, "and a whole lot more."

That wasn't any kind of answer, but it put a cork in me. So I did what I was told. I stood guard. Mr. Fishguts lay curled up in that busted-up fetal position. Barnes drew a skinning knife from a leather scabbard on his belt and started cutting off the corpse's clothes. I couldn't imagine what the hell he was doing. A minute later, the driver's corpse was naked, razored teeth grinning up at us through his lipless mouth.

Barnes knelt down on that unmarked road. He started to read.

First from the book. Then from Mr. Fishguts's skin.

The words sounded like a garbage disposal running backward. I couldn't understand any of them. Barnes's voice started off quiet, just a whisper buried in the fog. Then it grew louder, and louder still. Finally he was barking words, and screaming them, and spitting like a hellfire preacher. You could have heard him a quarter mile away.

That got my heart pounding. I squinted into the fog, which was getting heavier. I couldn't see a damn thing. I couldn't even see those corpses glued to the road anymore. Just me and Barnes and Mr. Fishguts, there in a tight circle in the middle of County Road 14.

My heart went trip-hammer, those words thumping in time, the syllables pumping. I tried to calm down, tried to tell myself that the only thing throwing me off was the damn fog. I didn't know what was out there. One of those inside-out grizzlies could have been twenty feet away and I wouldn't have known it. A rat-faced spider could have been stilting along on eight legs, and I wouldn't have seen it until the damn thing was chewing off my face. That minotaur thing with the centipede dreadlocks could have charged me at a dead gallop and I wouldn't have heard its hooves on pavement…not with Barnes roaring. That was all I heard. His voice filled up the hollow with words written in books and words carved on a dead man's flesh, and standing there blind in that fog I felt like those words were the only things in a very small world, and for a split second I think I understood just how those cocooned bloodfaces felt while trapped in that rat-spider's web.

And then it was quiet. Barnes had finished reading.

"Wait a minute," he said. "Wait right here."

I did. The deputy walked over to the Chrysler, and I lost

sight of him as he rummaged around in the car. His boots whispered over pavement and he was back again. Quickly, he knelt down, rearing back with both hands wrapped around the hilt of that wrought-iron trident we'd found in the car that very first day, burying it in the center of Mr. Fishguts's chest.

Scarred words shredded, and brittle bones caved in, and an awful stink escaped the corpse. I waited for something to happen. The corpse didn't move. I didn't know about anything else. There could have been anything out there, wrapped up in that fog. Anything, coming straight at us. Anything, right on top of us. We wouldn't have seen it all. I was standing there with a shotgun in my hands with no idea where to point it. I could have pointed it anywhere and it wouldn't have made me feel any better. I could have pulled the trigger a hundred times and it wouldn't have mattered. I might as well have tried to shotgun the fog, or the sky, or the whole damn universe.

It had to be the strangest moment of my life.

It lasted a good long time.

Twenty minutes later, the fog began to clear a little. A half hour later, it wasn't any worse than when we left the lodge. But nothing had happened in the meantime. That was the worst part. I couldn't stop waiting for it. I stood there, staring down at Mr. Fishguts's barbed grin, at the trident, at those words carved on the corpse's jerky flesh. I was still standing there when Barnes slammed the driver's door of the pickup. I hadn't even seen him move. I walked over and slipped in beside him, and he started back towards the lodge.

"Relax," he said finally. "It's all over."

HAT NIGHT IT WAS QUIETER THAN IT HAD BEEN IN a long time, but I couldn't sleep and neither could Barnes. We sat by the fire, waiting for something...or nothing. We barely talked at all. About four or five, we finally drifted off.

Around seven, a racket outside jarred me awake. Then there was a scream. I was up in a second. Shotgun in hand, I charged out of the house.

The fog had cleared overnight. I shielded my eyes and stared into the rising sun. A monster hovered over the beach—leathery wings laid over a jutting bone framework, skin clinging to its muscular body in a thin blistery layer, black veins slithering beneath that skin like stitches meant to mate a devil's muscle and flesh. The thing had a girl, her wrist trapped in one clawed talon. She screamed for help when she saw me coming, but the beast understood me better than she did. It grinned through a mouthful of teeth that jutted from its narrow jaws like nails driven by a drunken carpenter, and its gaze tracked the barrel of my gun, which was already swinging up in my grasp, the stock nestling tight against my shoulder as I took aim.

A sound like snapping sheets. A blast of downdraft from those red wings as the monster climbed a hunk of sky, wings spreading wider and driving down once more.

The motion sent the creature five feet higher in the air. The shotgun barrel followed, but not fast enough. Blistered lips stretched wide, and the creature screeched laughter at me like I was some kind of idiot. Quickly, I corrected my aim and fired.

The first shot was low and peppered the girl's naked legs. She screamed as I fired again, aiming higher this time. The thing's left wing wrenched in the socket as the shot found its mark, opening a pocket of holes large enough to strain sunlight. One more reflexive flap and that wing sent a message to the monster's brain. It screeched pain through its hammered mouth and let the girl go, bloody legs and all.

She fell fast. Her anguished scream told me she understood

she was already dead, the same way she understood exactly who'd killed her.

She hit the beach hard. I barely heard the sound because the shotgun was louder. I fired twice more, and that monster fell out of the sky like a kite battered by a hurricane, and it twitched some when it hit, but not too much because I moved in fast and finished it from point-blank range.

Barnes came down to the water. He didn't say anything about the dead monster. He wanted to bury the girl, but I knew that wasn't a good idea. She might have one of those things inside her, or a pack of bloodfaces might catch her scent and come digging for her with a shovel. So we soaked her with gasoline instead, and we soaked the winged demon, too, and we tossed a match and burned down the both of them together.

After that, Barnes went back to the house.

He did the same thing to those books.

FEW DAYS LATER, I DECIDED TO CHECK OUT THE TOWN. Things had been pretty quiet...so quiet that I was getting jumpy again.

They could have rolled up the streets, and it wouldn't have mattered. To tell the truth, there hadn't been too many folks in town to begin with, and now most of them were either dead or gone. I caught sight of a couple bloodfaces when I cruised the main street, but they vanished into a manhole before I got close.

I hit a market and grabbed some canned goods and other supplies, but my mind was wandering. I kept thinking about that day in the fog, and that winged harpy on the beach, and my deputy. Since burning those books, he'd barely left his room. I was beginning to think that the whole deal had done him some good. Maybe it was just taking some time for him to get used to the way things were. Mostly, I hoped he'd finally figured out what I'd known all along—that we'd learned everything we really needed to know about the way this world worked the day we blew apart the inside-out grizzly on County Road 14.

I figured that was the way it was, until I drove back to the house.

Until I heard screams down by the lake.

Barnes had one of the bloodfaces locked up in the boathouse. A woman no more than twenty. He'd stripped her and cuffed her wrists behind a support post. She jerked against the rough wood as Barnes slid the skinning knife across her ribs.

He peeled away a scarred patch of flesh that gleamed in the dusky light, but I didn't say a word. There were enough words in this room already. They were the same words I'd seen in those books, and they rode the crazy woman's skin. A couple dozen of them had been stripped from her body with Roy Barnes's skinning knife. With her own blood, he'd pasted each one to the boathouse wall.

I bit my tongue. I jacked a shell into the shotgun.

Barnes waved me off. "Not now, boss."

Planting the knife high in the post, he got closer to the girl. Close enough to whisper in her ear. With a red finger, he pointed at the bloody inscription he'd pasted to the wall. "*Read it*," he said, but the woman only growled at him, snapping sharpened teeth so wildly that she shredded her own lips. But she didn't care about spilling her own blood. She probably didn't know she was doing it. She just licked her tattered lips and snapped some more, convinced she could take a hunk out of Barnes.

He didn't like that. He did some things to her, and her growls became screams.

"She'll come around," Barnes said.

"I don't think so, Roy."

"Yeah, she will—this time I figured things out."

"You said that when you read those books."

"But she's a book with a pulse. That's the difference. She's alive. That means she's got a connection—to those lesser demons, and to the things that lord it over them, too. Every one of them's some kind of key. But you can't unlock a gate with a bent-up key, even if it's the one that's supposed to fit. That's why things didn't work with the driver. After he piled up that Chrysler, he was a bent-up key. He lost his pulse. She's still got hers. If she reads the words instead of me—the words she wrote with a knife of her own—it'll all be different."

He'd approached me while he was talking, but I didn't look at him. I couldn't stand to. I looked at the bloodface instead. She screamed and spit. She wasn't even a woman anymore. She was just a naked, writhing thing that was going to end her days cuffed to a pole out here in the middle of nowhere. To think that she could spit a few words through tattered lips and change a world was crazy, as crazy as thinking that dead thing out on County Road 14 could do the job, as crazy as—

"Don't you understand, boss?"

"She digs up graves, Roy. She eats what she finds buried in them. That's all I need to understand."

"You're wrong. She knows—"

I raised the shotgun and blew off the bloodface's head, and then I put another load in her, and another. I blew everything off her skeleton that might have been a nest where a demon could grow. And when I was done with that little job I put a load in that wall, too, and all those scarred words went to hell in a spray of flesh and wood, and when they were gone they left a jagged window on the world outside.

Barnes stood there, the girl's blood all over his coat, the skinning knife gripped in his shaking hand.

I jacked another shell into the shotgun.

"I don't want to have this conversation again," I said.

FTER BARNES HAD GONE, I UNLOCKED THE CUFFS AND got the bloodface down. I grabbed her by her hair and rolled her into the boat. Once the boathouse doors were opened, I yanked the outboard motor cord and was on my way.

I piloted the boat to the boggy section of the lake. Black trees rooted in the water, and Spanish moss hung in tatters from the branches. It was as good a place as any for a grave. I rolled the girl into the water, and she went under with a splash. I thought about Barnes, and the things he said, and those words on the wall. And I wished he could have seen the girl there, sinking in the murk. Yeah, I wished he could have seen that straight-on. Because this was the way the world worked, and the only change coming from this deal was that some catfish were going to eat good tonight.

The afternoon waned, and the evening light came on and faded. I sat there in the boat. I might have stayed until dark, but rain began to fall—at first gently, then hard enough to patter little divots in the calm surface of the lake. That was enough for me. I revved the outboard and headed back to the lodge.

Nothing bothered me along the way, and Roy didn't bother me once I came through the front door. He was upstairs in his room, and he was quiet…or trying to be.

But I heard him.

I heard him just fine.

Up there in his room, whispering those garbage-disposal words while he worked them into his own flesh with the skinning knife. That's what he was doing. I was sure of it. I heard his blood pattering on the floorboards the same way that rat-spiders' blood had pattered the cement floor in the football stadium. Sure it was raining outside, but I'd heard rain and I'd heard blood and I knew the difference.

Floorboards squealed as he shifted his weight, and it didn't take much figuring to decide that he was standing in front of his dresser mirror. It went on for an hour and then two, and I listened as the rain poured down. And when Deputy Barnes set his knife on the dresser and tried to sleep, I heard his little mewling complaints. They were much softer than the screams of those cocooned bloodfaces, but I heard them just the same.

Stairs creaked as I climbed to the second floor in the middle of the night. Barnes came awake when I slapped open the door. A black circle opened on his bloody face where his mouth must have been, but I didn't give him a chance to say a single word.

"I warned you," I said, and then I pulled the trigger.

HEN IT WAS DONE, I ROLLED THE DEPUTY IN A SHEET AND dragged him down the stairs. I buried him under the swing set. By then the rain was falling harder. It wasn't until I got Barnes in the hole that I discovered I didn't have much gas in the can I'd gotten from the boathouse. I drenched his body with what there was, but the rain was too much. I couldn't even light a match. So I tossed a road flare in the hole, and it caught for a few minutes and sent up sputters of blue flame, but it didn't do the job the way it needed to be done.

I tried a couple more flares with the same result. By then, Roy was disappearing in the downpour like a hunk of singed meat in a muddy soup. Large river rocks bordered the flowerbeds that surrounded the lodge, and I figured they might do the trick. One by one I tossed them on top of Roy. I did that for an hour, until the rocks were gone. Then I shoveled sand over the whole mess, wet and heavy as fresh cement.

It was hard work.

I wasn't afraid of it.

I did what needed to be done, and later on I slept like the dead.

ND NOW, A MONTH LATER, I TOSSED AND TURNED IN Barnes's bed, listening to that old swing set squeak and squeal in the wind and in my dreams.

The brittle sound of gunfire wiped all that away. I came off the bed quickly, grabbing Barnes's .45 from the nightstand as I hurried to the window. Morning sunlight streamed through the trees and painted reflections on the glass, but I squinted through them and spotted shadows stretching across the beach below.

Bloodfaces. One with a machete and two with knives, all three of them moving like rabbits flushed by one mean predator.

Two headed for the woods near the edge of the property. A rattling burst of automatic gunfire greeted them, and the bloodfaces went to meat and gristle in a cloud of red vapor.

More gunfire, and this time I spotted muzzle flash in the treeline, just past the place where I'd stacked a cord of wood the summer before. The bloodface with the machete saw it, too. He put on the brakes, but there was no place for him to run but the water or the house.

He wasn't stupid. He picked the house, sprinting with everything he had. I grabbed the bottom rail of the window and tossed it up as he passed the swing set, but by the time I got the .45 through the gap he was already on the porch.

I headed for the door, trading the .45 for my shotgun on the way. A quick glance through the side window in the hallway, and I spotted a couple soldiers armed with M4 carbines breaking from the treeline. I didn't have time to worry about them. Turning quickly, I started down the stairs.

What I should have done was take another look through that front window. If I'd done that, I might have noticed the burrowed-up tunnel in the sand over Roy Barnes's grave.

IT WAS HARD TO MOVE SLOWLY, BUT I KNEW I HAD TO KEEP my head. The staircase was long, and the walls were so tight the shotgun could easily cover the narrow gap below. If you wanted a definition of dangerous ground, that would be the bottom of the staircase. If the bloodface was close—his back against the near wall, or standing directly beside the stairwell—he'd have a chance to grab the shotgun barrel before I entered the room.

A sharp clatter on the hardwood floor below. Metallic…like a machete. I judged the distance and moved quickly, following the shotgun into the room. And there was the bloodface…over by the front door. He'd made it that far, but no further. And it wasn't gunfire that had brought him down. No. Nothing so simple as a bullet had killed him.

I saw the thing that had done the job, instantly remembering the sounds I'd heard during the night—the scrapes and scrabbles I'd mistaken for nesting birds scratching in the chimney. The far wall of the room was plastered with bits of carved skin, each one of them scarred over with words, and each of those words had been skinned from the thing that had burrowed out of Roy Barnes's corpse.

That thing crouched in a patch of sunlight by the open door, naked and raw, exposed muscles alive with fresh slashes that wept red as it leaned over the dead bloodface. A clawed hand with long nails like skinning knives danced across a throat slashed to the bone. The demon didn't look up from its work as it carved the corpse's flesh with quick, precise strokes. It didn't seem to notice me at all. It wrote one word on the dead kid's throat…and then another on his face…and then it slashed open the bloodface's shirt and started a third.

I fired the shotgun and the monster bucked backwards. Its skinning knife nails rasped across the doorframe and dug into the wood. The thing's head snapped up, and it stared at me with a headful of eyes. Thirty eyes, and every one of them was the color of muddy water. They blinked, and their gaze fell everywhere at once—on the dead bloodface and on me, and on the words pasted to the wall.

Red lids blinked again as the thing heaved itself away from the door and started toward me.

Another lid snapped opened on its chin, revealing a black hole.

One suck of air and I knew it was a mouth.

I fired at the first syllable. The thing was blasted back, barking and screaming as it caught the door frame again, all thirty eyes trained on me now, its splattered chest expanding as it drew another breath through that lidded mouth just as the soldiers outside opened fire with their M4s.

Bullets chopped through flesh. The thing's lungs collapsed and a single word died on its tongue. Its heart exploded. An instant later, it wasn't anything more than a corpse spread across a puddle on the living room floor.

HEY, OLD SCHOOL," THE PRIVATE SAID. "HAVE A DRINK."

He tossed me a bottle, and I tipped it back. He was looking over my shotgun. "It's mean," he said, "but I don't know. I like some rock 'n' roll when I pull a trigger. All you got with this thing is *rock*."

"You use it right, it does the job."

The kid laughed. "Yeah. That's all that matters, right? Man, you should hear how people talk about this shit back in the Safe Zone. They actually made us watch some lame-ass stuff on the TV before they choppered us out here to the sticks. Scientists talking, ministers talking…like we was going to talk these things to death while they was trying to chew on our asses."

"I met a scientist once," the sergeant said. "He had some

guy's guts stuck to his face, and he was down on his knees in a lab chewing on a dead janitor's leg. I put a bullet in his head."

Laughter went around the circle. I took one last drink and passed the bottle along with it.

"But, you know what?" the private said. "Who gives a shit, anyway? I mean, really?"

"Well," another kid said. "Some people say you can't fight something you can't understand. And maybe it's that way with these things. I mean, we don't know where they came from. Not really. We don't even know what they *are*."

"Shit, Mendez. Whatever they are, I've cleaned their guts off my boots. That's all I need to know."

"That works today, Q, but I'm talking long term. As in: what about tomorrow, when we go nose-to-nose with their daddy?"

None of the soldiers said anything for a minute. They were too busy trading uncertain glances.

Then the sergeant smiled and shook his head. "You want to be a philosopher, Private Mendez, you can take the point. You'll have lots of time to figure out the answers to any questions you might have while you're up there, and you can share them with the rest of the class if you don't get eaten before nightfall."

The men laughed, rummaging in their gear for MRE's. The private handed over my shotgun, then shook my hand. "Jamal Quinlan," he said. "I'm from Detroit."

"John Dalton. I'm the sheriff around here."

It was the first time I'd said my own name in five months.

It gave me a funny feeling. I wasn't sure what it felt like.

Maybe it felt like turning a page.

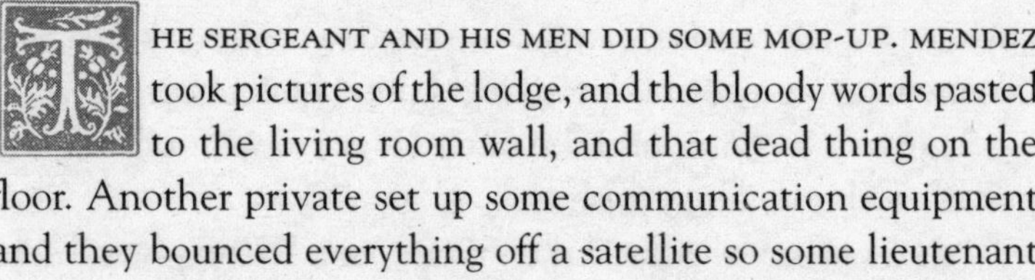

THE SERGEANT AND HIS MEN DID SOME MOP-UP. MENDEZ took pictures of the lodge, and the bloody words pasted to the living room wall, and that dead thing on the floor. Another private set up some communication equipment and they bounced everything off a satellite so some lieutenant in DC could look at it. I slipped on a headset and talked to him. He wanted to know if I remembered any strangers coming through town back in May, or anything out of the ordinary they might have had with them. Saying *yes* would mean more questions, so I said, "No, sir. I don't."

The soldiers moved north that afternoon. When they were gone, I boxed up food from the pantry and some medical supplies. Then I got a gas can out of the boathouse and dumped it in the living room. I sparked a road flare and tossed it through the doorway on my way out.

The place went up quicker than my house in town. It was older. I carried the box over to the truck, then grabbed that bottle the soldiers had passed around. There were a few swallows left. I carried it down to the dock and looked back just in time to see those birds dart from their nest in the chimney, but I didn't pay them any mind.

I took the boat out on the lake, and I finished the whiskey, and after a while I came back.

THINGS ARE GETTING BETTER NOW. IT'S QUIETER THAN ever around here since the soldiers came through, and I've got some time to myself. Sometimes I sit and think about the things that might have happened instead of the things that did. Like that very first day, when I spotted that monster in the Chrysler's trunk out on County Road 14 and blasted it with the shotgun—the gas tank might have exploded and splattered me all over the road. Or that day down in the dark under the high-school football stadium—those rat-spiders could have trapped me in their web and spent a couple months sucking me dry. Or with Roy Barnes—if he'd never seen those books in the backseat of that old sedan, and if he'd never read a word about lesser demons, where would he be right now?

But there's no sense wondering about things like that, any more than looking for explanations about what happened to Barnes, or me, or anyone else. I might as well ask myself why the thing that crawled out of Barnes looked the way it did or knew what it knew. I could do that and drive myself crazy chasing my own tail, the same way Barnes did with all those *maybes* and *what ifs*.

So I try to look forward. The rules are changing. Soon they'll be back to the way they used to be. Take that soldier. Private Quinlan. A year from now he'll be somewhere else, in a place where he won't do the things he's doing now. He might even have a hard time believing he ever did them. It won't be much different with me.

Maybe I'll have a new house by then. Maybe I'll take off work early on Friday and push around a shopping cart, toss steaks and a couple of six packs into it. Maybe I'll even do the things I used to do. Wear a badge. Find a new deputy. Sort things out and take care of trouble. People always need someone who can do that.

To tell the truth, that would be okay with me.

That would be just fine.

An Eldritch Matter

ADAM NISWANDER

Adam Niswander is the author of the Lovecraftian novels The Charm *(Integra, 1993) and* The Serpent Slayers *(Integra, 1994), the first two of a series of novels set in the Southwest. The third and fourth novels of the series,* The Hound Hunters *and* The War of the Whisperers, *appeared in 2008 and 2009 from Hippocampus Press. His short stories have appeared in numerous magazines and anthologies.*

 AM TERRIBLY CONFUSED.

I am not the adventurous type, if you know what I mean.

I like things to be a little dull, as a matter of fact.

Yesterday, my life was normal and perhaps a bit predictable, and I was happy. My wife loved me, my children looked up to me, I had a good job, and all the people we knew seemed to like me—to like us. The bills were paid on time, the house was a real home, and the biggest uncertainty in my life was not knowing if my wife would choose to prepare pork chops or spaghetti for our supper.

Then, this morning, while waiting for the bus, I happened to look down and saw a little metal disk on the curb. You wouldn't think something as silly as a hunk of cheap pot-metal could mess up your life, would you?

It didn't look like anything all that unusual to me at the time. It was just a disk of white metal with an engraved sort of tentacled—something surrounding a big red eye in the middle. I picked it up, looked at it, and figured my son, Arnie, would find it interesting. I put it in my pocket and promptly forgot about it.

When I arrived at the office, I grabbed a cup of coffee in the lobby kiosk and took the elevator to the eighth floor. I went straight to my desk, settled in, and began to begin work on a proposal that is due by the end of the week. The client is important, representing a big percentage of our total business.

I had been sitting there only minutes when, without warning, I felt a terrible stabbing pain on my right thigh. It was excruciating…as if something had taken a bite out of me, or some giant insect had stabbed me with a stinger. I jumped up and slapped at the spot, hopping around, but the pain did not abate. It burned.

And it began to spread.

And I fell to the floor.

I was yelling by now.

Several of my co-workers came to see what all the ruckus was about. Despite my obvious suffering, no one could see anything wrong. Whatever was attacking me was covered by my clothing, and my flailing gyrations kept everyone at least an arm's length away. The pain was like a palpable thing, like a flame that crawled up my leg leaving agony in its path.

And it seemed there was nothing I could do about it, no way I could alleviate it.

Bob Shaw had knelt by me and was trying to ask me what was wrong.

"What is it, Thompson?"

And I felt…well, some…weird…thing. Even through the pain, my right leg suddenly didn't feel like a leg at all, really. It felt kind of…well, boneless. And as I clutched at it through my trouser leg, my fingers didn't find anything solid. I moved my left hand down to my knee, but I didn't feel a knee. It felt the same as the upper part of my leg, and curiously not solid. And the feeling was crawling up and down my leg simultaneously. It scared the crap out of me!

If I had been yelling in pain before, now I was screaming in terror. I looked down and discovered my shoe had come off. My sock was still on, but the foot inside it was horribly shapeless—and by now my entire right leg was curved in a very unnatural way.

My co-workers had pulled back away from me.

I heard Bob Shaw on the phone. "No, I don't know what's

wrong with him," he shouted, "but send an ambulance right away. The man is dying!"

But the pain was not through with me yet. It spread across my groin, scalding like acid. I can't even begin to describe my horror as it passed through my genitalia and then into my left leg, once again racing down and feeling as if it was burning my bones away.

I could not stop screaming.

The speed with which it spread through me seemed to be increasing. In moments, my left leg, like my right, was strangely limp, and I found I could no longer hold myself upright. I flopped backward just as the pain and burning began to climb up my spine.

I began to be racked by spasms that set my legs thrashing about, but they no longer bore much resemblance to legs. They rippled and squirmed, they seemed to slither across the floor. My right sock had now slipped completely off and the obscenely pink flesh it had revealed did not resemble a foot. There were no signs of toes or nails, or ankles and soles, only a featureless fleshy tube tapering gracelessly to a rounded tip. Worse, it had begun to itch mercilessly.

By now, the siren could be heard on the street below and the screech of tires braking on asphalt. I hoped the paramedics would hurry.

My co-workers, my office-mates, had backed as far away as they could, and panic spread among them.

"Oh God! Look! His skin is writhing."

"What's happening to him?"

"It's like his bones are melting!"

"Do you think it could be catching?"

That last question sent some of them fleeing to the elevators and the rest strained to back yet further away.

I wanted to sit up and gain control of myself, but I could not. The strange tide of transformation continued unabated and the pain seemed to be increasing. I fear my yelling had degenerated into bursts of sound that hardly resembled anything human. I was exhausted, my throat raw from screaming at the top of my voice. My cries now were more a harsh bleating and moaning.

Strangely, no matter how my body was being changed, I could feel my heart steadily beating. It was a hypnotic rhythm that was at once petrifying and weirdly reassuring.

The feeling of something coursing through me had now reached my neck and shoulders, and spread rapidly into my arms. I was still thrashing about, but it was as if I had been trapped inside my head and was being forced to watch as everything about me—everything that went into my concept of me—was irrevocably changed.

Then, suddenly—mercifully—the pain stopped.

And I looked over to see my left hand, which had been flailing uncontrollably, and saw no hand at all. My eyes grew wider as I stared in terror. It looked as if some giant pink worm was crawling out of my coat-sleeve.

There was a commotion over by the door and three paramedics came bustling through, pushing people aside. Two maneuvered a gurney and the third carried the medical bag. But even as they approached, I felt/heard/guessed the final transformation occur. My head sank back squishily and I knew that my skull had just gone the way of the rest of the bones in my body.

As the lead medic knelt by me, I attempted to speak and tell him I was in no pain. I could not lift my head, yet I still was under the delusion that I would be able to communicate. I was wrong. What issued from my mouth was a gelatinous baritone belch, accompanied by a horrible stench.

I think I was as shocked as the medic.

Certainly his face revealed his disgust. "What the hell is this?" he asked angrily.

Shaw stepped up and stared at me with consternation. He cleared his throat and, after a few false starts, he managed to say, "Until a few minutes ago, he was our co-worker, Mr. David Thompson. This is his desk. He was sitting there working quite normally before whatever…happened…began…er… happening."

"Are you telling me this is a human being?" asked the medic.

"Yes, as far as I know," said Shaw.

Had I been able to control my movements, I would have embraced him then and there. I was filled with gratitude. I tried to lift my arms and found that it did set the worms into motion. The pink protuberances seemed to leap up from the floor like writhing tentacles, but I had no control.

The medic jumped back, a look of fear on his face. Shaw and everyone else backed further away as well.

I tried again to speak, but this time all I managed was a noisy exhalation of noxious gases.

I then discovered that it was very difficult to get a breath. It was as if some giant was sitting on my chest. I gasped.

The medic approached again. Tentatively, he reached out to me, trying to take my wrist, but I really no longer had one. He stopped that movement, and then placed a stethoscope on my chest. He face relaxed a little when he heard my heart beat.

"What happened?" he asked aloud.

Shaw shrugged. "I don't know. He was working at his desk and then cried out, as if in pain. He fell to the floor and began to writhe about, and, over the course of several minutes, he seemed to collapse in upon himself. We tried to help him at first, but the changes were dramatic, startling, and frightening. His thrashing about became dangerous and we all had to pull back. That's when I called for you."

"We'll take him in," said the medic. He gestured to his companions. "Load him on the stretcher."

What happened next might have been funny had it not been so macabre.

The two other medics collapsed the gurney, placed it by me, and moved to lift me onto it. They each took an arm—or what used to be an arm—and pulled, but the transformed limbs just seemed to stretch impossibly and the bulk of my body lay where it had been.

The lead medic moved in to help. They folded my long tubular limbs atop my body. The three of them got their arms under my torso and what had been my hips, and tried to lift me up.

I guess it was like trying to move a puddle of Jello with toothpicks. They tried several times before realizing it wouldn't work.

Finally, they simply rolled me over the edge and up onto the stretcher, rearranging my limbs as best they could and using my clothing as a sort of sling.

Mercifully, they threw a sheet over me as they rushed the gurney to the elevator, to the ground floor, the waiting ambulance, and, at last, to the local hospital with sirens screaming.

T HAS BEEN SOME HOURS NOW. THEY CHECKED ME IN, put me in a private room, and left me here. I wish I could say I lost consciousness, but I did not.

The strangest thing was that my mind remained my own. No matter how traumatized I had been, the cessation of pain brought a kind of detachment, almost as if I was floating above myself. I did not understand my transformation, but I then became curious.

If I had no skull, what was protecting my brain? What remained of my face was pressed into the bed with some amount of my own flabby body forcing it into the padding, yet I had a sense that I was unharmed. If I had no ribs surrounding it, how did my heart continue to beat? Yet it did, with a strangely reassuring regularity.

I concentrated on moving one of my limbs—what had been my right arm. It twitched.

I focussed my thoughts on reaching up to touch my face. The appendage hesitantly squirmed toward my eye.

I knew an illogical sense of jubilation. For the first time since the onset of the pain, I began to sense that I might have some minute, fragmentary, miniscule, bit of control over something.

Ever so slowly, painstakingly, I guided my right arm. When it finally, tentatively, brushed my face, I discovered two things.

First, that I could still feel things with the limb, changed though it might be. In fact, the sensation of touch seemed to have been enhanced—as if the entire limb had the sensitivity of a fingertip.

Second, what had been my skull was not completely gone. A hard but malleable kind of gristle formed a protective cage around my poor human brain, a cartilaginous cranium, and some kind of similar ridges protected my eyes.

My mouth, however, had been transformed into a lipless, toothless maw that seemed to exude a viscous liquid. My nose was simply gone—not even nostril slits remained.

But I was still breathing…in some way.

That was when I began to hear the Bronx-cheer buzzing again, and realized it sounded from what had once been my neck. I focussed on moving the arm again and managed to brush it over a place where ripples of flesh seemed to rise up when I exhaled and draw down when I inhaled.

Sudden realization swept over me. Gills? Great God, I had gills!

BUSTLING SOUND CAME FROM THE DOORWAY AND A whites-mocked male figure entered the room, closely followed by two nurses.

He stopped when he reached the foot of the bed and looked at the chart. "This is supposed to be a David Thompson," he said sarcastically. He threw back the sheet in front of him, exposing my midsection and upper thigh. "This is not a human. Is this a hoax?"

I felt his hands move over what had been my hip and over what used to be my thigh.

"Wait!" he said suddenly. "What's this?"

I felt him squeeze the skin of my former thigh together and felt an uncharacteristic lump under the skin.

"I bet I can get this without even requiring a local," he muttered to himself. He looked around and took a scalpel from a tray, then made a sudden quick, small incision. I felt a bit of pressure and then something seemed to pop. I can't describe it any other way. It actually clattered on the tray.

"Some sort of round metal object," he observed, picking it up carefully. "It's about the same size as a bottle cap." He turned to the second nurse. "Suture that incision closed. I'm going to look at this through the lab microscope."

But he took only a few steps before he seemed to freeze. "What the fu…!"

He never finished what he was saying. His voice rose up in a rapid wail and became a scream. His hand snapped into a fist around the object, and he fell heavily to the floor. There he continued to writhe, his screams growing more shrill.

I could not sit up to see clearly, but I guessed immediately what was happening.

Poor bastard, I thought. Now there are two of us.

Substitution

MICHAEL MARSHALL SMITH

Michael Marshall Smith is a widely published British author of novels, short stories, and screenplays. His novels include Only Forward *(HarperCollins, 1994),* Spares *(HarperCollins, 1996), and several novels published as by* Michael Marshall*. Among his short story collections are* What You Make It *(HarperCollins, 1999) and* More Tomorrow and Other Stories *(Earthling, 2003). He is a five-time winner of the British Fantasy Award.*

ALFWAY THROUGH UNPACKING THE SECOND RED BAG I turned to my wife—who was busily engaged in pecking out an e-mail on her Blackberry—and said something encouraging about the bag's contents.

"Well, you know," she said, not really paying attention. "I do try."

I went back to taking items out and laying them on the counter, which is my way. Because I work from home, I'm always the one who unpacks the grocery shopping when it's delivered: Helen's presence this morning was unusual, and a function of a meeting that had been put back an hour (the subject of the terse e-mail currently being written). Rather than standing with the fridge door open and putting items directly into it, I put everything on the counter first, so I can sort through it and get a sense of what's there, before then stowing everything neatly in the fridge, organized by type/nature/potential meal groupings, as a kind of Phase Two of the unloading operation.

The contents of the bags—red for stuff that needs refrigeration, purple for freezer goods, green for everything else—is never entirely predictable. My wife has control of the online ordering process, which she conducts either from her laptop or, in extremis, her phone. While I've not personally specified the order, however, its contents are seldom much of a surprise. There's an established pattern. We have cats, so there'll be two large bags of litter—it's precisely being able to avoid hoicking that kind of thing off supermarket shelves, into a trolley and across a busy car park, which makes online grocery shopping such a boon. There will be a few green bags containing bottled water, sacks for the rubbish bins, toilet rolls and paper towels, cleaning materials, tins of store cupboard staples (baked beans, tuna, tinned tomatoes), a box of Diet Coke for me (which Helen tolerates on the condition that I never let it anywhere near our son), that kind of thing. There will be one, or at the most two, purple bags of frozen beans, holding frozen peas, frozen organic fish cakes for the kid, and so on. We never buy enough frozen to fill more than one purple carrier, but sometimes they split it between a couple, presumably for some other logistical reason. Helen views this as both a waste of resources and a threat to the environment, and has sent at least two e-mails to the company about it. I don't mind much as we use the bags for clearing out the cats' litter tray, and I'd rather have spares on hand than risk running out.

Then there are the red bags, the main event. The red bags represent the daily news of food consumption—in contrast to the contextual magazine articles of the green bags, or the long-term forecasts of the purple. In the red bags will be the Greek yoghurt, blueberries, and strawberries Helen uses to make her morning smoothie; a variety of vegetables and salad materials; some free-range and organic chicken fillets (I never used to be clear on the difference, but eleven years of marriage has made me far better informed); some extra-sharp cheddar (Helen favours cheese that tastes as though it wants your tongue to be sad), and a few other bits and pieces.

The individual items may vary a little from week to week, but basically, that's what gets brought to our door most Wednesday mornings. Once in a while there may be substitutions in the delivery (when the supermarket has run out of a specified item, and one judged to be of very near equivalence is provided instead): these have to be carefully checked, as Helen's idea of similarity of goods differs somewhat from the supermarket's.

Otherwise, you could set your watch by our shopping, if you'll pardon the mixed metaphor—and this continuity of content is why I'd turned to Helen when I was halfway through the second red bag. Yes, there'd been spring onions and a set of red, green, and yellow peppers—standard weekly fare. But there were also two packs of brightly coloured and fun-filled children's yoghurts and a block of much milder cheddar of the kind Oscar and I tend to prefer. And a family pack of deadly-looking chocolate desserts. Not to mention a six-pack of thick and juicy-looking steaks, and very large variety pack of further Italian cured meats holding five different types of salami.

"Yum," I said.

I was genuinely pleased, and a little touched. Normally I source this kind of stuff—on the few occasions when I have it—from the deli or mini-market, which are both about ten minutes' walk away from the house (in opposite directions, sadly). Seeing it come into the house via the more socially condoned route of the supermarket delivery was strangely affecting.

"Hmm?" Helen said. She was nearing the end of her e-mail. I could tell because the speed of her typing increases markedly as she approaches the point when she can fire her missive off into space. She jabbed send and finally looked up properly. "What's that you said?"

"Good shop. Unusual. But I like it."

She smiled, glad that I was happy, but then frowned. "What the hell's that?"

I looked where she was pointing. "Yoghurt."

She grabbed the pack and stared with evident distaste at the ingredient list. "I didn't order those. Obviously. Or *that*." Now she was pointing at the pile of salamis and meats. "And the cheese is wrong. Oh, bloody *hell*."

And with that, she was gone.

I waited, becalmed in the kitchen, to see what would unfold.

A quick look in the other bags—the greens and purples—didn't explain much. They all contained exactly the kind of thing we tended to order.

Five minutes later I heard the sound of two pairs of footsteps coming down the stairs. Helen re-entered the kitchen, followed by the man who'd delivered the shopping. He was carrying three red bags and looked mildly cowed.

"What it is, right," he muttered, defensively, "is the checking system. I've told management about it before. There are flaws. In the checking system."

"I'm sure it can't be helped," Helen said, cheerfully, and turned to me. "Bottom line is that all the bags are correct except for the red ones, which both belong to someone else."

When I'd put all the items from the counter back into the bags I'd taken them out of, an exchange took place. Their red bags, for ours. The delivery guy apologised about five more times—somehow making it clear, without recourse to words, that he was apologising for the system as a whole rather than any failure on his part—and trudged off back up the stairs.

"I'll let him out," Helen said, darting forward to give me a peck on the cheek. "Got to go anyway. You're all right unpacking all this, yes?"

"Of course," I said. "I always manage somehow."

And off she went. It only took a few minutes to unpack the low-fat yoghurt, sharp cheese, salad materials, and free-range and organic chicken breasts.

A FUNNY THING HAPPENED, HOWEVER. WHEN I BROKE OFF from work late morning to go down to the kitchen to make a cup of tea, I lingered at the fridge for a moment after getting the milk out, and I found myself thinking:

What if that had *been our food*?

I wasn't expressing discontent. We eat well. I personally don't have much of a fix on what eating healthily involves (beyond the fact it evidently requires ingesting more fruit and vegetables per day than feels entirely natural), and so it's a good thing that Helen does. If there's anything that I want which doesn't arrive at our door through the effortless magic of supermarket delivery, there's nothing to stop me going out and buying it myself. It's not as if the fridge or cupboards have been programmed to reject non-acceptable items, or set off a siren and contact the diet police when confronted with off-topic foodstuffs.

It was more that I got a sudden and strangely wistful glimpse of another life—and of another woman.

I was being assumptive, of course. It was entirely possible that the contents of the red bags I'd originally unpacked had been selected by the male of some nearby household. It didn't feel that way, however. It seemed easier to believe that somewhere nearby was another household rather like ours. A man, a woman, and a child (or perhaps two, we're unusual in having stopped at one). All the people in this family would be different to us, of course, but for the moment it was the idea of the woman which stuck in my head. I wondered what she'd look like. What kind of things made her laugh. How, too, she'd managed to miss out on the health propaganda constantly pushed at the middle-classes (she *had* to be middle class, most people in our neighbourhood are, and *everyone* who orders online from our particular supermarket has to be, it's the law)—or what had empowered her to ignore it.

We get steak every now and then, of course—but it would never be in the company of all the other meats and rich foods. One dose of weapons-grade animal fats per week is quite risky enough for this household, thank you. We live a moderate, evenly balanced life when it comes to food (and, really, when it comes to everything else). The shopping I'd seen, however foolishly, conjured the idea of a household which sailed a different sea—and of a different kind of woman steering the ship.

I was just a little intrigued, that's all.

COUPLE OF DAYS LATER, I WAS STILL INTRIGUED. YOU'D be right in suspecting this speaks of a life in which excitement levels are relatively low. I edit, from home. Technical manuals are my bread and butter, leavened with the occasional longer piece of IT journalism. I'm good at it, fast and accurate, and for the most part enjoy my work. Perhaps "enjoy" isn't quite the right word (putting my editing hat on for a moment): let's say instead that I'm content that it's my profession, am well paid and always busy, and feel no strong desire to be doing anything else, either in general or particular.

But…nobody's going to be making an action movie of my life any day soon. And that's perhaps why, sometimes, little ideas will get into my head and stick around for longer than they might in the mind of someone who has more pressing or varied (or viscerally compelling) things to deal with on a day-to-day basis.

I was still thinking about this other woman. This different girl. Not in a salacious way—how could I be? I had no idea what she looked like, or what kind of person she was (beyond that spoken of by her supermarket choices). That's the key word, I think—difference. Like any man who's been in a relationship for a long time (and doubtless a lot of women too, I've never asked), every once in a while you beguile a few minutes in fantasy. Sometimes these are sexual, of course, but often it's something more subtle which catches your internal eye. I've never felt the urge to be unfaithful to Helen—even now that our sex life has dropped to the distant background hum of the long-term married—and that's partly because, having thought the thing through, I've come to believe that such fantasies are generally not about other people, but about yourself. What's really going on, if you spend a few minutes dreaming about living in a scuzzy urban bedsit with a (much younger) tattooed barmaid/suicide doll, or cruising some sunny, fuzzy life with a languid French female chef? These women aren't real, of course, and so the attraction cannot be bedded in them. They don't exist. Doubtless these and all other alternate lifestyles would come to feel everyday and stale after a while, too, and so I suspect the appeal of such daydreams actually lies in the shifted perception of yourself that these nebulous lives would enshrine.

You'd see yourself differently, and so would other people, and that's what your mind is really playing with: a different you, in a different now.

Perhaps that insight speaks merely of a lack of courage (or testosterone); nonetheless, the idea of this nearby woman kept cropping up in my mind. Perhaps there was also a creative part of my mind seeking voice. I don't edit fiction and have never tried to write any either. I enjoy working with words, helping to corral them into neat and meaningful pens like so many conceptual sheep, but I've discovered in myself neither the urge nor the ability to seek to make them evoke people or situations which are not "true." With this imaginary woman, however—not actually imaginary of course, unless it *was* a man, it was more a case of her being "unknown"—I found myself trying to picture her, her house, and her life. I guess it's that thing which happens sometimes in airports and on trains, when you're confronted with evidence of other real people leading presumably real lives, and you wonder where everyone's going, and why: wonder why the person in the seat opposite is reading that particular book, and who they'll be meeting at the other end of the journey that you, for the moment, are sharing.

With so little to go on, my mind was trying to fill in the gaps, tell me a story. It was a bit of fun, I suppose, a way of going beyond the walls of the home office in which I spend all my days.

I'm sure I wouldn't have tried to take it further, if it hadn't been for the man from the supermarket.

WEEK TO THE DAY AFTER THE FIRST DELIVERY, HE appeared on the doorstep again. This was a little unusual. Not there being another order—Helen considerately books the deliveries into the same time slot every week, so they don't disrupt my working patterns—but it being the same man. In the several years we've been getting our groceries this way, I'm not sure I've ever encountered the same person twice, or at least not soon enough that I've recognised them from a previous delivery.

But here this one was again.

"Morning," he said, standing there like a scruffy Christmas tree, laden with bags of things to eat or clean or wipe surfaces or bottoms with. "Downstairs, right?"

I stood aside to let him pass and saw there were a couple more crates full of bags on the path outside. That meant I had a few minutes to think, which I suddenly found I was doing.

I held the door open while he came up, re-ladened himself, and tramped back downstairs again. By the time he trudged up the stairs once more, I had a plan.

"Right then," he said, digging into a pocket and pulling out a piece of paper. He glanced at it, then thrust it in my direction. "That's your lot. Everything's there. No substitutions."

Before he could go, however, I held up my hand. "Hang on," I said, brightly. "You remember last week? The thing with the red bags?"

He frowned, and then his face cleared. “Oh yeah. That was you, right? Got the wrong red bags, I know. I’ve spoken to Head Office about it, don’t worry.”

“It’s not that,” I said. “Hang on here a sec, if you don’t mind?”

I quickly trotted downstairs, opened one of the kitchen cupboards, and pulled out something more-or-less at random. A tin of corned beef—perfect.

Back up in the hallway, I held it out to the delivery guy.

“I think this should have gone back into the other person’s bags,” I said. “I’m not sure, but my wife says she didn’t order it.”

The man took the can from me and peered at it unhappily. “Hmm,” he said. “Thought most of the delivery goods was branded. But it could be. Could be.”

“Sorry about this,” I said. “Didn’t notice until you were gone.

I…I don’t suppose you remember where the other customer lived.”

“Oh yeah,” he said. “As it happens, I do. Vans in this area only cover a square mile each day, if that. And I had to go through the bags with her, see, in case there was a problem with it, what with you already unpacking it here.”

“Great,” I said. His use of the word “her” had not been lost on me.

“Didn’t say nothing about something being missing, though,” he said, doubtfully. He looked down at the tin again without enthusiasm, sensing it represented a major diversion from standard practices, which could only bring problems into his life. I looked at it too.

“Hang on,” he said, as a thought struck him. He gave the tin to me. “Be right back.”

I waited on the doorstep as he picked up the crates on the path and carried them back to his van. A couple of minutes later he reappeared, looking more optimistic.

“Sorted,” he said. “As it happens, she’s next but one on my

list. I'll take it, see if it's hers."

I handed the corned beef back to him again, thinking quickly. I was going to need my house keys. Oh, and some shoes.

"Don't worry about bringing it back, if it's not," I said, to hold him there while I levered my feet into a pair of slip-ons which always live in the hallway.

This confused him, however. "But if it's not hers, then…I can't just…"

"It's just I've got to go out for a while," I said. "Tell you what—if it's not hers, then just bring it back, leave it on the step, okay?"

I could see him thinking this was a bit of a pain in the neck—especially over a single tin of canned meat—but then realising that my solution meant less disruption and paperwork than the likely alternatives.

"Done," he said, and walked off down the path.

I trotted to my study, grabbed the house keys from my shelf, and then back to the front door. I slipped out onto the step and locked up, listening hard.

When I heard the sliding slam of a van door, I walked cautiously down the path—making it to the pavement in time to see the delivery vehicle pull away.

THERE FOLLOWED HALF AN HOUR OF SLIGHTLY ludicrous cloak and daggery, as I tried to keep up with the supermarket van without being seen. The streets in our neighbourhood are full of houses exactly like ours—slightly bigger-than-usual Victorian terraces. Many of the streets curve, however, and two intersections out of three are blocked with wide metal gates, to stop people using the area as a rat route between the bigger thoroughfares which border it. The delivery driver had to take very circuitous routes to go relatively short distances, and bends in the street meant that, were I not careful, it would have been easy for him to spot me in his side mirrors. Assuming he'd been looking, of course, which he wouldn't be—but it's hard to remind yourself of that when you're engaged in quite so silly an enterprise.

Keeping as far back as I could without risking losing him, I followed the vehicle as it traced a route which eventually led to it pulling up outside a house six or seven streets away from our house. Once he'd parked I faded back forty yards and leaned on a tree. He'd said the stop that I was interested in was not this one, but the next, and I judged him to be a person who'd use language in a precise (albeit not especially educated) way. He wouldn't have said "next but one" if he meant this house, so all I had to do was wait it out.

Whoever lived here was either catering for a party or simply ate a lot, all the time. It took the guy nearly fifteen minutes to drag all the red, green, and purple bags up the path and into the house—where a plump grey-haired man imperiously directed their distribution indoors. This gave me plenty of time to realise I was being absolutely ridiculous. At one point I even decided just to walk away, but my feet evidently didn't get the message, and when he eventually climbed back into the van and started the engine, I felt my heart given a strange double thump.

She would be next.

I don't know if the delivery driver had suddenly realised he was behind schedule, but the next section of following was a lot tougher. The van lurched from the curb as though he'd stamped on the pedal, and he steered through the streets at a far brisker pace than before. I was soon having to trot to keep up—all the while trying not to get *too* close on his tail. I don't exercise very often (something I take recurrent low-level flak from Helen over), and before long I was panting hard.

Thankfully, it was only a few more minutes before I saw the

van indicating, then abruptly swerving over to the curb again. The funny thing was, we were now only about three streets from my house. We were on, in fact, the very road I walked every morning when I strolled out to the deli to buy a latté to carry back to my desk—a key pillar in my attempts to develop something approaching a "lifestyle."

I waited (again, taking cover behind a handy tree) while the delivery man got out, slid open the van's side door, and got inside. He emerged a few minutes later carrying only three bags. They were all red, which I found interesting. No frozen food. No household materials. Just stuff to go straight in the fridge—and probably meats and charcuterie and cheeses that were a pleasure to eat, rather then feeling they were part of some obscure work-out.

There were only two front paths that made sense from where he'd parked, and I banked on the one on the right—sidling up the street to the next tree, in the hope of getting a better view. I was right. The man plodded up the right-most path toward a house which, in almost every particular, was functionally identical to the one in which Helen and Oscar and I lived. A three-story Victorian house, the lowest level a half-basement slightly below the height of the street, behind a very small and sloping "garden." I was confident this lower floor would hold a kitchen and family room and small utility area, just as ours did—though of course I couldn't see this from my position across the street.

The man had the bags looped around his wrist, enabling him to reach up and ring the doorbell with that hand. After perhaps a minute, I saw the door open. I caught a glimpse of long, brown hair…

And then a sodding lorry trundled into view, completely obscuring the other side of the street.

I'd been so focused on watching the house that I hadn't seen or even heard the vehicle's approach. It ground to a halt right in front of me, and the driver turned the engine off. A gangly youth hopped down out of it immediately, busily consulting a furniture note and scanning the numbers of the houses on the side of the street where I was standing.

I moved quickly to the left, but I was too late. The supermarket delivery man was coming back down the path, and the door to the house was shut again.

"*Bollocks*," I said, without meaning to.

I said it loudly enough that the delivery man looked up, however. It took a second for him to recognise me, but then he grinned.

"You was right," he called across the street. "Was hers after all. Cheers, mate. Job done."

And with that he climbed back into his van. I turned and walked quickly in the other direction, thinking I might as well go to the deli and get a coffee.

Maybe they could put something in it that stopped middle-aged men being utter, *utter* morons.

HAT EVENING HELEN HAD AN ASSIGNATION WITH TWO of her old university friends. This is one of the few occasions these days when she tends to let her hair down and drink too much wine, so I made her a snack before she went out. After she'd gone and Oscar had been encouraged up to bed (or at least to hang out in his bedroom, rather than lurking downstairs watching reality television), I found myself becalmed in the kitchen.

I'd got almost none of my work done that afternoon. Once the feelings of toe-curling embarrassment had faded—okay, so the supermarket guy had seen me on the street, but he'd had no way of knowing what I was doing there, no reason to suspect I was up to anything untoward—I'd found myself all the more intrigued.

There was the matter of the corned beef, for a start. I knew damn well that there had been no error over it. I'd bought it myself, a month or two back, from the mini-market. I like some corned beef in a sandwich every now and then, with lettuce and good slather of horseradish. I'd fully assumed that the tin would make its way back to me. And yet, when presented with it, the woman had decided to claim it as her own.

I found this curious, and even a little exciting. I knew that had Helen been in a similar situation she would have done nothing of the sort, even if the item in question had been totally healthy and certified GM-negative. This other woman had been given the change to scoop up a freebie, however, and had said "Yes please."

Then there was her hair.

It was infuriating that I hadn't been given the chance to get a proper look at her, but in a way, just the hair had been enough. Helen is blonde, you see. Really it's a kind of very light brown, of course, but the diligent attentions of stylists keep it mid-blonde. A trivial difference, but a difference all the same.

Trivial, too, was the geographical distance. The woman lived just three streets away. She paid the same rates, received cheery missives from the same local council, and would use—probably on a more frequent basis than we do—the services of the same takeaway food emporiums. If she went into the centre of London, she'd use the same tube station. If it rained on our back garden, it would be raining on hers. The air I breathed stood at least some chance of making it, a little later, into her lungs.

This realisation did nothing to puncture the bubble which had started to grow in my head over the previous week. I can't stress strongly enough that this was not a matter of desire, however nebulous. It was just interesting to me. Fascinating, perhaps.

Difference doesn't have to be very great to hold the imagination, after all. Much is made of men who run off with secretaries twenty years younger than their wives, or women who ditch their City-stalwart husbands to get funky with their dreadlocked Yoga teacher. Most affairs and marital breakages, however, do not follow this pattern. Helen and I knew four couples whose relationships had clattered into the wall of midlife crisis, and all amounted to basically the same thing. Two men and two women had (in each case temporarily) set aside their partner for someone who was remarkably similar. In one case—that of my old friend Paul—the woman he'd been having a semi-passionate liaison with for nine months turned out to be *so* similar to his wife that I'd been baffled on the sole occasion I'd met her (Paul having had the sense, after two months, to go back to Angela and the children, tail between his legs). Even Paul had once referred to the other woman by the wrong name during the evening, which went down about as well as you'd expect.

And this makes sense. Difference is difference, whether it be big or small, and it may even be that the smaller differences feel the most enticing. Most people do not want (and would not even be able) to throw aside a lifetime of preference and predilection and taste. You are who you are, and you like what you like. Short of being able to have their partner manifest a different body once in a while (which is clearly impossible), many seem to opt for a very similar body that just happens to have a slightly different person inside. A person of the same class and general type, but just different enough to trigger feelings of newness, to enable the sensation of experiencing something novel—to wake up, for a spell, the slumbering person inside.

Difference fades quickly, however, whereas love and the warmth of long association do not, which is why so many end up sloping right back to where they started out. Most people don't end up in liaisons with barmaids or other exotics. They get busy with friends and co-workers, people living in the same tree. They don't actually want difference from the outside world. They want it within themselves.

I realised, after mulling it over in the quiet, tidy kitchen for nearly an hour, that I wanted to be someone different too, however briefly. So I went upstairs, told my son that I was popping out to post a letter, and went out into the night.

T WAS AFTER NINE BY THEN, AND DARK. AUTUMNAL, too, which I've always found the most invigorating time of year. I suppose it's distant memories of changes in the school or university year, falling leaves as an augur of moving to new levels and states of being within one's life.

I didn't walk the most direct route to the house, instead taking a long way round, strolling as casually as I could along the deserted mid-evening pavements, between lamps shedding yellow light.

I was feeling…something. Feeling silly, yes, but engaged, too. This wasn't editing. This wasn't ferrying Oscar to and from school. This wasn't listening to Helen talk about her work. The only person involved in this was me.

Eventually I found myself approaching the street in question, via another that met it at right angles. When I emerged from this I glanced up and down the road, scoping it out from a different perspective to it merely being part of the route to my morning latté purveyor.

The road ended—or was interrupted—by one of the traffic-calming gates, and so was extremely quiet. There'd be very little reason for anyone to choose it unless they lived in one of the houses I could see.

I stood on the opposite side of the street and looked at

the house where the woman lived, about twenty yards away. A single light shone in the upper storey, doubtless a bedroom. A wider glow from the level beneath the street, however, suggested life going on down there.

My heart was beating rapidly now, and far more heavily than usual. My body as well as my mind seemed aware of this break in usual patterns of behaviour, that its owner was jumping the tracks, doing something new.

I crossed the street. When I reached the other side I kept going, slowly, walking right past the house. As I did so I glanced down and to my right.

A single window was visible in the wall of the basement level, an open blind partially obscuring the top half. In the four seconds or so that it took me to walk past the house, I saw a large green rug on dark floorboards and caught a glimpse of a painting on one wall. No people, and most specifically, not her.

I continued walking, right the way up to the gate across the road. Waited there a few moments, and then walked back the same way.

This time—emboldened by the continued lack of human occupancy—I got a better look at the painting. It showed a small fishing village, or something of the sort, on a rocky coast. The style was rough, even from that distance, and I got the sense that the artist had not been trying to evoke the joys of waterfront living. The village did not look like somewhere you'd deliberately go on holiday, that's for sure.

Then I was past the house again.

I couldn't just keep doing this, I realised. Sooner or later someone in one of the other houses would spot a man pacing up and down this short section of street and decide to be neighbourly—which in this day and age means calling the police.

I had an idea, and took my mobile out of my trouser pocket.

I flipped it open, put it to my ear, and wandered a little way further down the street.

If anyone saw me, I believed, I'd just be one of those other people you notice once in a while—some man engaged in some other, different life, talking to someone whose identity they'd never know, about matters which would remain similarly oblique. It would be enough cover for a few minutes, I thought.

I arranged it so that my meandering path—I even stepped off into the empty road for a spell, just to accentuate how little my surroundings meant to me, so engaged was I with my telephone call—gradually took me back toward the house. After about five minutes of this I stepped back up onto the curb, about level with the house's front path.

I stopped then, taken aback.

Someone had been in the lower room I could see through the window. She'd only been visible for a second—and I knew it was her, because I'd glimpsed the same long, brown hair from that morning—starting out in the middle of the room, and then walking out the door.

Was she going to come back? Why would she have come into what was presumably a living room, then left again? Was she fetching something from the room—a book or magazine—and now settling down in a kitchen I couldn't see? Or was she intending to spend the evening in the living room instead, and returning to the kitchen for something she'd forgotten, to bring back with her?

I kept the phone to my ear, and turned in a slow circle. Walked a few yards up the street, with a slow, casual, leg-swinging gait, and then back again.

I'd gone past the point of feeling stupid now. I just wanted to see. When I got back to the pavement, I caught my breath.

The woman was back.

More than that, she was sitting down. Not on the sofa—

one corner of which I could just make out in the corner of the window—but right in the middle of the rug. She had her back to me. Her hair was thick, and hung to the middle of her back. It was very different in more than colour to Helen's, who'd switched to a shorter and more-convenient-for-the-mornings style a few years back.

The woman seemed to be bent over slightly, as if reading something laid out on the floor in front of her. I really, really wanted to know what it was. Was it perhaps *The Guardian*, choice of all right-thinking people (and knee-jerk liberals) in this part of North London? Or might it be something else, some periodical I'd never read, or even heard of? A book I might come to love?

I took another cautious set forward, barely remembering to keep up the pretence with the mobile phone still in my hand.

With my slightly changed angle I could now see her elbows, one poking out from either side of her chest. They seemed in a rather high position for someone managing reading matter, but it was hard to tell.

My scalp and the back of my neck were itching with nervousness by now. I cast a quick glance either way up the street, just to check no one was coming. The pavements on both sides remained empty, distanced pools of lamplight falling on silence and emptiness.

When I looked back, the woman had altered her position slightly, and I saw something new. I thought at first it must be whatever she was reading, but then realised first that it couldn't be, and soon after, what I was actually seeing. A plastic bag.

A red plastic bag.

Who unpacks their shopping in the living room? Other people do, I guess—and perhaps it was this link with the very first inkling I'd had of this woman's existence (the temporary arrival of her food in the kitchen of my own house, in the very same kind of bag) that caused me to walk forward another step.

I should have looked where I was going, but I did not. My foot collided with an empty Coke can lying near the low wall at the front of the woman's property. It careered across the remaining space with a harsh scraping noise, before clattering into the wall with a smack.

I froze, staring down at her window.

The woman wrenched around, turning about the waist to glare up through her window.

I saw the red plastic bag lying on the rug in front of her, its contents spread in a semicircle. She was not holding a newspaper or magazine or book. In one hand she held half of a thick, red steak. The other hand was up to her mouth and had evidently been engaged in pushing raw minced beef into it when she turned. The lower half of her face was smeared with blood. Her eyes were wide, and either her pupils were unusually large, or her irises were also pitch black. Her hair started perhaps an inch or two further back than anyone's I had ever seen, and there was something about her temples that was wrong, misshapen, excessive.

We stared at each other for perhaps two seconds. A gobbet of partially chewed meat fell out of her mouth, down onto her dress. I heard her say something, or snarl it. I have no idea what it might have been, and this was not merely because of the distance or muting caused by the glass of the window. It simply did not sound like any language I've ever heard. Her mouth opened far too wide in the process, too, further accentuating the strange, bulged shape of her temples.

I took a couple of huge, jerky steps backward, nearly falling over in the process. I caught one last glimpse of her face, howling something at me.

There were too many vowels in what she said, and they were in an unkind order.

I heard another sound, from up the street, and turning jerkily I saw two people approaching, from the next corner, perhaps fifty yards away. They were passing underneath one of the lamps. One was taller than the other. The shorter of the two seemed to be wearing a long dress, almost Edwardian in style. The man—assuming that's what he was—had a pronounced stoop.

In silhouette against the lamp light, both their heads were clearly too wide across the top.

I ran.

I ran away home.

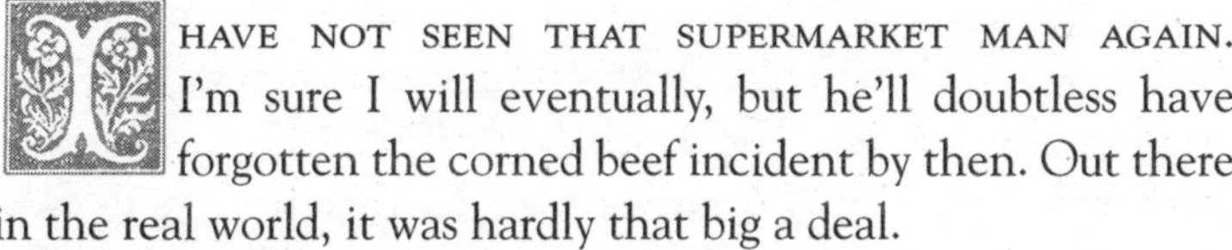

I HAVE NOT SEEN THAT SUPERMARKET MAN AGAIN. I'm sure I will eventually, but he'll doubtless have forgotten the corned beef incident by then. Out there in the real world, it was hardly that big a deal.

Otherwise, everything is the same. Helen and I continue to enjoy a friendly, affectionate relationship, sharing our lives with a son who shows no sign yet of turning into an adolescent monster. I work in my study, taking the collections of words that people send me and making small adjustments to them, changing something here and there, checking everything is in order and putting a part of myself into the text by introducing just a little bit of difference.

The only real alteration in my patterns is that I no longer walk down a certain street to get my habitual morning latté. Instead I head in the other direction and buy one from the mini-market instead. It's nowhere near as good, and I guess soon I'll go back to the deli, though I shall take a different route from the one which had previously been my custom.

A couple of weeks ago I was unpacking the bags from our weekly shop and discovered a large variety pack of sliced meats. I let out a strangled sound, dropping the package to the floor.

Helen happened to be in the kitchen at the time and took this to be a joke—me expressing mock surprise at her having (on a whim) clicked a button online and thus causing all these naughty meats to arrive as a treat for the husband who, in her own and many ways, she loves.

I found a smile for her, and the next day when she was at work I wrapped the package in a plastic bag and disposed of it in a bin half a mile from our house. There's a lot you can do with chicken, and even more with vegetables.

Meanwhile, we seem to be making love a little more often. I'm not really sure why.

Susie

JASON VAN HOLLANDER

Jason Van Hollander's fiction and nonfiction have appeared in Weird Tales, Fantasy and Science Fiction, *and other publications. His macabre artwork adorns books published by Arkham House, Golden Gryphon Press, Subterranean Press, PS Publishing, Tor Books, Night Shade Books, and Ash-Tree Press. He has illustrated books and stories by Thomas Ligotti, Fritz Leiber, Ramsey Campbell, William Hope Hodgson, and Clark Ashton Smith. He has won an International Horror Guild Award and two World Fantasy Awards.*

USIE, ANGUISHED WITH THE BURDEN OF A THOUSAND Unborn, curses the frailty of human life as Doctor Farnell clamps cool fingers around her chin. "Sip slowly," urges the physician in a voice devoid of emotion. "We can add sugar to the next dose." He lowers the fluted glass. "Your sister has been asking about you," he adds.

Alkaloid bitterness spirals down her gullet. Sitting up is difficult. The single pillow, which is too thin, slips down the headboard of the hospital bed. As the nurse fluffs the pillow Susie licks her lips, sifts through unfamiliar memories. Sister? Her thoughts are mazy. *The little one under the earth?* "Emeline?" she wonders aloud. "Didn't she die when she was six?"

Her query floats away unanswered. Doctor Farnell taps her wrists, which she notices are bound with surgical gauze. Even through the miasmas of delirium and the lingering effects of anesthesia the doctor's expression is troubling. Unmanageable anxieties banished her to this Gothic Revival Palace of Moan, whose inmates roam the halls, shuffling in slippers, lost in the folds of ill-fitting stained frocks.

Eventually the nurse explains, "Tomorrow your sister wants to visit."

"Lillie Delora? Annie?"

"One of your sisters."

Susie's bewildered response: "*Which one am I?*"

Her unanswerable question drifts beyond the curtains drawn around the bed. A late May breeze, sea-scented, mixes with the acrid scent of carbolic acid that wafts down the women's infirmary of Butler Sanatorium. Other than Susie and the doctor and the portly nurse, the ward is unoccupied. Shivering, the dying woman squirms. Her bedclothes and sheets are damp with sweat. Doctor Farnell leans closer, manipulates her eyelids, gawks as if peering deeply into unfathomable pools.

"What about your son—didn't you say he's some sort of astronomer?" asks the physician. "Surely a star-gazer would want to gaze upon his mother during her convalescence. Surely he intends to visit."

"He is a poet of the highest order," Susie hears herself say. "But he is too frail to visit, too sickly. His appearance…he really doesn't like to walk upon the streets."

"Is there some sort of infirmity?" inquires the doctor.

"He must avoid places where people could stare at him. Illness…and the constellations…accentuate the deformity. The hideous face"—she pauses to catch her breath—"when the host-form sickens the displaced identity surfaces. And the host form dissolves. This is why I'm here, this is what is happening to me."

A flicker of understanding passes between nurse and physician. Exhausted, Susie closes her eyes.

"The fever will break," F. J. Farnell avers in a medical man's voice that is heartless and reassuring at the same time. "Depend on it: the surgery was completely successful, the obstruction removed, the biliary colic resolved. Get some rest. Get some sleep. Palliatives will be provided."

Susie opens her eyes. Her vision is blurred. The nurse seems to be proffering an empty glass; the edges shimmer. An unconvincing simulation of a smile mars the physician's face as he intones: "The tincture is efficacious but it clouds the mind. Nurse Grady will try to remember to sugar the next dose."

"My head aches." Susie—the unusurped portion—tries to gather her thoughts. "Everything is collapsing. Years ago my husband collapsed. My child will collapse. How will we manage, how will we fare? Our situation is dire…"

"It's the fever. When it breaks you'll feel better."

"*I will live only to suffer*," Susie whispers as the doctor swirls through the curtains. Her statement is objective, not a contradiction. Human ingenuity is insufficient. The doctor and his medicaments are primitive, the nurse is impertinent, traipsing in and out of the curtained partition with her sour Sapphic glower.

The dying creature shuts human-seeming eyelids, tests the failing sensorium. Listens to the click-clack of cleats of high-button shoes on floors of tile and marble. Inhales institutional odors: green soap, floor-wax, ammonia. Disinfectant.

Nurse Grady returns, brandishing the fluted glass. It glistens with opium and water and spiraling granules of sugar that are magically descriptive, nebular, galactic in implication. Flushed, the nurse fidgets, sputters, "Don't think I'll be forgetting the terrible things you said to me, what you accused me of yesterday!"

"You are the heavyset nurse. The one who bathes me."

"Accusing me of…improprieties. When all I did is what I'm paid to do: a sponge bath for patients that sweat through their gown and dirty themselves."

"You touched me. Your hands lingered," Susie reminds the porcine woman.

"All I did was to perform my duty as a nurse."

"You kept staring at my nakedness."

"Your belly-skin had tattoos, symbols in strange colors, scurrying around like beetles. Especially near the sutures. And someone put furry boots on your legs. They looked like goat-feet."

Susie stared at the ceiling, warding off realizations. "Is my body changing?" she wonders.

"By the time the ether wore off…by the time you stopped vomiting, the tattoos vanished. I don't know how you got rid of the boots. Maybe it was some sort of trick. Anyhow," huffs the nurse, "I was just performing my duty as a nurse."

As evidence the porcine woman points at her uniform, which is starched, unnaturally white, overbright in the sunlight slicing through the bars of the sanatorium windows. *Silicated*, decides the efficiency that is fused with Susie. "When you washed the host-body, your hands lingered," avers the pluralized Susie. "You caressed the host-body."

"Lookie, Missus. I don't never touch the Host except when the priest places it on my tongue."

"You touched *this* flesh." Susie, unable to move, gestures with her chin. "The flesh of *this* body."

Abruptly the nurse throws open the curtains, muttering, "Godless and raving sick in a madhouse, and I'm justifying myself to her."

Shanty-Irish sow. The human insult, a regional construction, flits through Susie's overmind. Communication is futile, a distraction. As the dying body lurches there is a sense of gauze tightening on wrists. This is because hands and ankles are bound to the hospital bed. Two thrashes confirm constraint. Her slender fingers clench the sheets. Suddenly she comprehends that the host-body is wracked with pain from the surgery. Just for a second the steely intention in front of Susie's mind unclamps. "*This husk is in agony*," she gasps. "*Help me!*"

HE HOSPITAL BED IS EQUIPPED WITH A RUBBER PAD to protect the mattress. Nonporous, the pad repels moisture, spew, discharges, fluids. By preventing evaporation the unyielding rubber pad promotes perspiration. This is why Susie's sheets are sweat-damp, her gown sweat-sodden. Her temperature climbs. Delirium convinces her that the pad and length of her body form a human-skinned flying carpet. Over Providence she soars, lying on a mesh of discontinued selves. Surcease is a formula etched on the aethers, magically descriptive, nebular, galactic in implication. Her many-selved mind aches with pluralized yearnings. How many selves crouch and hide in the swirling formulae?

Ideations, viscid geometries, larval letterforms.

Strands of her consort are woven into this carpet of dreams. *Winfield, animalistic whiskers sprouting from his upper lip.* His illness was the illness of this accursed planet, which crawls with absurd cavalcades, husk armies, ritualized and valueless spawnings...while her Thousand Unborn swirl in the aethers like the spindrift of Eternity.

In the midnight hospital room the dying entity jolts awake. The plight of her Unborn Brood knifes into her. Her helplessness is unbearable. To open time she summons a tangible ideation of her consort and bleats *Iä! Iä! Iä!* without uttering its truest name.

Proceeding into the room is a crowd-sized tangle, mostly Winfield, partly the Butler Hospital room in which he died, partly the unnamable efficiency. Fully aroused, the avatar mounts her, thrusts, groans, boasts, its mind maggoty with spirochetes. *Iä!*

Between her thighs Susie feels the potent fecundating seed of death.

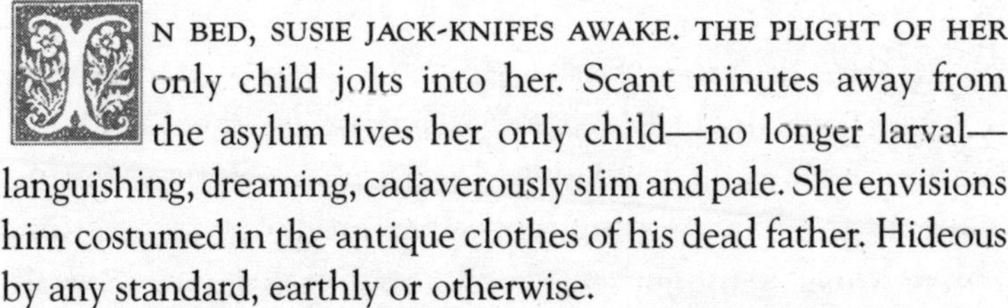

N BED, SUSIE JACK-KNIFES AWAKE. THE PLIGHT OF HER only child jolts into her. Scant minutes away from the asylum lives her only child—no longer larval—languishing, dreaming, cadaverously slim and pale. She envisions him costumed in the antique clothes of his dead father. Hideous by any standard, earthly or otherwise.

In a midnight hospital room Susie forms a tangible ideation of her child ("*a poet of the highest order*"). Because she's fatally depleted the phantasm is runt-sized. It drifts near the ceiling fan. Sliced into wisps by the slow rotation of blades, it recombines but loses volume, substance, lacks luminosity. Willed to do so, it alights onto a wall calendar, budging a leaf (May 24, 1921). Then it alights on her wrist. By any earthly standard its expression is hideous, the choreatic tic pronounced. Tiny as it is, the lantern-jaws manage to chew through the gauze, freeing one hand. Susie unknots the other wrist, but not before an avalanche of pain engulfs the right upper quadrant of her torso. There, the phantasm suckles, drawing nutrient ooze from the partially unstitched wound. Then and there she expects discontinuation, as the brown rat-like minikin cleaves and burrows into her flesh. Pain is everything. Yet everything is nothing compared to the plight of the Thousand Unborn, whose fate must devolve on her beloved, sublimely gifted, weakling invalid useless child.

IS INVOLVEMENT IS ESSENTIAL: BELATEDLY, SUSIE realizes this. Suddenly the undermind bursts through. *What do you expect from my child?* demands Sarah Susan.

"He must tend to his mission," answers the usurper in a goatish bleat. "He must...he must devote his energies to the Thousand Unborn. And usher in the Dawn of the Thousand Young."

He is too frail, he will collapse.

Susie feels the ideation of her son brush against her cheek, licking teardrops. It is odorless, breath-textured. Inexplicably, it smiles as it slithers through the bars of the window, a slow silvery comet staining the air with a trail of luminous symbols, viscid geometries, larval letterforms.

Breathing is no longer necessary: Susie realizes this

belatedly. When her body is discovered her mouth is open. In repose she appears to be glancing out the window. At midnight the sky of Providence is tinctured with hues of the morgue and the stars. To the eyes of the dead this is a scroll of endless night…with symbols and the language of Time etched on the aethers, magically descriptive, cosmic in implication.

ABOUT THE EDITOR

S. T. Joshi is a leading authority on H. P. Lovecraft and the author of *The Weird Tale* (1990), *The Modern Weird Tale* (2001), *The Rise and Fall of the Cthulhu Mythos* (2008), and other critical and biographical studies. His biography, *H. P. Lovecraft: A Life* (1996), won the British Fantasy Award and the Horror Writers Association award; it has now been published in an unabridged edition as *I Am Providence: The Life and Times of H. P. Lovecraft* (2010). Joshi has prepared corrected editions of Lovecraft's fiction, poetry, and essays, and is working on a long-range project to publish Lovecraft's collected letters. He has also done work on Ambrose Bierce, H. L. Mencken, Lord Dunsany, and other writers. He has received the World Fantasy Award, the International Horror Guild Award, and the Distinguished Scholarship Award from the International Association for the Fantastic in the Arts. He lives in Seattle, Washington, with his wife, Leslie, and numerous cats.

ALSO AVAILABLE FROM TITAN BOOKS

Black Wings of Cthulhu

VOLUME TWO

EDITED BY S. T. JOSHI

The modern masters of Lovecraftian horror offer up more brand-new and utterly horrifying tales, taking their inspiration from stories by Lovecraft himself. Well-known writers such as Caitlín R. Kiernan, Steve Rasnic Tem, Chet Williamson, Jason V Brock, Nick Mamatas, John Shirley and Darrell Schweitzer delve deep into the psyche to terrify and entertain. S. T. Joshi, the world's leading expert on Lovecraft, has assembled another star-studded line-up essential for every horror library.